SHIFTING SANDS

A DESERT ROSE NOVEL

MICHELLE A DARNELL

HIDDEN LAKE PUBLISHING LLC

Cover design by: Ravven at ravven.com

eBook ISBN: 978-1-962809-16-0
Paperback ISBN: 978-1-962809-17-7
Hardback ISBN: 978-1-962809-18-4

First edition: November 2025

Dedicated to Rachel and Ryan Murphy.

Thank you for keeping me sane during grad school, and for making sure I ate better fare than arak and coconuts during our finals weeks.

Contents

Character Glossary

CHARACTERS:

Aaron – the leader of the Tenaran assassins

Abram Lastro – head of The Mage College in Elysia

Astra – a merchant from Tenara

Ayda (AY-duh) – a member of the Elysian Mage College

Coram – a royal guard of Elysia

Divinius Morganis III – Crown Prince of the Fae Realm and Holder of the Seven Orbs of Femora

Gin – Desert Rose

James – an assassin from Tenara

Lady Sapphora Saussec – a lady at Elysian court

Lady Taniela Shanera – a lady at Elysian court and a member of the Elysian Royal Guard

Lord Belieu (Bay-lee-EW) – Elysian noble

Lord Suzac (SOO-zach) – Elysian noble

Roland – proprietor of The Golden Gosling tavern

Sana Mistwater – the leader of the Elysian assassins

Simon – captain of The Siren's Revenge

Taeral (TAY-rall) – steward to Queen Lillia Cordelia Morganis, Queen of the Fae Realm and Heir to the Rings of Reimar

Tarred (TAR-red) – healer to the Elysian royal family

Thea – healer for the assassins in Tenara

Vin – an assassin from Tenara

Warlord Akre – Gin's master, ruler of Kadena

Warlord Orion Lycis (Or-RYAN LIE-sis) – Gin's former fiancée

MAGIC WORDS:

Aga — Fire

Bharama — Illusion/disguise

Darasana — Vision (reveal magic)

Jhalaka — Reflect

Khula — Open

Pakara — Grip/hold/secure

Pharo — Hold/Freeze

Samajhana — Comprehend

Sudha karana — Purify

Vadha — Vocal Projection

Chapter 1
Gin

I would never get tired of killing. That probably made me some sort of sociopath, but after seven years enslaved to someone as evil as Warlord Akre, it was to be expected. Assassinating people was the one way my master allowed me to blow off some steam.

And I was nothing if not full of steam, so it was good he had a never-ending list of targets.

I pushed myself up against the inside of the stone fence lining the spacious property as the night watch marched down the street. My favorite set of stiletto daggers pressed into my hips as their metal sheaths ground across the rock.

"What's that?" Sand and gravel scraped together under the guard's footsteps as he approached.

I froze, not daring to breathe. The noise had been little more than a whisper, hardly worth catching the man's attention or investigating. I winced. It would be just my luck if I'd gotten saddled with a squad of brand-new night watch recruits. They'd doubtless look to investigate every little detail to prove themselves to their superiors. Dropping one of them without making a scene would be simple enough, but a whole patrol right outside my target's window? Not even I was that good.

Fighting the urge to squeeze my eyes shut and melt into the shadows, I wrapped one hand around the handle of a stiletto and pulled it loose as the footsteps approached. There was some truth to the saying we never truly knew what we were capable of until faced with it. I was, after all, Desert Rose, the best assassin in the realm. Maybe I could murder an entire night watch squad in my target's front yard minutes before sending the unfortunate nobleman to his grave. Tonight was as good as any to find out because the warlord's punishment for my failure would be a thousand times worse than anything the guards or my target could dish out—Akre would kill me if I botched this job. Death by his magic would be slow, and as painful as he could make it.

I shivered. Few things scared me in this world, but Akre and his power made my soul tremble. Not like I'd ever admit that weakness to anyone, especially him. He'd use it against me any chance he got.

The ink of my facial tattoo itched—a surefire indication the bastard was watching. He was almost as bloodthirsty as I was. It would be a toss of a coin as to if the night guards' deaths would please him or if the deviation from the plan would warrant a punishment.

Knowing him, it would be both. Any excuse to inflict pain was reason enough.

My dagger's hilt creaked as my knuckles went white. A trickle of dampness slid down my temple, cool in the overheated desert air. I could deal with anything Akre could throw at me, as long as it wasn't the water wheel.

If I'd had magic, the first thing I'd do was assassinate all seven warlords and free the population of Obron from their tyranny. But since only the warlords had magical powers, that would make me one myself, and I would never stoop so low. My parents had raised me better.

The guard's footsteps paused on the other side of the fence in front of the gate, a mere two paces away. The full moon, barely cresting the horizon, cast its shadow over the cobbled walkway.

If he walked away now, not only would he save the lives of his entire squad, but I might be spared Akre's wrath for deviating from the plan. Emphasis on the might.

My palms turned damp, slickening my grip on the blade. Without warning, my brain manifested the phantom press of cool water smothering me until my vision exploded with white lights, and my chest burned so badly the only relief was to inhale the liquid.

The water wheel was the warlord's favorite punishment when I failed.

I took a deep breath. Air, not liquid, filled my lungs. My chest heaved. I wasn't there. I was safe, for now.

Overhead, the leaves of the palm trees bordering my target's garden rustled in the hot desert breeze. The sweet scent of night blooming jasmine and orange blossoms tickled my nostrils.

It was as if Akre had sent me the watery image as a threat, knowing how close I was to being caught. He certainly enjoyed instilling a little terror mid-job to remind me of my place, and for his sick entertainment.

Shaking off the premonition, I glared at the wall, as if I could see through it by sheer force of will. Worrying about the future would do nothing more than get me killed here and now. I knew better than to let Akre, or anything else, distract me in the middle of an assignment. Bending my knees I took a deep breath, preparing to lunge as soon as the guard's head popped into view. If only he would turn around and walk away, taking the rest of the patrol with him.

The blood rushed past my ears, threatening to drown out everything else. I leaned forward, ready to prove my reputation yet again. Desert Rose—Warlord Akre's personal assassin.

The wrought iron gate jerked once against its latch. Twice.

My heart skipped a beat as I reined in the urge to stab through the slats. I pressed the soles of my shoes into the sandy dirt, grounding myself.

Patience. It would be much easier to land a strike and retreat if I didn't have to worry about maneuvering my arm between the decorative metal bars on the gate. Nobles and their opulent finery would be the death of me. Why couldn't they have a regular, solid fence like the rest of us?

"Collin!" Another voice hissed from across the street. "You'll wake the whole neighborhood."

The guard grunted. The sound would've been too low for me to hear, had I not been practically on top of him. With a shake of his head, he spun and retreated.

I relaxed the grip on my blade and shook out my hand. The tension between my shoulders released. That had been too close.

The itching faded from my tattoo. Akre's attention focused elsewhere. It looked like I'd avoid the pool in the bowels of his dungeons tonight, after all. I wiped the last of the phantom sensation of water away from my face. Grit from my dirty hands scraped across my skin.

What would the guards do if I ran after them and admitted who I was? If I turned myself in?

I nearly scoffed at the idea. Akre owned everyone and everything in the city of Kadena, the capital of the former kingdom of Obron. A country that now existed only in name, torn into seven shards by the seven men known as the warlords when they'd overthrown the monarchy and executed the royal family.

A knot twisted in my gut, sending a spike of fire exploding through my torso. I shoved those memories back into the locked box in the back of my mind where they belonged and ripped my focus back to the present.

Running after the guards would be no use. They'd rough me up a little, throw me in the stockade for a few days, then turn me back over to Akre once they'd had their fun. And then we'd go down to the dungeon and things would get really interesting.

No. Anyone who might be able to aid me in escaping was loyal to Akre. Those who weren't, well, they didn't have the power to help themselves, much less someone else.

Taking a deep breath, I brushed a loose strand of hair from my face and turned my focus back to the immediate problem.

The estate loomed before me. The adobe structure was of a similar design to the rest of those in the city, but the stone fixtures adorning the edges, as well as the window trim made of actual, real wood boasted of wealth. Not to mention the garden that would've sparkled so many shades of green in the daylight in a truly ostentatious display of wasted water. Only the warlord's inner circle could afford such extravagance.

I always wondered what my targets had done to fall from Akre's graces. Not like it mattered—if I was coming for them, they were already dead. But the small, reckless part of me was always curious. Maybe, someday, I'd have the courage to ask one of them before I sent them to their graves.

The crux of it, though, was I was afraid of what I'd learn. Afraid the response would simply be "nothing," and I'd discover Akre had been sending me to murder innocents. If I didn't know, I could pretend they were all criminals who had merely had the misfortune of crossing paths with a more dangerous predator. Then I could maintain the illusion that by assassinating Akre's targets, I was leaving the world a little safer for the people of Kadena, of Obron. That, I could live with.

With a glance over my shoulder in the direction the patrol had disappeared, I slid across the lawn, moving from shadow to shadow. The squish of verdant grass beneath my feet was a welcome contrast to the usual sand and gravel.

I chewed on my lower lip and studied the mansion's façade. This house had been vacant for months. The new owners must be making serious waves to have earned a visit from me so soon. Doubly so, because Akre insisted on this being done tonight, rather than giving me a few days to scout the building and my target. Bloodthirsty as Akre may be, he was cunning enough to recognize the value of a well thought out plan. His lack of patience crawled up my spine like tiny sand spiders, ready to sink their poison fangs into the base of my skull.

Thorns from the long-stemmed black rose that was my calling card, and was currently tucked into my waist, jabbed into my side. Akre demanded I leave one at every assassination. They ensured I was a legend throughout the city—Desert Rose. But some legends are also warnings, especially to Akre's enemies.

Personally, I thought he enjoyed the drama, like all small men with more than a little bit of power. It also too-conveniently marked each of my kills so when it was my turn to anger him, he'd have an easy way to pin everything on me before ordering my very public execution. But I should've been dead seven years ago, so whatever.

The ink in my tattoo itched again.

It was time to get moving unless I wanted to pay for it in a few hours.

Adjusting the stupid rose so it wouldn't be a distraction, I knelt at the front door and glanced behind me. The street was still clear. Pulling out my lock picks, I returned my focus to the door and got to work.

Less than twenty heartbeats later, the third and final tumbler fell into place. The latch sprang open with a quiet click. For all their money, you'd think the nobles of Obron would spend a little of their wealth on security. Even a standard bodyguard or butler would be better than a keyed lock with only three tumblers. I stood, secreting the thin strips of metal back into their spot on my belt. Gently, I turned the handle and cracked the door.

The parlor was dark, as it should be at midnight. The owner had gone to bed right after sunset, no doubt exhausted from a full schedule of shopping and socializing that seemed to be all the upper crust was good for. No one cared that people like me starved to death on the dusty streets, as long as the nobles still had their banquets and money.

I rubbed some oil from a small vial just for this purpose over the hinges in case they squeaked.

One day, none of this would be my problem. At some point in the comfortably blurry future, I'd kill Akre and steal enough coin to get my tattoo removed and set myself up with a comfortable life somewhere far away, where no one had ever heard of Genevieve Trushade, Desert Rose, or even Obron.

As soon as I managed to figure out how to end a warlord, and how to get rid of this cursed slave tattoo.

Slipping inside, I pulled the door closed behind me.

It took a few heartbeats for my eyes to adjust to the darkness. The room was as empty as it had initially appeared. Only a pair of lounge chairs and a solitary settee filled the middle of the room, along with a handful of paintings on the walls whose designs I couldn't quite make out.

Not like it mattered. I was an assassin, after all, not an art thief.

Keeping to the wall, I slunk through the parlor and up the stairs to the second level. Somewhere up here lay my target, sleeping the last peaceful dreams of a dead man.

The hallway was covered with a finer carpet than the palace itself boasted. Perhaps I was here because Akre was jealous of this man's wealth? My master was usually too cunning to fall prey to useless emotions like jealousy. Wasn't he? If that was all this was, it may be a weakness I could exploit in my bid for freedom. With a slight shake of my head, I set the thought aside to chew on later, when I had the luxury of time to think.

I paused, pressing my foot down to test the padding. Not only did the floor not creak beneath my weight, but the plush weave provided more support than the castle's mattresses. If the owner could afford such things in areas of his house guests didn't see, surely he had excess funds lying around somewhere I could repurpose for my escape? Someone like this may have the fifty thousand marks I needed to remove Akre's slave tattoo. That would be the first step of whatever I planned.

I bit my lower lip to hold back a grin. Perhaps tonight wasn't going to be a waste, after all.

The first door on the right was closed but not locked.

I pressed my ear to the thick wood, listening for any noise within.

Twenty heartbeats. Thirty. The only sound was the blood rushing through my own ears. I clenched my teeth and turned the doorknob oh-so-slowly.

The door slid open on well-oiled hinges.

The smell of leather with a hint of vanilla and almonds tickled my nostrils. An oversized wooden desk dominated the middle of the room, backed by a chair and endless shelves of books.

I stepped inside, pulling the door mostly closed behind me. Speaking of excess coin...

Where else would wealthy people hoard their valuables but in their study? I had no doubt most of my target's net worth was in investments, banks, and the like. But rich people were too scared of being separated from their money to not keep at least a little bit on hand. And although thievery hadn't been part of the original plan for tonight, as long as my mark still slept, I had a few minutes to spare for the possibility of a sizeable payoff.

Starting with the desk, my fingers ran lightly over and under each surface. None of the drawers locked, but one did have a false bottom that would've been much more interesting if anything had actually been in said space beyond a withered parchment with faded ink written in a language I couldn't read.

With a disappointed sigh, I turned away and faced the books. There were probably over two hundred here. Hopefully the money wasn't hidden in a hollowed-out volume or two. I hardly had time to flip through all of them. But I could jostle the tomes and see if their weight felt off.

Starting on the left, with the highest shelf I could reach, I tipped the top of the first book toward me. It slid as it should and didn't feel too heavy or too light. Frowning, I bit back a sigh and shoved it into place, moving on to the next.

Near the end of the third row, I grabbed the upper spine of a thick tome and tilted it forward. It was stuck. I flashed my teeth in a wide grin.

Found something.

On closer inspection, the last five books on this shelf were false, their covers glued together to cunningly hide that fact. A few minutes of wiggling and prodding with my lock picks had the book-door's latch springing open.

The face of a small safe stared back at me.

Tingles ran up my skin, blooming into a warmth in my chest that brought a genuine smile to my lips. What luck! The ability to finance my freedom may be only heartbeats away.

I fought the urge to rub my hands together and jump up and down like a child. Pressing my nose to the shelf, I studied the front of the strongbox, and the visible sliver of each side for any maker's mark. Running my fingers around the edges, three bumps caught my attention on the underside.

No way...

Crouching, I squinted at the bottom.

The stamp was in the shape of an inverted triangle. A stylized eye sketched in between them stared back at me as the hope blooming in my gut turned to ice.

Sand demon's spit. It was an Akun safe, crafted by the dwarves. Every wall would be lined with two thin sheets of metal with a layer of liquid that, if exposed to air, would turn into a poisonous gas and kill everything in the vicinity.

I immediately took back all the crap I'd said earlier about nobles needing to invest in more security. Why did it have to be an Akun?

It would take me too long to get this unlocked here. I'd have to take it with me after-the-fact, and pray it had something worth the effort inside. Then I'd have to find somewhere outdoors, far away from anything living, so I could spring the trap and force it open.

I bared my teeth and growled.

Stupid aristocrats.

Well, once I was finished here, I'd stash the safe at my favorite tavern, The Golden Gosling, while I decided what to do with it. The owner, Roland, owed me a favor—he would hold onto my prize for me for a few days.

A snarl, followed by something heavy crashing to the ground had me jumping and whirling toward the door, which I'd left ajar. My heart leaped into my throat, threatening to choke me.

A shadow with yellow eyes yowled before it stalked into the room. The cat arched its back and fluffed its fur at me. A stack of books lay scattered on the floor at its feet.

I hissed, trying to wave the animal away. My knees buckled with relief at the realization I hadn't been discovered, at least, not by a human. However, the noise had been loud enough to warrant investigation for all but the deepest sleepers.

The feline leaped to the window frame. With one last tail flick, it curled up and settled onto the rim, fixing me with a pointed glare.

I raised a finger and shook it, whispering, "If you've botched this for me..." Pausing, I pulled up short. I'd what? I may be an assassin, but not even I would kill an innocent cat for being, well, a cat.

I took another deep breath and listened for any further movement hinting the animal had disturbed its owner.

Several heartbeats later, the house remained still, and white sparks danced at the edge of my vision. I exhaled, relieving the burning in my chest. All was silent. Something was going right tonight, at least.

I tiptoed to the door, watching the dark hall as I counted to two hundred.

Nothing moved. It looked like tonight's target was a heavy sleeper.

Thank the fates.

I pointed at the cat. "Do not mess with my safe." With one last glare at the fuzzy intruder, I stalked into the hallway. I'd come back for it on my way out.

The next door opened to what was likely supposed to be a music room. All the noble houses had them in a vain attempt to appear more cultured, usually with an heirloom instrument of some sort, a manichord, a full set of pan pipes, or something equally impressive, that the rest of the room centered around. Rarely could said nobles play the instruments, at least, not with any skill. This room was devoid of any furnishings.

I liked this nobleman. He didn't seem to care about putting on airs like the others. He might have been someone I'd have befriended in another life. Not like that would stop me from carrying out the assassination. When it came to him or me, I'd always choose myself.

The third and final room was more promising. This door was locked. Heavy breathing, not quite snores, rasped gently through the wood.

My lock picks made quick work of the latch as I quietly popped the bolt. Pouring the rest of my oil over the hinges and taking my time, I eased the door open.

Poking my head around the edge of the frame, I studied the interior. Despite the full moon, this side of the house was bathed in darkness. Across the space, a figure lay on a large bed beneath an exotic black silk sheet that covered him from the waist down.

His back was to me. Perfect.

I ignored the way the shadows highlighted the ridges and planes of his muscles as he breathed.

A door on the far wall, presumably leading to a closet or second room, was closed. A writing desk sat next to it. A few swords in various designs hung like prized art. I could make out at least one scimitar, a falchion, and a much larger version of my stilettos.

I approved of his practical decoration choices. It was too bad this noble had to die—if the world had been different, we definitely could've been friends.

Overall, the room had a very sparse layout, which was all the better. Less clutter meant fewer obstacles and things to go wrong. I'd be back in my room with enough time to catch half a night's sleep, if I was lucky.

I freed one of my blades and slid the black rose into the emptied sheath.

This would be quick and easy. I smiled, tiptoeing across the room.

My target rolled as I reached the edge of the bed. I froze, my heart in my throat, mentally checking off the list of things I could've done to alert him to my presence. There was nothing—I'd made no noise, tripped no alarms.

As his eyes remained closed, I allowed my muscles to relax. He was no more than a restless sleeper.

The man before me had a strong jaw with well-defined cheekbones that were doubtless the subject of many women's dreams. Wisps of dark hair curled around his forehead.

I frowned. He was quite attractive. An odd sense of familiarity settled in my gut.

It was almost too bad Akre wanted him dead. There were far too few beautiful people in the world as it was.

Again, I wondered what he'd done. Not like he would tell me, if he knew. And I'd have to be a fool for asking questions I didn't want to know the answers to. Which I wasn't.

I shook my head. It was a stupid thing to want. All that mattered was the warlord had ordered me to assassinate him.

I squeezed the stiletto until my knuckles creaked. At least I was professional enough to make it quick and painless. Aligning the blade at a forty-five degree angle so it would slide between the man's skull and his spine, I leaned forward, making a slight adjustment to the right with my wrist.

The target spun, throwing the thin sheet to the ground. A sword whistled through the air.

I flung myself to the floor with a grunt. The scimitar swung through where my neck had been a heartbeat before.

I rolled under the bed and popped up on the far side, brandishing both stilettos. So much for the decent half-night's sleep. With the energy suddenly rushing through my blood, however, that wouldn't be happening anyway. At least now I'd have the opportunity to work off some pent-up nerves.

"Who's there?" His voice was rough with sleep.

Expecting me to answer was as fruitless as my wondering what he'd done to earn Akre's ire.

He sounded familiar, though. I took two steps out of range as I clawed through memories to identify him.

He waved one hand in a gesture I didn't recognize. "Aga."

A candle on his nightstand and two torches in sconces flared to life, casting a dangerous orange light across the room.

The floor dropped from beneath my feet as the walls spun around me, closing in. My target was a mage.

A sand-blasted mage.

My mind stuttered to a halt. Akre had sent me against a rival warlord! I was dead. This was Akre's way of executing me, likely hoping I'd take out his rival as I went.

As my panicking thoughts shut down, instinct took over. With a growl, I flung one of my blades at his face.

He ducked. The stiletto flew by and embedded itself in the wall. "Stop!" he yelled.

I wasn't going down easy. Desert Rose didn't cower before Akre, there was no way I would do so in front of this bastard. "Go pick a fight with a sand demon. As if preying on peasants isn't enough for you warlord scum." The words rasped past my vocal cords, trapped by the heat of slow-burning rage pushing a sour taste into the back of my throat. It was almost sufficient to break through my terror.

I may be the best, but even the fabled Desert Rose couldn't go up against a warlord and expect to survive.

He stepped off the bed and flared his palms, lightning crackling around his fingers. His eyes traced from my feet to the onyx flower at my hip and up to my face, covered in a black mask. "Desert Rose, I presume?" A muscle at the corner of his mouth twitched as his tone pitched lower. "I like a challenge."

The hint of his smile caused a curl of heat to uncoil below my navel in contrast to the ice his voice sent through my veins. The conflicting sensations were almost enough to send me off balance as I ripped my whip from the back of my belt with my free hand, unfurling it with a crack. "Now you've got one." I snapped the weapon at his left eye as I leaped to the right, dodging around the edge of his bed.

He ducked, catching my lash on one wrist while snapping his other, flinging an arc of onyx-colored lightning my way.

The sizzle made the hairs on my arm stand on end. The bolt slammed into the wall behind me. My eyelids stretched as wide as they could go. Akre had never thrown his magic at me, or anyone else. Even I couldn't hope to out-dance lightning.

But I had survived too much at this point to let some asshole male chauvinist pig get the better of me without a fight.

I lunged over the bed, swinging the stiletto as I yanked on the leather strap, now hopelessly tangled around his forearm.

He stumbled forward, using the opportunity to claw at me, ripping the mask from my face along with several handfuls of hair.

I screamed and sliced at his fingers with my dagger, dropping the useless whip.

The black veil joined the sheets on the ground.

"Genevieve?"

Oh, shit. Terror clenched my heart and squeezed at the use of my full name. This man knew who I really was—if news got back to Akre, my slim chance of surviving the night would be gone, and it would be like the last seven years had never happened.

I sprinted to the wall and ripped the falchion I'd noticed earlier from its mounting. Spinning, I swung for my target's neck.

"Genevieve, stop!" He mumbled something I didn't understand and countered my swing with a sword of his own, one that appeared to be made entirely out of black lightning.

I refused to be impressed by the precise control such an action obviously required. I was so dead. And with the possible exception of Roland, no one would miss me or care. In fact, if word got out Desert Rose was gone, the vast majority of Kadena would probably sigh in collective relief, believing themselves safer, though that was the farthest thing from the truth.

The warlord lunged, aiming for my stomach. I leaped to the right, trapping his crackling blade between my elbow and waist, and kicked him in the face. The electric shock and smell of seared flesh where his weapon touched my skin threw me back as I cried out.

I slammed against the wall, my shoulder numb. Forcing the fact that I was fighting a freaking warlord into the darkest recess of my brain before panic could take over, I growled, switching my sword to my other hand. Losing the use of one arm just for a solid hit to the head probably hadn't been the best choice in terms of risk versus reward. If I'd managed to keep my wits about me instead of panicking, I'd have thought things through a little better.

I could give in to the hysteria later. No doubt there would be plenty of time to do so in Akre's dungeon, assuming I was lucky enough to escape with my life. And if I wasn't, well, then it wouldn't be a problem, now, would it?

My opponent spun from the force of my kick and ended up facing away from me, bracing himself on the back of a chair that had been tucked neatly next to a small writing desk. I snarled, shoving to my feet. Stalking toward him, I aimed the tip of the falchion at his neck. "I was going to make this painless for you, but not anymore."

As I stepped within striking range, he kicked my hand. My sword flew across the room. The momentum spun me off-balance as the rug I'd been standing on slid out from beneath me. I landed on my back, staring up at him. The air exploded from my lungs with a whoosh.

He bent, arms extended as if to strangle me.

Fates! If I let him get his hands around my neck, I was done for. There was no way I was going to make it easy for him, or any warlord.

I jammed my heel between his legs, and while I missed my true target, it was enough to throw him off-balance. He tumbled to the right. I somersaulted to the left, bouncing to my feet and kicking the traitorous rug out of the way.

Ha! Eat that, bastard!

I wasted a heartbeat sucking huge gulps of air into my lungs. My knees shook, mirroring the tremble in my gut. I was in over my head and wasn't going to live to regret it.

The warlord used the edge of the bed to pull himself upright and spun to face me.

I might not survive the night, but at least I could leave a mark, maybe even do some permanent damage to someone who had actively destroyed the kingdom I'd grown up in and turned it into the cesspool it was today.

I lunged and threw a right hook followed by a sloppy uppercut from my lightning-weakened arm. Yeah, now would've been a good time to have two functional fists. Sometimes, I truly was an idiot.

He stepped back, spitting a mouthful of blood, and glared at me.

Stepping forward and grabbing a fistful of his hair, I pulled his head down until it connected with my knee. His nose collapsed with a satisfying crunch as he tumbled to the ground.

Blinking hard, he crawled away.

Hardly believing I'd landed such a solid hit on an actual warlord, I stumbled back, scanning the floor for any of my weapons. Anything at all. Now was my opportunity to end this and get back to Akre, with a new, warlord-sized notch on my belt. The scimitar and both stilettos were on the far side of the room. I couldn't see my whip. Crap.

I leaped into a back handspring and managed to kick my opponent in the temple with my second foot.

Taking a step back, I shook my head, clearing the strands of loose hair that had freed themselves from my braid. Heaving, I rubbed my arm across my upper lip. It came away red.

At least I felt better than he looked. His nose gushed blood down his muscular chest and onto the floor.

He stood, balled up his fist and threw lightning.

It crashed into my gut and slammed me against the wall with an ominous crack.

I gasped as the air burst from my lungs. My vision went white with sparkles. A fiery knife rammed into my side. I'd broken a rib, maybe two.

No. No, no, no... My slim chance of survival was slipping through my fingers.

The heel of his foot caught me across the jaw, snapping my head around so hard my teeth rattled.

"Stop fighting me!" He grabbed a fistful of my hair and yanked my face up to look at him.

I blinked once, twice, as his face finally came into focus. The world tilted sideways. I was going to faint. "Rion?" My voice was a dry husk in my throat. My heart pounded against my ribs, burning as my breath hitched.

Orion Lyncis. My childhood best friend, the one I was supposed to have married in another life. Before Akre had swooped in and killed everyone I knew and loved, including him.

And yet, here he was. A warlord, like my master. The worst type of villain.

Nausea roiled through my gut. No...

I gasped at the implication, coughing up blood as my stomach heaved. Shaking my head, I tried to dislodge his grip. Unfortunately, my arms and legs weren't working right. My clumsiness fed the heat taking hold in my chest until it became a raging inferno. "You're supposed to be dead." Or... he'd left me to die. The other possibility, that he'd participated in the coup that killed my family and crashed the world down on my head, was far too outlandish to consider.

"Shut up!" He slammed his hand against my jaw and blasted me with lightning.

I screamed as my flesh burned, as though he was flaying it from my bones. By the fates, I'd take the itching of Akre's watchful eye over this any day. This was it—the moment I died and never had to worry about Akre or anything else ever again.

I'd been so intimately acquainted with death for the last seven years, I'd had no idea it would hurt so much when he finally came for me.

Something in the back of my mind shattered with a snap I felt more than heard over my own screams.

I turned my head and bit down on the joint where Orion's thumb joined his palm until I tasted blood.

He cried out, flinging me away. The pain ended as soon as his fingers left my skin.

I pushed onto all fours, my chest heaving. Was I dead? No... I ached too much. Raising one hand, I placed it against my sternum, as if I could hold my thunderous heart inside my broken ribs. "You're no better than the rest of the warlords," I hissed through lips nearly too swollen to form words. I heaved myself from the floor. I was still alive. Why? "You should kill me while you have the chance." Because as surely as sand demons lived in the desert, I would hunt him down and avenge my parents, my kingdom, if it was the last thing I did.

Not just because he was a warlord, though that was certainly reason enough. Orion knew who I was. Who my parents had been. If word got out and Akre realized, I'd be executed as publicly as the rest of my family. The ice in my gut coalesced into steel.

Orion frowned at whatever he saw in my face and leaned in, his mouth opening.

Without waiting to hear what he had to say, I reached out and raked the fingernails of both hands down his perfect face. I gouged as deeply as I could as I screamed my pain into the void. Unfortunately, I missed the bastard's eyes.

He stumbled backward with a cry, flicking his wrist in my direction.

Instinct took over. I flung myself to the ground. A blade of lightning slashed across the room where my neck had been. It slammed into the wall with enough force to shake the unused swords to the floor.

What was Akre thinking? Sending me after another warlord, with no warning? If I returned in failure, my best hope was a night on the water wheel. Worst case, Akre would kill me himself.

If I stayed, Orion would end me as surely as Akre would. Just like he'd left me for dead seven years ago. He'd been everything to me once, my future, the kingdom's, and here he was now—the full evidence of his betrayal staring me in the face.

My eyes and the back of my throat burned. I blinked, holding the tears back. What was wrong with me? I'd pulled myself out of much worse situations than this before. One didn't become the best assassin in Obron by backing down at the first sign things weren't going my way.

But my thoughts were too foggy. Orion was here, not dead. Not only that, he was a warlord.

And it was my job to kill him or die trying.

My temples pounded in time to my racing heartbeat under the increasing pressure to make a decision. To do something.

I may be a hardened butcher, but even I couldn't murder someone I'd once loved. Swallowing, I bit the inside of my lip. But could I end the person who had double-crossed me, my family and the entire kingdom?

I clenched my jaw so tightly, I practically felt my molars crack. Yes. Yes, I could, and I would. No one betrayed me and lived.

Across the room, as though controlled by an invisible poltergeist, one of the pair of sconces holding torches screeched in protest and crashed to the ground, spilling flaming oil all over the floor.

Orion spun to face the new threat.

This was my chance. I scrambled for the door, snatching the whip from where he had apparently dropped it near his rug. I had no choice but to abandon my lost stilettos.

The black rose lay on the bed, its petals smashed and scattered across the sheets.

Forget this. I lunged down the dark stairway. Possible future torture or death at Akre's hands was better than my imminent demise at Orion's. My ankle caught the final step at an angle, sending me stumbling. Or maybe it was just the unnaturally plush carpet. I somersaulted to my feet and charged for the exit, pumping my arms to give me speed.

Any minute now, the heavy thud of Orion's footsteps would echo behind me. I hadn't damaged him nearly as much as he had me. If he caught me and we fought again, he'd emerge the victor.

I dropped my shoulder and slammed into the front door, which flew open with a loud crash. Metal shrieked as the hinges bent. Hopefully the patrol of guards was out of earshot. I didn't look back as I tore through the grass.

Orion Lyncis was a warlord, and he was coming to kill me. I needed some time to lay low and come up with a plan.

Whose hands would it be less painful to die by? The truth was, I had no idea. Akre was depraved, and he'd drag my death out, making it as painful as possible, but he did lack creativity when his wrath took over. Orion... Orion was a wildcard. He could be better or so much worse.

I'd been seventeen, he'd been two years older, and absolute perfection. His muscular build was evidence of few days spent outside the training ring, but even with all his strength, he'd never been anything but gentle with me. And nothing had made me feel as good as his smile.

I could've done nothing but listen to his laugh for the rest of my life and been happy. But that was before.

Tonight, the hard set of his face told me he hadn't laughed in a long time. Nor had he been tender. No. Whatever he'd been through the last seven years, the man who had once been my everything, and the future of Obron, was dead. Whatever monster existed in his place, well, hopefully I wouldn't have to find out.

I reached the iron gate marking the entrance to the property. A glimpse over my shoulder revealed a lush garden devoid of pursuers. My knees turned weak as I fought to not collapse against the bars. Maybe he wasn't going to chase me after all?

Two steadying breaths later, I placed my hand on the top of the railing and vaulted onto the road.

Fortunately, the guards from earlier were long gone. With one quick glance in each direction, I sprinted for the Golden Gosling. Roland would hide me. I could grab a drink or two to calm down and figure out what I was going to do.

It was a matter of only about a quarter of an hour to duck through random alleys and climb a few fences—much slower than normal due to my painful ribs—to ensure Orion wasn't following.

Once outside the noble district, I dropped to a jog and eventually to a walk. Running through Kadena's slums was an excellent way to attract unwanted attention, which was the last thing to do when I was already beaten and bloody.

What I needed was a safe place and the time to fall apart mentally and put myself back together. That would let me wrap my love for Orion in a noose and hang it from a sharpened edge of my broken heart where it could rot. And then I could formulate a plan to deal with both Orion and Akre. I wanted nothing more than to cross my arms and curl into a ball somewhere while the world straightened itself out, but I couldn't permit my rage and the strength that came with it to ebb until I reached Roland's. Allowing myself to be overcome with weaker emotions—hurt, pain, regret—would get me killed here just as certainly as the warlords.

Instead, I strode down the middle of the ghetto, shoulders back and my head held high, daring any passer-by to challenge me. All the inhabitants I encountered were smart and stayed out of my way. That was fortunate, because it was hard enough to focus on placing my feet in front of me through the ache of my swollen face and broken rib. I wasn't sure I was up to putting down anyone who challenged me right this instant.

Though my breathing calmed, my heart still slammed against my chest. Blood rushed through my ears with each beat, whispering Orion's name over and over.

Best Friend. First love. Betrayer. Murderer.

I ran my fingers through my hair, freeing it from the destroyed braid. If only my thoughts could be untangled so easily. Ripping through the knots, I re-plaited the strands as I walked.

The pain of his betrayal was a knife in my heart; it cut every time I moved, even more than my broken rib. Which was stupid because I had no idea how deep his treachery truly went. I wasn't naïve enough to think he'd come back to Kadena looking for me. Judging from his expression when he'd said my name, he hadn't known I'd survived, either. Genevieve Trushade, princess of Obron, was supposed to be as dead as he was.

He could have realized seven years ago the coup was going to be successful and switched sides mid-event. That was easier than believing he'd been in on the entire thing from the beginning, because that would mean I'd been played from the start, and everything he'd done had been a setup to snatch power. That romancing me was just one long con.

There was no Warlord Lyncis, however. At least, not the ones I knew of. So, he'd changed his name to hide his identity. That might be a secret worth some currency with Akre. Perhaps enough to save my life.

If Orion wasn't here for me, then there was only one reason a warlord left his territory and breached another's. The last thing the city of Kadena needed was to be caught between two power-hungry tyrants in a quest for more land and power.

It was too bad I couldn't just kill them both and be done with it.

On second thought, maybe I should let them go at each other. Then I could swoop in and finish off whoever survived, when they were at their weakest. But that would leave hundreds if not thousands of bystanders dead, and while I was an assassin, even I balked at massacring innocents.

Bracing myself with the last bit of fortitude I possessed, I pushed the door to the Golden Gosling open and strutted inside as though I truly belonged here. The familiar rush of noise, the bitter smell of smoke and the clamor of many voices all talking at once washed over me. The tension between my shoulder blades released. I was safe, at least for now.

The Golden Gosling was nothing short of brutish, with blood and shattered glass crunching underfoot. The furniture and walls were crusted the same brown as the drinks. But arak was arak, and it tasted disgusting no matter where I got it. Besides, I'd never worried about mingling with the dregs of society. After all, no respectable warlord would grace such a den with his presence.

Catching the bartender's eye, I made my way around the crowded tables and collapsed into a stool at the counter.

Roland wiped his cleaning cloth across the bar in front of me. "Hey, Gin." It was hard to tell which was dirtier—the rag or the wood, but I appreciated the effort. He disguised his surprise by raising an eyebrow as he studied the no doubt impressive swelling on the side of my face. There was probably still blood caked below my nose, too. Fates. I should've tried to clean myself up a little before walking in here. I closed my eyes and dragged my sleeve across my mouth, hoping to wipe most of the mess away. If I hadn't been so distracted by thoughts of Orion...

Something inside me crumbled. My spine curled in on itself as I hunched forward, bracing my elbows against the bar and pressing my palms into my eyes, as if the pressure would hold back the tears.

"Looks like you've had a rough night." Roland waited until I nodded before continuing, "What can I get for you?"

He had no idea, and it was only going to get worse when Akre got his claws into me. Not like I could run—the magical tattoo guaranteed that. At best, I had minutes until he realized something had gone wrong. I may as well drown myself in booze before I had to face whatever punishment he had waiting for me.

I scanned the shelves behind Roland, even though it was pointless. The answer to my problems didn't lie among the bottles of liquor displayed there. Slaves didn't have the funds for the good stuff. Arak, the muddy concoction provided by the warlords, was always free to the masses. It contained sufficient calories to keep us from starving, with enough alcohol to dull our senses and make us less prone to revolt. "Just a mug of arak." I sighed, dropping my head to my hands.

Fates, what a messed-up world. For the first time in longer than I cared to admit, I missed my parents. I longed for the feeling of their arms wrapping around me as I cried out the pain of losing my first love for the second time.

But my parents were long dead, and that was likely at least partially Orion's fault. And I was no lovesick teenager. I was a grown ass woman who was strong enough to stand on her own and deal with the punches life threw at me, no matter how it hurt. I could suck it up like every other person out there.

Roland filled a mug to the brim and slid it in my direction.

Arak was somewhat of an acquired taste, but if I held my breath and chugged it, the bitter flavor didn't bother me too much. Plus, it worked just fine to dull the pain. At least, temporarily.

"Who'd you go after tonight?" he asked, his gaze searching mine.

I narrowed my eyes. Usually, he was smarter than to pry into my business, or that of any of his regulars.

Holding his palms toward me, he stepped back. "No offense meant. I was just wondering if you needed to talk."

As if he could help me straighten my mess out. Besides, Desert Rose was never vulnerable enough to share her feelings with anyone. I wasn't certain I'd know how, even if I wanted to. I opened my mouth to tell him to go pick a fight with a sand demon, but stopped. I couldn't confide in my parents, but Roland had always been a good friend, had gone out of his way to make sure I had somewhere I could go after a hit to decompress and put myself back together.

I studied him as the ever-present flush from too much sampling of his own wares drained from his face, leaving his skin looking yellowish and enhancing the pale spider veins tracing his jaw.

He handed me his rag, which I promptly ran down my face, scrubbing off the dried blood before handing it back. The cloth was gross, but my face was likely even worse.

The fabric was now more red than gray. Fates. I was in bad shape. My gut twisted. No wonder Roland looked so freaked out. That's what I got for tangling with a warlord. Mages had quite the advantage over everyone else—it was how they managed to hold onto power with such an iron fist, despite all being craven despots.

Roland grabbed a half-finished mug of arak from beneath the counter and chugged it. "I'm sorry, Gin. It's just..." He swallowed. "You look like

Akre had you kill your own mother, or something. And she gave as good as she got."

Not my mother, but a close second. I eyed Roland. Sometimes, I wondered if the man had a seer somewhere back in his family bloodline. "My mother was killed in The Purge." That was what the peasants called it when the warlords took power. Telling Roland that didn't reveal any great secret—a good percentage of the people of Kadena died, both common and noble. Orion was supposed to have been dead, too. If not during the initial attack, then in the weeks following when they exterminated everyone who had an ounce of magical ability. Other than themselves, of course. Sand demons forbid anyone beyond the high-and-mighty warlords have access to magic.

If Orion had survived, maybe others I'd known had, also?

I wrapped my fingers around the mug and, with a deep breath, poured half of the burning concoction down my throat. The aftertaste was more bitter than usual. "Ugh." I shoved the glass across the counter. Whoever came up with an arak blend that didn't taste like camel piss would never have to work again. "I think you've got a bad batch." Either that, or he'd sourced his water from a non-approved well to save coin. Not like he'd admit it, of course.

Roland's gaze snagged on something behind me. He nodded, and I didn't get the impression he was confirming the quality of his draft.

My blood chilled as lead pooled in my gut. I'd seen that expression before, and nothing good ever came after it.

Fighting the urge to spin in my chair to see who he was signaling, I turned slowly. Deliberately. Nothing caught my eye as being out of place. Tension creeped onto my back, forming a knot underneath my right shoulder blade, making my spine and neck ache. My ribs sent a shooting pain up my side as I adjusted my weight to relieve the pressure on them.

With a quick smile at me and the other patrons at the counter, Roland sat his glass below the bar, tossed the rag over his arm and disappeared into the back.

My stomach grumbled. Hopefully when he returned, it would be with some sort of meat or hearty stew for dinner. On the house, of course, because it wasn't like I had the coin to pay for it. Maybe he'd let me start a tab, on account of my rough night and all.

Any minute now, my tattoo would itch as Akre called me home for my debriefing. Then, he'd punish me, possibly even kill me.

I paused, my hand hovering a finger-width above the bar. My face hadn't itched since the fight, when Orion had blasted me with his lightning. Maybe there'd been some sort of mystical blow-back that had injured Akre. Perhaps even knocked him out.

Was such a thing possible? I didn't know too much about how magic worked, but if so, that would be amazing. My mind promptly served up an image of an unconscious Akre laying on the floor of his room, blood leaking from a broken nose.

I bit back a snort. As if I'd be so lucky. It was more likely Orion's power had damaged the nerves on my face, and I simply couldn't feel Akre's pull anymore. That was a blessing but would also be a problem when I couldn't tell when he was summoning me. If I didn't know when Akre was watching, or calling me, I'd be dead sooner rather than later.

Pressing one hand flat against the bar before its trembling called attention, I lifted my other fingers to my jaw. I disguised the action by rotating my head to the side to pop my neck as I dug my fingernails into the swelling surrounding the tattoo.

Crescents of pain shot up my face from my nails.

Nope, definitely not numb.

Sand demon spit.

The ink had itched since the day Akre had forced it on me. But unless he was checking in on me directly, the sensation was mild enough I'd learned to ignore it. So why did it not itch now?

As Akre's primary weapon against Orion, it would be in Orion's best interest to get me out of the way. What better way than to have Akre kill me himself by messing with my tattoo? That seemed like a lot more work than just zapping me with lightning, though. Perhaps this was a fail-safe in case I'd beaten him and escaped. Like I had. With warlords, there were always plots within plots. However, with the tattoo telling Akre exactly where I was and what I was up to, it was impossible to gain my freedom.

Unless I managed to secretly drum up fifty-thousand marks to pay a back-alley healer to remove the magic in the tattoo. Doing so was illegal, and any healers with the knowledge kept that fact closely guarded to protect their own lives. But there was one I'd contacted several months ago who'd promised to do so for the astronomical sum of fifty-thousand marks. Then all I'd have to worry about was hiding the residual facial ink from any who may see it and know what it meant.

I ran my fingers through my tangled hair that was falling out of its braid, pulling it away from my face as I rested my elbows on the bar and exhaled forcefully. The mug in front of me blurred in and out of focus. I blinked hard, forcing the tears back inside where they belonged.

I had to think. The money in Orion's library would go a long way toward buying my way out of this dust bowl, but no way was I sneaking back into his house to steal it. Not tonight, assuming I survived Akre's wrath. Not until I could guarantee Orion and I wouldn't cross paths. Then I could go somewhere safe and formulate a plan on how to take both warlords down. There was a certain level of satisfaction knowing Orion's downfall would be financed by his own coin.

"Gin?"

Blinking, I focused on Roland's face. His brow was pinched, the outer corners of his lips turned down.

"You seem rather distraught. Is everything okay?"

What an idiotic question. I opened my mouth and closed it a few times. Oh, screw it. Roland had watched my back for the last seven years. He'd more than earned my trust. I peered over my shoulder and down each side of the bar, confirming no one was close enough to overhear. Taking a deep breath, I curled my finger at him and whispered, "There's another warlord in town." Surprisingly, something in my gut lightened as I spoke the words out loud.

Roland's eyes bugged out as his skin turned pale. "Who?" He glanced down the counter and leaned in until our breaths mingled. "Did Akre send you after him?"

I nodded.

He scooted closer. "And? He's dead?"

Shaking my head, I broke his gaze. Grabbing the mug, I pushed it in slow circles in front of me. "No. I was caught completely by surprise." I couldn't believe I'd just admitted that. A sudden wave of dizziness washed over me. Grabbing the counter, I steadied myself.

That was one bad batch of arak. I'd probably be sick for a week from drinking it.

Several heartbeats passed as the gears in Roland's brain turned. He tilted his head like an owl evaluating a rodent. "What does Akre gain by sending you in blind?"

I shrugged. "That's what I can't figure out." There was no way I was going to admit out loud what I suspected—Akre was trying to get rid of me and was using Orion to do it.

"Hmm." Roland stroked his chin with a finger and thumb. "Maybe he's worried about a leak somewhere in his court and didn't want news of your assignment reaching this other warlord's ears?"

I chewed on the inside of my cheek as I contemplated his words. Sometimes, Roland was smart. Smarter than me, anyway. I was fairly certain Akre didn't know who I really was, or my connection to Orion, but he probably didn't want to risk me approaching his rival and offering to switch sides.

"Sand demon spit."

I raised my eyebrow at Roland's curse.

"This other warlord. He's most likely got people out looking for you right now, huh?"

Any competent tyrant would. I nodded, swallowing down a wave of nausea.

"We should get you out of sight, then."

I bit back a smile. This was why I loved Roland. He didn't insult me with stupid questions like, "Were you followed?" or "Did you lead them to my tavern?" He knew better.

"Come on." He waved me to the side. "You can hang out in the kitchen until the coast is clear and you can get back to Akre."

The mention of my master's name shriveled the warm fuzzy feelings in my gut stemming from his concern. I still had to figure out why my tattoo didn't work before I could go back home. Akre would be livid. While the Golden Gosling wouldn't be the first place his people looked for me, it wouldn't be the last. I'd already lingered here too long. My best bet would be to find a roof or somewhere else I could lay low for a few days.

The tiny hairs on my arms stood on end, and I ran my palms over them absentmindedly. I could sneak out the back and go to ground until I figured things out.

The doors to the Golden Gosling slammed open. Roland froze.

I winced at the sharp noise and glanced over my shoulder.

A dozen guards in red and black uniforms—Akre's colors—poured into the room. Patrons leaped from their tables, upending ale and food, and scrambled out of the way. Screams battered my ears.

By the fates. They'd found me. My blood chilled, settling into a ball of ice in my stomach that my pumping heart did nothing to dispel. My breath caught in my throat as I gasped, the edges of my vision darkening.

No, not yet. I wasn't ready, hadn't had time to come up with a plan...

Roland winced at the crack of breaking chairs and glassware as he yanked me around the bar toward the kitchen. He tugged me through the door so quickly I tripped and lost my balance.

Slamming into me, he grabbed my upper arms as the shock of the impact rattled my teeth. "Steady on there, Gin." His now-gloved hands were coated with a glittery purple dust.

I stepped back, brushing at the oddly colored handprints, which clung stubbornly to my sleeves. "What are you doing?" This was beyond weird, even for Roland. And that was saying something.

My irritation should have risen, but my head, my brain felt cloudy and sluggish.

He took a few steps away, his throat bobbing with an exaggerated swallow. Beads of sweat dotted his forehead as he peeled off the gloves and dropped them.

I froze at the anticipation on his face. Icy dread flashed through me. The dizziness, the slowed thoughts and reactions...

"You drugged me!"

My heart was beating too fast, my chest burned so hot I couldn't breathe. A second betrayal in less than an hour. Terror welled through my chilled veins, the emotion oddly dulled by the fog smothering my head. I had to fight off whatever he'd given me. Falling unconscious now meant being helpless at the hands of Akre's men. Who knew what hellscape I would awake to if I succumbed.

I stumbled back, glancing over my shoulder to check the progress of the guards. "You're a dead man," I choked past paralyzed vocal cords. My temples throbbed, my thoughts were too fuzzy.

Roland's hair rose from his shoulders until it was sticking straight up.

Fear clamped invisible steel bands around my ribs and sealed off my throat. "What did you do?" I mouthed, but no sound came out. Sparkles flickered in the periphery of my vision. No. No, no, no...

He glanced away and bit his lower lip. "Gin, I'm sorry—"

A thunderclap exploded above me, and everything went white.

Chapter 2

Divinius Morganis III, Crown Prince of the Fae Realm and Holder of the Seven Orbs of Femora

I glanced up from a particularly dusty grimoire as the door opened, signaling, yet again, an impending intrusion on my solitude. Why, oh why, couldn't the denizens of my parents' courts leave me alone, today of all days?

My mother's steward appeared, backlit by the bright sunlight spilling in from the hall.

I clenched my teeth and bit back a sigh. "What is it?"

The wretch bowed, almost fast enough to hide the scowl on his face. Almost.

My magic zipped over my skin, raising the fine hairs on my arms. It wanted to zap the little bastard as much as I did.

"Your Highness," he said, "Your mother inquires when you will be attending court tonight? Many of the young ladies are bemoaning your absence."

Ugh. Not this drivel again. I waved my hand in a flippant gesture. "Please convey to my mother that, while I of course appreciate the well-deserved attention, I'm occupied with my studies of the deep and mysterious." Two adjectives that were the exact opposite of every single one of those 'young ladies' that followed my mother around like well-behaved pets. I turned back to the grimoire.

Instead of accepting the dismissal, the steward shifted his weight back and forth. The action would've had more effect if the man weighed more than one hundred twenty-five pounds soaking wet.

I didn't bother hiding the sigh this time. "Was there something else, Taeral?"

He cleared his throat. "Indeed, Highness. With it being your birthday, the queen has requested your attendance. Tonight's party is for you, and as the honored guest, your presence is expected."

With the third sufficiently dramatic exhalation in less than a minute, I shut the thick tome—a gift from my father this morning. His first official acknowledgement of my abilities, in fact. An olive branch of sorts. The gesture made me feel some sort of warm fuzziness inside that was pleasant, but uncomfortable due to its lack of familiarity. But I suppose the secrets to the source of magic would have to wait, because fates forbid the queen not get her way, even on my special day. But there would be consequences tomorrow if I angered her tonight. "Very well. Please inform my mother I will be there in half an hour, since I am not appropriately attired for such a momentous occasion."

Taeral bowed, spun on his heel and exited my library.

With a grunt that was more frustration than pain, I stood, leaning backward until my spine cracked and the knot beneath my shoulder blade released.

"You'd think, being my birthday, I'd have a choice in how I spend my time," I muttered. But heavy were the burdens of the head that would one day wear the crown, and my adoring fans awaited.

I left the grimoire where it lay. My librarians knew better than to disturb my things.

Fortunately, my rooms were but a brief walk from the library. I pushed my door open. Mumbling under my breath sent a flicker of power from within my core to the chandelier. The energy flared, lighting the candles high above. Hundreds of crystals reflected the tapers' light around the spacious room. The warm glow matched the heat that flooded my veins at the flare of magic. Sure, I could turn the lights on the normal way—the switch was right next to the door—but showing off, even when it was to no one but myself, was a guilty pleasure.

At my nod and exhale, the wardrobe on the far side of the room opened, displaying my various outfits. I approached, frowning at the assortment. I pulled out each item, shook my head, and replaced it. Fashion was becoming increasingly constrictive of late, and unlike other people, I preferred to breathe.

Probably because my magic required the ability to do things like speak. The people at court, the normals, didn't seem to worry about such trivialities.

The last two options were my mage robes. I chewed on the inside of my cheek. Mother wouldn't be thrilled, but... Yes, one of them would do for this evening, a not-so-subtle dig at the queen and her insistence that I attend what was certain to be yet another boring parade of eligible-but-undesirable women. I pulled both from the closet and turned to face the mirror.

Which went best? Navy or eggplant?

I stared at my reflection, admiring the strength of my chin, the symmetric points of my ears, and the way my hair waved, just so, to catch the light from overhead.

The blue looked better with my eyes tonight.

I shoved the purple garment where it belonged and closed the door. Shrugging into the robes, I spun, making sure the silver embroidery flashed in the glow from the chandelier overhead. Despite its loose fit, the front was cut in such a way that it highlighted the breadth of my shoulders and the slimness of my hips.

I stepped back. Splaying my hands to my sides, I mumbled the Old Elvish word for fire. "Aga." Two fireballs appeared, hovering just above my palms. A mere parlor trick, of course, but it looked impressive as hell. I looked impressive, and ready for an evening at my mother's court.

With a flourish, I dismissed the magic and flicked my wrist to flare the robes dramatically as I turned and headed out the door.

"His Royal Highness, Divinius Morganis III, Crown Prince of the Fae Realm and Holder of the Seven Orbs of Femora." The herald bowed and stepped out of my way.

I halted at the top of the stairs and looked down on the room. Literally. This was such a waste of time—I don't know why she insisted I attend. It wasn't like I didn't already know everyone, and my social skills were not lacking. With my lips plastered in a thin smile, I nodded to my mother, who was, as expected, perched on her throne like a vulture. Opulent velvet curtains in purple and silver draped behind her, artfully directing attention to where she sat. The royal scepter lay across her lap. Gems in her delicate tiara sparkled enough to rival the embroidery on my robes.

She smiled and patted the cushion of the chair next to her.

I know what that look meant... she'd expected me half an hour ago, and there would be hours of groveling on my part before she'd let it go.

Keeping the false smile pinned in place, I descended the imperial staircase slowly, giving my mother's fawning minions time to prepare for my presence. It seemed like all fifty noble families were in attendance. Despite the large crowd, my footsteps echoed off the landing like some sort of death march leading me into what was yet another boring and pointless evening. Of late, my mother had taken to throwing me to the fish, just as one would a worm on a hook, for the sheer entertainment of watching everyone flock to me as I was crushed by the throng. It was no exaggeration to say court had become a torture session and would remain so until the queen got bored and moved on to something else.

As I stepped off the mezzanine, the music resumed. Several young ladies crowded at the bottom of the steps at my approach, dropping into deep curtsies. They batted their eyes and called out to me.

"Hello, Your Highness."

"Happy birthday!"

"Prince Divinius, over here."

"Ladies, ladies." I turned and gave them a more genuine smile, making eye contact while I gestured to myself. "There will be plenty of this to go around." At least, until I could come up with an excuse to leave. "But regrettably, my mother requires my presence at the moment." I accepted a few random hands, kissing their knuckles as I passed, with a wink and grin for each.

I didn't blame the nobles, not really. Court was a battle of influence and power—those who had it, and those who wanted it. The easiest way to climb to the top was by close association with my mother or, by extension, with me. The queen was far too fond of that game, nothing would change until I took the throne, which would likely be centuries from now.

I nodded to a group of men my age, standing at the edge of the room in their cliques. A few of them tilted their heads in my direction, though most kept their backs to me, their attention focused on something at their feet.

An odd pang hit my chest. Their disrespect was strange. I'd have to check in with them later. Perhaps someone brought a new pet to the party?

The crowd parted in front of me. I moved toward the white marble dais where my mother waited.

The queen grinned as I settled in the chair beside her. "Happy birthday, my son."

"Good evening, mother." I sat upright, my posture rigid.

She wore a burgundy gown which accentuated the gold of her throne. At least I'd decided against the purple robes. It would be uncouth to wear clashing clothes.

"So kind of you to join us."

I raised an eyebrow. Sarcasm? In public? She was usually more refined than that. She must truly be angry at my tardiness. No doubt I'd pay for it tonight, and for many days to come. Queen Lillia was the best in the realm when it came to holding grudges.

But she wasn't furious enough to disinherit me, so I could tolerate whatever she threw my way.

Shrugging a shoulder, I glanced across the room. The din from the crowd was more than sufficient to keep our words from carrying. "I was researching. Where's father?"

"At an emergency council meeting, which you'd know if you pulled your nose out of those dusty books once in a while."

Of course, His Majesty hadn't bothered to send a page and spare me an evening at court. Just because the king and the Mage College had their differences, that was no reason to exclude the crown prince from a council meeting. I pushed my annoyance aside. One day, when I sat on the throne, I would work with the mages rather than against, for the benefit of the realm.

My mother leaned close, keeping her voice low. "Divinius, you're of age. It's time to take up the mantle of your title and honor the royal obligations."

The what and what? Why couldn't she ever just say what she meant like a normal person? "Mother, what's that supposed to mean?"

She tilted her chin up and stared down her nose. "It's time for you to choose a mate and produce an heir." She handed me a folded piece of parchment. "I've done the hard work and prepared a list of suitable women from among the acceptable families."

With a sinking pit in my stomach, I unfolded the paper and scanned the twenty names.

Shelar Rogella, Pyria Loralei, Taniela Shanera... This was ridiculous. Now I couldn't help but wonder if she hadn't conspired to keep me out of the council meeting just to drop this on me. This sort of manipulation was right up her alley.

"Mother," I hissed, "you know I'm focused on my studies. I've no time for this." Refolding the letter, I held it between two fingers and handed it back to her.

She fixed me with a glare and leaned to whisper in my ear. "You will make time, or your father and I will select one for you. You have one week."

I blinked, frozen in surprise. Seven days? To choose the future queen? Why the sudden rush? The king and queen were young by fae standards...they'd rule for many decades or centuries to come.

Studying her face, I sighed at her expression and shoved the list into the deepest pocket of my robe. There was no arguing with her when she used that tone.

Happy birthday to me.

If only my parents valued my magical abilities half as much as the Mage College did.

The sound of the orchestra and the lighting was more muted now, as the room took on a foreboding, almost sinister atmosphere. The sparkling chandeliers overhead seemed to mock the black pit settling in my gut. My shoulders drooped as I scanned the crowd, picking out each of the women on the top five of my mother's list, and mentally crossed them off.

Too loud, too quiet, too bold, too whiny...

"Enjoy the party, my son. I suggest you use the time to...become acquainted with the selected ladies."

My mother stood, and I echoed her action. She banged the end of the scepter against the marble floor. Music and bodies froze, the attendees turned, bowing or curtseying as she passed. Her Majesty, Lillia Cordelia Morganis, Queen of the Fae Realm and Heir to the Rings of Reimar, ascended the stairs and disappeared.

Abandoning me in the middle of this unwanted celebration.

Great. Thank you, Mother. I should have refused to come or made myself harder to locate. But that was ridiculous, of course. One didn't disobey the queen's commands; I'd tried once as a child and still regretted it. The incident resulted in the single scar that marred my flawless skin. At least it wasn't in a visible location.

If I left now, someone would inform my mother even before I escaped to my rooms. And then she would disinherit me, and everything I'd been working toward regarding uniting the Mage College and the monarchy would crumble like a sandcastle at high tide.

I plastered a smile on my face that felt even more fake than the one I'd entered with and headed for the food. If I had to waste the evening, at least I could do so on a full stomach.

I waited for the butler to pour me a glass of wine and sipped it without tasting the sweetness, perusing the assortment of offerings that stretched from one end of the wall to the other. Ripe elderberries and dragon fruit competed for limited counter space with savory bear stew. Somewhere further down, a dish of spiced gooseberry pie hid, if my nose was to be believed. Not that I'd likely have time to enjoy the buffet—the noble-women would swarm me any moment now.

It was all such a waste. Even twice the attendees would be hard-pressed to eat half of this.

Taniela Shanera, woman number three on my mother's list, stepped up beside me. She leaned in close to select a choice strawberry. "Happy birthday, Your Highness. Are you enjoying the evening?"

I held back a snort and schooled my expression. My frustration with my mother was not Lady Shanera's fault. "I am, thank you. All the more for your presence. And you?"

She stuck the end of the berry in her mouth, pooched her lips, and bit off its tip as she stared into my eyes. As an extra measure, she leaned over, giving me a superb view of her ample cleavage.

Wait... I glanced around the room. All the eligible women were acting oddly, doing their best to attract my attention while also being obvious in their attempts to not watch me.

I hadn't seen so many hair flounces and eyelash battings outside a Coming-of-Age Ball. I turned my focus back to Taniela's sultry gaze. This was going to be even worse than I'd imagined. My mother must have let slip—accidentally, of course—the topic of her list, and now the entire court knew I'd been ordered to find a wife post-haste. Though, since no one had burst into tears or abruptly excused themselves, they couldn't know whose names were or were not listed.

Perhaps I should leak it. That would at least eliminate half of the women from the competition and get them out of my hair. With the next breath, I dismissed the idea. Doing so would only make the remaining ladies more brazen. My mother had well and truly cornered me.

Valek.

I narrowed my eyes and studied the crowd. Hopefully, they wouldn't start circling me in truth.

Taniela wrapped her arm around mine and pulled me toward the vacant space in front of the orchestra. "Would you like to dance with me, Your Highness?"

As if she was giving me a choice.

She ignored the glares of the other women. The music faded out mid-song as the musicians noticed our approach. Movement ceased.

My limbs felt numb and heavy as resignation settled on my shoulders. The only thing to be done was to get through this night. I would corner my father tomorrow and have him help talk some sense into mother.

Bracing myself, I nodded to the conductor and placed my hand at Taniela's waist. The orchestra struck up a classic waltz and I spun her in time to the beat.

How many dances would be considered acceptable before I could take my leave? It was likely I'd need to dance with all the women on the list to please my mother's informants. Twenty songs, back-to-back, would be exhausting for anyone, even if they were enjoying all of this. Which I most certainly was not.

With my position, my abilities and admittedly stunning good looks, I'd never lacked for female attention. It was, after all, my due. But the difference between lighthearted flirting and tonight's predatory intensity made me feel like I was on a battlefield with no weapons.

Taniela batted her eyelashes and tilted her head. "So, my prince... what qualities do you think are important for a future queen?"

I frowned, yanking my focus back to her. She was going right for my throat. No subtlety or ability to read social cues at all. "I'm sorry?"

She licked her full lips, using the gesture to hide the flicker of annoyance that flashed across her features. "What qualities do you think make a good queen? Intelligence? Beauty?" She pooched her mouth again and winked at me. "Stamina?"

Well, Taniela was certainly beautiful, though I doubted the other two applied to her. But she would expect pretty words in my response. I thought back to my mother's maneuverings. The true answer was the ruthlessness to do whatever one must to achieve her goals. Though my mother thought more about herself than her kingdom when it came to said desires. I could hardly admit that a cunning and manipulative nature sprung to my mind, however. That would be tantamount to announcing hunting season on me, and this coming week was going to be rough enough already.

Beneath my feet, the ground wobbled. My heart skipped a beat as Taniela clung to me with a little more fervor than was likely warranted.

I glanced around as exclamations of alarm rang out from across the room. Elysia hadn't had an earthquake in over a thousand years.

Had I consumed too much wine? But that was ridiculous, of course. I'd only had one sip before Taniela hauled me away. My stomach twisted.

Perhaps it would unsettle the nobles enough that court would adjourn early. That would be the best birthday present I could ask for.

The music faded before I had to come up with a response to Taniela's innuendo. At least the conductor seemed to be on my side. Maybe all the songs tonight would be so short.

I met the man's eyes and nodded my thanks.

Woman number seven on The List used her ample hips to nudge Taniela out of the way.

Mentally crossing off the first of tonight's forced dances, I let her go with a quick bow and a kiss to the back of her hand before turning to the newcomer. "Lady Sapphora, how pleasant to see you." Lies, lies, lies.

The room dimmed for a heartbeat as the music started up again.

Pressure squeezed against my ears. What in Naraka was going on?

The hairs on my arms stood on end as the telltale scent of ozone tickled my nose.

I glanced around. No one else seemed to notice anything awry, but the realization settled deep in my bones. A shiver ran up my spine.

Valek! Someone was performing magic!

At least now I had something to do beyond dancing with my would-be fiancées, for the few moments it would take me to clear it up, anyway. Unless they were invited by the king or queen, mages were prohibited from attending court functions. With the exception of myself, of course.

I closed my eyes, not losing a beat as I guided Sapphora in a twirl and whispered the Old Elven word for vision. "Darasana."

I opened my eyes. A multilayered blue-black cloud hung overhead, crackling with bits of lighting.

According to the Mage College, navy was the color of conjuration, which had been outlawed for seven generations. My jaw went slack. Who was stupid enough to be conjuring, and at my birthday party, nonetheless? The last thing court needed was a demon summoned into their midst. Or worse.

As the only other magic user present, it was my solemn duty to handle it. Giddiness at the chance to show off warred with the sour taste of apprehension at the back of my throat. I'd never counteracted a conjuring before. I snorted—there were likely no mages alive who had ever opposed a conjurer.

One side of my mouth ticked up. I would be the first.

I dipped a blissfully unaware Sapphora, taking the opportunity to check behind me.

There it was. A pulse of warm satisfaction burst through me.

A thin tendril of power snaked from the haze to the corner of the room, where I'd noted the young men clustered earlier. No matter how I strained, I couldn't ascertain the mage's identity, hidden in the dark recesses of the alcove—not from the dance floor, at least.

A herd of sea demons swam through my gut. Now that I'd found the mage, I would actually have to confront them, would have to risk failing in a truly spectacular manner and in front of everyone who was anyone in Elysia. I was under no illusions—someone brazen enough to sneak into court just to conjure Helani-knew-what in the queen's presence would be no novice. I'd be going up against a master, who would have more training and knowledge than myself. My only hope was that my raw power would neutralize those handicaps.

Warm fingers snaked over my shoulders and around my neck, the shivers they left in their wake demanding my attention. "Your Highness?" Sapphora pulled me close, crushing her chest to mine.

"Yes?"

She stuck out her lower lip in an exaggerated pout that many men had likely found endearing but only stirred my ire. "Is everything okay? You seem rather distracted."

I shook my head and gave her what I hoped was an apologetic smile. "I'm sorry, my dear." I pressed a kiss to one of her hands and guided her off the floor. "Duty calls. I must apologize for cutting our dance short." I mentally winced at my next words. "I'll make it up to you."

Her disappointment vanished at my last sentence as she curtseyed.

I smiled, patting down the wayward tendrils of her hair that were sticking up from the magical static in the air then headed toward the source of the spell.

The orchestra faded out, leaving an eerie silence in its wake. The rustle of paper and a few small gasps reached me. I glanced back. Sheet music peeled off the musicians' stands, floating to the floor. Women and men desperately held their hair down at the oppressive atmosphere building around them.

The power was ramping up fast. My heart gave a single warning thump against my ribs. I should've untangled myself from Sapphora sooner. Picking up my pace, I broke into a sprint as my pulse pounded through my ears.

A loud explosion shook the stones under my feet. My eardrums popped. I lost my grip on my magic and the navy cloud disappeared from my vision as if it had never been. A trickle of sweat worked its way down the back of my neck. With a growl, I wiped it away.

Valek! Concentrate!

Tiny bits of mortar fell from the ceiling, peppering those below. I threw my arms over my head protectively as I ran. If I didn't hurry, the entire castle could collapse on top of us.

Behind me, a high-pitched voice screamed as the ground trembled.

Footsteps pounded through the hallway beyond the grand staircase. Voices called out in alarm in the entry.

As one, the nobles surged toward the exits—bottlenecking at the large double doors to the balcony overlooking my mother's gardens, or up the stairs into the main hall. Caught in the middle, I fought against the rising wave of bodies. Frustration rose, pushing acid up my throat that drowned out my too-quick breaths.

"Vadha," I mumbled, willing the magic to project my voice above the din. "Get out of my way!" The conjurer couldn't be allowed to escape.

Behind me, the grand chandelier crashed to the ground, sending crystal shards throughout the room.

Someone in a forest green ball gown brushed past. The static discharged where their arm touched mine with a painful spark.

The spell was building to a crescendo. If I couldn't block it, we would have more than an explosion and fallen masonry to worry about. Any moment now, some horrible creature from the under-deep would manifest in the middle of court and start devouring the bodies and souls of my mother's courtiers. My feet moved as though I was running through water, each step heavy and slow as I fought against the force of the conjurer's spell.

The push of the crowd disappeared as I stumbled into the now vacant corner.

"Darasana!" The magic responded, and the navy cumulonimbus cloud blinked into view once again. It towered overhead, filling the room. Angry currents of power roiled within.

Blood drained from my face as my skin turned to ice.

The spell was too big, had collected too much magic. I couldn't hold it back alone. If only I'd spent more effort studying and wasted less time at court, maybe I'd be strong enough to stop this.

I had no training as a war mage. I would be useless against a demon or other denizen of the underworld. Remaining here would only get me killed.

The only hope now was in catching the caster and physically stopping them.

"Valek!" I whirled around, searching for the tendril that would link the conjurer to their power. A pale blue filament trailed outside.

They were too far away. I had no chance of finding them before the spell took hold.

The heat that had been building in my chest since I'd exited the dance floor exploded as full-blown panic burst through my muscles. "Brace yourselves!" I shouted, my voice swallowed by the cries of the fleeing nobles.

The screams in the hallway above changed timber. "The king is dead! The king's been murdered!"

No! My heart stopped, my blood freezing in my veins. My father was not dead. He couldn't be. The elf had his entire council and a squad of royal guards to protect him. An invisible steel band squeezed my ribs, crushing the air from my lungs. My vision blurred as the room tilted sideways. Father! Mother!

This couldn't be happening.

I swallowed. I wasn't ready to rule. Would never be ready.

I spun, staring at the suddenly vacant room with wide eyes.

The magic crackled as the spell crested, tumbling toward me. A bolt of lightning caught me in the forehead as everything went white.

Chapter 3

Gin

A strong arm snaked around my waist, pulling me against a firm torso. His thumb rubbed light circles over my stomach. A smile danced on my lips as my hands clenched the balcony railing overlooking the city of Kadena, the capital of Obron. The sun was just cresting the horizon, the morning air still pleasantly cool.

Orion's chin brushed the skin near my ear, his breath sending pleasant tingles down my spine. "How did you sleep?"

He knew the answer to that, he'd been with me all night. His fingers threaded through my hair as he tugged gently.

I tilted my head to the side and back against his chest, exposing my neck.

A heartbeat later, his lips descended, kissing the spot that caused heat to explode in my core. He knew exactly what I liked.

I moaned. His skin on mine always felt so good, I'd never get enough of it, even if we had a hundred years together. It had been such a long time since we'd touched. Longer than it should have been.

My toes curled, the delicious warmth building below my navel. I closed my eyes with a quiet moan, enjoying the sensation.

He nipped at the soft spot behind my ear. "Genevieve?" Fates, I could melt at the sound of his voice. I arched my back, pressing harder against his chest in demand.

His free hand ran lightly up my arm, across my collarbone that was exposed by the unbuttoned clasp of the night gown and up my neck. No, it wasn't his fingers—it was a rose. A black rose.

We'd spent many mornings on this balcony, overlooking Kadena. Never once had he brought me a flower.

He slid the petals to my lips, their light scent wafting beneath my nose.

Wait. A black rose, like the one I'd just tried to give him, along with a quick death. I stiffened, pulling away as the dream fog lifted from my thoughts.

His arm wrapped around my chest, locking me in place against him. "What were you doing in my room last night?"

"God's Teeth!" My fingers brushed my aching forehead, finding yet another goose egg. What in sand demon's spit was up with people knocking me out today? There ought to be some rule about how terrible a day could be before the universe gave you a free pass for the next twenty-four hours. I rubbed the phantom press of rose petals away from my lips as Orion's voice echoed in my ears.

Something hard pressed into my back—stone. The air smelled fresh, with a hint of moisture that didn't match the dankness of Akre's dungeon.

The heat in my veins cooled faster than slickrock after sunset.

Akre had sent me to die. But compared to the weight of Roland's drugging me piled on top of Orion's betrayal, Akre's actions seemed almost inconsequential and expected. A hoarse laugh escaped me, sounding more like a wheeze.

A cool breeze tickled my skin, brushing a few locks of hair across my forehead.

My eyes burned as the lump rose in my throat. I covered my face in my hands as I squeezed my lids shut, as if that would hold back the welling tears. Orion and the other warlords had cut everything I'd known out from beneath me seven years ago. Tonight, I'd lost the last person I could rely on when Roland chose Akre over me, drugging me and handing me over to the guards.

So why wasn't I in Akre's dungeon, locked in a dank cell waiting my turn on the water wheel?

I dropped my hands, rubbing them over my cheeks to wipe away the betraying wetness there. Sniffing, I glanced around before slamming my eyes shut against the sunlight. I was lying on the ground, on some sort of smooth, cool rock, completely at odds with the sun being so high in the sky this time of year.

A ball of snakes curled through my stomach. Whatever this was, it was Roland's doing.

I clenched my teeth in a noiseless snarl as my rage crested, forcing an acid taste up my throat. I'd trusted the man like a second father. How could he do this? I'd gut him and leave his bones for the sand demons to suck the marrow. I opened my eyes, squinting until they adjusted.

What was going on? Orion was a warlord, and I'd tried to kill him. Then Akre's guards found me and Roland drugged me. Regardless of the outcome, I should be either Akre or Orion's prisoner, awaiting whatever fate they saw fit. So, where was I, and what was their game?

The lump in my throat shifted, the muscles in my neck tightening. I couldn't breathe! My lungs felt like I'd been on the water wheel Akre liked to tie me to when I failed him. Blindfolded, he would turn the crank at unpredictable speeds, dunking me in and out of the pool. Opening my mouth, I tried to inhale, but my ribs wouldn't expand.

The world was collapsing in on me. Every nerve in my body burst into flames. I crab walked backward, as if that would help me escape the terrors that plagued my mind.

I ran into a pile of boulders hard enough to knock the air from my lungs. It whooshed up my throat, throwing me into a coughing fit. I curled onto my side as I wretched up the arak Roland had served me.

The spasm broke the panic as my brain caught up with what my body was trying to tell me.

I wasn't tied down, and they hadn't stationed any guards nearby. At least, not that I could see. And there was no water in sight, other than what I'd just thrown up. I needed to calm down, take a deep breath, and think.

Squinting, I studied my surroundings. I was not in Akre's dungeons—the sun would never penetrate those crypts.

There was no clinking or telltale weight of manacles around my wrists or ankles. I didn't appear to be under arrest.

At least, not yet.

I pushed myself to my feet, leaning on the rocks behind me and looked down, brushing the last of the purple dust that had been on Roland's hands off my sleeves. Whip, check. Missing stilettos, unfortunately check. Other than the headache and aching ribs, I didn't seem to be any worse for wear. And I still had one weapon.

The idiots who'd kidnapped me from The Golden Gosling hadn't even bothered to disarm me. A wave of indignation slammed into me as

I clenched my jaw until my teeth creaked, reminding me I had a split and swollen lip. "Don't you know who I am?" I yelled at the surrounding stones.

A mocking echo was the only reply.

"Come out and fight me, you cowards!" I turned in a circle, trying to watch all directions at once.

They had to come out, to make themselves known, because my brain was finally processing what my eyes had been telling me since I woke up: I was nowhere near home. The smooth grey rocks were of a type I'd never seen before. They were covered with scattered patches of thin verdant strands that grew in the cracks and filled a clearing that was walled off with green vegetation that climbed into the blue sky. Nothing like the deserts of Obron with their sandstone formations in vibrant tans, oranges and reds.

My outrage settled, chilling in my bones at the very real possibility that I was alone, lost in this strange place with no supplies and idea how to get back home. A hollow opened in my gut. I almost preferred Akre's dungeons—at least those were familiar, and I knew what to expect.

"What do you want?" I hollered.

Again, there was no movement, no response.

I'd kill someone to have my tattoo itch right about now, but it was annoyingly silent.

Being more careful, I held my hand up to shield my eyes and peeked through my eyelashes. The sun shown on a tangle of miniature palm trees that resembled those cultivated on the warlord's estate with much care and wasted water. Unlike those, these specimens were no taller than my knees.

They were so green. Were they fake? I brushed the vascularized leaves with my fingertips. Drops of dew fell to the ground. I rubbed the foreign wetness between my fingers. It highlighted the dry, cracked blood underneath my nails.

Orion's blood, from when I'd gouged his too-perfect face.

I glanced at the clearing again.

I was sitting on the edge of a crumbled gray stone floor I'd originally mistaken for scattered boulders.

Where was I?

Several eroded columns covered in robust vines formed a circle around some sort of dais in the center of the room. The roof overhead had long since disappeared. Plants of all varieties lined the outer rim, determined to reclaim the ruins.

A speck of color amongst the green caught my eye and I crept toward it. Yellow flowers glowed in the sun, giving off a sweet odor that reminded me of the overused perfumes worn by the women in Akre's court.

Somewhere, invisible behind the maze of plants, a fountain trickled.

I licked my cracked lips and swallowed past a sandpaper tongue. The aftertaste from vomiting and whatever drugs Roland had used on me roiled my stomach. I'd never longed so badly for something, anything, to drink. I'd even take something from the old kegs that lay forgotten in the back room of The Golden Gosling at this point.

But the plants were so strange; some might be poisonous, or harbor other unknown dangers. Did I dare brave them to find the stream? Would it even be drinkable? In Kadena, water was muddy and not safe to consume—that was why everyone drank arak, which was made with water specifically purified by the palace.

I glanced at my hands and feet. I was definitely dehydrated, and sitting here would accomplish nothing. Shaking my head, I scowled at my weakness. I was Desert Rose, the most feared assassin in all of Obron. No way would I cower before some stupid foreign plants standing between me and the chance to assuage my thirst.

I pulled out my whip and sliced through a handful of miniature palms. The fronds tumbled to the ground.

Someone cleared their throat behind me. "What did those ferns do to you?"

I spun, lash held at the ready, eyes wide as I searched for the intruder.

A man a good hand taller than me stood just out of reach. He wore long dark blue robes with silver runes embroidered onto them. The cloth matched the exact shade of his eyes. Pointed ears peeked out from a full head of lightly waved hair. The sun highlighted the angle of his strong jaw, high cheekbones and perfectly defined mouth.

I'd never given much care to my appearance. At least, not in the seven years since Akre had taken over. It didn't matter what I looked like when the only people who would be seeing me up close and personal were marked for death. But facing this elf who could have stepped straight out of the divine realm, I was suddenly far too aware of my bruised face, swollen eyes and disheveled hair. I must look like I'd crawled out of the sand demon spawning pits.

Heat flooded my face. "Who are you?" My voice snapped off the stone.

He crossed his arms and fixed me with an annoyed glare, as if he was mortally offended I couldn't identify him on sight. "I am Divinius Morganis III, Crown Prince of the Fae Realm and Holder of the Seven Orbs of Femora. You may address me as Your Royal Highness."

Not a god, then. Good. Though from his tone, he was self-absorbed enough to consider himself one. "Right. And I'm a warlord's consort." I studied him. "On second thought, I don't give a sand demon's left tooth who you are. Send me home now."

The elf blinked, brows knitted like I'd insulted him. "You think I conjured us here?"

Irritation sparked in my gut, sending that burning sensation up my throat again. I spread my arms, gesturing to the clearing, leaving myself wide open, inviting an attack. "I don't see anyone else here, do you? I know I didn't drop us in the middle of...wherever we are."

"Interesting." He stepped back and glanced around, writing me off. Just like that. Like I wasn't a threat.

My jaw dropped. I should kill him for that insult alone. Except, it was oddly comforting to find another person in this forsaken place. Even if he was too egotistical for his own good and not smart enough to respect me for the danger I was.

"Clearly," he continued, "a normal like yourself couldn't manage such a feat."

I frowned, squinting at him. "A what?"

His gaze darted back to me before returning to our surroundings.

I flicked my whip so it snapped in the crisp air. "I said, a what?" If he was going to ignore me, I'd kill him. I'd just have to settle for being alone to figure this mess out.

He stared at me for several heartbeats then heaved an exaggerated sigh. "A normal. Someone without magical talent."

I blinked. He'd called me that like it was an insult. Bastard. "The ability to use magic is reserved for the warlords." As if everyone didn't know that. Oh, sand demon spit. I tightened my grip on my weapon as the implication slammed through me. "You're a warlord then?"

Fates... I couldn't stand against two warlords in the same day, even at my best. And after my fight with Orion and this thing with Roland, I was leagues away from top form right now. The universe was throwing everything it had at me to finish me off.

The blood drained from my face. My knees went weak as I stumbled backward, catching myself on one of the vine-covered pillars. I squeezed my eyes closed, bracing for the blast of magic that would end me.

"You don't listen very well, do you? I told you, I am Divinius Morganis III, Crown Prince of the Fae—"

My eyes snapped open and I cut him off. "Of the Fae Realm, blah, blah, fancy words, blah. Crown Prince, Warlord, whatever." Titles were transient, the only thing that mattered was power. As a warlord, he had it... I didn't. Not without a crap ton more weapons and weeks' worth of preparation.

Oddly enough, he didn't seem inclined to kill me right this moment. I glanced around. Maybe he was waiting for his armies or some other sort of backup? Other than Orion, I'd never seen another warlord fight their own battles. And in Orion's case, that had been a very specific situation where he hadn't had time to summon his guards when I'd attacked him. After a few heartbeats when no one appeared, I turned my attention back to the elf—Divinius. "So, you didn't bring us here?"

He stared at me like I'd grown a third eye. "Why would I bother with a human who stinks of sweat, blood and dirty leather? Especially one who was obviously fighting in the pits with the dogs."

Heat rushed to my face in response to the flames that exploded in my chest. My knees stabilized and I pushed away from the pillar. I'd forgotten in the last seven years how much I hated royalty. "Sorry," I snapped. "I didn't have time to brush myself down after my kidnapping."

"Kidnapping?" He scrutinized me as though seeing me for the first time. The sun cast a red sheen to his dark brown hair that was far too shiny for its own good. One curl fell forward to rest on his sharp cheekbone, as if a sculptor had specifically placed it there to highlight the fineness of the prince's features.

I fought not to shift my weight. I clenched my jaw as his gaze scraped up and down my raw nerves. Needing to distract him before my discomfort betrayed my weakness, I swallowed and licked my lips. "Where are we, anyway?"

He shrugged. "Helani if I know. I thought you brought us here." He turned his nose up, staring at me with that haughty expression all royals seemed to perfect by puberty. "Of course, I realize it was a ridiculous assumption, now that I've spoken with you."

The nerve! If I had just a little more energy and my ribs hurt just a bit less, I'd wrap my whip around his throat and... Taking a deep breath, I used all my remaining mental strength to rein in the impulse. Right now, I would lose that fight. After everything I'd gone through in the last twenty-four hours, I did not want to die. "Are you trying to goad me into killing you? Because I've got enough to deal with today without having to make your death look like an accident."

He brushed his hand over his eyes. "As if... What did you say your name was?"

I bit back a snort. As if I'd trust him with anything personal. "I didn't. You can call me Desert Rose."

He gave me the same look I'd likely given him when he identified himself. "*The* Desert Rose? Assassin extraordinaire?"

My chest swelled despite myself as I threw him a crooked smile. "I see my reputation precedes me. All the way to...?" I let my words trail off, the silence in the clearing building.

He rolled his eyes and sighed. "Elysia."

I frowned, trying to recall the map of the world that had hung in my father's study when I was a small child. Since I'd been enslaved, there'd been no need to bother with international geography. "Is that where we are, then?" Sand demon spit... Elysia was weeks away from Obron, even with horses. On foot, it could take me a full moon to return to Kadena, assuming everything went smoothly. Without supplies or coin, I wasn't foolish enough to hope the trip would be easy.

Shaking his head, Divinius crossed his arms. "You're a long way from home, Rose."

I flashed my teeth at him, the memory of the black petals scattered across Orion's sheets springing unexpectedly into my mind. "Don't call me that."

"What? Rose?"

I nodded, a muscle in my jaw twitching. Those stupid flowers...

"I refuse to address you by a moniker. If you won't share your name, then I'll call you as I see fit."

I stepped toward him, flicking my whip. My patience was at an end. Maybe I would lose my life today, but I'd do my best to take this bastard with me. "Then you do want to die."

He widened his stance and held his arms out, palms facing the sky. "Aga." Two balls of fire appeared in the air above his hands. "Careful who you threaten, assassin."

I met his hard glare with one of my own as I wrestled down the ball of snakes in my gut that arose with my terror at the blatant display of power. That was the same word Orion had used, and my body remembered exactly how much his magic had hurt.

Pulling my mental shield up and stuffing the fear into the dark recesses of my mind where it belonged, I tilted my head. What was the chance I could get him with my whip before the fireball hit me? Pretty good, actually. But the chances of getting him before he threw the fire was less likely. Either way, I'd end up fried to a crisp. I wouldn't be able to kill Akre, Roland or Orion if I was dead.

I narrowed my eyes and glared at him.

His gaze traveled from my toes to my forehead. Several heartbeats passed.

My white knuckled grip on the lash was so tight my hand was starting to tremble.

Finally, he flicked his wrists and the fireballs disappeared. "Listen, Rose—"

"If you refuse to call me what I ask," I interrupted, fighting a shudder, "at least call me Gin."

A satisfied smirk danced across his face. I had the strongest urge to slap some sense into him, but he was a warlord. One didn't assault warlords unless they were looking to die a very slow and painful death. Like I almost had with Orion.

A dagger of ice slashed through my heart. It would be easier if I knew how deeply Orion's betrayal went. Had he participated in the uprising that had ended my parents' lives? Or killed someone who had and taken their place after-the-fact? It wasn't like I could ask him, much less expect him to answer.

"There. That wasn't so hard, was it?" The hint of a dimple creased Divinius' right cheek.

I bared my teeth in a grimace. I didn't know him nearly well enough to trust him with my name, but anything was better than Rose.

His shoulders drooped into a slouch as he exhaled. He dragged his fingers through his hair, pulling it away from his face. I ignored the shine of the dark waves as they reflected the sunlight. "Listen, Gin. My palace was under attack when I was banished, my father assassinated. I have no idea how much time passed before I woke up here, but by now, my mother's likely dead, too. It's vital I get back to my realm immediately and set it to rights."

I scoffed. "What do I care? Royals are killed all the time. Parents die. It's a fact of life. You'd best get used to it." As a warlord, he'd probably murdered more than his fair share of people. Of innocents. It seemed the height of hypocrisy to be so torn up when it was someone he cared about.

His mouth opened and closed several times, as though my flippant response had left him speechless.

A small tendril of satisfaction uncurled in my stomach. Warlord or not, I was not going to subjugate myself; I would not bow to his will.

"W-well." He glanced around the clearing as he lifted a hand to the back of his neck and turned to me. "I suspect you have pressing business to attend to back home, also?"

"Of course." My blood boiled at the reminder. My knuckles went white as I squeezed the handle of my whip. Roland needed to die, along with any of his conspirators. Then Orion, and Akre. Though maybe not in that order...

Divinius raised an eyebrow and cleared his throat, bringing my attention back to him. "Well, it seems to me you're more apt to get back where you belong with my aid than by yourself. And I'm more likely to survive long enough to return to Elysia with someone like you by my side." He took a step forward.

I matched it by taking one back, brandishing my whip. "Stay away from me."

"It's not in your best interest to kill me, nor I you."

I blinked and threw him the sort of smile that always irritated Roland. "Yet."

Divinius studied me and cleared his throat. "What do you say you put your weapons away, I promise not to use any magic on you, and we figure out where we are?" He held out his hand. "What do you say, partner?"

I stared at the elf, then at the arm he'd extended to me. He didn't seem to be lying—he was too frustrated to feign innocence. But then, I hadn't seen Roland's betrayal coming, either. Or Orion's.

However, the fae did have a point, and I needed to get home.

"Fine." I coiled my whip and secured it to my belt, ignoring his hand. Besides, a good assassin didn't need a weapon when surprise was on their side. If push came to shove, I could take him to the ground before the brain beneath that perfectly tousled hair realized what happened.

"Excellent." He took a step toward me, dropping his arm. "Now, how do we figure out where we are?"

"I have no idea, elf." I braced my hands on my hips. "I don't see a convenient map with 'You Are Here' inked on it. Can't your magic tell you?"

He shook his head. "I don't study Divination. I can't pull knowledge out of thin air."

Well, that was probably a lie, but I could play that game if he insisted. "Whatever." I brushed my palms on my pants and turned my back to him. It was a risk, but his posture was relaxed. He'd be hard-pressed to get the jump on me without warning. I gestured to the flora. "I hear a fountain. If these plants are real, maybe the water's safe to drink."

I practically heard his eyes roll. "Of course, they're real. And why would the water not be drinkable? It's water."

I glared at him over my shoulder. Typical warlords and their privilege. "Most in Obron is too dirty to drink. That's why the arak brewers have such a raging business." That, and after a few swigs, even Roland's booze tasted decent.

I swallowed past the bitter aftertaste in my mouth from whatever the bastard had used to drug me.

Well, usually arak was okay.

I pushed a handful of plants out of the way with the tip of my boot and stepped into the thick undergrowth. Trails of dew dripped down my legs and arms, leaving cool, muddy streaks in their wake. The sound of running water loomed closer.

"Hey, wait up!"

Footsteps trampled the foliage behind me. I didn't bother to respond or pause. Apparently the warlord didn't like being left alone, either. Good to know.

Tall trees with thin trunks and fat leaves spread above, shading the forest floor. Goosebumps pebbled my skin. The foreign but refreshing scent of petrichor tickled my nose.

This place was magical.

Too bad I had business to handle and couldn't stay here.

The vegetation thinned, revealing an emerald-green pond with a small waterfall on the opposite end.

My jaw dropped. I fell to my knees at the pool's edge. The water was clear—I could see all the way to the bottom. It was stunning, the most beautiful thing I'd ever seen.

I took a deep breath. It smelled amazing.

Cupping my hands in a bowl shape, I dipped them into the liquid and brought it to my mouth. Refreshing coolness washed the sensation of sand and grit from my tongue. It soothed my aching throat.

This was delicious. I had no idea water could taste so good. I cupped another handful.

Thin tendrils of red-brown stained the pool where my hands had been. I was dirty—it was probably no safer for me to drink from my cupped palms than it was from unapproved Obronian wells, but I didn't care. The liquid was the most decadent thing I'd ever tasted.

I bit back a groan.

The crown prince of whatever-it-was perched on a rock beside me, being careful to arrange his robes so they didn't touch the mud or water. "You act as though you're dying of thirst."

Because I was blade free at the moment, I swallowed a retort about how he could die of a dagger to the throat. And I didn't feel like getting into another fight with a warlord today. I'd rather drink more of this. Gesturing to the pool, I said, "You're missing out, Div. Try some."

From the corner of my eye, I caught the edges of his mouth hardening at the nickname. "You will address me as—"

"You refused to call me what I asked," I reminded him, victory churning in my gut. I fought to keep my mouth from curling up in a triumphant grin. "Why should I do any different for you?"

He frowned and blinked at me for several heartbeats before he shook his head and rolled his eyes. "Impertinent human. How my father deals with your kind, I'll never understand." He paused. "I mean, how he used to deal with you."

I caught the twitch of pain across his features when he corrected himself to past tense, but I didn't care. I slurped another handful.

This elf was unlike any of the warlords I knew, and I had no clue what to do with him.

Sliding forward, Divinius dipped a long finger in the pool then, with a grimace, touched his tongue. "It's normal water. What's the big deal?"

"Normal water?" I blinked. Was he for real? "The merchants in Elysia would make a fortune if they could transport this to Obron. Our wells are full of mud, good for little more than sustaining the warlord's palm trees. It tastes like dirt and will only make you more thirsty."

He raised his eyebrow. "What about your rivers?"

I laughed, liquid streaming down my chin leaving what I was certain would be embarrassing dark marks behind. "In the desert?"

He harrumphed. "Perhaps you should bathe. The dirt on your face makes it look like you have a beard." He sniffed. "It would take care of the stench, too."

What an asshole. I was so tired of being judged by those who considered themselves my superiors, on top of being physically and emotionally exhausted. I put my hands on my hips and whirled to face him, hoping he interpreted the flush on my face as coming from anger rather than embarrassment. "What do you expect after a full night of assassinating warlords and getting kidnapped?" Or failing to assassinate them, but he didn't need to know that.

Divinius ignored me and pushed to his feet. "I'll wait for you back in the ruins. Be thorough but try not to take too long." He turned on his heel with a flare of his robes that had me ducking to avoid getting hit in the face before disappearing back the way he'd come.

"Be thorough but try not to take too long," I muttered, parroting his words like the mature adult I was.

Bastard. He really needed a good punch to the gut.

Shoving him from my thoughts, I stared down at the water. I'd kick his ass later. Right now, there was a whole pool, and I had it all to myself.

Stripping down to my undergarments, I stepped into the pond.

Tight bands wrapped themselves around my ribs and I was suddenly back in Akre's dungeon, tied to the water wheel by my wrists and ankles.

Soft mud squished between my toes. It tickled.

Squeezing my eyes closed, I clenched my jaw. I wasn't there. The sun beat through the leaves overhead, warming my skin. I took a deep breath, holding it for the count of five before exhaling.

When I was turning on the wheel, the liquid always hit my face first. Here, it was only covering my feet, and I was in complete control. I could enter the pond as slowly as I wanted, my legs and arms free to move as I wished. And I wouldn't submerge my face.

It took several minutes for the burning in my chest to subside until all that lingered was the dull ache from my broken rib. It took me even longer to work my way into the pool, when I found a good spot to sit that would keep my head above the surface.

The pool wasn't deep, which was good because I had no idea how to swim. I sat and untied the leather thong that held my braid, tossing it on the bank with my clothes and whip. Combing my braid out with my fingers, I took a slow breath. Steadying myself, I dipped my head back as the water flowed over my scalp. It swayed with the current.

As soon as I felt the phantom sensation of liquid flowing over my face, I sat back up. That was enough hair washing for the day.

Brushing the soaking strands out of my eyes, I looked down.

A cloud of filth and blood spread from me in every direction. The pool's bottom was no longer visible.

Oh. That had been what His Royalness had been talking about. My face burned. No one I normally interacted with would have cared that I was so dirty. I swallowed the painful tightness in my throat and lowered my head. Scrubbing at my skin, I watched more scum slough off. Taking a deep breath, I closed my eyes and pretended I was standing over a simple basin of water instead of a pool big enough to drown in and splashed my face to get rid of any mud that may be lingering.

Some time later, I climbed to my rock on the bank, re-braided my hair and watched the dirt settle as the pond slowly cleared. With my locks again tied back, I reached for my pants.

They were also filthy.

Taking them in both hands, I slapped them as hard as I could against the boulder Divinius had sat on earlier. I smiled, imagining with each hit I was striking his high-and-mightiness.

Clouds of dust and grit exploded into the air. I sneezed.

When the debris quit flying, I grabbed my tunic and did the same. Somewhere along the way, I'd gotten a faint sheen of Roland's purple powder across the back of my shirt. I wiped it off with my hand.

I'd trusted him, gone so far as to consider him a friend.

I would kill Roland for his betrayal, if it was the last thing I did.

I stepped into the clearing, my hair leaving a trail of drips behind me on the stone. My face and neck may still be swollen and bruised, but my eyes felt less puffy and at least I no longer smelled of fear, sweat and blood. Maybe, just maybe, I could face the rest of whatever this day chose to throw at me and crawl out the other side.

The prince's robes lay in a jumbled pile in the middle of the ruins. My heart leaped into my throat. Had I taken so long he'd lost patience and left? If so, it didn't make much sense for him to ditch his clothes only to run off. But he was an elf and a warlord—who knew what to expect from him? My hand drifted to the handle of my whip as my muscles tensed, bracing for an attack. "Divinius?"

"Up here!" His voice floated down from above.

Holding one hand over my eyes to shield them, I turned toward the sound. He was perched at the top of one of the thin-trunked trees, his torso obscured by their large leaves.

"What in the warlord's name are you doing up there?" As soon as the words passed my lips I winced. Perhaps I shouldn't have used the word warlord in vain. He might consider it blasphemous and punish me for it.

He shimmied down the tree trunk faster than anyone should be able to. At least he was wearing pants. Unfortunately, I couldn't say the same for his upper half.

I studied his face and body language. He didn't seem angry. Maybe he hadn't even noticed my slip-up?

"I was scouting. There looks to be a settlement in that direction." He paused halfway across the clearing, his eyes raking over my face as a slow smile curled one side of his mouth. "See anything you like?"

Heat flooded my face as I realized I was staring. I was so not even going to dignify that with an answer. "You should put a shirt on," I said, pointedly turning my attention away. "What will your lady admirers think?" I squeezed my braid and grinned at the cascade of drops that splattered at my feet. It was still hard to believe I'd had an entire pool to myself. The city of Kadena had public bath houses the wealthiest of the population could make use of, but since I'd become the property of Warlord Akre, those were off-limits. The only time my hair got wet anymore was when I was on the Water Wheel. I suppressed a shudder.

Divinius smirked, pulling his robe over his head, obscuring the well-defined planes of his chest and abdomen that I didn't notice. Not at all. "I don't see any ladies around here." He winked, flashing that dimple at me with a smarmy smile. "And they've never minded before."

Ugh. I rolled my eyes. As if I would be stupid enough to fall instantly head-over-heels for some self-absorbed prince. "I'm sure." I swung my braid over my shoulder and pointed in the direction he'd indicated. "The settlement's that way? How far?"

He shrugged. "It's a ways, but hard to say with the jungle. Maybe a few leagues?"

"Don't sound too certain, *partner*." I eyed the tree he'd climbed, trying to decide if it was worth the effort to go up and confirm what he'd said. I didn't know him, or how good he was at judging distances. Reigning in the urge, I stepped back. Neither one of us had food, and I had no idea how long it would be until we got some. Best not to waste energy when it wasn't needed.

I headed in the direction he'd indicated, not waiting to see if he followed. Who knew what sort of creepy crawlies would come out of the jungle if we were still here after dark. Not to mention if it was this pleasant during the day, the nights were likely to be chilly. "Come on, I don't want to be stuck out here when the sun goes down."

Chapter 4
Gin

It turned out the so-called settlement was a thriving metropolis. I had no idea what His Royal Highness-ness considered a city, but this looked like it had its own market, piers, and even some super-fancy houses on the hill overlooking the bay. I was pretty sure anything I wanted or needed could be found here, for the right price.

I leaned against the lamp post and picked a rock from my sandal. The sun hung low in the sky, casting my shadow down the street. "Only a few leagues, huh?" At least there had been plenty of water available and the weather wasn't sweltering. I could deal with sore feet if it meant we'd reached civilization.

My stomach growled.

Divinius flung his arms wide and turned to me. "I said 'maybe.' I've never been here before, either."

I snapped my mouth shut and glared at a passing farmer who eyed us too curiously.

Studying the avenue and the locals' practical attire, I leaned closer to Divinius. "Your robes attract too much attention. We'll have the guard here in no time." Assuming this area had regular patrols. But what city with rich people didn't?

I froze, my hand going to my cheek as my stomach convulsed into knots. What if someone recognized my tattoo? Just because His Royal Highness obviously hadn't didn't mean anyone else wouldn't.

"My robes?" Divinius spun toward me, his voice rising. "What about your clothes?"

I raised my eyebrow and glanced down at my dark tunic and pants. "What about them?" They were as generic as they came, without the fancy symbols embroidered with shiny thread, and, most importantly, they hid blood exceptionally well should the need arise.

Divinius gestured at the locals filling the street. They were dressed in earth tones, in rigid cloth and black boots, all going about their own business.

Neither of us fit in here. Regardless, a thin curl of relief uncoiled in my stomach. At least we'd washed up in a human land. That would make it easier for me to navigate, but only as long as no one identified me as a slave or got the local law involved. Maybe I could find a hat or some sort of facial scarf, even though I hadn't seen any of the people surrounding us wearing such items. Or some makeup, but then I'd have to explain to my endearing companion why I was trying to hide my face. A shirt with brass buttons in the style reminiscent of Kadena's guard uniform flashed through the crowd. Sand demon spit.

I grabbed Divinius' arm to steer him off the street.

He shook me off. "Unhand me!" Something like lightning snapped across his eyes, reminding me he had magic and was more dangerous than he appeared.

Rolling my eyes to disguise the sudden twist in my gut, I stepped back, holding my hands up. Note to self, don't touch the warlord without his permission unless I wanted to get fried. "Okay, fine. Let's just get somewhere quieter and see what we can learn about where we are."

Divinius oh-so-graciously allowed me to lead him down a side road for several minutes before he stopped and pointed. "Hey, wait! There's a cartographer's shop. We could get a map."

My stomach rumbled again. "Why waste the money? A map is no good until we figure out where we are." I smirked. "Do you think it won't raise suspicions to ask the cartographer to write 'You Are Here' on it?"

He opened and shut his mouth as I pulled him past the storefront.

"I promise, we'll come back once we have a plan and know where we need to go."

"But it'll be closed soon!"

Exactly. Not that I'd tell him that.

With a sigh, I rolled my eyes and turned to face him. "Look, Div—"

He scowled, dragging us to a stop. The expression in his eyes would probably send most humans scurrying for cover. But not me. I'd faced down two warlords in the last day and somehow lived to tell the tale. Plus, the more time I spent with the mage, the more I suspected he wasn't a warlord. Despite his haughtiness, he didn't have their cruel streak.

I flashed him a too-tight smile and batted my eyelashes. Apparently I'd found a nickname that annoyed him as much as Rose bugged me. Good. "I'm hungry. Let's go find a tavern where we can sit in a dark corner and listen. We'll learn more that way, and it'll look less suspicious."

He sighed, flicking his hair for the added dramatic effect. "Fine. I can see you let your stomach rule your thinking."

"We've all got to eat, elf, even you." I took a deep breath, counting to five as I inhaled and again as I exhaled. My fingers itched for a blade that I could whirl around and slam into his annoyingly well-built chest. But even I wasn't that reckless. I hadn't forgotten that he needed me to get back home. And having an elven prince, who controlled the fabled armies of Elysia, in my debt would make it all the easier for me to put Akre, Orion, and all the others in their places. Only when all the warlords were wiped from existence would I truly be free.

I studied the entrance to the cartographer's shop. The door was the obvious entry point, but I didn't see any locks on the front window shutters, either.

"I may not know you very well," he said, crossing his arms as we stood in the middle of the street, "but I do know that look. You're planning something." He tilted his head, studying me like a cat that's uncertain of a new toy. "What are you up to?"

I flashed my teeth in a wide smile. "Of course I'm plotting something." Many somethings, in fact. Not that I'd ever tell him any of them. "When I figure it out, I'll let you know."

A muscle in his jaw ticked. "I am the crown—"

Oh, for sand demon's sake! I spun and slapped my hand over his mouth. "Announce your title here," I hissed, "and you may find yourself in more trouble than you bargained for." I studied the street, and the few people who passed us by, for any who were showing signs of being too interested in us. One slightly older man caught my gaze before he slunk away. A warm burst of satisfaction ignited in my chest as I fought to keep a smile from my lips. I might be lost in a foreign country with no connections or support, but I was still strong enough to protect myself.

Divinius' eyes flashed as he slapped my hand away. "How dare you assault me!"

My heart squeezed as I clenched my jaw so hard my teeth creaked. Of all the stupid… I'd show him assault. Taking a deep breath, I punched him in the solar plexus.

Bending over, he gasped.

"Shut up, you idiot! Everyone here is out for themselves. Do you have any idea what they could do with access to a royal ransom?"

Divinius took two steps back as his mouth fell open, his chest still heaving for air.

I shook my head, stepping forward so I could drop my voice. "Think about it. There's got to be some reason we were sent here, and I don't think it was for either of our health." What had Roland been thinking? No doubt, drugging me had been the stupidest thing the old alcoholic had ever conceived, but even I could admit it took a lot of magic to transport someone so far away. After all the years I'd known him, I was certain Roland had no magical inclination. He was no warlord. Which meant in sending me here, he'd been working with one—Orion, or Akre.

Probably Orion. If Roland had been loyal to my master, he would have just let Akre's guards take me after they stormed The Golden Gosling. Orion must have given Roland something to get me out of the way, but why?

Other than the obvious, that Orion was in Kadena to overthrow Akre and claim his territory and position as his own, what did Orion gain by getting me out of the way when it was already so clear he could wipe the floor with me in a fight? It would've been less effort and risk to just kill me rather than involving Roland.

Thinking back, it seemed like Orion had been as surprised at my appearance as I'd been to see him. Though I couldn't tell if that was because he'd found an assassin in his bed chamber, or if it was because I was still alive.

I shook my head, setting that particular line of thought aside. It wasn't like I'd ever have the chance to ask him. Turning my focus back to the male who was more of an immediate problem, I studied the elven prince.

He straightened his robe, still fighting to breathe after my punch.

When it was clear Divinius wasn't going to say anything further, I continued. "I don't suffer fools, even royal ones. Stick with me, don't be stupid, and I'll get you home." I hoped. In the meantime, we desperately needed to figure out why we'd been sent here.

I glanced down the street. "Let's try that inn."

"The Swaying Palm. Well," Divinius said, "it sounds high-end at least. Hopefully they'll have a bottle of red."

I paused, frowning as I turned to glance at him. "Red?"

He stared at me.

I rubbed my forehead, which was about the only part of my face I could be sure wasn't swollen and bruised. "Did I grow a third eye or something?"

"Elven wine, of course." He scoffed. "I wouldn't expect a human like you to understand."

I grunted, letting the implied insult roll off my back like water. Whatever. "Are all elves as annoying as you?"

He flashed me a smug grin that showed just a hint of one fang.

I pursed my lips and exhaled as I led the way up the steps. His Royal Highness needed to reevaluate his priorities. Maybe I should check mine, too. If I wanted access to his armies, I would need to tolerate his ego and lack of common sense. I'd have to get him to trust me and that meant at least pretending to befriend him.

The sound of laughter and wafts of pipe smoke drifted from behind the closed doors.

I turned the latch and stepped inside, blinking for several heartbeats while my eyes adjusted. There appeared to be only one exit—the front entrance—though a staircase in the back did go up, so there was the possibility of a secondary escape route that way.

The patrons seemed a normal mix of farmers, poor merchants, and a few more muscular people who might be mercenaries, laborers or thugs. Maybe all three. Across the room, a cold hearth sat next to a bar. A handful of half-occupied tables were scattered throughout the space.

This would be perfect. It was a much tamer version of The Golden Gosling back home. I smirked. I could handle this.

A vacant spot in the back beckoned. "Come on," I said, waving over my shoulder to the gawking prince. I claimed the corner seat.

Divinius glared at the remaining chair, which would put him with his back to the room.

I raised my eyebrow as my gut hardened. "Don't make a scene, Div." If he did, this tavern would be burned and we'd have to go find another one. And would probably have to repeat the process multiple times during the night unless he could get his royal ego under control.

He sighed, pulled out the stool and collapsed into it. "I suppose, of the two of us, you'll do a better job of watching my back in a place like this than I would." Divinius turned, gaping at the heads of dead animals that adorned the walls.

I nodded, a satisfied smile creeping over my face. At last, some common sense manifested in that thick elven skull. It was about time. "Careful, princeling. That almost sounded like a compliment. But I'm glad you're learning." I studied him for a few minutes. His face was annoyingly... symmetrical, and I couldn't deny it was worth staring at. Above his high cheekbones, his eyes were reminiscent of the lapis lazuli jewels the ladies of Akre's court favored. Letting him get close would be a very dangerous mistake—one countless women willingly made, no doubt. "You've never been in a human tavern before, have you?"

He shook his head. "No. I'd never be caught dead in such a low-class establishment." He met my gaze and winced. "Well, under normal circumstances."

I rolled my eyes. So much for common sense and compliments. I scanned for a bar wench so we could order dinner. I wouldn't be sad when we parted ways. The elf really was quite tedious. And the most annoying thing was he didn't even realize it.

Blasted royals. They were the same, no matter which kingdom they hailed from.

The smell of unwashed bodies and sickeningly sweet alcohol overpowered any scent that would hint at what was being offered as a meal. No one glanced my way except the bartender across the room. He was wiping a glass with a towel that was only slightly cleaner than what it cleaned. Something he and Roland had in common.

I clenched my jaw at the thought of Roland. But I couldn't do anything about that betraying, friend-drugging scumbag at the moment, and I was getting hungry.

"Wait here," I said, sliding out of my seat.

I wove between the tables to the large counter, polished to a fine sheen from the oil of many hands. I caught the bartender's eye. "How much for dinner?"

The barkeep eyed me up and down. His gaze fixed on my tattoo and outfit for several heartbeats.

My pulse skipped as I resisted the urge to reach for my whip. I couldn't kill him if I wanted to eat instead of dodging guards tonight.

Clenching my fists hard enough for my fingernails to dig small crescents into my palms, I held them at my sides. Forcing my spine straight, I met his stare with a brazen one of my own, daring him to challenge me.

The man jutted his chin out. "Three shivs."

"Each?" I scratched the back of my neck. What in sand demon's spit was a shiv? Meeting his eyes, I mentally shook myself. I couldn't let him know I had no idea what he was talking about, not unless I wanted to be taken advantage of and set up as a mark for other unscrupulous characters.

He nodded.

Pressing my lips into a thin line, I reached into my purse, pulling out three marks. "Will this do?"

The bartender shoved my coins off the edge, where they clinked to the ground at my feet. "We don't take foreign currency here." He raised his voice. "You got no money, get out."

Bending over, I picked up the marks and pocketed them. It hadn't occurred to me that we would have a problem even purchasing food. Fortunately, I had one belonging that would probably still work. "Fine." I pulled the gold and obsidian ring off my finger, ignoring the hollow feeling in my chest at its absence. I swallowed past the sudden lump in my throat at the loss of the one thing of value I still owned.

Holding the band out to the man, I asked, "Will this cover two dinners?" I may not know what a shiv was, but I was well aware of the piece's worth.

His eyes sparkled as he nodded, snatching it from my fingers.

The jewelry disappeared almost faster than I could follow. Almost.

"And a room for tonight." I bit the inside of my lip, marking which pocket my ring had vanished into.

I'd be back to reclaim it later.

The innkeeper reached beneath the bar and produced a key, which he tossed to me. "Upstairs, second room on the right."

Pocketing it, I pivoted on my toes and returned to my seat.

Divinius raised an eyebrow as I settled. "What's for dinner?"

I shrugged, trying to ignore the hallow ache in my gut and the naked feeling of my ring finger and failing miserably. "I don't know. I didn't ask."

He shoved his chair back with a screech and stood. "You didn't?" His voice echoed across the tavern. "You probably didn't order my wine, either, did you?"

Yanking him back down into his chair, I shook my head. "Trust me, they don't have it." And even if they did, I wasn't going to fund his drinking binge. I studied the room, ignoring the barkeeper who was staring at us with far more interest than I was comfortable with. "Judging from what everyone else is eating, I'm guessing some type of stew and hardtack."

His oh-so-Royal Highness dropped his head into his hands. "What have I gotten myself into?"

"Relax, your highness-ness. One night in this place won't kill you." At least, not while I was there. "We can find accommodations more to your liking tomorrow, after we deal with a minor currency issue."

Divinius opened his mouth when a serving girl set two bowls of porridge and a plate with meat and bread on the table. "What'll you have to drink?" she asked.

"Water," I said. Hopefully it tasted the same as it had in the jungle.

Divinius cleared his throat. "I'll take your finest elven red."

Stupid, egotistical fae royalty. I sighed. Divinius was proving to be more of an annoyance than he was worth. Perhaps I'd get lucky and someone would spike his precious drink and knock him unconscious. At least then, it'd get his stubbornness out of my hair for the night while I figured out what to do.

The bar wench's eyebrows climbed beneath her bangs at his request, but she nodded and disappeared into the crowd. A few minutes later, she re-appeared with a mug of water and a goblet of wine she set in front of us.

"Praise the mages," Div mumbled, bringing the glass to his lips. Before I could blink, he spewed it out onto the floor. "What in Naraka is this drivel?"

"What are you doing?" I hissed. "I said to not make a scene." I peered over his shoulder at the room, noting those who glanced in our direction.

"Don't tell me what to do," he said, holding the drink out to me. "This is not elven wine."

I shoved the alcohol away. "I already told you they wouldn't have any. And even if they did, we couldn't afford it. They don't take credit here." I relaxed as the last of the too-curious locals finally turned back to their business.

Divinius gasped. "What are you talking about? Of course they do. They'll take the credit of House Morganis."

I fixed him with a hard stare. "No, they won't. This is not some high-end restaurant that caters to the nobility, whose owners would have the connections to redeem royal debts." No, this was a tavern parked squarely in the middle of the seediest part of town I could find. The people that frequented businesses like this actively avoided anything to do with the royals, nobles or law enforcement.

He blinked. The affronted expression on his face would be comical in any other situation. "Are you insinuating my family doesn't make good on their debts?"

I banged my fist on the table. By the fates, I'd knock him unconscious myself. Right here, right now. "Ugh! No. I'm saying they don't accept foreign currency. And you're way too eager to announce yourself."

He narrowed his eyes and studied me. "Announcing who I am is the most efficient way to get what I want. Which, at this moment, is elven wine. And, if we don't have money, then how did we get dinner?"

I shrugged, feigning nonchalance as I peered at the bartender. "They do, apparently, barter." I eyed his robes. "What've you got on you that's worth a glass of your precious red?"

Divinius patted his pockets and sighed, slumping against the back of his stool. "Very well, I'll bite. What did you trade them?"

"Excuse me, I believe this is yours?"

My ring tumbled across the table to rest next to my mug.

Divinius snatched the metallic band as I spun my gaze to the newcomer.

The human had blond hair styled into spikes taller than my fingers. His tresses were so white it almost had a blue sheen to it. His coppery skin was tattooed down both sides of his neck in a pattern that looked a lot like lizard scales. Warm cerulean eyes that were so vibrant they reminded me of fractured diamonds crinkled at the corners as he smiled. A red velvet cloak hung over the man's shoulders above a tan vest and matching trousers with perfectly polished boots. He didn't seem to have any weapons on him.

My lips curled into a frown. Something about this stranger didn't feel right, like acid in the back of my throat. What sort of person returns another's bartered property with no ulterior motive? I narrowed my eyes, trying to figure out what this man wanted.

"Aren't you going to say thank you?" he asked.

"Thanks," I said, glancing over at Divinius. My ring was no longer visible. By the sand gods... It'd be hell to get it back from him. I might have to take a finger, or maybe a whole hand.

The stranger pulled a vacant chair to our table, turned it backward, and straddled it. "So, what brings an elven mage and an—" he eyed me, "—Obronian to our town?"

I met the blond man's gaze. He was dressed like a trader, but something hovered behind his eyes that had my instincts screaming there was more to him than what the surface revealed.

"We're just passing through." I crossed my arms, leaned back, and sent him a glower that dared him to call me a liar.

"I see." He glanced between me and Divinius. "I'm Astra. A merchant by trade. I'd be happy to switch any foreign currency you have for..." he paused, "a thirty percent cut. To compensate me for buying back your ring, of course."

I opened my mouth but Astra waved me silent. "Don't worry. The idiot at the bar didn't know its true value. He charged me less than a quarter fair market price."

That was still well over what I saw in a year. There was no way I'd be able to reimburse the merchant, even if I gave him everything I had on me. I met Divinius' gaze with a raised eyebrow.

His Royal Highness shrugged.

Fat help he was going to be.

If only I knew what the exchange rate was on a shiv. Thirty percent seemed incredibly low, considering my sudden debt to Astra. He must want something else, but he wasn't studying me like most men who sought something besides money. That probably had something to do with my bruised and swollen face, though some males liked this look on their women.

I glanced around the bar. This time of day, the currency exchange booths and banks were likely closed, assuming we were even able to find them. This was our only option at the moment unless I wanted to spend an inordinate amount of time wandering the city looking for alternative options. I'd just have to be on the lookout for when the other shoe dropped regarding Astra's motives. "Okay." I turned to the merchant. "But only because you saved me the trouble of stealing my property back."

He burst out laughing. "You're my kind of person, lady."

Divinius stared at me, wide-eyed. "You'd steal back what you traded fairly for food?"

I snorted. Apparently, my definition of fair was very different from his. But then, he hadn't had to give up any of his belongings, so... "Of course. That ring would've covered room and board in any inn for at least a month. The bartender was taking advantage, and he knew it." An unexpected blade twisted in my gut at the disappointment on Divinius' face.

And that thought alone was disturbing, because I didn't care what he thought of me.

I didn't.

A wave of heat rose to my cheeks. I glared at him. "Don't judge me. You haven't the right."

Divinius met my gaze for several heartbeats before he shrugged, dropping the topic.

Astra stared between us as he brushed his palms on his pants. "Alright, how much have you got?"

Swallowing the bitterness at the back of my throat, I emptied my too-light purse onto the table. A few breaths later, he'd matched them with a small pile of coins in shapes and sizes I was unfamiliar with and slid my funds into his pocket.

"Very well." He stood, rubbing his hands as though cleaning them of dirt. "It was a pleasure doing business with you both. Welcome to Tenara."

Chapter 5
Gin

I crouched in the narrow space between the cartographer's shop and the apothecary. The overwhelming smell of herbs and poultices stung the inside of my nostrils and made my temples pound.

At least the guards didn't come around more than every half-hour or so. I peeked out at the avenue. They were due any minute, then I'd be free to take my time hunting down the information Div and I needed.

A few blocks away, a whistle sounded.

The patrol must have found some poor beggar or street urchin somewhere they shouldn't have been. At least it wasn't me.

But the signal meant they were close. I ducked deeper into the darkened recess. My foot landed on something that crunched. The sound sent shivers that felt like invisible sand spiders up my spine. A rancid stench filled the air as I stepped back. The crushed half-rotten body of some unknown rodent met my gaze.

Ugh. I shook my head, more than eager to let the patrol pass so I could get on with the evening's activities.

Heartbeats later, footsteps pounded down the walkway outside the shop. A figure two-thirds my size ducked into the space in front of me, not bothering to confirm if the narrow corridor was already occupied.

The child leaned hard against the rough wall, ribs heaving as he fought to catch his breath.

I froze, willing myself to be invisible. Curse my luck. Now the guards would be on high alert and focusing on the area. And I was still in need of a sword.

I'd spent some time on the streets, immediately after Akre had murdered my parents and taken power. At seventeen, I lacked most of the street smarts growing up homeless like this boy would have granted me. Hunger and the lack of survival skills would've probably pushed me into the brothels had Akre not found me. Chewing the inside of my cheek, I studied the interloper. I'd been on my own for a few weeks before being yanked back into the castle. This child, judging from the way his bones jutted from his skin, had been there for years. But he had his freedom, whereas I'd been well-fed but enslaved. It was disconcerting that I couldn't quite decide which fate I would have preferred.

As long as the tattoo marred my face and the warlords lived, freedom was outside my reach. Longing for it would accomplish nothing.

The intruder pulled a piece of bread from beneath his tunic and stuffed his face, chewing desperately.

There was a bakery somewhere to my left. By the smell of the loaf, the proprietor was more skilled at his trade than the cooks at The Swaying Palm. My mouth watered.

Two sets of boots pounded toward us. Seconds later, a pair of soldiers rushed down the street, their blue uniforms standing out in the darkness.

"Damn," the closest one said. "Lost him."

"Let's split up. He can't have run far."

The guards separated, one going out of view to my right, and the other to my left.

Sand demon's spit. I looked up. The roof would be easy to reach, but not without attracting the attention of the interloper in front of me.

If we stayed here, we'd both be caught.

The thief turned his back to the wall and sighed. Then he noticed me and jumped.

I put my finger over my mouth to command his silence and pointed at the roof. The overhang would make it hard to climb onto, but once there, the rough texture should provide more than enough grip to escape, even with the steep slant.

The boy's eyes grew round as he peered at where I'd indicated before glancing back at me. He nodded frantically at the question in my eyes.

I braced my back to the wall of the cartographer's shop, my feet against the apothecary, and shuffled myself halfway up. Turning, I reached down to the boy. "Where's the bakery?" I whispered. If I was going to save his sorry hide, the least he could do was make my evening a little easier.

He blinked twice and tilted his head, indicating the direction. "Five buildings down, on the corner."

"And the blacksmith's forge?" Surely there would be a loose sword laying around that needed to be put to good use.

His brow furrowed as the corners of his lips turned down. "Just across from the bakery."

That worked. Nodding, I grabbed his outstretched hand and hauled him up. He stood in my lap and boosted himself over the roof's edge.

"Thanks, lady!" he whispered before his head disappeared.

One of the guards called from down the street. "Hey—check that alley!"

I shuffled the rest of the way up and pulled myself onto the rooftop as their footsteps approached. Pressing flat, I forced my breathing to slow. The residual heat from the day leeched through my tunic and into my skin. It felt good on my tense muscles.

The space between the buildings lit up as one guard held his lantern aloft. The thief I'd rescued was nowhere to be seen.

"Nothing here."

One edge of my mouth curled up at the disappointment in his voice. Outsmarting guards and depriving them of their prey were two of my favorite pastimes.

I relaxed with a sigh. Now all I had to do was lay here until they went away. And hope Divinius didn't wake up and find me missing.

I gave the patrol a count to one hundred before I dropped to the ground and pressed my face close to the cartographer's window. Pulling out a thin dagger I'd pickpocketed from a passing watchman, I slid it between the two shutters and lifted the inside latch.

The slats of wood swung open.

What a soft people, to not even bother with basic security. All it would take was a little knowledge or determination to clean them all out. The inn hadn't employed anything beyond simple locks on the room doors, either.

I slipped through and closed the shutters behind me. The room had several diamond-shaped cubbies against the long back wall with scrolls sorted into them, and two tables in the center of the space, complete with ink bottles and quills. Workstations.

A lantern rested on the edge of one table.

I sprung the latch and flicked the spring that banged the flint and steel together. The resulting spark caught on the wick and lit the room with a warm glow. I shuttered three of the four sides to keep the light from bleeding out onto the street.

Leather scraped against gravel outside.

Heart in my throat, I ducked behind a desk. The door rattled.

"Garren must have left his lights on again," the familiar voice filtered through the shutters. The front lock clicked open as the guards stepped inside.

Sand demon spit. I'd apparently been too quick to write off the city watch. I bit my lip hard enough to draw blood at the novice mistake. Just because this town was soft didn't mean the guards were idiots. It was quite possible I deserved to be caught for being so overconfident.

Their steps circled to my right. I scooted around the edge of the table with the blasted lantern and tucked myself up tight between the work stool and the desk. The quiet rasp of my pants against the floor made me wince. I crossed my fingers that the light had ruined the men's dark vision enough that the shadows from the table's overhang would protect me.

"Hey, did you hear anything?"

One of the guards stepped into the room, attention on the wall covered with racks of scrolls. "Probably the wind on the maps. You left the door open, idiot."

I glared at the soldier's back as he studied the endless piles of papers crammed into the wall's cubbies. Taking a deep breath, I squeezed my eyes closed.

Go away, go away, go away, go away!

Messing with the night watch when I had the advantage was one thing, but being cornered like a wild animal was significantly different.

"Well, nothing to be done about it right now," the other guard said. "Garren's an early enough riser he may be here before we're finished clearing the streets. You can tell him then."

They approached the table. I jerked at the metallic clank as the final side of the lantern slammed down. The room plunged into darkness.

I strained past the thumping of blood in my ears as their footsteps faded. The front door slid closed with a click.

Just my luck, to break into the shop of someone who actually lived by the old adage early to bed, early to rise.

After another count to one hundred, I came out of hiding. Now, all I had to do was decipher the mapmaker's filing system.

I grabbed a few scrolls from the nearest cubby and spread them on the desk. With a quick glance at the door, I re-opened the lantern. Behind me, the entire shelf of papers slid out and crashed to the floor.

I ducked back below the table as the blood rushed past my ears loud enough to drown out the sound of any impending footsteps.

How stupid could I be to not ensure I didn't unbalance the remaining rolls?

I definitely deserved to be caught.

It took several minutes for my heartbeat to normalize. The guards didn't return.

With a sigh, I unceremoniously scooped up the pile of parchments and stuffed them into their cubby. The cartographer would no doubt notice they were out of order upon close inspection, but they looked fine to my cursory gaze.

I selected a few more scrolls—more carefully this time—and turned back to the table.

A quarter hour later, I growled in frustration. There were plenty of documents containing detailed depictions of certain neighborhoods within Tenara, and other cities I'd never heard of. But for the life of me, I couldn't find anything that hinted at Tenara's position relative to the rest of the world. Nothing that would tell us which way Elysia was, or anywhere else outside the local municipality.

The cartographer must draw those from memory, unless he kept his reference scrolls for the outlying areas in another location. Maybe Tenarans just weren't interested in traveling to other countries? That was the more likely explanation. And I needed to move—if what the guards had said was true about the proprietor being in early, I was running out of time. It would be impossible to explain my presence if I was caught.

I frowned at the papers scattered in front of me. It would be obvious someone had been in here.

I shrugged. Oh, well. It wasn't like we'd be in this town long enough for it to matter, anyway.

Perhaps the Merchant's Guild would be better. Traders were always traveling, and a city of this size would surely have such an office. I should've shadowed Astra last night and maybe I'd have a few more answers, but leaving His Royalness unsupervised at the inn would've been disastrous. Who knew what sort of problems Divinius would get us into without me there to rein him in.

Hauling my tired legs up the stairs, I made my way down the hallway to our room above The Swaying Palm. The weight of the dagger and falchion I'd pilfered from the blacksmith was soothing. They weren't the prettiest weapons I'd ever wielded, but they were well-balanced with keen edges, and that was all I really needed. My stomach twisted as I anticipated eating the cheese bread I'd snatched from the bakery with as much fervor as the street urchin I'd helped this morning.

I froze. The door to the room I shared with Divinius was cracked open. I'd locked it when I'd left. It was far too early for spoiled elven princelings to be out of their cozy beds. While his physique indicated he wasn't slothful or prone to excess, no royal was up before the sun without reason.

Slinking to the doorframe, I whispered, "Divinius?"

Something fell to the ground and shattered just out of my line of sight.

I slammed the handle, flinging the door wide. It crashed against someone hard enough to ricochet back at me.

An unfamiliar voice cursed, "Mingering bint!"

I flung myself around the door, my stolen dagger at neck level. I grabbed a fistful of the hooded cloak and shoved the intruder to the wall, blade to their throat.

"Darasana!" The two lamps in the room flared to life, lighting the space as though it were high noon.

Throwing up my hand to protect my eyes, I squeezed them closed against the blinding onslaught. What in sand demon's spit did that stupid idiot think he was doing? In one action, he'd incapacitated me. By the time I recovered, the situation would be resolved, likely with a sword to my gut.

"Who do you think you are, breaking into my room?" Divinius' voice, deeper than usual, reverberated through my bones. The strength of his magic crawled over my skin with the same painful bubbling sensation Akre's did.

Fates!

My heart leaped into my throat as the panic Akre had trained into me when exposed to that much power exploded to the surface.

But this wasn't Akre, and I was still fairly certain Divinius was no warlord.

I wrangled my anxiety under control and used that energy to slam the dark figure into the wall again as I blinked furiously, willing my vision to adjust to the bright light. "You heard the elf. Who are you?" My voice hardly cracked at all. Good for me.

The intruder's hood fell back.

I squinted into the shadows. "The bartender?" My knees threatened to buckle. "Why are you breaking into our room?"

The fool tried to heave me away, but froze at the cold press of my steel against his throat.

I tilted my head and pinned him with a stare. Every inch of my instincts told me the larger threat was the mage behind me, but I didn't dare tear my gaze away from the intruder.

Crap. I had no idea what to do. As easy as it would be to drag my dagger across the bartender's neck, I now had a witness, and I didn't know how Divinius would react. It wasn't usually legal to kill someone just for breaking in, and I couldn't afford any potential entanglements with the town guard if I wanted to avoid catching Akre or Orion's attention.

This was going to get messy.

"Divinius?" I called over my shoulder.

The mage stepped into view, tugging his robes into place. "What?" He gave me a glance from the corner of his eye. "I'm surprised you haven't killed him already."

The bartender's face paled.

I pressed my lips into a thin line. Perhaps Divinius didn't skirt the side of the law I'd assumed he did. "I would have, if you'd given me warning before blinding me." Tilting my head and giving the human a pointed glare, I continued, "I still can. That would be the cleanest solution." I nudged the door closed with my toe. "At least, in the metaphorical sense." Blood spray was a bitch to get out.

Divinius shook his head. "No. We should turn him over to the watch. They can investigate and let the justice system handle it."

So much for my hopes in his law-abiding nature, or lack thereof.

I raised an eyebrow. "Or, we could kill him and not have to worry about anyone coming after us once he buys them off."

He gaped at me. "Gin! Have you so little disregard for the city watch?"

I snorted. "As if Elysia's guards are any different than the warlords'. Don't be ridiculous. We don't have the time, or the funds, to bribe them to make sure he's punished appropriately."

"A bribe!" He turned wide eyes to me. "No wonder you're so barbaric."

I bared my teeth at him as bile crept up my throat. Grabbing the bartender, I threw him against the bed. Using one of the sheets, I tore it into strips and used them to tie his wrists to one bedpost and his ankles to the other.

"There." I patted the man's cheek. "You just stay put until we figure out what to do with you." Bracing my shoulders, I whirled on His Royalness. "Since my barbaric self has only one solution to this, what does your all high-and-mightiness suggest we do? Can you magic an explanation out of him?"

"Aga." Fire flared over one of Divinius' fists, which he brought close to the intruder's face.

A drop of sweat trailed down my prisoner's temple.

I wrapped my anger at Divinius calling me a barbarian around myself like a blanket and used that as a shield against the urge to flinch and cower away from his use of magic. The impulse only served to heighten my rage at my weakness. It wasn't like he was directing it toward me, after all. There was no reason for me to be reduced to a quivering ninny.

"No," Divinius said, "but I can cause a lot of pain if he doesn't explain himself immediately."

I blinked, raising an eyebrow. This was a side to Divinius I hadn't seen before, and it did remind me of Akre, just a little. My blood chilled as I studied the hardness in his gaze and the confidence in his posture. He sure looked like he meant what he said. I wouldn't push him, if the bartender's and my positions were reversed.

With the prisoner secured, Divinius could likely handle things, at least for a few moments.

Shoving my blade into its sheath at my waist, I ducked into the hallway where I'd left the food. The scent of herbed cheese and warm bread permeated my nostrils. My stomach rumbled with impatience as I stepped back into the room. Plopping down on a stool near the shaky wooden construction that was supposed to pass as a table, I ripped a roll apart and stuffed a chunk in my mouth as I settled in to see just how dark the crown prince of the fae could be.

Mmmm.

"What's that?" the dark prince asked.

"Breakfast."

"Excellent!" His fireball forgotten, Divinius moved toward me.

"No, you don't." I pulled my bag of goodness out of reach. "Us barbarians only share with other savages. You'll have to forage your own." I gave him a pointed stare before glancing at the bartender. "After you get us answers."

"I'm sorry," Divinius said. "I didn't mean to say you were a barbarian."

Sand demon's spit. I held back an eye roll. "No, you're not, and yes, you did."

He shook his head. "I apologized. What more do you want?"

I frowned, pretending to consider as I stuffed another chunk of cheese bread into my mouth. When I was certain His Royalness was about to start drooling, I nodded at the barkeep. "Magic him. Find out why he's here."

The man tied to the bed spit at me. It barely made it halfway across the room.

I laughed.

Divinius rolled his eyes. "I already told you, I don't study divination. I can't just 'magic' knowledge out of thin air."

"For goodness sake, Div." I plopped a half-eaten roll on the table and heaved to my feet, pushing his useless corpse aside. I kicked the chair I'd been sitting on back into place with a loud screech. "Did you fail Interrogation Training or something? He hasn't said anything. Make him scream until the truth comes out, like you said you would."

"Oh, erm..." Divinius stared at his boots and scratched the back of his head.

God's teeth. I knew it was all for show. Part of me was annoyed that the princeling couldn't back up his threats, but the other half—the woman who remembered all too well what happened when Akre's voice rang with that threatening tone—was grateful. Besides, I could be plenty dark enough for both of us. Pulling the dagger from my waist, I brandished it in front of the barkeeper's face as I leaned over him. My weight caused the loosely stuffed mattress to cave dangerously. "Now, then. What possessed you to let yourself into our room in the middle of the night?"

The man's eyes went wide, his mouth flapping open and closed several times.

I dragged the tip of the blade down the side of his face and along his jaw, not hard enough to break the skin. Yet. "I'm losing patience. Talk!"

"I ain't telling you nothing, harlot." His breath smelled of stale ale and some sort of pipe smoke.

I flicked the knife across his cheekbone, pointedly keeping my focus on the human so I didn't see the expression of disgust that would no doubt grace the prince's face. A thin line of red welled up. "Ever heard of Death by a Thousand Cuts?"

I gave him a matching slash on the other cheek, letting him see the hardness in my eyes. "That's two. It's a slow, painful way to die." And an unprofessional execution method for someone of my skill level, but it sounded badass. "Most people pass out between five and six hundred."

He flinched, shaking the bed frame. "Okay, okay! I figured if you were so quick to part with that black and gold ring, you must have other, more valuable pieces!"

"Yeah, right." I stuck out my lower lip in a pretend pout as I pondered his words and stared at the freshly whitewashed wall just an arm's reach from my face. "You tried to rob us because you thought we were rich?" The possibility was as likely as what I'd feared—that Akre or Orion had somehow known where I was and had sent him.

Divinius burst out laughing. "Rich? And staying in a place like this?" He scuffed the sole of his boot across the rough wood floorboards.

I flashed my teeth at him. The irony was, as the elven crown prince, Divinius probably had more wealth than the rest of this city combined. "Be quiet!" I hissed. "Do you want to wake the whole town?"

Divinius wiped a tear from his eye before spearing the bartender with his gaze. "Clearly, you have no idea who we are, or you'd never have done such a stupid thing."

I glared at the elf. "Shut up." I was going to have to gag him. There was no way around it, no matter how hard that would be to explain to the townsfolk and any travelers we came across in our journey.

He snapped his jaw closed.

Good. Now was the perfect time for his non-existent common sense to kick in.

I tore a strip of cloth from the barkeeper's cloak and shoved it into his mouth, tying it tight behind his head. "There. That'll keep him quiet until we're long gone." I stood, gathering my things.

"Wait." Divinius moved to stand in front of me. "Where are you going?"

I grabbed the last few rolls from the table. Where did he think? "We need to leave. What's the big deal? You didn't want to stay here, anyway."

He snatched one of the cooling rolls from my hands and bit into it with relish.

I snatched the rest of the bread away and hauled him out the door. "Come on. We can eat on the way."

Chapter 6
Divinius

I followed Gin through the doorway into the Merchant's Guild.

I dragged a hand through my hair. What was I doing? My mother would have me whipped if she caught me associating with someone like Gin. I froze for half a heartbeat. Or worse—she'd disinherit me.

Assuming she was still alive, of course. Which was a big if, but I couldn't let myself consider the alternative.

I was nowhere near ready to rule. There was still so much I needed to learn about magecraft that I wouldn't have time to study once the crown rested on my head. Not to mention the responsibilities of the kingdom and ensuring the continuation of my line with heirs...

An image of my mother's list flicked through my mind. I shuddered, shoving the thought aside. Now was not the time for that.

The oak flooring creaked beneath our feet as we stepped from the relative quiet of the entry into a bustling office. Scribes sat at desks to my right with long lines of well-dressed people queued in front of them. Couriers disappeared with scrolls almost faster than the clerks could produce them. To my left, there was some sort of auction going on. It was louder than the tavern from yesterday. The room tingled with energy and the smell of wet ink.

I slowed, focusing on the man with unnaturally red curls at the auctioneer's podium.

One would think they'd save the vending of their goods for the marketplace. Except that unlike traditional auctions, the prices here seemed to be going down rather than up.

"Baron Kesselier's silk and spice run to Nadrus! Going once, going twice... Sold! To Mr. Lavold."

Shipping contracts. They were searching for the lowest bidder. That explained it.

Gin pushed me forward to a familiar figure with blue-blond spiky hair who stood in an eddy of calm in the middle of the room.

"Astra!" Gin's voice was nearly lost in the din.

The merchant turned, a smile on his lips. "Ah, my friends. Greetings! I'm afraid I didn't catch your names last night." He gestured to the room. "What brings you to the guild? Hoping to pick up a shipping contract?"

Gin stepped in front of me. "We're heading to Elysia, looking for bodyguard work."

Honestly, it surprised me she'd agreed to escort me home so easily—Obron was in the opposite direction and, as annoying as she was, someone with the tenacity to build the reputation Desert Rose had wasn't stupid. She had to have a plan, even if it was just expecting me to send one of my ships to deliver her back home. Alternatively, said plan could be as complicated as her being a part of the uprising that had led to my father's assassination. Or anything in between. I needed to ferret that out before she got within striking range of Elysia, not just for myself, but for my country. I'd sent my magic toward her a few times since we'd met, looking to pick up her surface thoughts to see if I could figure her out.

Unfortunately, all I'd gotten were images of some overly muscled human and black silk sheets, along with an overwhelming desire for murder.

For as calm as she appeared on the outside, the woman's mind was a toxic pit of rage. I almost felt bad for the male but truly, anyone with the stones to sleep with Desert Rose had best be able to deal with the... unusual repercussions when the relationship turned sour.

"I see." Astra rubbed his chin, drawing my attention back to the strange merchant. "I happen to have an oil and wine shipment headed in that direction." He met Gin's gaze, like she was the one in charge instead of me. Rude, but not entirely unexpected from the lower class. Likely the two of them related to each other better due to their similar social standings.

"In fact," Astra continued, "it leaves tomorrow. Is that too soon for you?"

"It's perfect," I said, a weight evaporating from my shoulders. I could be home within a few weeks. Then I could finally learn the fate of my mother and deal with any traitors she hadn't already taken care of.

"Too perfect," Gin mumbled.

I glared at her, but she refused to acknowledge my attention.

If Astra heard her words, he didn't react. "Excellent, excellent." He slapped her on the shoulder with a good-hearted chuckle. "Let's go somewhere a little more private, and we can discuss the details."

He leered at me while steering us into a small meeting alcove I'd failed to notice burrowed into the walls. It was one of many such cubbies that lined the large room.

I ignored the look. After all, I'd been trained from birth to correctly interpret and ignore all manner of reactions from the lower class in response to their jealousy. After all, there was plenty to be envious of—my social skills, rank, magical abilities and yes, even my physical appearance. Most of the population would never be graced with two of those features, and here I was with all of them. For that, I could handle a little envy on the merchant's part.

We settled around a small table as Astra leaned forward. "Now, the lady's qualifications are quite apparent." He eyed the dagger, falchion and whip tied expertly to her side before turning and fixing me with an intent stare. "Yours, my dear sir, are not so. Are you trained with a sword?"

I scoffed. How dare the little man assume my skills were insufficient compared to a woman who claimed to be the near-mythological assassin, Desert Rose.

"I need no weapon," I said, letting the same haughtiness I'd heard so many times from my mother creep into my tone when someone underestimated her and she was about to make them regret it. Favoring the human with a thin-lipped smile, I leaned back in my chair and flicked my wrist at the table. "Aga."

A ball of fire appeared, hovering in front of us. I blinked and exhaled as the magic washed over me with a gentle caress. The fireball split into three spheres, which spun around us before vanishing.

Astra clapped his hands, practically jumping up and down in his seat like an excited toddler. "A mage! Wonderful! Wonderful. We don't get many of your kind in these parts."

He mumbled numbers to himself, counting on his fingers. Several heartbeats passed until Astra nodded. "The going rate for convoy protection is twelve shivs per day."

Gin cleared her throat. "How long until we reach Elysia?"

Astra tilted his head. "The first part of our journey will be by ship, with the last portion over land." He paused, his gaze unfocusing for a moment. "We should arrive at Faegate Port to make that transition in four days, assuming no problems, my lady."

I raised an eyebrow at him addressing Gin as a lady, but decided to let it go. At least now that she'd washed her face, clothes and hair, she looked human. Instead, I turned my focus back to the merchant and nodded. Faegate would put me with only the mountains blocking me from my home. "What's the fastest your convoy has ever made the journey?"

Astra frowned. "Twelve days, but that was a light load, and things rarely go smoothly over the Beartooth Range." The mountain chain lining the western border of Elysia was populated with all manner of predators from cave bears to ice lynx.

My heart skipped a beat. "Wait, we're going through the pass?"

Nodding, Astra focused on me. "The window between summer snowmelt and the fall storms is narrow, and it takes far too long to go around to be profitable."

Gin narrowed her eyes, glancing between us, clearly not following the geography. Apparently, she didn't do much international traveling—there must be enough assassin work in Obron to keep her busy. Though to be fair, I didn't make a habit of visiting other countries, either. That was what the royal couriers were for.

I met her eyes and nodded once.

She turned her full attention back to Astra. "Twelve shivs per day." Her gaze flicked to me. "Each."

I kept my expression flat. The pay rate was insultingly low, but it did get me back home relatively safely and efficiently. I had to at least give Gin that—when she had a goal, she was apparently quite competent at achieving it.

I briefly wondered who would win if my mother and Gin came blow-to-blow with court politics. The image was so vibrant in my thoughts I almost missed Astra's nod.

Gin's hand settled on her whip, though her body language was relaxed. Well, more so than usual, which was saying a lot. "When and where do we meet you?"

Astra stood. "Sunrise, Pier Five. The ship's called *The Ashwing*. I provide food, but anything else you need, bring it with you." He shook both our hands before bowing and ducking out of the room. The pointy spikes of his hair disappeared into the crowd.

Gin crossed her arms and slumped back in her chair. "Well, this is a little too convenient for my tastes."

I turned to her, my jaw slack. "Why are you complaining? You're looking a gift horse in the mouth."

She swallowed, running a hand over her tresses to smooth down any stray strands. "I still don't like it. Everything fell into place too easily. What are the chances the first person we meet here just happens to be the perfect one to help us?" She met my gaze. "This whole thing feels like a setup."

I raised an eyebrow, irritation creating a sour aftertaste in the back of my throat. "Are all assassins this paranoid, or just you?"

She narrowed her eyes as the edges of her mouth hardened. "Only those of us who survive long enough to make a name for ourselves. The world doesn't just hand out opportunities like this."

I frowned. That was where she had it wrong. "Sometimes, it does."

She snorted, crossing her arms. "Sure. If you're the elven crown prince. The rest of us aren't so lucky."

Well, that stung. I cleared my throat as she pushed herself up and marched out the door.

"Hey, wait!" I jogged after her. "Where are you going?"

"To get supplies," she said, barely glancing over her shoulder at me. "If we're hiking over a mountain range, I'm going to need more than these sandals." She jingled a purse that was suspiciously heavier than when she'd emptied it for Astra last night. "I'm going to see what my money can buy."

I frowned. Her coffers shouldn't be that full, especially if she had purchased breakfast this morning and her two new blades. In fact, she should be in the red judging by the quality of the steel. Opening my mouth I paused, shook my head, and closed it. I shouldn't ask questions I really didn't want to know the answers to.

But by Naraka, I had to know. As we stepped into the sunlight, I grabbed her arm, pulling her to a halt. "Gin, what did you do?"

She turned, her expression somewhere between confused and far too innocent. "What do you mean?" Batting her long lashes at me, she stared at my face.

I frowned, a ball of lead congealing in my stomach. I'd seen that same countenance on many a lady's face at court when they'd just been out maneuvered and cornered. "How much did you spend on breakfast?"

She shrugged out of my grip. "What are you, my personal banker now?"

I shook my head, frowning. That was what treasurers and secretaries were for. "Don't be ridiculous. Of course not. But if you're arrested for theft, it's going to put a serious kink in my plans to get home and reclaim my throne."

She chortled and took a step back. "It's good to know you care, Div."

"Valek! I mean it! Don't do anything stupid." I spread my arms and stepped toward her.

"Stupid? That's bright, coming from you after last night." She pulled a dagger and brandished it at me.

Me! The crown prince of the fae!

"You think I'm a child who can't handle herself?" she asked.

I slapped the blade away. Of all the idiotic things to say. "Of course not!" I clenched my teeth and groaned, resisting the urge to thread my fingers through my hair and rip it out. "You are so infuriating!"

"You said you needed my help to get home!"

I shook my head. "No, that's not what I—" I paused. No... that was pretty much exactly what I'd said to her. But it had been a moment of weakness, of disorientation from the teleportation spell.

She tucked the dagger into her belt. "So, trust me to do what needs to be done, and above all, don't patronize me!"

Of all the frustrating, infantile, low-class things to say! "I wasn't! You know what? Never mind." I pushed her away. "Go, do whatever it is you're going to do. Just don't come crying to me for help when you find yourself in trouble and needing a rescue."

"Don't worry, I won't," she muttered, her voice darkening to a tone that reminded me of black velvet and steel. No doubt many a mortal had trembled when she spoke like that. It was like death. And something in the back recesses of my psyche woke up with sudden interest.

Turning on her heel, Gin stormed off toward the market. People scrambled out of her way as they caught a glimpse of her expression.

Hopefully she'd listen and not get into trouble.

She was probably more familiar with danger than I'd ever know, but it didn't matter. What was important is we'd never agreed on a time or location to meet up.

Valek. I had no idea where I was going. But no way was I going to chase after her.

I studied the Merchant Guild. Fortunately, no one seemed to have taken notice of our spat.

I glanced around the square. A woman washed laundry in a fountain in the middle of the intersection, just steps away from another who drew a pitcher of drinking water. Humans scurried about on their way to or from various errands. No one paid me any attention.

Well, I had nothing pressing to do until tomorrow at sunrise. Perhaps I could find a place to stay tonight that was more appropriate to my station. Somewhere the owner wouldn't try to steal from me in the dark hours of the morning. I chuckled. I'd never been robbed before. No one in Elysia would dare.

What would've happened if she hadn't been there?

Best not to think about it. Surely the inns in the noble quadrant would accept my family's credit. My name would be safer to use in the upper-class areas, as well. If Gin cooled down and apologized, I'd show her what a luxury hotel was like.

I glanced left and right. Which way? Swallowing, I put my back to the docks and started walking.

I passed underneath the sign for The Satin Ribbon.

This seemed like a quality establishment, with no hint of the low characters who had frequented the inn Gin had chosen last night. I wouldn't have to worry about being assaulted or robbed here.

I took a deep breath. The scent of spiced meat tickled my nostrils. Yes, even the food smelled better.

With a flare appropriate to one of my station, I used a small tendril of magic to push the door open and stepped inside. My robes billowed dramatically at my heels. At this time of day, the tavern was mostly empty. A bartender polished glasses behind the bar, and a scullery maid mopped the already shining floors. A fire crackled merrily in the hearth on the far end of the room.

The attendant glanced up from a paper he was studying at the pedestal near the doorway. "Good morning, m'lord. How may I help you today?"

I cleared my throat. "Good day. I would like reservations for luncheon, dinner, and a room for tonight."

The valet nodded. "Very good, m'lord. Lunch will be boiled lamb with tubers, and supper will be pork loin with cornbread and honey. Meals are six shivs, and the room is ten."

Twenty-two shivs. I should've paid more attention to Astra and Gin when they were working out an exchange rate. Not that Elysia used Gin's Obronian marks, but it would've been a starting point.

I pulled out my purse and jingled the coins inside. "And what is the price in Elysian dalasi?"

The attendant frowned. "I'm sorry, sir. For that, you'll need to go to the Central Bank. We don't accept foreign coin here."

My stomach hardened, pushing the tightness in my chest up my throat. Stretching myself to my full height, I braced my hands on my hips. "I am Divinius Morganis III, Crown Prince of the Fae Realm and Holder of the Seven Orbs of Femora. Will you insult me by refusing the credit of the royal family of Elysia?"

I had to admire the man's backbone. In the face of my wrath, the attendant barely flinched.

Instead, he bowed. "I do apologize, Your Highness. Perhaps you will allow one of our pages to courier your funds to deposit on your behalf, and return when your coins have been exchanged? We will be happy to serve you an early lunch while we wait."

I bit back a scoff. As if I'd let my limited money out of my sight. I exhaled forcefully, holding back an eye roll. Humans. "No, that will not be necessary." I paused. "Being new to the area, however, I would appreciate the services of said page to direct me, so I can make the exchange myself."

"Very well, Your Highness." He gestured to a boy no older than seven I hadn't noticed earlier who was sitting on the edge of the room. "Please escort the prince to the bank and, when he has finished his business, back here."

The young lad bowed to me and led me out the door.

At least the child had manners. I shook my head as I followed my young guide.

Several hours and a trip to the bank later, I sat in the dining room and put the last bit of cornbread with honey in my mouth. Flavor exploded over my tongue. This was more like it. The staff had done everything possible to make sure I was comfortable, even reserving a dinner table just for me, in a prime location near the fire. My room was acceptable, as well, with a freshly stuffed down mattress. The food, while not the quality I was accustomed to in the castle, was at least palatable.

If Gin ever experienced luxury like this, she'd never want to set foot in a low-class tavern again.

I'd have to arrange for someone to put a rooster outside my window tomorrow morning. If I slept past the ship's departure, I'd likely never hear the end of it.

Speaking of Gin, hopefully she'd found some lodgings of her own, safer accommodations than the night before.

I raised my hand in the air. "Gaston!"

The attendant from earlier approached and bowed. "Yes, Your Highness?"

"I'm going to retire for the evening. Will you please send up a bottle of elven red?"

Something sparked in the man's eyes, but it was gone too fast for me to identify.

A ball of pit vipers churned in my stomach, reminding me of how I felt each time I faced my mother in court. I glanced over my shoulder just to make sure someone wasn't sneaking up behind me with the intent of burying a dagger in my back.

"Very well, sir. Is there anything else I can do for you?"

I shook my head. The man was likely just jealous of my station and rank. It didn't matter, as long as he continued to do his job well. After tonight, we would part ways and never see each other again. Then, his opinion of me would be inconsequential. "At the moment, no. Thank you. You may attend to your other duties."

The man nodded and disappeared into the crowd.

With a hearty pat of my stomach as the food settled, I ascended the stairs and opened the door to my room with a bronze key that matched the finish of the doorknob and hinges. The space itself was rather cramped compared to the royal suite I was used to, but it was likely spacious by more common standards. In the far corner opposite the bed, a copper tub waited.

I should've asked them to prepare a bath while I was at dinner. Shrugging, I heaved a mental sigh. Oh, well. I'd request it when my wine was delivered.

Inspecting the limited offerings on the bookshelves, I selected a promising one titled <u>A Treatise on the Political-Economic Relations Between Gorlinia and Brachia</u>. If I was going to rule Elysia now that the king and queen were murdered, I needed all the information on other countries I could find.

Arranging my robes so they wouldn't get wrinkled and ignoring the sharp twinge of pain in my chest at the thought of my parents, I settled in the chair near the hearth and cracked the book open.

My eyes were getting heavy when the knock on my door finally came.

"It's about time," I muttered, standing. "I ordered that wine over an hour ago!"

I opened the door, but instead of the attendant, three burly ruffians with smiles full of yellowed and missing teeth greeted me.

The center man punched me in the jaw, flinging me into the middle of the room.

Pain exploded across my face. I gasped, the impact driving the air from my lungs and making my vision go double.

"Gag him, boys! So he don't do no magic on us!"

A rough cloth that tasted like someone's dirty sock was shoved between my teeth and tied behind my head. The knot pulled at my hair and the binding caused the corners of my lips to crack. Blood seeped into my mouth, bringing with it a coppery tang that coated my tongue.

"This is an outrage! Do you have any idea who I am?" The words came out muffled and nearly incomprehensible, even to my own ears.

I lunged toward the closest one, but missed as a well-aimed kick rammed into my ribs from the other direction.

"Grab him! Tie his wrists!"

Scarred and calloused fingers took hold of my arms and ankles, binding me with coarse rope that chafed my skin.

"You'll pay for this," I rumbled through the gag, glaring at them as if the expression in my eyes could convey my intent.

Rough hands shoved a bag over my head and threw me over their shoulder like a sack of potatoes.

"Take him out back, quick, before someone comes to check on the noise."

Chapter 7
Gin

I dangled a leg over the side of the mansion's roof as I munched on a slice of melon and watched the sun go down. Seagull cries and the scent of brine carried on the breeze, even this far away from the docks. A pack with my recent purchases, including a new pair of boots and a blanket, sat safely near the edge. On the street below, the last few people scampered about their business, wrapping up the day's activities before returning home to dinner and fluffy beds.

I smiled. This was my kind of place.

I could live here, happy in my anonymity, for the rest of my life.

At least, if I didn't have that pesky little thing known as Orion's betrayal to deal with. And freeing myself and all of Obron from the warlords. I shoved the image of Orion's muscular torso wrapped in black silk sheets from my mind, ignoring the tendril of heat uncurling behind my navel. Instead, I pulled out my dagger and used it to clean underneath my nails. It would feel so satisfying when I finally slid it between Orion's and Akre's ribs and into their hearts. My knuckles went white around the handle until they popped, the faint stabs of pain bringing me back to the present. With a shake of my head, I put the blade away.

This rooftop was as good a place as any to spend the night. The rising sun would be guaranteed to wake me, and the pier was only a fifteen-minute walk away.

I had no clue where His Royalness had gotten to. I probably should've followed him to make sure he didn't do something stupid and get into trouble, but he was an adult and a future king—he should be able to look after himself.

Should being the operative word. I grimaced. Royals.

I glanced at my pack. If I'd tailed him, I might not have had time to get supplies, or dinner. I licked the last of the melon juices from my fingers.

He had better not miss our departure time tomorrow. No matter how much I loathed to admit it, I wasn't getting home anytime soon without his help. And it would be a lot easier to have my revenge with his army at my back.

I studied the buildings surrounding me, the orange lights from candles inside fading into the distance in an expansive wave of humanity. Tenara was a big city. I had little chance of tracking him down tonight, anyway.

He was no doubt somewhere nearby in the noble quadrant, likely patronizing a far-too-expensive cushy inn and spending the last of his money on that and company from a high-end bordello. How many inns could there be that catered to the super wealthy? Judging from what I'd seen today, there weren't any other upper-class elves running around Tenara. He'd stick out, especially if he was still wearing those ridiculous robes. And if he wasn't, well, then the scenery would probably bring the vast majority of the local women to their knees...

Either way, a few whispered words with coins dropped into the right hands, maybe I'd get lucky and track him down.

The streets below were empty now. I'd get no help there.

I'd definitely sleep better knowing he'd be ready to go tomorrow.

"Sand demon's spit." I threw one last glance at the roof that was meant to serve as my bed for tonight, strapped on my pack, and leaped over the side. Adjusting the weight on my shoulders, I headed down the street.

Two blocks later, I ducked into a slit between two store fronts as the local guards rounded the corner.

"Did you hear about the upset this evening at The Satin Ribbon?" one asked.

There was a dark chuckle. "I didn't think you'd care about some elf getting killed."

Killed? My blood turned to ice as I stepped into the shadow of a hedge. I definitely should've followed him. If Divinius was dead, then I was back at the starting point with no Plan B.

Crap.

Maybe I was jumping to conclusions. Sure, we hadn't seen any other elves in Tenara, but that didn't mean there weren't any. Divinius had magic, just like the warlords. And the gods knew how hard it was to kill a warlord, even if they were taken by surprise. My fight with Orion was more than enough to prove that.

It was some other elf. It had to be. Knowing Divinius, he'd show up at the pier early tomorrow morning, his eyes sparkling with that cocky, self-assured smile and his annoying dimple as he judged me for the dark circles under my eyes. Because now there was no way I wasn't going to spend the whole night searching for him, as fruitless as those efforts would most likely be.

I mentally kissed the thought of sleep goodbye.

"There was a lot of blood, but no body," the guard continued, as if he hadn't just tilted my entire world sideways. "Since when does the Assassin's Guild bother to dispose of their corpses?" There was a rustle of cloth sliding over cloth. "No. I think they'll ransom him. Assuming he actually is who he claimed to be, of course."

I frowned as lead settled in my gut, making me regret eating the whole melon earlier. That was definitely Divinius. I'd told him to keep a low profile, to shut his mouth. Stupid idiotic fae royal.

Why hadn't he used magic to send the assassins to the Night Gate? Surely he had to know he was most likely going to end up dead before they finished with him.

I stepped into the street, intending to back the guard against the wall with my blade and make him tell me everything he knew, but I stopped. There weren't just two officers down the block, there was a whole squad. Even if I could pinpoint the one who'd been talking, I couldn't take on a dozen guards by myself.

"Sand demon spit," I muttered, slinking back into the shadows as the patrol moved on.

I had to get info, fast. Unfortunately, I had no connections in Tenara, and my funds for buying information were limited.

The best place to hunt down gossip, at least in Obron, was a seedy tavern. There would be several down by the docks, but I needed one that catered to the locals, not the sailors.

The assassins weren't likely to stash Divinius anywhere near the noble quadrant, where the authorities had full control. Maybe the Industrial section of the city?

I adjusted my pack with a sigh. I shouldn't have let the idiot out of my sight. Usually, I was smarter than that.

Less than an hour later, I leaned back and rested my feet in the empty chair next to me. The din from so many voices threatened to blow out my eardrums, but this was exactly the type of tavern I needed. I eyed my untouched mug where it sat on the counter. In a place like this, likely as not, the ale was probably spiked with something stronger. And getting drugged in a foreign country wasn't my idea of a good time.

I caught the bartender's eye and flashed my purse at him.

The man wove his way over to me. He looked like someone had smashed his face with a shovel—his jaw was square with a cleft that went for miles, a flat nose and dark beady eyes. He pointedly stared at my drink, then back at me. "You want something else?"

I leaned in and pitched my voice low enough he had to bend closer to hear. "Information."

He raised his eyebrows. "On?"

I pulled out two silver shivs and set them on the counter. "The location of the Assassin's Guild."

He scrutinized my money, then at me, seeming to notice for the first time my leather armor and the plethora of visible weapons. I held back a grin at the thought of him wondering how much steel I had on me he couldn't see.

Yes. I might be an assassin. And I might kill him for not telling me where the sand-blasted guild was. Or I might end him for spilling their secrets.

Both options flashed through his eyes as he paused long enough to confirm he knew the info I wanted.

I added another silver piece to the counter. "Don't make me ask again, barkeep."

He chewed on the inside of his cheek as his Adam's Apple bobbed. The man leaned in, his breath tickling my ear. "Five blocks down, take a left. Two blocks down, on the right. It's a large building with a turret and iron gate."

My coins disappeared into his pocket as he stood. "Watch your back, girl. Nothin' good comes out of that place."

I fixed him with a flat stare and blinked once. He had no idea.

Shrugging, he turned away, our conversation apparently forgotten. Or stored away for future use in case someone else came looking.

I marked his appearance, in case I needed to come back later and kill him. Leaving my untouched mug where it sat, I left the bar while checking the position of my knives.

Time to rescue the elven princeling.

The bartender hadn't been kidding about the iron gate.

I crouched in the hedges across the street, studying the mansion housing the local Assassin's Guild. A wrought iron fence surrounded the lot, the shoulder-high spikes a not-so-subtle warning to outsiders. Multiple thin windows stretched from floor to ceiling on both levels. Two gothic-style tiers crowned the building.

The second story was inset a few feet from the bottom, allowing for a narrow ridge of roofing that would be easy enough for me to stand on while I figured out which upstairs window would be my entrance point.

Architectural taste aside, I'd think a bunch of assassins would be more cautious about their presence. But they didn't have to deal with a power-hungry warlord like I did. Perhaps here, intimidation and bribes to the local gangs was all they needed to keep the riffraff like me in check.

It was a relief of sorts, to finally be doing something I knew how to do, something familiar. International travel while babysitting an elven royal was way out of my comfort zone, but some simple breaking and entering that would likely end in a murder or two? That was a warm blanket on a cold winter's night. I latched on to the feeling of familiarity, letting it steady my nerves and drain some of the tension that had been present ever since Orion had thrown his first ball of lightning at me.

Fates, was that only yesterday? It seemed like a lifetime ago.

Light flickered from the far side of the upper level of the assassin's mansion, casting shadows across the backyard. The front of the house was dark, but that didn't mean there wasn't someone there, keeping watch.

My calf muscles cramped so I shifted my position to relieve the pressure.

If the assassins did have a sentry, they were good—they hadn't moved in over half an hour.

This late at night, the streets were deserted. It would be impossible to cross unnoticed. I'd have to backtrack several blocks and come at them from the other side of the street. But now that I'd had time to scout, I had my return approach mapped out.

This would be as easy as Roland drinking arak.

Heat roiled in my gut. I frowned at the reminder of my old friend and his betrayal.

I grunted. That bastard.

The phantom brush of rose petals skated up my arm, the pressure as diaphanous as spider silk. I startled, but there was nothing there. Brushing my hand up and down my bicep to dispel the sensation, I exhaled. As long as the warlords lived, I'd be on the run, always looking over my shoulder. Always jumping at the slightest unexpected touch or noise.

First, I had to rescue Divinius. Then I could focus on my revenge. I shoved all thoughts of Roland and Orion into the tiny black box at the back of my mind where they belonged and slammed the lid closed.

A fluffy cloud floated across the moon, giving me precious moments of deeper shadows along the walkway. I pushed myself out of the bush and made my way down the street, creeping from shadow to shadow.

Several minutes later, I stood inches from the iron fence, the neighboring house at my back. A fly buzzed by my ear. Absent-mindedly, I brushed it away.

I crouched, alert for any indication someone had seen the movement. The insect flew near my face again. I blew a puff of air in its direction. It tumbled into the railing and disappeared with a buzz and white spark.

I took an involuntary step backward. What in sand demon's spit was that?

Glancing around, I picked a small branch off the ground. With a furtive peek at the Assassin's Guild, I tossed the stick at the bottom of the wrought iron.

It collided. A shower of sparks exploded, burning after-images into my vision. Smoke tickled my nostrils as the blackened twig fell at my feet.

What sort of sorcery was this?

I'd have to grill Divinius on it when I got him back. Because I would get him back.

This complicated things. I'd have to get over the fence without touching it. It would be so nice if something would go smoothly tonight. Just one thing... Was that really too much to ask?

It seemed like the fates were not in the mood to grant me favors, unfortunately. It looked like, as always, I was on my own.

I counted to two hundred. There was no movement from the house. The lightning spell must not be an alarm, then, just a deterrent.

The neighbors had a tree halfway down the property that would at least get me off the ground. It was too close to the light spilling from the back windows of the Assassin's Guild for my comfort, but it appeared to be my only option.

I scurried to the tallest branch that would hold my weight. Pulling my whip from my belt, I flicked it across to the other house where it wrapped around the drainpipe. I gave it a few tugs to ensure it was secure. Hopefully it wouldn't collapse on me. Unfortunately, the only way to find out was to jump.

Closing my eyes to mumble a quick prayer to whichever gods would listen, I took a running leap.

My feet cleared the fence by mere itches. I released the lash as I ducked and rolled into the side of the mansion. I lay there for several heartbeats, catching my breath and listening for any indication I'd been heard. No one came rushing to investigate the commotion and, as a bonus, I wasn't fried by a replica trap of whatever magic they'd incorporated into their fencing. My muscles relaxed with a tremble.

As much as I wanted to stay here and celebrate my victory, if I didn't want the assassins to find me, I needed to get up and move.

I rolled to my feet and slid into the shadows against the outer wall of the mansion. My fingers yanked on the knot at the end of my whip while glancing over my shoulder. I was too exposed here.

Come on, come on! My heart raced like the legs of a sand beetle stuck at the top of a dune at midday. I couldn't make it this far, get this close, only to be caught now.

Finally, the leather strap came free. I coiled the length around my arm and reattached it to my belt before shimmying up to the second floor using the same drain pipe that had granted me access over the fence.

Pulling myself over the edge of the roof, I pressed against the siding. Hopefully, any sentries were only watching the front of the house. I leaned over to the closest window and peeked in.

An empty bedroom greeted me. The bed was made, and the door was closed. Raised voices, too muffled for me to make out words, filtered through the door.

This was as good a place as any.

I turned my focus to the windowsill.

Damn. The latch was a quality one, securing the glass into the frame with a deadbolt from the inside. Go figure, assassins would be the ones to lock their second floor windows. There'd be no subtle way of opening it from where I was.

Fortunately, there was always more than one way to solve a problem, as long as one didn't care about the consequences. And this time, the ends justified any means.

Wrapping the bottom hem of my shirt over my dagger's pommel, I rammed it into the pane. The glass shattered with a quiet tinkle. I ran the dagger around the edge, clearing the last shards from the frame, reached inside and undid the lock.

I was through before the window finished swinging open.

Crossing the room on soundless feet, I cracked the door. If they locked their windows, it would be unlikely they'd also station guards upstairs, unless Divinius was somewhere up here. At least, if I headed the guild, I wouldn't waste resources like that. Peeking one eye into the hall, I stared in one direction then the other. Nothing moved. Taking a deep breath, I drew my sword and crept into the corridor.

"Boss, Joe's late." A nasally voice trickled to my ears from downstairs.

"I know, Vin. I don't need you to teach me how to tell time." The second voice was more of a baritone with that buttery quality that always seemed to reduce noblewomen to bumbling ninnies.

It sounded like Orion's. Millions of miniature ice daggers twisted in my veins before I shoved that bastard of a traitorous warlord back into the wooden box in the far recesses of my brain where he belonged and slammed it shut.

"So, what about the elf? We're assassins, not babysitters."

"Patience, Vin. Remember every assassin's first lesson: even the best plans go awry. You know that. The payout is worth a little wait."

I edged down the hall until I was at a banister overlooking the living room below. Divinius sat in a chair to the side, head and ankles bound. I rolled my eyes. A thick gag ran around his head and between his teeth. One of his eyes was an angry purple and swollen nearly shut.

How cliché. It was like they didn't consider him a threat, holding him out in the open like this. Only idiots didn't think warlords, or any magic users, were dangerous.

The base of my neck tingled. I clenched my jaw, willing them to go into more details about the payout and who'd hired them. I slunk closer to the edge until I risked them seeing me if they looked up.

"Sitting here waiting to be double-crossed isn't my idea of a good time," the one called Vin said. He wore a burgundy shirt that clashed with his fire-red hair.

A man with a blue tunic stretched over an impressive chest rounded on Vin. "You will wait, because I say so."

Hello, Mr. Butter-voice. I narrowed my eyes as I assessed the threat. He had at least fifty pounds of muscle on me, and I probably didn't even come up to his shoulder. Based on the way he paced, he had strength and control, which meant I'd need to rely on my agility to get past his guard to take him down.

Three others glanced among their leader, Divinius, and Vin, clearly nervous but not anxious to get between Vin and the man with the sexy voice. The timid minions wouldn't be the primary threat. I'd have to take their boss down quickly, though, or they might get it into their head to rush me at once. If it turned into a five-on-one fight, I'd be dead.

"I say we kill him and be done with it."

Butter-voice whirled on Vin. "Go watch the front. Let me know when Joe arrives."

"But—"

The man held up a hand, silencing Vin's objection. "I said go. I'll not have you here making problems and costing us this payout."

Vin sighed and headed up the stairs.

My heart leaped into my throat as I scrambled behind a chest of drawers. The assassin stormed by, his footsteps vibrating through the floor.

I squeezed my eyes shut. *Please don't go into the bedroom, please don't go into the bedroom, please don't go into the bedroom.*

Vin stalked past the room I'd entered through and proceeded down the hall. A door slammed at the end of the corridor.

My shoulders relaxed in a slow exhale.

I crawled to the banister again. Divinius glanced up, his gaze meeting mine, almost as if he'd sensed my presence, which was a stupid thing to think. His eyes widened and he shifted in his chair.

I drew my hand across my throat before holding a finger in front of my lips. Be quiet and don't move, idiot!

He seemed to get my meaning, because he froze and pointedly redirected his attention to the remaining four assassins.

One of the others, with long brown hair and light eyes, spoke. "Aaron, I think Vin may be right. I've got a bad feeling about this. And keeping such a high-profile target here… I think we should cut our losses and walk away."

At least now I had a name for the man with the too-smooth voice.

"Cowards!" Aaron whirled around and stormed over to Divinius. "Did I train you so poorly? He's just a mage, totally powerless when he can't talk." He pulled back his fist and slammed it across Divinius' jaw with a crack.

I winced. That had to hurt, especially for someone who wasn't used to being punched.

Divinius groaned.

My gut twisted. Hopefully he was okay.

"See? Even royalty bleeds red." Aaron shook his hand and turned away.

Now was as good a time as any. If I waited much longer, Divinius would be dead. I put one hand on the banister and vaulted over. Hitting the ground, I rolled, popping up in front of Aaron.

The hardwood floor beneath my feet was polished to such a shine it was slippery.

His flicker of surprise was gone almost before I could recognize it, replaced with steely determination and cunning. "Stay out of this," he said to the room. "The bitch is mine."

I brought my sword up toward his gut. He batted it away with a dagger that materialized in his hand. Candlelight from the iron sconces on the wall reflected off it. The metal was scarred and unpolished from repeated use, but the edges were sharp.

I leaped, aiming a kick at his face just to see how he'd react. He dodged as my foot flew harmlessly past his ear. I smiled—that was exactly how I'd hoped he'd respond. Grabbing his shoulder, I tucked my leg behind his neck. My momentum spun me around as I kicked his dagger away and seated myself firmly on his shoulders. Freeing my whip, I wound it over both of my wrists and pulled, catching his throat with my makeshift garrote.

Aaron seized me and yanked, stumbling backward. Throwing his enormous weight into the move, he rammed me into the wall. One of the heavy framed pictures down the way clattered to the ground, the glass shattering upon impact. I bit back a curse as my broken rib shot a burst of blinding pain up my side. White bursts sparkled on the edge of my vision. Sand demon spit, that hurt. He bent over, grabbed both of my arms and hurled me across the room as I fought to not pass out.

My head hit with a crack before I slid to the floor. Stars exploded behind my eyes to match the stabbing ache through my temples. Blinking rapidly, I pushed myself up, ignoring the throbbing from my broken rib. If I let that overwhelm me, I was dead. Divinius would no doubt follow, though to be fair, since it was his fault I was in this situation in the first place—with him getting kidnapped and all—maybe he deserved it. I pulled a dagger from my belt, flipped it so I held the blade and threw it, burying the steel in Aaron's right shoulder.

He flashed his teeth as he wrapped his free hand around the handle and tore the weapon out, which was about the stupidest thing he could do if I'd nicked an artery. At least if the knife was left in, it would seal the wound until it could be tended. Perhaps I'd get lucky and the bastard would bleed out. Instead, he charged, bringing his fist down at me in a crushing punch.

I somersaulted to the side, past a mahogany end table and out of his reach. He had training, for sure. But his moves were not nearly as honed, or as powerful, as Orion's. And he didn't have magic.

Bracing against the wall, I kicked the table out of the way and lunged at him again. I feinted toward his head and drew my blade up to slash his torso.

My weapon came away red. I fought back a grin. Gin two, Aaron zero.

Aaron growled as his fist cracked into my cheekbone. My sword clattered to the floor, bouncing out of reach.

Pain radiated over my entire face as my vision bled crimson.

"Get her, boss," someone called from across the room.

I dropped to the ground and swung my leg out blindly, catching his ankle. Clenching my teeth against the burning ache in my side, I yanked.

He fell prone, the breath exploding from his lungs.

The bigger they are, the harder the fall. Pride swelled, the warmth rushing through my muscles, giving me the energy to somersault to my feet. Glass from the shattered picture crunched underneath my shoes.

Contracting his abs, Aaron leaped up as though I'd tossed him onto a feather-stuffed mattress.

He made it look so easy. In my arrogance, I might have bitten off more than I could chew when I picked this fight. At this rate, my body would give out before he so much as bruised. But I'd survived Orion, a sand-blasted warlord. No way was some bastard assassin taking down Desert Rose.

Rage flashed in Aaron's eyes as we glared at each other, our chests heaving as we sucked in air.

I may be over my head, but I would not die today. With a scream that tore from the deepest corners of my lungs, I met his strike with one of my own.

He blocked me with his left forearm, swatting me aside like I was nothing but a gnat.

I barely ducked the punch for my head I should've seen coming. His unopposed swing threw off his balance, so I drove my heel into his knee. Something popped, but he kept upright.

I cursed his excessive muscles. Taking out one of his joints was going to be harder than I'd realized.

Aaron swung a dagger at my neck with his off hand.

I bent backward and kicked, meeting satisfying resistance as my foot made contact with his chin. I completed the backflip and held both hands to my side, beckoning him to attack. I wasn't going to lie—pulling off that move had been mostly luck, but it looked darn impressive, judging from the gaping jaws of the three assassins in the corner. Divinius' eyes were also wide, and something warm curled in my chest.

I didn't think he had any remaining doubt I was, in fact, Desert Rose. At least something good would come out of this, and I'd finally have the prince's respect. That was Step One when it came to acquiring his army.

Aaron worked his jaw for a heartbeat and tilted his head to one side then the other, cracking his neck. "You're dead, you are."

He lunged.

I grabbed his arm, ducked, and using his momentum against him, tossed him over my shoulder.

Mid-throw, he caught my wrist, flipping and pulling me with him. As he rolled to his feet, his other hand found my throat and squeezed, lifting me off the ground.

Fates, he was strong. An acidic taste welled on the back of my tongue as invisible bands constricted around my ribs. I'd let him get his hands on me! If I didn't break his hold in the next few heartbeats, I was dead. I kicked at him. My chest heaved as I fought to suck air past his fingers pressing into my windpipe.

He slammed me into the wall again. The wooden paneling creaked beneath my skull.

I felt to either side, searching for a photo or a sconce, something I could pull down and use as a weapon to free myself. There was nothing. My lungs burned as an invisible band tightened over my ribs.

I opened my mouth to groan but nothing came out. My vision cleared as his dagger swung for my face. I brought both hands up, latching onto his wrist and shoving as he used his weight to push the blade toward me.

The dagger wobbled, hovering between us, the point only a few finger-widths from my eye. Another second and it would ram right through my skull.

Disregarding the fingers still wrapped around my throat, I jerked to the side, throwing us to the floor and slamming his arm against the hardwood. His grip on me loosened.

The weapon skittered away, coming to a stop beneath one of the other assassin's boots.

My gaze tracked it and landed on my sword, just within reach. Snatching it, I leaped to my feet, gulping as much air into my lungs as possible. By the fates, my neck hurt. No doubt the bruises would be impressive.

Aaron followed suit. He punched, but his aim was too far to my left. I twirled, trapping his shoulder between my elbow and the wall. I pushed against it until something popped.

He screamed as the joint separated.

I yanked him away, reached under his arm and slammed my fist into his jaw. Grabbing him by the face, I pulled him backward, over my knee. He spun through the air twice and landed face-down on the ground.

He shoved himself onto all fours, the muscles in his arms trembling.

I straddled him, wrapping his hair around my fingers and rested my blade at his throat.

"I'm Desert Rose." The words were a rasp over my strained vocal cords, barely audible. "Maybe you've heard of me?"

His Adam's Apple bobbed beneath the edge of my sword.

Warmth spread through my gut. Excellent. "Good. You have. I'm taking over this guild, effective immediately." I swallowed, fighting the urge to cough. I needed to quit talking and give my voice time to recover. As thready as it was, it did nothing to add to my intimidation factor.

"Like hell you are," he growled.

I drew my steel across his throat. He collapsed at my feet with a wet gurgle.

Piercing the other three assassins with my gaze, I straightened my spine to lend strength to my words and asked, "Who's in charge here?"

"I am, now."

I turned to find Vin standing several paces away.

"Wrong answer!" I glared at him, my blade dripping blood over the polished hardwood. I forced my suddenly weak legs to take two solid steps toward him, hopefully looking as menacing as I felt. "Who's in charge here?"

Vin stared at Aaron's body, cooling in a pool of red at my feet. His gaze drifted back up to mine. "You are." He cleared his throat. "Desert Rose."

"Good." I cowed each man with a cold stare before turning to the one standing closest to Divinius. Crossing my mental fingers that my expression was intimidating enough to not have to speak anymore, I swallowed. Doubling over in a coughing fit would not only shred my poor vocal cords, it would undermine every bit of respect I'd just earned. And the consequences of that would be deadly.

Vin took a tentative step forward. "Will you show me that move you used?"

Pausing, I glanced over my shoulder at him and raised an eyebrow.

"The first one, where you spun around Aaron's neck and strangled him with the whip?" he said.

I bit back a smile. Yeah, that had been pretty impressive, if I did say so myself. "Maybe later, if there's time." Which there wouldn't be. I studied Divinius. He was in bad shape, worse than me. Beyond the black eye and swollen jaw, blood dripped down his nose and from a spit lip. We'd be hard-pressed to convince Astra that Divinius was worth paying protection wages with his face black and blue.

Blast it.

"Cut the elf loose," I rasped. "The deal's off."

"Cut him loose?" Vin's mouth was slack. "What about the payout?"

My head throbbed with the beginning of what was sure to be a terrible headache. I probably had a concussion, maybe two. "Is there an echo in here? Don't make me repeat myself." I massaged my temples and nudged Aaron's corpse with my foot. "Someone take care of this." The floor wobbled but I tightened my core to keep my balance. The last thing I needed was the other assassins realizing how badly I'd hit my head, how almost out-of-it I was. That I was so vulnerable.

I hated being weak.

I walked over to Divinius as the other man cut the ropes binding him.

His Royalness spit the gag on the ground. "You came for me." The disbelief in his gaze twisted something uncomfortably low in my gut.

I fought back a flinch. "Of course I did." With one hand braced on the back of his chair, I pulled him to his unsteady feet. "I need you to get me home." I paused. "Partner."

He turned wide eyes to me. "You are Desert Rose."

There it was. I raised an eyebrow. "You didn't believe me?" A warm curl of smugness unraveled in my chest.

Scoffing, he shook his head. "Of course not. Any woman alone with a stranger in the jungle could make such claims to protect herself."

I rolled my eyes. Men. I accepted my whip from one of the assassins—when had that gone missing?—and tucked it into my belt where it belonged. "Satisfied?"

Pressing his lips into a thin line, Divinius nodded.

I turned to Vin. "Do you have a doctor on retainer?"

The assassin nodded a little too vigorously, the beginnings of what I suspected to be hero worship glittering in his eyes. "Yes. She's just a few blocks away."

I propped Divinius' arm over my shoulder, as much to support him as to camouflage the fact that my knees were wobbling like I'd had a night bingeing Roland's arak. My broken ribs burned. My throat felt like I'd swallowed a flagon of molten ore. No doubt I sported an impressive necklace of fingerprint-shaped bruises.

After several heartbeats, Divinius' hand tightened over my shoulders, stabilizing me. Either he had good instincts, or he'd noticed my trembling muscles.

Taking a deep breath, I turned to Vin. "You're my second?"

He brought his fist to his breastbone in a salute and nodded. "It's an honor to serve under Desert Rose."

I held back a snort. Right. "Okay. Stay here, get things sorted out. Inform the guild members of the change in management. I reward loyalty, and I protect those loyal to me." I tilted my head toward Divinius. "Like him. Follow his example, and I'll do the same for you, too. Betray me, and you won't see your death coming." I studied the other two assassins, standing awkwardly off to the side. Clearing my throat, I asked, "Which one of you is going to help me get him to the healer?"

They glanced at each other and stared at the ground.

"I don't need a doctor, Gin," Divinius whispered.

"Sand demon's spit." He must have hit his head along the way, too. "You do if you're going to be of any use to me tomorrow."

He grumbled, but didn't protest further.

Smart man.

I turned back to the others. "You, with the green shirt. Yes, you. What's your name?"

A man with sandy blond hair stepped forward. "James, um, at your service."

"Well, James. It's your lucky day. You get out of clean-up duty. Show us the way." I swallowed, adding as an afterthought, "Please."

He glanced at his colleagues before walking around me and Divinius, giving us a wide berth. "Of course. Come with me."

I held back a snort. The man was afraid of me. Good. But I didn't need to be within arm's reach to kill him.

My rib sent a jolt of white-hot pain up and down my side.

Divinius turned his head and whispered in my ear, "I hope you know what you're doing."

Yeah. Me, too.

"James, what happened?

A wizened crone shuffled into the parlor of the home the assassin had led us to. With the deliberate slowness of one in advanced age, the woman found my gaze.

I blinked. I'd expected rheumy eyes clouded by cataracts to be staring from the folds in the healer's face. Instead, clear green met mine.

The old woman's lips curled in a bitter smile. "You're new. Not what you anticipated, then, am I?"

Divinius stiffened, forcing his swollen lids open enough to get a solid look at the woman. He gasped. "You're a mage!"

She nodded as she analyzed him. "The magic takes its toll, as you well know, elf."

I peeked sideways at Divinius. There was a cost to using magic? Why hadn't I thought to ask him that before? That could be another weakness I could use against Akre and Orion. I'd have to remember to talk to His Royalness the next time we were alone.

The healer turned her attention to James. "What trouble have you guys gotten yourselves into now?"

Their escort nodded to me. "Thea, meet Desert Rose. The new head of the Guild."

The healer's eyes widened as she studied me. "I see. I'll put this on the Guild's tab, then." She waved us to the back room. "That must be some story, James. You'll have to tell me about it while they're recovering."

I shifted Divinius' arm over my shoulder. He tensed, but I tugged him forward before he could protest.

Thea led us to a small room with a bed covered in clean linens. "Lay him there." A handful of candles flickered in the corner.

Divinius settled on the blanket with a muffled groan. "My head's spinning."

So was mine, but I wasn't about to admit it.

Thea nudged me away as she pulled a stool to the edge of the mattress.

The momentum sent me stumbling for the only other chair in the room, which I unceremoniously collapsed into. My head and ribs screamed. I scrunched my face to bite back my shriek.

"I'm not surprised," Thea said, completely ignoring me as she took out a small mirror and used it to reflect candlelight into Divinius' eyes one at a time. "The good news is you don't seem to have a concussion." She pocketed the silvered glass and placed her hands on either side of his temples, then closed her eyes. "Broken nose, two cracked teeth, and lots of swelling."

She opened her eyes and met my gaze. "Nothing I can't fix."

I nodded. "Do it."

Keeping her eyes shut, she mumbled foreign words under her breath.

Divinius relaxed with a sigh. I gaped as his nasal bone straightened itself with an audible crack and the puffiness in his face disappeared over the course of several heartbeats. The angry purple-black bruises turned yellow and faded from sight.

"That's amazing!" I forced myself to watch even though I wanted nothing more than to close my eyes and crawl into a bed where I could pull the blanket over my head and sleep through this headache. Nausea curdled in my gut, pushing a sour taste up my throat. The dark paneling of the walls spun around me. I squeezed my eyes closed and gripped the armrests.

I couldn't vomit here. Not in front of James, or even Thea, when word might get back to the other assassins.

Thea wiped the back of her hand across her forehead. "That's magic."

I blinked, trying to remember what I'd said that she was responding to. My brain came up blank.

Divinius pushed himself up on his elbows. "Thank you, Thea. I feel incredible."

The healer looked as though she wanted to shove him back into the pillows. "Relax for a few days, at least. Your body will need to replenish itself. Healing takes a lot of energy." She turned to me. "Now you, young lady. On the bed."

"What? Me?" I shook my head, which only made the dizziness and nausea worse. "No, I'm okay."

"Gin," Divinius said, "You look terrible. Probably as bad as I did."

I raised my eyebrow, not because he realized he wasn't completely put together like usual, but because he'd actually admitted it out loud.

Thea nodded. "He's right. And there's a worrying lump on the back of your head I need to check."

"This is nothing. I'll be fine." Bruises and bumps were barely worth mentioning. I'd had much worse when I was fighting Orion.

The healer braced her hands on her hips. "You may be the new head of the Guild, but in my house, I'm in charge. On the bed. Now."

Divinius chuckled as he sat up and moved aside, making room for me on the narrow mattress. "You remind me of my mother. She'd either love you or kill you."

Something in his tone made Thea pause. She studied him. "You're serious, aren't you?"

Being compared to the likely dead queen of Elysia was probably intended as a compliment, though I doubted Thea knew that. I glared at Divinius, willing him to keep his mouth shut. Frowning, I navigated the braided wool rug adorning the center of the room to make sure I didn't do something embarrassing like trip over it, then flopped down on the bed before he could tell yet another person about his royal lineage.

"Ow!" I winced. Today's fight hadn't done any wonders for my broken ribs. Or my head. My vision blurred at the edges. Maybe I needed to have a healer examine me, after all.

Thea reached for me.

I flinched, leaning away before I realized what I was doing.

"Let the lady do her job, partner." Divinius rotated his hand around his wrist and whispered, "Jhalaka."

My heart leaped into my throat at his use of magic. I tensed, ready to leap off the bed.

A silver mirror glowing with a haunting teal light appeared in the air in front of me.

Swallowing past the tension in my chest, I leaned forward and poked at the swollen black blotches on my cheek, jaw and neck. Sand demon spit...

"Don't want to show up tomorrow looking like that, do you?" His taunting words echoed what I'd thought about him less than an hour ago.

I glared at him. "It looks more serious than it feels."

Thea's hands reflected in the polished silver, hovering over my temples. "I assure you, young lady, it's just as bad as it appears. Worse, even. You've got bleeding in your brain." She shook her head with a tsk. "And all of this with an already broken rib? You have quite the pain tolerance."

The mirror disappeared.

I rolled my eyes. Whatever. I hated to admit Divinius was right. If I was this battered tomorrow morning, Astra would likely fire us as soon as he laid eyes on us. "Fine. Let's get this over with." I stared up at the ceiling. Someone had covered it with plaster then used some sort of brush to create a design of overlapping half-circles, staggered in such a way that they reminded me of fish scales.

Thea's warm palm rested against my forehead. My vision turned gold, and the periphery sparkled like light reflecting off a lake. Tiny effervescent bubbles crawled along my skin, searching out each ache, coalescing in a surge of pressure before washing away the pain like a summer rain.

It could have been two minutes or two hours, but when the sensation faded and I opened my eyes, I couldn't help but gasp. For the first time since my fight with Orion, nothing hurt. Bending at the waist, I pushed on my broken rib.

There was no pain.

Thea caught my gaze with a shy smile. "Fixed that up, too. Don't worry. I don't leave a job half done." Bracing on the mattress, Thea heaved to her feet. "Now, stay here for the remainder of the night. Your bodies need to recover."

She reached out to James, who came at her beckon. "I must also rest. Please help me to bed and make sure the front door is secured before you go?"

He nodded and escorted her from the room.

My ears weren't good enough to pick up on their whispered conversation as a door closed behind them.

Divinius chewed the inside of his cheek as he watched them go. "Do you think there's something between them?"

I didn't bother to answer. It wasn't my business. Instead, I turned to him, still sitting beside me. "That was amazing. Can all mages do that?" The warlords only ever utilized their magic for pain and their own selfishness. It had never occurred to me it could be used for anything else.

Maybe not all magic users were evil. At least, not all of the ones outside Obron.

Divinius shook his head, still staring after Thea and James. The candles flickered behind him, silhouetting his profile. "No. Healing is a rare gift, and she's exceptionally talented. I'd love to know what she's doing in the slums. With talent like that, she could be working for kings, living in the luxury someone with her skill deserves for as long as she can."

I raised an eyebrow. "What do you mean?"

He stared at me as if I were stupid. "Did you not hear her? Magic always takes its toll." He paused, his brows furrowing as he studied me. "How old do you think she is?"

I shrugged, thinking back. "Maybe seventy?" Except for her eyes.

He shook his head. "No. She's probably barely half that."

I cringed. "Fates." That was one hell of a price.

"Humans don't bear the cost of spellcrafting as well as the other races. It wears them down and shortens their lives, even more so than they already are." His eyes flicked back to the door. "Thea's price appears to be physical. Sometimes, the toll is cognitive, leaving a demented mage in a young body. Or something else." His voice drifted off, as though his thoughts wandered.

I studied him as my brain churned. If magic came with a cost, then the warlords had a weakness I hadn't known and could be exploited. "And what's yours?"

He sputtered, his jaw going slack. "That's a very personal question. And rude."

"Why? Sensitive about aging, are you?" I already knew Akre's price wasn't physical or mental. He hadn't aged a day since taking power, and unfortunately his mind was just as sharp. I needed more examples to help narrow it down.

"Don't be ridiculous. Of course I'm not." Divinius turned away.

The silence stretched between us until he finally sighed. "It gives me an upset stomach and headache." He studied the floor at his feet.

The prince had just lied to me. Interesting. Why?

Clearing his throat, he brushed his hair out of his face. "That whole battle with the assassins was amazing. You were amazing. I've never seen anyone fight like that."

With a sigh, I let him change the subject, tabling the argument for later. Because there would be a later. I couldn't afford not to explore every possible weakness in my enemies. "No life-and-death brawls in the castle, huh?" I had a little time before I needed to discover Akre and Orion's weaknesses. All I'd need to do was keep needling Divinius and eventually I'd build my list of possibilities.

I also had to figure out if there was a way to bring the Tenaran assassins with me to Obron. A squad of professional killers would be useful in undercutting the warlords and overthrowing them.

Divinius huffed once and ran his fingers through his hair again. "I find this difficult to say, but..." He swallowed, his eyes still glued to the floor. "Thank you. For coming for me. I thought I was dead."

Warmth bloomed in my chest. It had been so long since anyone had thanked me, since I'd done anything worth the appreciation. I cleared my throat, glancing to the side, my skin suddenly prickling. I rubbed my hands over my arms. "You would've been." Or worse. I still wasn't sure who they were going to give him to. I glanced at the door James and Thea had disappeared behind, but decided against interrupting them and instead made a mental note to ask James or Vin tomorrow morning. "But you're welcome." I threw him a half-smile and punched him gently in the arm. "After all, I couldn't very well show up to Astra's in a few hours without you, could I?"

He chuckled, his voice dropping. "I suppose that would've been awkward to explain, in light of the fact we're supposed to be bodyguards."

"Yep." I crossed my arms. "So, tell me what happened."

He told me about the thugs forcing their way into his room at the inn. I paused him several times, making him repeat things and asking questions about details he clearly hadn't been paying attention to.

"Come on, Div. You didn't notice what colors they were wearing or anything?" The smallest thing might give us a clue as to who had sent them.

"Of course not. It was dark, and everything transpired so fast. You act like kidnapping is an everyday occurrence or something."

I raised my eyebrow at him. As a noble, it should definitely have been something he'd been prepared for. It was a very real possibility for those in Obron, at least. Could Elysia really be that different?

"I've only had people try to kidnap me since I've met you," he said, eyes narrowed on me.

I found that hard to believe. "I haven't even known you for forty-eight hours and you've been the subject of attempted kidnappings twice now." Okay, technically the first time was a robbery, but still... "Maybe if you quit flashing your title and name to anyone who will listen, it would happen less."

He glared at me. "I'm not like you."

A wave of burning indignation crested, tightening my chest. I curled my hands into fists. "I'd have expected you to move past the barbarian thing by now."

"Valek!" He ran his hand down his face. "That wasn't what I meant. You know a lot more about..." Gesturing around the room, he rolled his eyes. "About things like this than I do."

Clearly. "Then maybe you should believe me when I tell you to quit name-dropping." I couldn't keep the snap from my voice.

He flinched but nodded.

A dagger twisted in my heart, and I had the overwhelming sensation I'd kicked a puppy or something. Shaking my head, I pushed a few loose strands of hair out of my face. "They didn't let any names slip? None?"

"Not that I recall. I was, however, a little busy at the time, fighting for my life and all."

I sighed. "I'd bet three gold coins the innkeeper sold you out." Or one of the staff members.

"Does it matter? We're leaving tomorrow. Well, today, I guess."

"Div, of all people, a crown prince should know how far-reaching politics can be. You've got someone out there who wants you out of the way, if not dead. Don't you want to know who that is?" Didn't he say he was deposed, his parents murdered? "It's likely the same person who stands to benefit from your parents' deaths."

His lips pressed into a thin line. "Don't patronize me. I know that better than anyone, including you."

Then he needed to quit being so stubborn and act like the future king of Elysia. Otherwise, there was every likelihood neither of us would survive. "So, tell me, then. Who's behind this? Because I can't keep you safe if I don't have all the facts."

He shrugged. "Where should I begin? The list is very lengthy. I'd be able to pare it down if I knew who claimed the throne once my parents and I were out of the way. Or even if my mother still lived, as she has a long lineup of both allies and enemies herself."

That wasn't surprising. All royals did. I kept my face expressionless as I waited for him to continue.

He laid against the wall and sighed. "I do know there was a magic user involved in the plot, the one who banished me to this forsaken land. But the Mage College as a whole and I were frequently accomplices when it came to political matters. If it had been them, logic dictates they'd murder my parents and leave me in charge."

I flinched, shrinking into myself. "Forsaken land? This country has all the water it could ever need, with comfortable temperatures and wind that doesn't flay skin from bone." A nation that was soft enough a person could take over a guild just by killing the leader. That would have never worked in Obron.

Would anyone other than Akre notice I was gone? I swallowed past the tightness in my throat. Unlikely. I wasn't known to the kingdom as anything beyond Desert Rose, someone who only stalked the darkness of their nightmares.

"Is Elysia truly so idyllic that Ternara is terrible in comparison?" I shuddered to imagine what he'd make of Obron.

"What?" He glanced at me and changed his tone at whatever he saw in my face. "Of course not. I just meant, it's not home."

Despite his opinion, this place could be my home. I rubbed the tattoo on my cheek absently. Even if I could live my life with the shadow of Akre and Orion always at my back, I'd never truly be free as long as they lived. And I owed my parents to not leave the country and the people they'd loved under the control of such tyrants.

There was nothing that said I couldn't take my revenge, put someone on the throne who would rule justly, and retire Desert Rose. Then I could come back here to reside in the relative comfort of a peaceful city with a temperate climate and no shortage of water.

I shook my head. Who was I kidding? If I left Tenara, I wouldn't be back. Obron was in my blood. If Akre or Orion didn't kill me, I'd spend the rest of my life mopping up the mess the warlords had made out of some stupid sense of loyalty to a people who knew me as nothing but something to fear. Who would probably never know me as more than that.

It would be nice, though. To live in a place like this, with something to drink other than Arak.

I blinked. Divinius was staring at me.

Resisting the urge to rub my hands up and down my forearms to brush off the weight of his regard, I shifted from side to side. "I'm sorry, did you say something?"

He shook his head and closed his eyes. "Go to sleep. Tomorrow's going to be a long day."

I turned my back on him and curled into a ball. A few hours of rest were better than nothing. Unfortunately, I still had things to do.

I counted to two thousand before Divinius' breathing evened out. Moving slowly, I pushed myself from the bed and snuck out the door.

Chapter 8

Divinius

I awoke as the first gray light of morning breached the windows. I tilted my head to one shoulder then the other, cracking my neck in an attempt to alleviate the crick that had developed overnight.

That was what I got for sleeping while sitting up. Inhaling, I searched in vain for the slightest scent of fresh-brewed tisane, or the crackling of bacon to hint breakfast was on its way.

The dull smell of antiseptic, old blood and musky linens greeted me instead.

The events of the previous evening rushed back to me. My heart skipped a beat as heat raced through my body. The walls closed in, invisible hands wrapping around my chest. I took a deep breath through my nose and exhaled, once, twice. I needed to be calm. Last night's ordeal was in the past.

Speaking of behind... "Gin?"

Her half of the bed was empty, the bedding unwrinkled. "Gin?" Where had she gone? I hadn't gotten the impression she'd had any intention of abandoning Astra's job or her promise to get me home...

"Div?"

I followed the sound of her voice to a dark corner of the room. My shoulders sagged in relief. She sat in a rocking chair, rubbing some sort of oil into her whip. Strands of her hair stuck out in odd directions, and her clothes looked even more rumpled than last night.

She tossed something onto the floor by the bed. It snagged on the edge of the rug and came to rest just out of my sight.

Peering over the mattress, I frowned. A short sword in a well-crafted leather scabbard lay against the wooden frame.

"That's for you. I assume you know how to use it?" Even in the darkness, the raised eyebrow and taunting curve to one side of her lips were visible.

I picked it up and drew the blade from the sheath. "Of course. The basics, at least. Once it became clear I was magically inclined, there was no reason for further training."

She scoffed. "Uh, huh. And because of the 'no cost to you' for the magic thing, right?"

Valek. She hadn't bought last night's fib like I'd hoped.

I flashed the sword in the meager light, inspecting each edge of the weapon and the folds crafting the intricate pattern in the metal. "Among other things. Members of the royal family do not participate in duels."

She approached, her footsteps echoing in the silence "Nor do they defend themselves in the event of an insurrection?"

Ouch. That stung more than it should have. I brushed my hand over the coarse sheets. "That's what magic is for." At least, in my case.

"The thing that only costs you an upset stomach?"

I ground my teeth together and shoved the sword into its sheath. "Drop it. Please."

She coiled her whip, attaching it to her belt. "Fine."

I adjusted the scabbard on my waist, even though it sat oddly over my robes. "Thank you." It made sense to have one if I was going to play bodyguard. "Where did you get it? Or do I not want to know?" I wouldn't put it past her to steal it... it wasn't like her purse was flush based on her and Astra's dealings last night.

"The Assassin's Guild. Where do you think?"

I raised an eyebrow at the bite in her tone. Was she mad at me or something? "No sleep makes you cranky."

She shrugged, ignoring my comment, and smoothed down the errant strands of her hair. The onyx tresses faded into the shadows behind her. "It's my guild now. As are the contents of the armory." She flashed her teeth at me in a wicked smile that stirred the magic running beneath my skin.

I braced myself. There was something in her expression...

A sense of foreboding settled on my shoulders. "What?"

"And its treasury."

I blinked, my gaze settling at the bag at her feet. "How much did we get?" I asked, reaching for the satchel.

She kicked it out of my reach. "I got a bunch of silver and gold coins. Maybe enough to set me up for life after all this. But I left them with most of what they had."

If it really was hers, why not take it all? I sighed. Humans, they made no sense. Whatever. "You can't carry so much money around while we're on the road. Someone will steal it."

She glared with narrow eyes. "I'd like to see them try."

I shivered at her expression. One would never guess it from her appearance when I'd first met her, but there was a deadly, unbendable strength to Gin that the women in my mother's court could never hope to match. "I didn't say I would." I wasn't stupid enough to piss off Desert

Rose, the one who had taken on an entire guild of assassins to rescue me. If anyone could keep her gold safe, it would be the woman before me.

I wiped my face with my free hand. By Naraka. My mother would be so proud of the company I was keeping lately.

My stomach twinged. Assuming the queen still lived.

I shrugged my robes into place. "Come on. We should be going."

Gin stood. "Do we say goodbye to..."

"Thea?" I glanced at the door the healer and James had disappeared behind last night. "I doubt they'd welcome the interruption."

Gin added her sack of gold to her backpack and slung it over her shoulder with a sigh. "I need to stop at a bank and drop this off on the way. You ready?"

I groaned. Every muscle in my body hated me today. How did regular people function without a proper bed?

"What's the matter, Highness-ness? Not used to sleeping on mattresses that aren't filled with goose feathers?"

Well, yes. "No." I rubbed my eyes and yawned. "The hour is indecent. The sun isn't even up."

Gin opened the door and stepped onto the street, turning toward the docks. "You'd best be grateful it's not. If we're late to meet Astra, we'll lose the job. Then we'd have to make it back to your castle by ourselves."

I jogged to catch up with her. The cobblestones were rough beneath my shoes. I tensed my legs to keep my balance on their uneven surface. "You're right, of course. I'd kill for some tisane to help me wake up."

She tossed me her canteen. "Here. Have some water."

"Is it hot?" I stared blankly at it like the half-asleep moron I was. "Can we make tea?" That was ridiculous. There was no fire here, no stove to heat the liquid. Though the off-chance her container was charmed to warm beverages was worth fantasizing about.

Ahead of us, a few humans moved along the street, hurrying off to their early morning tasks.

Gin looked at me like I'd sprouted a second head, her eyebrows furrowed. "Why on earth would you want to do that?"

So much for that hope. "Um, because it tastes better?" I held back an eye roll. Obronians.

Gin scoffed. "Trust me. Nothing is as delicious as the water they have here."

I raised my eyebrow. Clearly, she'd never had a good bottle of elven red.

She shook her head. "Why you would want to heat and flavor perfectly good water is beyond me."

I opened my mouth to argue but paused as my awakening brain caught up. She was from the high desert. Cold anything was a luxury, especially water. I shrugged. At least I could make an effort to get along, since she'd saved my life last night and all. Opening the waterskin, I took a long drink.

Surprisingly, the cool liquid sliding down my throat did make me feel a little more awake.

Gin smirked in that irritating better-than-thou way she had. It reminded me of the piranhas at court when they'd pulled off a particularly crafty political maneuver. "See, I told you." She snagged two pieces of fried fish from a street vendor and tossed one to me.

The smell was mouth-watering. Whatever combination of spices the human used had my stomach growling. I took a bite. For peasant fare, it was juicy and flavorful, but not enough to quench my appetite. Especially if I wasn't going to be getting any tisane this morning.

The sun crested the hills at our backs and the number of people milling about increased until I felt like we were wading up a stream. We had finally hit the docks after a quick stopover for Gin to open an account at a local bank. Pages scurried about underfoot. The fishmongers were already barking today's catch on the piers as they cleaned their nets. Some had grills right on the waterfront.

My stomach growled at the smell, still hungry. I stepped toward the nearest one.

"Excellent!" A familiar voice sounded. "I was worried you two wouldn't make it." Astra strode across the pier and stopped a few paces away, sizing us up.

I froze mid-step and turned to face the merchant. Today, Astra's hair was a stunning violet.

He nodded, his gaze straying to the array of weapons dangling from Gin's waist. "Yes, you'll both do. We're almost loaded up. A couple more minutes and we'll be on our way."

He spun on his heel and waved over his shoulder, beckoning us to follow him onto the dock. "The first several days of the journey will be by sea. We'll hit Faegate Port and travel inland from there, along the river until we reach the mountains."

A sudden breeze whipped the heavy canvas of the sails in the ships lining the pier. The salty scent of brine and rotting seaweed assailed my nostrils as a few strands of loose hair danced across my forehead.

I glanced at Gin. Her face betrayed no emotion, but her eyes flicked over the scene before us. She was probably identifying threats and mapping escape routes, despite the bored affectation to her posture rivaling any noble's. I couldn't help but wonder what sort of life or training she'd had that would make such a thing second nature to her. Unlike royals, commoners weren't surrounded by guards whose sole duty was to keep them safe, but most people didn't step into each room or new area always expecting a trap.

I dodged a burly sailor who wove down the pier rolling a full-sized barrel. The weight of his burden had the boards creaking beneath my feet as he passed.

Astra called above the din, "Paul! That had better be the oil and not the wine!"

"Don't get your panties in a twist," the man yelled back. "I know how to do the job you're paying me for."

I pursed my lips imagining Gin's response if someone said something similar to her. There'd be one less head attached to a neck if that ever happened. Catching Astra's eye, I asked, "You let him talk to you that way?"

Astra smiled. "All sailors are a little coarse around the edges. Paul's one of the best."

Behind the merchant, Gin froze. I nearly bowled her over. Her gaze was riveted to the next dock over.

"Gin, what is it?" I asked, frustration welling in my chest at the interruption. I resisted the urge to send a tendril of magic her way to pick up her surface thoughts. My slip-up last night had left me feeling more than a little guilty about the invasion of her privacy, but it was a relief to know she did actually intend to help me regain my throne, even if it was only to facilitate her return to Obron to dethrone the warlords.

The corners of her lips hardened. She grabbed her blades.

Across the way, a group of fishermen heaved barrels of fish guts into a skiff that rocked in the waves. I followed her stare to the line of people staggering toward the shore under the crack of a whip. The clank of chains rose above the screams of the seagulls.

Oh.

She pressed her pack into my hands. "Here, hold this. I'll be right back." Spinning on her heels, she took off down the dock, her footsteps echoing off the warped planks.

I blinked. She'd handed me the last of the coin she'd been so possessive of less than half an hour ago. "Gin, wait!"

"Where's she going?" Astra asked, staring after her.

I turned to meet his raised eyebrows. Shrugging, I hauled her pack over one shoulder gently, so as to not betray its contents. "Who knows why Gin does anything?" But if it was at all like the display she'd put on inside the Assassin's Guild, this was going to be a show.

The twinkle left Astra's gaze as he frowned. "Is she going to be a problem?"

I scoffed and took a few steps in the direction of the merchant's vessel. "Gin? She's worth five times any trouble she causes." I swallowed. At least, I hoped.

Chapter 9
Divinius

I crossed my arms as a surge of irritation burst through my chest. My magic crested in response, tingling across my skin. Gin was gone, as if our entire plan of getting me home was no longer of consequence, shoved to the back burner for... whatever this was. And while I was always down for a good show of Gin kicking ass, especially when my life wasn't on the line, a quick glance at Astra's pinched expression had a wave of unease roiling in my stomach that rivaled the surf crashing into the beach.

My focus zeroed in on the column of slaves trudging across the opposite dock. The crack of a whip had most of them flinching, followed by a sharp cry from the slaver's unfortunate target. The clatter of chains was like nails on slate, sending shivers up my spine. No wonder my parents disliked slavery. I hadn't spent much time thinking on the plights of those wretches, as it had never affected me or anyone I knew. But we had more important things to focus on right now—namely, getting me home and restored to my throne.

Gin's reaction was a little extreme for someone with Desert Rose's reputation. Based on how she reacted to the warlords, and to me when we'd first met, it was obvious she didn't like people in positions of power. Maybe she'd been bullied as a child and had never dealt with the trauma. But there were healthier ways to deal with problems than murder.

I thought back to the coup that had thrown me into her path. Well, most of the time, there were better methods.

My father would've searched for a diplomatic solution to any problem rather than risking a direct conflict. Gin seemed to know nothing beyond confrontation and escalation. But, as a beneficiary of said escalation, since I wasn't dead in some assassin stronghold, I didn't have much ground to stand on when it came to criticizing her methods.

Gin had a spine. There was a core of strength and competence to the woman I'd never have guessed.

A youth dressed as a sailor, possibly a cabin boy or cook's apprentice, saw Gin coming as she sprinted up the dock. Even from this far away, the speed at which his face paled was almost comical. He threw himself into the water rather than face her. The splash of his exit was swallowed by the churning ocean.

Salty spray covered my face, plastering my hair to my forehead but I hardly noticed.

Gin drew her sword and slashed it across the slavemaster's neck before he'd managed to whirl around to face her.

I flinched, my mouth going dry at the brutal violence.

Gin's opponent dropped the rope in his hand as he collapsed to his knees. She ripped a key ring from his belt and tossed it at the nearest slave. Her lips moved, but I was too far away to make out her words.

Heavy footsteps pounded against the dock as she turned to face the newcomer. Every action, every movement embodied strength and grace, which, for a human, was impressive. She fought almost as well as the warriors in the Elysian Royal Guard.

Her new opponent was a large man, someone who had likely been an imposing wall of muscle in his younger years but now had a layer of what I considered 'hard fat' overlying any remaining muscles. The man was strong, but nowhere near as intimidating as he'd been in his youth.

I clenched my hands into fists, resisting the urge to call out a warning. I bounced up and down on my toes, the planks beneath my feet bending with my shifting weight.

Gin feinted toward her opponent's neck with her sword but dropped to the ground as his scourge hissed through the air where her head had been a heartbeat ago. She swung her blade as she kicked in the opposite direction, likely hoping to catch his leg in the scissor-like move. The sailor was more agile than he appeared, leaping out of the way as her weapon sailed past.

She was a stunning, murderous beauty.

My heart rate sped up, sending a flush of blood to my face and extremities. Warmth pooled low in my stomach as my muscles tensed.

The first few slaves in the chain were free, having managed to unlock their shackles.

Astra stepped into view, the scowl on his face cooling some of the heat unfurling in my torso. "What in the name of the fates is she doing?" The tattoo along the sides of his neck tightened, giving the ink an almost 3D appearance, as though the scales were ridged.

Did he mean other than kicking ass? Raising an eyebrow, I peered at him from the corner of my eye.

I cleared my throat, catching the words before they crossed my lips. Instead, I went with the obvious response. "It looks like she's freeing the slaves."

The sun beat down on us as the tense silence stretched. The reflection off the slaver's blade was blinding to the point of distraction.

Astra's fingers settled around my bicep, squeezing to draw my focus away from the spectacle that was Gin.

"Unhand me!" I jerked back out of the way, my mage robes flapping in the wind and getting in the way. "What do you think you're doing?"

Astra narrowed his eyes and turned the full weight of his attention on me. "What am I doing?" He waved his free hand toward Gin with enough force it seemed as if he wanted to stab her. "What is she doing? This is one of the main ports I operate in! She's going to get my trade permits cancelled!"

It was on the tip of my tongue to snap I didn't give a dung beetle's horde about his permits, but in the name of international relations, I kept that thought to myself. Instead, I chewed the inside of my cheek as I turned my attention back to Gin, who was somersaulting away from the older soldier with the scourge. "Only if she gets caught."

Astra grabbed my arm again and jerked me to face him. No, to face the shore, where a group of guards assembled wearing uniforms of navy with gold sashes.

Valek.

My gaze swiveled back to where Gin fought. She hadn't noticed them yet.

Her opponent had his lash wrapped around her wrist. He yanked, spinning her in a half circle that had her slamming into the dock. She cried out as she landed, the air exploding from her lungs.

My heart leaped into my throat as my thoughts helpfully served up images of the slaver stabbing the cutlass at his belt into her gut or slicing it across her throat.

I grabbed Astra's arm. "We have to help her."

"Help her?" He scoffed, waving me off. "Hells, no. I'm firing her, firing both of you. I don't need to be associated with this sort of drama."

A cold slash sliced through my torso, as though someone had stabbed me in the ribs with a frost blade. No, I couldn't allow it—this job was my ticket home. "You can't do that."

Astra's ice-blue eyes flashed red. Actual blood-red.

By Helani. I took a step back, shaking my head. It must have been a trick of the morning light. I couldn't have seen what I saw.

Astra followed, shoving his face in front of mine. "I can do anything I want, elf. I hired you, and I can fire you without cause before you've even started." He waved toward Gin as she slammed her sword through the slaver's gut with a wicked cackle that sent zaps of energy up my arms and neck. "You're both too unpredictable."

Well, that was hardly a fair assessment. I flicked my eyes between Gin and Astra. The pier guards were already piling onto the dock, cutting off Gin's escape route. The only way she could get away now would be to swim for it, just like the child had done when she'd first approached the slave line.

"We are not," I protested.

Astra froze, the expression on his face was almost comical as he raised one eyebrow, glancing pointedly at Gin. "Oh, really?"

Okay, so perhaps Gin was slightly, occasionally unpredictable. But me... I spread my arms wide. "I'm here, aren't I?" Maybe Astra would still take me, and at least I could get home.

There was a large clank as Gin crossed blades with yet another man, this one had a scimitar with a wickedly serrated blade. I had no idea what purpose the serrations served, beyond looking intimidating, but the quality of the weapon was impressive.

The guards fanned out across the beginning of the dock, blocking off her escape but in no hurry to get in between the two combatants.

Gin sidestepped as her newest opponent threw himself forward. Two slaves leaped out of her way, somehow entangling her foot with their chain. She wobbled on the edge of the pier, her arms windmilling as she fought to shift her center of gravity back far enough to avoid plunging into the ocean.

Her sun-kissed skin went pallid as her eyes bulged, giving her a harried, wild appearance. I'd never seen sheer terror on her face before, but there it was as she stared into the churning sea below. Her mouth opened and closed as if she couldn't catch her breath.

The famed Desert Rose was afraid of water. That was... odd. Perhaps she wasn't all brazen steel, after all. Maybe, under the façade, she was a regular person with normal fears and weaknesses. And she'd still faced down an entire guild of assassins to save my life.

My knees locked, every muscle in my body straining to throw myself toward her. She'd risked her life for me. It wouldn't be very princely of me to abandon her when I owed her a life debt. "We need to help!"

Astra shook his head. "No. She brought this on herself. Getting involved will only get me kicked out of port and you fired." He peered at me from the corner of his eyes. "That's assuming, of course, you still want the work?"

From the edge of my vision, I caught movement as one of the slaves grabbed Gin's arm and pulled her away from the brink.

I pressed my lips into a thin line and turned the full fury of the Morganis Glare onto Astra. "We both still want it, and you are not firing anyone."

Astra harumphed, leveling a flat stare at me. "As the captain of my fleet, I have every right to decide who I do and don't fire."

My intimidating expression crumbled under his lack of capitulation. Few in Elysia had ever stood up to my father or mother when they used the Morganis Glare. Maybe I was losing my touch.

Perhaps the merchant was so motivated by greed he didn't care about the implied threat against his person. Regardless, it was time to try a new tactic.

"Look at how great a fighter she is." I gestured at Gin as she jumped into a backflip, bounced off her opponent's outstretched arm and sailed above his head. Wrapping her legs around his upper torso, she stretched her whip tight across the slaver's neck. I bit back a smile. That was the same move she'd used in the Assassin's Guild—and then another of the men had asked her to teach them. "Isn't that someone worth having on hand to protect your goods? Your people?"

Astra shook her head. "Impressive as she may be, I can't trust her to not run off and abandon her duty at the first distraction."

I stepped forward, putting myself directly in Astra's line of sight. The surge of irritation had my magic crackling across my skin until it coiled, ready to explode. Sparks danced through the edges of my vision as I put the full force of my power behind the words. "Yes, you can. Save her, or I will burn your ship to cinders."

Astra braced himself, as if fighting the urge to step back. His gaze hardened as he stared at me. "Threatening me is not wise, and not the way to get what you want, elf."

Something dark loomed in his expression, and I suddenly felt like a rabbit in a fox's sights. Like I was prey. With a sigh that was as casual as I could make it, I released my magic. Time for a different approach. "Get us both out of the port and into Elysia, and I can guarantee you the position of Most Favored Trader in every Elysian post for the next," I paused, "twelve months. Imagine, a full year of premium docking space and priority loading and unloading. You'll save yourself several days off each voyage, especially in the busier ports."

The only sign of Astra's surprise was the two slow blinks he gave me before his eyes roamed from the tip of my head to my feet and back again. "The only way to get that is through royal decree."

I tensed, willing my gaze to burn through his thick skull. "I can arrange that."

The silence stretched between us as the sound of Gin's blade crossing with the slaver's echoed across the pier. Sails snapped in the wind behind Astra as the breeze picked back up. We'd need to leave soon or we'd miss the tide.

Astra crossed his arms. "Five years."

I bit the outer corners of my mouth to hold back the victorious smile. "Three."

"Done!" He narrowed his eyes and pointed a dagger at my throat.

My forehead knitted. This wasn't how deals were sealed in Elysia. And I hadn't even noticed him drawing the blade. Gin would no doubt roll her eyes at my lack of observation skills.

"But I warn you, mage," Astra said, as if my surprise hadn't been written across my face, "if you can't keep to your half of the bargain, I'll throw you over the side of the boat and keelhaul you."

I had no idea what that meant, but judging from Astra's hard expression, it wouldn't be pleasant. But it didn't matter because I had every intention of making good once I reclaimed my throne. I studied the smooth sides of the ship towering behind us, looking for any clues as to how his keel was a threat, but found none. The hull was polished to a sheen, no doubt to help it speed through the water. "Agreed." I held out my arm.

Shoving the dagger back into the concealed sheath at his waist, Astra took my hand and we shook.

With a sigh, Astra took a deep breath and turned his back on me. "Damien!"

A head appeared from the deck above us. "Captain?"

"Drop the dinghy!" Astra said.

A few heartbeats later, a small rowboat crashed to the surface of the water, where it bobbed along the edge of the pier.

"Come on," Astra waved to me as he marched up to the tiny vessel and dropped into it. I followed suit as Gin rolled the final slaver's body off the dock. It disappeared with a splash.

The slaves were long gone, only the empty shackles and chains remained.

I grabbed one set of oars as Astra settled at the other. "Stroke!" he called, setting a pace almost as furious as my racing heartbeat. I swallowed the irritation at being given orders and pulled on the oar with all my strength.

Gin stood, brushing her palms on her pants as she stared out to sea.

The guards were storming the wharf. She turned to face them, her hand curling around her whip.

As badass as she was, not even Desert Rose could take on a whole contingent by herself.

"Gin!" I pulled a fine thread of power, using it to project my voice over the ruckus.

She whirled, her eyes frantically scanning.

"Down here!" I paused my rowing and waved my hands.

She stepped to the edge of the dock and peered over the side.

Her face relaxed as her gaze met mine. Astra's little rowboat banged into one of the pilings holding up the pier.

I sat back, gesturing for her to join us. "Get in!"

"Yes," Astra growled through clenched teeth. "Before the port master gets here and has us all arrested."

The visible tremble of her relief had me wanting to reach for her, but Astra's presence drew me up short. That, and the fact that she still had a death grip on her sword. I had no desire to be stabbed today.

She scrambled over, her feet slipping as our boat rocked. Releasing her hold on the rough planks of the dock, she collapsed onto a pile of netting on the floorboards.

Astra pushed off. "Stroke! One, two, three..." He took up the rapid rhythm again.

My back ached at the unaccustomed strain, and I was sure I'd have at least four blisters and several slivers from the unpolished oars before this was over. But Gin was safe, and the two of us still had jobs, so that was something.

Once the wharf was an acceptable distance away, Astra glared at Gin. "What in the name of the Seven Sea Gods were you thinking?"

She stammered, "I—"

He cut her off with a sharp head shake. "You weren't! You'll get me banned from this port! Do you have any idea how hard it will be to do business in Tenara after this stunt?" He pointed over her shoulder at all the guards who swarmed the pier she'd stood on moments before.

Plastering a smile on her face, Gin leaned back. "If it's so much trouble, why come to my rescue?"

Astra redirected his ire to me. "Your partner was... insistent." He dropped his voice. "Violently so."

I frowned. I didn't think offering him Most Favored Trader status counted as violent, though I had threatened his boat with my magic.

Shrugging, I turned back to Gin. Astra could think whatever he wanted in order to sleep better at night.

Gin raised her eyebrow. I let one side of my mouth curl up and winked.

She bit her lower lip and took a deep breath. "Thank you," she mouthed.

I shook my head. "Next time, warn me before you run off and do something hot headed. You do know there are more appropriate ways of dealing with problems than killing everyone, right?"

She scrunched her face at my words, as if I'd tried to tell her the sky was purple. "No, there's not."

I turned the Morganis Glare on her.

The resolve in her eyes crumbled a little around the edges. Well, that was something, at least. In the future, hopefully she'd think before running headfirst into poor life choices.

I sighed. "Politics, Gin. Politics." I pulled back on the oars. "What have you done here? Rescued twenty slaves? In the process, you've likely gotten Astra banned and if we're lucky, we won't be caught and arrested before we can escape." I yanked on the paddles again. "With political maneuvering and negotiations, it would take time, but you could work for the freedom of every slave, here and beyond. Assuming the wretches are worth that much effort." Not like patience was one of my skills, nor did I consider it a virtue, but in this case...

Something in her demeanor crumbled, reminding me of a sandcastle assaulted by incoming waves.

After several heartbeats, Gin rolled her shoulders back and scoffed. Jutting her chin forward, she met my gaze with a furious one of her own. "Politics is nothing more than power-hungry aristocrats trying to get a one-up on their peers. Not one nobleman or woman I've known would spend more than a breath on someone other than themselves, much less a slave." Pulling her knees to her chest, she glared at me like a petulant toddler. "When those in charge won't stick up for us, the only option we have left is to defend ourselves."

She'd definitely been picked on as a child and had needed to learn the hard way to stand up for herself. Maybe she'd grown up on the streets? If she'd been an orphan and had to fight to survive, that would explain her exceptional combat skills and her inability to follow the law. "Not everyone bullies their peasants." In fact, my parents had worked tirelessly for the benefit of their people and those in the surrounding countries. Now that they were both likely dead, I'd have to decide which of their policies were worth continuing and which would change.

Gin snorted like I'd said something funny, or incredibly naïve.

I furrowed my eyebrows. "What?"

"Just wondering how much time you've spent looking outside your own castle walls."

I frowned. Petulant Gin was not a good look. Ice sprouted in my chest, tensing my muscles. "Your poor experience doesn't give you the right to judge me or my life. And your issues with authority are not my problem!"

Astra cursed under his breath, interrupting us. "They're commandeering the slaver's ship! Looks like we're in for a pursuit!"

Chapter 10
Gin

I glanced over my shoulder as I gripped the sides of the far too tiny rowboat until my knuckles turned white. As much as I hated to admit it, Divinius was right. I'd risked the entire mission, my only chance at securing an army and getting revenge, on freeing less than two dozen slaves. Most of whom would probably be recaptured by the end of the day. I'd let my emotions get the best of me and had compromised everything.

Sand demon spit. I should've handled the slavers better. In losing control, I'd almost botched the whole plan.

I took a deep breath of the salty sea air, held it for a count of five, then exhaled, willing the heat of anger and embarrassment to drain from my face as I turned my attention to the pier. To the mess I'd made.

The navy uniforms had boarded the slaver's vessel and were running around like a nest of upset sand-wasps.

Divinius paused his rowing, earning him a glare from Astra. "Aga!"

A large fireball hurled across the bay, exploding against the largest mast on the doomed boat. Flames licked the sails, casting an orange pallor over the water's surface.

With a satisfied grin, Divinius picked up the oars. "That should hold them."

Astra's eyes widened for half a heartbeat before he nodded. "Aye. It should, if we hurry. Though it's a shame to lose such a marvelous vessel."

I frowned as I studied the ship, its deck engulfed in fire. Anyone who would consider a transport used for slavery to be a 'marvelous vessel' had questionable tastes.

A sharp creak of metal against metal echoed across the bay.

Astra cursed in a language I didn't understand as Divinius and I whipped around toward the harbor's entrance.

A thick chain anchored between the two towers guarding the port rose, dripping a curtain of water and seaweed. The barrier would keep any arriving vessels out, and us trapped inside.

My gut crashed through the wooden planks at my feet and sank into the waters below. We were going to be caught, and it was all my fault. Divinius and Astra were probably destined for the brig, and I'd be packed right back to Akre or Orion as soon as the city constable set eyes on my tattoo.

I met Divinius' wide-eyed gaze, the same desperation I was feeling mirrored in his face.

Astra snarled. "Get us back to the ship! Now!"

Blinking as he schooled his features, Divinius leaned forward and back, ripping the oars through the water. The exertion rippled up his arm muscles and across his torso. A sheen of perspiration highlighted his toned body.

I caught myself admiring the view and glanced away before he noticed my stare. Heat rushed to my face. Now was not the time to develop a crush on someone who was a means to an end, especially when we were in the middle of fleeing for our lives.

Astra shifted his focus to the vessel floating behind us. "Weight anchor and hoist the mizzen!" he yelled.

I turned to find the crew raising a large sail at the back of his ship while other sailors scrambled around on deck. Turning my attention to Astra, I frowned, narrowing my eyes. "Are you planning on running?" Why do such a thing when there was no escape, and he could avoid most of the consequences of today's actions by just handing me over?

Astra grunted, the edges of his mouth hard. "I'm already neck deep in this. If they catch you, they get me, too. Besides, we're on a tight schedule with this delivery. If we miss the tide, we'll have to wait to leave until tomorrow, and late deliveries mean less profit."

I chewed the inside of my cheek as we pulled into the shadow of his ship. Waves lapped against the hull, spraying fine droplets across my arms and face. What was Astra carrying that he didn't want the authorities to find? Had we stumbled our way onto a smuggler's vessel? That didn't feel right, though... what smuggler would take on the added risk of passengers? Even if those individuals were capable bodyguards to protect the merchandise, Astra had no way of knowing we would be trustworthy around his illicit goods.

Something was off, like when Akre had forced me to attempt to assassinate Orion on a rushed timetable. My instincts screamed we were walking into a situation just as deadly.

I met Divinius' eyes, his focus pinned on me as our boat rammed the other vessel. His dark gaze told me his thoughts were likely running along the same lines.

Something heavy splashed into the bay twenty paces away. Waves crashed over the side, soaking us to the bone.

"Cannon fire!" someone above decks called out as a twisted net of ropes flew over the side to us. It slammed against the ship's planks inches from my face.

Astra cursed again as he grabbed the netting. "Hurry! Climb aboard!" The ship jerked and creaked as the wind caught the unfurling sails.

Another projectile rammed into the water, close enough to spray Divinius.

No one needed to tell me twice. Shoving my unease regarding Astra aside, I clutched the rough-hewn rope and hauled myself onto the deck.

Kicking my legs over the railing, I landed on my back. The polished wood was much more stable than the rowboat had been. Rolling to my feet, I stepped away to allow Divinius and Astra on board as the ship tipped sideways. Losing my balance at the sudden upset, I tumbled to the ground.

The nearest sailors chuckled.

Growling, I reached for my blade. An explosion and cloud of smoke sounded from the beach. A sharp whistling hit my ears that increased in pitch as the next cannonball sped overhead to splash into the water beyond.

"What are you lot laughing about?" Astra pulled himself onboard. The tone of his voice brought me up short. "I said cast off! Now! Before they blow a hole in the hull!"

The deck exploded into action. Canvas snapped above, yanked taught by the wind. I crawled into an out-of-the-way corner. Divinius joined me, making sure to keep one hand on the railing as he approached. Resting his elbows on the wood, he studied the horizon.

I sat, my back braced against the taffrail, as Tenara grew smaller. A weight lifted from my shoulders as the first step of my journey back home disappeared behind us. The ocean sparkled in the sun, a reflective mirror brighter than any in Obron. The constant breeze over my wet clothes raised goosebumps on my arms.

I turned to stare out at the open sea, where the string of black links hovered just above the surface. It was too low for us to hope to sneak beneath, but no part sunk into the water so we couldn't sail over it, either. "What do you think we're going to do about the chain?" I asked Divinius.

"Hmm."

He pressed his lips into a thin line. After several heartbeats, he said, "It looks like we're going to make a run for it. Though I can't see how that won't destroy this vessel and sink us all to the depths."

I swallowed the sudden rock in my throat. I'd rather be thrown in the brig and carted back to Obron than be on a sinking ship.

Divinius glanced at me, his expression changing at whatever he saw in my face. "Don't worry. I'm sure it won't come to that." He tilted his chin toward Astra, where the man stood at the front of the deck. "He's way too attached to this boat to risk its destruction."

Maybe. Hopefully. "I suppose it depends on how badly he doesn't want to be caught by the guards."

Divinius nodded. "Agreed."

"Lash six oil barrels to the prow!"

We stared, the furrows between Divinius' brows no doubt matching mine. Astra stepped out of the way as the sailors ran to do his command. A few minutes later, as the chain sailed ever closer, the casks were wrapped in netting and heaved overboard, three on each side of the dragon statue that adorned the ship's front.

Astra's eyes met ours across the deck as he headed toward us. Pinning Divinius with a hard stare as he approached, he stopped next to us, arms crossed over his chest. "I assume that little parlor trick with the fireball wasn't the extent of your fire-wielding ability?"

Divinius cleared his throat. "No. Why do you ask?"

"We're going to have to ram it." Astra gestured to the iron monstrosity hovering ahead of us. "We are fortunate half of our load is oil, but I need something to ignite it so we can weaken the links enough to snap them." He stared into Divinius' eyes. "It's time for you to start earning your keep, mage."

I blinked, my gaze flitting between the chain and Astra's face. Running into the chain? Was he serious?

"It seems to me," Divinius said, his expression schooled, "doing such a thing would destroy this ship. Either from impact, the force of the explosion, or the resulting flames." He narrowed his eyes and leaned forward. "Unless I'm mistaken that ships with the misfortune of catching fire tend to go up like dry tinder."

Like the slaver's vessel at the docks.

Astra's lips pressed into thin lines. "Usually, you'd be correct. But *The Ashwing* is made of sterner stuff." He patted the railing. "She'll see us through." He glared at Divinius. "Can you ignite the barrels for us when it's time?"

Divinius shrugged, the forced casualness of the action not softening the skepticism in his expression.

Astra nodded. "Good. Then you'd best come with me. The timing on this is going to be tight." He narrowed his gaze on me. "And then, young lady, you and I are going to have a talk."

A ball of sand-spiders roiled in my gut at his dark tone. The worst part was the dressing-down I was about to get was deserved. Even I could admit that. At least Astra wasn't likely to have a water wheel in the bowels of his ship. I probably didn't need to worry about him throwing me overboard, either. Otherwise, why rescue and bring me along in the first place?

With nothing else to do, I followed Divinius and Astra to the front of the vessel, making sure to hang on to the banister. The unpredictable movements of the deck continued to slide my legs out from beneath me at random intervals. I'd never been more grateful to have been born in the desert rather than in a coastal territory.

By the time I made it to the bow, the chain was clearly visible, each link at least the size of a person. Divinius was leaning over the railing, examining the barrels lashed to the front.

"How can you be certain the blast won't blow back and incinerate everyone on this half of the deck?" Divinius asked.

Astra's lips pressed into a thin line as he studied the obstacle, which was approaching too rapidly for comfort. "Do your part, mage, and trust me to do mine."

I glanced up at the sails and rigging overhead. All it would take would be one cinder...

An unseen fist clenched in my chest. This was all my fault. Astra's ship, the lives on board, were all at risk because of me. If I'd kept my stupid emotions in check...

I shook my head. But I hadn't, and there was nothing to do now except to surge forward. Astra was willing to gamble his vessel to escape the harbor. I wasn't under any delusions that urge had anything to do with me or Divinius, but we would be beneficiaries by association. I didn't have to trust Astra—because I didn't—but I could at least do what I could to help.

"What can I do?" I pulled myself up the steps to the upper deck.

Both men's heads whirled in my direction. I couldn't unsee the hard pinch in Astra's face. Okay, yeah, I deserved every inch of his wrath and disappointment for putting us in this position, but that didn't mean I wasn't capable in an emergency.

Astra's attention shifted over my shoulder. He lifted a finger and pointed. "Make sure they don't board us!"

I glanced behind me. While I'd been focusing on navigating the ship, another had snuck up on us, no doubt intent on preventing our escape. Drawing my sword with my free hand, I nodded as I retreated down the stairs. I could guarantee anyone who set foot on our deck wouldn't live to see another sunrise.

I'd cut loose three grappling hooks and dodged as many harpoons by the time we reached the chain. The pursuing vessel managed to haul itself close enough that in the next few minutes, the sailors would be able to swing aboard.

"Brace yourselves!" Astra yelled across the desk.

I dropped to all fours and curled against the railing, holding tight with both hands.

"Aga!" Divinius' voice echoed on the breeze, a heartbeat before a large blast shook my bones and rattled my teeth.

I glanced up front, his name a scream stuck in my throat.

A curtain of fire cascaded over the bow, imprinting the afterimage of the dragon figurehead in my vision. Astra separated his arms as if parting the seas, and the flames billowed harmlessly to either side of the deck.

Sand demon spit! Astra was controlling the explosion!

The wave of heat scorched my skin as the fireball enveloped the boat beside us. Sailors and guards screamed as they flung themselves overboard rather than risk being caught in the conflagration consuming their vessel.

Divinius waved his arms, though if he said something, it was lost to the roaring in my ears.

Astra was a mage, like Divinius and the warlords. God's teeth! I was stuck on a ship, on the freaking ocean, with not just one but two mages! What in the world of nope had I gotten myself into?

The fireball contracted, like it had turned in on itself and wrapped around the massive chain stretching in both directions in front of us.

The entire deck shuddered with a force that threatened to wrench me from where I huddled as it came to a sudden stop. A deep crack of splitting wood that reminded me of snapping bones ran up my spine like phantom sand-spiders. The boat was damaged. We were going to sink.

The edges of my vision went black. I couldn't get enough oxygen. My lungs burned as an invisible band constricted around my ribcage.

Oh, fates, fates, fates...

Clenching my jaw until it ached, I gasped. The air was still warm from the heat that concentrated on the iron links but didn't scorch my lungs. I couldn't lose control now. If I panicked, I'd be dead as soon as I plunged beneath the water's surface.

With the clank of metal, the chain snapped, both ends dropping into the ocean with a splash and loud hiss. A cloud of steam burst forth and washed over the ship as we sailed out of the harbor and into the open sea.

"Divinius, can you swim?" The explosion when we'd escaped port had apparently discouraged all other pursuit. And while Divinius swore left and right Astra was not a mage and there was no way the merchant could control fire, I couldn't deny what I'd seen with my own eyes. But there wasn't much I could do about it at the moment without risking being tossed into the ocean. And of everyone I knew, Divinius would be most likely to recognize another magic user. So, instead of confronting Astra, I occupied myself with staring over the railing at the large, gray fish with bottleneck noses swimming next to us. It was almost like they were keeping us company.

Divinius shifted his weight where he stood beside me, leaning his elbows over the banister as though this ship was a second home to him. My white-knuckled grip, in contrast, betrayed every inch of my discomfort. At any moment, the boat could pitch sideways, tossing us into the wet abyss. I was all too familiar with the feeling of liquid racing into my lungs and here, there would be no inquisitor to wrench the water wheel and raise me to the surface.

No. I'd sink into the darkness and be forever lost.

The damp cloth stretched over my face, with the rushing sensation of my feet being above my head. I opened my mouth, gasping for the last gasp of oxygen before I was plunged back into the pool. Liquid forced its way up my nose and down my throat. All I could do was close my lips and endure the spine-wrenching coughs that would do nothing more than force me to inhale more water.

I took a shallow breath, forcing air past the tight burning in my chest. My knuckles popped with the strength of my grip on the wood. The ocean would not claim me today. Not if I had anything to say about it.

"Can I swim? That's a random question." Divinius' hand brushed mine and I startled, putting several paces between us before I realized what I was doing.

He glanced at me, behind us where the port had disappeared hours ago, then back at me. His mouth turned down as he studied my reaction.

Sand demon spit. I shoved the loose strands of hair that had escaped my braid away from my face as I broke eye contact. Blinking hard, I took a few deep breaths to calm my racing heart. I couldn't lose control here, in front of the crown prince of Elysia, or the rest of the crew who were no doubt watching.

"Partner?" Divinius' voice was softer than I'd heard before.

Wrapping my arms around my torso, I turned away to hide my wince and the betraying wetness burning my eyes.

"I'm sorry." When I didn't respond, he cleared his throat. "Of course I can swim. I've been able to do laps in the royal pool almost since I learned how to walk." He opened his mouth to say more but glanced at me and snapped it closed at the last instant.

I focused all my attention on the frothy trail our ship left behind, grateful he'd not pushed. It looked so simple, swimming. The gray fish, even the slavers who'd escaped my wrath this morning, had done it with ease. Even His Royalness, who couldn't make his way down a side street without getting himself kidnapped and held for ransom could. "Can everyone swim?"

He shrugged. "I suppose so, if they're taught."

I stared at the animals, cutting through the sea below. Peeking at him from the corner of my eye, I took a deep breath and braced myself, hating the feeling of vulnerability. "I'd like to learn." There was no guarantee someone would be there to pull me back if I nearly fell in again. Also, maybe if I knew how, I'd quit having a panic attack every time I was near a body of water.

Divinius glanced at me and nodded. "Okay." He frowned. "But you're not a dolphin, and the ocean isn't the best place for beginners. When we get to Elysia, I'll make sure you're assigned a tutor."

The thought of trusting some unfamiliar person with my safety brought sand-crabs to my stomach along with an unexpected sensation of loneliness. "You wouldn't do it yourself?" I tilted my head and studied him. Maybe he'd been exaggerating his skill.

He shook his head. "There are better teachers."

More likely, he'd be too busy being the crown prince. I sighed, a ball of disappointment settling low in my gut as I took a deep breath. The crispness of salt and water filled my nose. "I think I like the smell of the ocean more without the rotting seaweed."

Nodding, one corner of Divinius' lips curled up. "Most people do."

I glanced at him again. "You look a little green. Are you sure you're feeling okay?"

"I'll be fine." He looked away, as if hiding his face would disguise its pallor. "I just need to get my sea legs under me."

I frowned, studying his shoes. From what I could see, they looked normal. He was much steadier on his feet since we'd climbed onto this fates-forsaken boat.

"I'm going to see where our beds are." He tottered off as the deck rocked beneath him, looking like Roland after a bad night of heavy drinking.

A stab of heat flooded through me at the thought of the traitorous innkeeper. My knuckles turned white as I grasped the railing. Roland, Akre and Orion would all get what was coming to them soon enough.

I could be patient.

The afternoon sun beat down on my back.

Astra strode to me, as though the ship wasn't bucking like a never-ending sandquake. The crew parted before him. They worked so seamlessly together, it was obvious they'd been a team for years, possibly decades.

I swallowed the sudden lump in my throat. The time and dedication it took to forge bonds of trust like that... Hopefully the merchant understood the blessing he'd been given to find such a thing.

Astra parked himself in the exact spot Divinius had been, studying the dolphins below.

He threw a meaningful glance at the tattoo marring my jaw. "I get your issue with slaves." I opened my mouth to protest, but he stopped me with a wave of his hand. "I do. But I expect professionalism from my employees, and your stunt was anything but."

I gulped as the guilt surged, overwhelming my discomfort at being so close to water. And at being in such proximity to someone who might or might not control fire. "I'm sorry," I choked out, the words tasting bitter on my tongue. "It won't happen again." My entire body itched with the urge to demand an explanation for the odd behavior of the fireball when we'd escaped Tenara, but the dark voice in the back of my head reeled me in, reminding me that all it would take would be one shove and Astra could hurl me over the railing and into the frothy waves below before anyone could stop him. I clenched my jaw so tight I was surprised I didn't crack a tooth or two.

He nodded. "See that it doesn't. Or the two of you are out of a job and dropped off on the nearest hunk of rock we can find, regardless of whatever threats your companion makes."

I bit my lower lip until I tasted blood as shame welled through me. He was right—I hadn't thought, only reacted. And in so doing, I'd jeopardized not just my chance at revenge, but Divinius' return to his homeland and, as little as I cared about the merchant, Astra's business was important to him, too.

"If it makes you feel any better," Astra continued, "the slaves are freed every seven years."

What? I wrinkled my forehead and studied him.

He nodded. "In Tenara, anyway. Some concession to the elves, I think, in exchange for certain trade rights. It's been a tradition now for close to twenty years."

The floor dropped from beneath me. I was fortunate to already be sitting down, or I'd have embarrassed myself in front of the crew yet again.

Who knew?

I swallowed past my dry throat. "When we rammed the chain..." My voice faded out.

Astra raised an eyebrow. "Yes?"

Licking my lips, I tried again. "There was a crack of wood. What broke?" I crossed my mental fingers and braced. Hopefully he wouldn't say it was the hull.

He studied the tense lines of my face. "The railing around the bow. It's what we tied the barrels to. The missing section is a safety hazard and annoying as all get-out, but the repair is relatively easy once we make port."

My lungs deflated in relief. Thank the fates we weren't taking on water.

I unfolded my legs and shoved to my feet. "Where'd Divinius get to?" I asked, more to distract myself from the urge that rose to demand an explanation for the fire's refusal to touch *The Ashwing*.

Astra raised his eyebrows but nodded toward the door below. "Your cabin's the second on the right."

Making sure to keep one hand clamped on the rail, I picked my way down as I fled Astra's presence. The sharp contrast in lighting belowdecks had me blinking as I fumbled for the indicated door.

"Divinius?"

Someone grumbled up ahead. That sounded like a cranky princeling, alright.

I blundered down the hallway until I reached our room. The knob turned in my hand. The ship rocked, throwing the door open, with me tumbling in behind it. I sprung to my feet, hopefully before Divinius noticed.

He lay on one of the two hammocks, one arm thrown over his eyes. He lifted his head and squinted. "Gin? What's wrong?"

"How can you stand this constant rocking? And it's so dark in here!"

I crawled into the second hammock. Only to spare myself the need to constantly balance, of course.

He threw me a dry smile and covered his eyes again. "Makes you appreciate the reason pirates wear a patch over one eye, doesn't it?

"What are you talking about?" Alarm shot through my muscles as I sat up, hitting my head on the beam above. "Sand demon spit!" I rubbed my scalp. "Do we have to worry about pirates?"

He chuckled. "Don't stress it. That's why we're here, remember?"

I wrinkled my nose. "They expect the two of us to fight off an entire crew by ourselves?"

"Relax. I am a mage, after all. I'll take care of it." He paused. "Maybe, if you ask nicely, I'll leave a few stragglers for you to pick off."

I rolled to face him. After everything we'd already been through today, he was teasing me. He had to be. "Ha ha, very funny." There was something about the way he was laying in the hammock, though. "Divinius... what's wrong?"

"Nothing, just a slight headache. The laughing and rocking boat isn't helping."

I laid back and stared at the dark ceiling. "I'm sorry. Thank you for coming after me."

Silence stretched between us for several heartbeats. "You're welcome. After all, you did the same for me."

Chapter 11
Gin

Something slammed against the side of the boat, hard enough to throw me from my hammock. The hull creaked ominously as I smashed face-first into the ground.

"What in sand demon's spit was that?" After two days, when I was finally able to walk like I hadn't binged too much arak... If Astra had sailed into a reef, I'd toss him overboard myself.

Countless feet pounded across the deck above as men screamed at each other, their words too garbled for me to make out.

"Divinius?" I squinted into the darkness.

His bed rocked in the air, empty.

The floor buckled beneath me again. This time, it felt like the impact was on the opposite side of the ship. Were we running aground? Or was it really big waves?

No, rocks would splinter the wood, and huge swells would just tip us over. I shivered at that image.

The boat shuddered from another collision. This one was closer.

There was something in the water. Something that was ramming into the hull. Repeatedly.

My heart leaped into my throat. I heaved myself up as the walls closed in around me. We were under attack!

Grabbing my sword and whip, I lunged out the door before my brain could think too much about the implications and fall into another panic spiral. The vessel tilted to the side with a loud crack that reverberated through my bones. I clutched at the banister as my feet slid out from beneath me. When the hull shattered, the last place I wanted to be was trapped belowdecks, with the water rushing in. As the floor leveled out, I scrambled up the stairs.

The main deck was in chaos. Sailors dashed back and forth carrying rope or canvas, cutting lines, and doing myriad other jobs I couldn't discern.

I grabbed the arm of the first man to run by. "What's going on?"

"Sea demon," he gasped, yanking out of my grip and continuing on his way.

A what?!

My brain helpfully served up an image of a sand demon swimming through the ocean. I froze, my knees locking as my thoughts screeched to a halt.

"Gin!" Divinius' voice carried over the uproar.

He stood at the bow, a thick rope tied around his waist that was anchored to the mast, like he was worried he'd be flung overboard.

My insides iced as my throat closed. I could fall into the water...with a sand demon.

A heavy weight descended on my shoulder. "What are you doing?" Astra screamed into my ear. "Get over there and do what I hired you to do! Kill it and protect the ship!"

I nodded. Right. I could do that, as long as I didn't focus on what it was. My vision blurred with a mix of terror and ocean spray. I stumbled blindly toward Divinius.

He handed me a rope I hadn't noticed and waited as I secured it around my waist. As the twine cinched tight, my throat relaxed. Gasping, I inhaled a lungful of air.

"What's a sea demon?" I asked, squeezing my eyes closed, hoping he wouldn't say it was like a sand demon.

Divinius raised an eyebrow before turning his attention to the murky water. "I imagine it's something like those sand demons you keep mentioning. Except, of course, in the ocean."

That confirmed it. Both of my worst nightmares combined into one. Great. I grabbed the railing so hard my hands went numb. My vision dimmed at the edges as I stared into the frothing darkness below. An invisible wet cloth slammed over my nose and mouth. I couldn't breathe!

Divinius' arms curled around my waist, steadying me. His lips were so close they tickled the fine hairs in my ear. "Stay with me, partner."

His voice brought me back from the precipice. The barricade between my lungs and the air evaporated. A shadow nearly the size of the ship flickered through the waves.

"Aga!"

A spear of fire lanced past and pierced the ocean's surface with a hiss seconds before the demon rammed the boat again.

The wood beneath me snapped, echoing in my ears as the railing slammed into my ribs.

I rubbed the tender area. It would be an incredible bruise later. Assuming we had a later. "We can't take much more of this."

He frowned, shaking his head. "No, we can't." He pointed to a thin trail of red in the sea foam. "But at least we've wounded it. Perhaps that'll be enough to scare it off."

I chewed the inside of my cheek. "Not if it's anything like a sand demon, it won't." Being injured would only serve to piss it off. I glanced at him, willing my pounding heart to calm before it exploded. "How can I help?" It wasn't like the thing would rise out of the ocean and challenge me to a sword fight

He studied me, eyes locking on my weapons. "Unless you've got some talent with a bow or a throwing weapon you're not worried about getting back, nothing until it decides to breach and get uncomfortably close." He shoved the edges of his sleeves up past his elbows. "And let's hope that doesn't happen."

I sighed, dropping my shoulders. Few things felt worse than being useless in a fight.

A sailor's cry pulled my attention to the far side of the deck.

I whirled to face the sound, a scream stuck in my throat. A triangle-shaped head crowned by a row of webbed spikes rose above the railing. Men cried out and scrambled out of the way. Cruel yellow orbs glinted at them from the black scales that flashed iridescent teal and blue in the sun. The sea monster opened its maw, exposing fangs as long as my arm. A snakelike tongue slithered between them as it screeched.

Oh, fates. It was exactly like someone had put one of those dolphins and a sand demon in a mixing pot and birthed this monstrosity. My mind spiraled through all the possible ways to kill it. Sand demons were only vulnerable in their mouths. But fish had gills, and this thing had eyes. So, there were three potential weak spots I could strike, if it got close enough and if I didn't faint from sheer terror.

Divinius hurled a ball of fire into the creature's face. It dove below with a cry.

The demon's tail flicked out of the water, flying through the air. It tangled in the rigging, only to smash against the central pole supporting the sails. With a victorious howl, it yanked the whole mess into the depths, along with the unfortunate sailors caught in its path.

I screamed as the men disappeared beneath the frothing waves.

The mast exploded.

"Look out!" Astra's scream echoed across the deck.

In slow motion, the pylon shuddered then teetered. We were tied to it. If it went overboard, so would we, just like those doomed crew members.

I snatched my sword and sliced through the ropes binding me and Divinius.

With a final groan of protest, the huge mast tumbled into the ocean, taking most of our sails with it.

Divinius glanced at me, his eyes wide and skin pallid. He licked his lips. "Quick thinking. Thanks."

He grabbed my hand as we sprinted to the far side of the ship. Bracing myself against the splintered remains of the railing, I peered over the edge. That was a mistake.

Foamy bubbles and debris circled the area where the sea demon had disappeared. No survivors materialized. We'd be next, hauled to our watery graves as soon as the creature resurfaced. Obron would be left at the mercy of bickering warlords, and I would fail my parents and their legacy.

An invisible band contracted around my ribs as my eyes burned.

Divinius ran his fingers through his hair. "Valek."

That was an understatement.

Beneath us, the deck groaned.

"Shore up the bilge!"

Astra's command breathed new life into the paralyzed sailors who stirred, racing below to carry out his orders.

"Divinius," I whispered as I stared at the watery maw. "Are we going to sink?" I couldn't decide if it would be better for the whole ship to go down, because then at least we'd have something under our feet, or for it to tip over and just dump us into the ocean.

He scoffed and waved his hand as though he could dismiss my fears. "Don't be ridiculous. These are experienced sailors with a stout vessel. Remember how we made it through the chain?" His confident smirk wavered. "I'm sure they face sea demons all the time."

His words no longer matched his expression. The pallid complexions of the crew further contradicted him. I raised my eyebrow at the discrepancy. He was trying to console me. I clenched my jaw—it wasn't working. "Divinius?"

"What?" He leaned over the railing, scanning the depths for the monster.

"You're a terrible liar."

"But you like me for it." He flashed me a half-smile then turned his attention back to the waves. "Let me know if you spot it before I do."

I swallowed what I'd been about to say about liking him. This wasn't the time. Astra had hired us to do a job, and if we failed, everyone was dead. "There!" I pointed at the ridge of fins that crested a wave several yards away.

"Aga!" Another firebolt scorched through the air. It sizzled as its mark dipped back below the surface.

"Sand demon's spit!" Not like hitting it in the ridges would likely do much damage, but maybe it would tick the monster off enough for it to breach so Divinius could get it in the face with another fireball.

The triangular head burst into view, drenching us in a shower of salty water.

I blinked, frantically trying to clear my vision. It was going to smash the boat! The towering behemoth blocked out the sun. How were we supposed to defend ourselves against something like this? Beside me, Divinius hurled bursts of fire as quickly as he could.

With a sand demon, if you could get to solid ground—a rock formation or something similar—you were safe. There was no safety out here, and it was staying too far away for me to be of any use.

It was too bad Astra's ship didn't have any harpoons or cannons like the Tenarans had. At least those would've been something I could've used.

My eyesight cleared just in time to see the sea creature open its mouth and roar at Divinius as he screamed, "Aga!" and launched another attack. The force of its breath redirected his magic back at us.

Divinius crossed his arms overhead. "Jhalaka!"

The air above us shimmered and the fireball rolled to the side as though it had bounced off a pane of glass.

The flames slammed into the deck and exploded in a fiery shower. The remaining rigging smoldered and smoked for a heartbeat before exploding.

Cries of "Fire! Fire!" flew back and forth.

The sea demon lowered its head to the level of the banister, as if selecting which of us would make its next meal. I swallowed past my dry throat as it narrowed its eyes on me and leaned forward.

It was in range. Finally, I could do something beyond sitting here!

"Let's see you do that to me!" I yanked on my whip, unfurling it with a crack. I flicked it toward a golden eye, doing my best to ignore the fact that each of my steps brought me closer to the churning water below.

The demon jerked backward, so the leather strip lashed across its cheek, opening a red welt. It snapped its jaw at me and lunged.

Divinius threw another fire spear. The creature dodged left, only to find my lash waiting. As long as it stayed between us, the princeling and I worked well as a team.

"Ha!" My strike hit home.

The creature cried out as the thong snapped against its eye. Roiling, it disappeared beneath the waves.

"Praise the mages," Divinius mumbled.

I inhaled, refusing to let the tension drain from my shoulders. "Is it gone?" If it truly was anything like a sand demon, then it was just regrouping and would most likely attack us from behind.

High above, something cracked, and the sound of tearing fabric sent prickles up my spine. I counted five breaths before it stopped and I dared to look up.

The sails were alight, bits of flaming canvas and rigging peppered the deck.

Someone yelled, "Abandon ship! The flames have reached the hold!"

My heart skipped a beat as lead pooled in my gut. The hold, with the rest of the oil barrels. My vision blackened at the edges.

No. No no no no.

Should we stay here and die a fiery death, or sink into the ocean and drown as the cold water filled our lungs?

That wasn't much of a choice, but given the two, I'd choose the inferno any day. Wouldn't I? Fire probably hurt more, but it would be over before I realized it. And I wouldn't have to face the sea demon's fangs.

A fist squeezed my heart, causing it to skip a beat.

"Belay that order," Astra called. "Clear the cargo into the dinghies, load them as high as you can!"

The floor shuddered as the hatch slammed open. Pulleys and bodies practically tumbled into the hold as the sailors raced against the flames. Winches creaked as they hoisted barrel after barrel onto the deck, where others rolled them to the edge, then tossed them over.

"Gin!" Divinius' hand wrapped around my upper arm, yanking me off-balance.

A beam crashed into the ground where I'd been standing, scattering flaming embers across the area.

With a curse, he disappeared.

I stared, my attention flicking back and forth between the spreading fire and the waves licking at the sides of the floundering boat.

My vision dimmed at the edges, my breaths coming too shallow as I heaved. I couldn't get enough air into my lungs!

A wave washed over the deck, washing any loose rigging overboard.

I backed away until the hard press of wooden planks that made up the ship's forecastle pressed into my back.

What could I do? I couldn't let the ocean take me.

The wet cloth that always accompanied Akre's water wheel slapped over my face as my vision dimmed.

No! I squeezed my eyes shut as I turned my head to the side, pushing my cheek against the wall at my back. This is a dream, it has to be. A nightmare.

I screamed as rough fingers spun me around until I was face-to-face with Divinius. "Come on!" He dropped something into my hands. My backpack. "Put this on. We need to go!" He pushed me in the direction of the barrels.

I dug my heels in, slapping at him. "No! Stop!" I clawed for the relative safety of my shelter but he wrenched me away. When had he gotten so strong?

He grabbed me and shoved his face in front of mine. "The boat's sinking! You want to stay here and drown?" He snatched my pack from my numb hands and maneuvered each of my arms through the straps, securing it where it belonged. I barely registered what he was doing, my focus entirely centered on the waves that washed over the deck, over us, at regular intervals.

"No!" The vessel felt pretty solid beneath my feet. Unlike the water. I tried to twist out of his grip. "That thing's still out there!"

"And when it comes back, the first thing it will do is attack the ship!"

The edge of the broken railing caught on my toes. I didn't even care about the tremble in my voice, the weakness it betrayed. "No, Div—"

The churning sea reflected the auburn and amber of the flames above.

"No, stop!" I clawed at the banister as Divinius pushed me overboard.

The cold plunged a knife into my lungs as the water filled my nose. It tasted of brine and raw fish. The salt scorched my eyes, blurring what little I could see. My backpack pulled on my shoulders, dragging me beneath the surface. This time, there was no wheel to bring me back up.

I fought against the water's pull, but my muscles were too uncoordinated to untangle myself from its clutches. The reflection of the fire drifted further away as the ice-cold water tore at my legs. Blackness swallowed me whole.

I jerked my head right and left. If the sea demon was coming for me, I wanted to at least face my death straight on. Millions of bubbles filled my vision as the waves tumbled me every which way until it was impossible to tell which direction was up.

I opened my mouth to scream and seawater rushed in. My lungs burned, seared from the inside out by the salt. I clawed at the water as my sight dimmed.

This was it. Karma had finally caught up to me—I was going to die. Akre, Orion, and the rest of the warlords had already won. I'd failed my parents and Obron one last time.

Something yanked on my collar, pulling me in the opposite direction I'd been trying to go. Endless heartbeats later, my head broke free. I pushed against the obstacle in front of me as I coughed up seawater.

Someone yelled something nearby.

The obstacle grabbed my arm and held it to my side.

A wooden creak above put me back in Akre's dungeon, the matching groan of the water wheel the only indicator I was about to be forced beneath the surface again.

"No!" I don't know if I screamed it, or the thought was just in my head. I pulled my knees to my stomach and kicked. My heels hit something hard and unforgiving.

My cheek burned as someone slapped it.

The impact stunned me. My vision cleared right as a wave plunged me into darkness.

My collar yanked again, and Divinius' waterlogged hair came into view.

"Gin, stop it! Calm down. I've got you. Look at me." He grabbed my chin and jerked it until I could see his eyes. "Look at me, partner. You're okay."

Instinctively responding to the commanding tone, I froze. Blinking like an idiot, I stared at him as my thoughts raced to catch up. I wasn't in Akre's dungeon. There was no water wheel.

My panic dipped.

A tangle of canvas, rope and wood fell into the waves behind Divinius.

I wasn't a prisoner—I was in the middle of the fates-cursed ocean with a sea demon who was sinking our boat! If the monster didn't devour us, the waves would. I couldn't breathe, but this time it had nothing to do with the water saturating my lungs and everything to do with the invisible bands tightening once more over my ribs.

Bracing my hands against Divinius' chest, I shoved him away.

He muttered something before turning his focus back to me. "We need to get away from the ship, or we may be sucked down as it sinks. Take a deep breath, lay on your back, and I'll pull you."

The weight of my pack was pulling me under again. I flailed, smacking at the water, hardly bothering to notice what I was doing. "No!"

"Come on, partner, trust me." Something in his eyes broke through the wall of terror that shielded my mind.

I inhaled and promptly vomited up all the seawater I'd swallowed. The back of his hand brushed my face, combing strands of my hair out of the way.

When I'd finished coughing, he leaned forward, holding my head above the surface. "Feeling better?"

Letting him take my full weight, I wiped my hand across my mouth. "Yeah." My ribs hurt, and my heart still beat at an impossible staccato, but my head was clear.

"Then be still while I get us out of here. Can you do that?"

I inhaled and nodded. It took all my control to remain still as the cold seawater permeated my hair and chilled my scalp. It flooded my ears, but stopped just before it covered my face. I squeezed my eyes closed at the sensation, images of the water wheel in Akre's dungeon slamming through my mind.

Divinius pulled me away from the lost ship.

An eternity later, the sounds of other voices reached me. I opened my eyes. Several of Astra's sailors clung to the edge of a dinghy piled so high with barrels it barely managed to stay afloat.

Divinius heaved me at the boat. "Here, grab on."

I scrambled to find a grip on the slippery wood, clinging to it as though it were my most valuable possession. He squeezed in beside me.

Astra's voice echoed over the waves, rising above the ringing in my ears. "Everyone, kick us toward land!"

Holding my arms out straight like those around me, I kicked. To my surprise, the craft lurched forward.

Divinius threw me a rakish half-smile as his tangled hair dripped rivulets of water across his face. It was absolutely not fair that he looked that good after coming through a battle with a sea demon and an actual shipwreck.

I narrowed my eyes at the sight of that sand-blasted dimple in his cheek. I ought to gut him for throwing me overboard.

Behind us, wood crumbled with an ear-splitting crack. I peeked over my shoulder. The sea demon had wrapped its lengthy body twice around Astra's ship. With one final groan, the hull collapsed as the monster dragged it beneath the waves.

On second thought, maybe I'd give Divinius a free pass this time.

On the opposite side of the dinghy, Astra swore.

I glanced toward the merchant.

His normally erect hair hung in bedraggled strands across his pallid forehead as he watched the death of his beloved vessel. "I've never seen a sea demon so big."

Divinius coughed, drawing Astra's attention. "How much cargo did you manage to save?"

Astra shook his head, his eyes red-rimmed as though he'd just lost his mother. "Less than a quarter, I'm afraid. Even in the best of terms, it won't cover expenses. Added to that the loss of property and life…"

I blinked and glanced to either side. So few sailors clung to the boat. Was this all who had survived? My solemn gaze met Divinius.' Based on his expression, he was thinking the same thing.

Astra shuddered. "Kick faster, men. Before that creature decides to come after us for dessert."

Redoubling my efforts, I kicked, propelling the craft toward the dark shadow of land in the distance.

Chapter 12

Gin

The dinghy ground to a halt as the hull scraped against sand. I dropped to my knees as waves pounded my back. Thank the fates.

"I'll never get on another boat as long as I live," I muttered. The air smelled crisp and fresh here. It didn't carry any of the rotten seaweed or fishy smell like it had in Tenara.

Divinius slapped me on the shoulder. "Well. How did you like your first swimming lesson?"

Forget that. I was never getting in another pool of water, either. Brushing my hair out of my face, I glared at him for his false levity. "I ought to kill you, you know." Except I couldn't really add him to my list of people to murder. It was already lengthy enough, and technically he had saved my life.

After throwing me overboard in the first place, a petulant voice in the back of my mind whined.

A large wave slammed into me, shoving my face into the sand. I surfaced to Divinius' roaring laugh.

"Don't you know not to turn your back on the ocean?" he asked between wheezes.

"I'm from the desert, you doorknob!" I scowled and hauled myself onto the beach, fully above the tide line. Stupid royal. I pulled my backpack off my shoulders with a huff and dropped it to the ground, pretending I didn't feel the heat that creeped across my face. Flopping down next to the bag, I stared at the azure sky, pointedly ignoring him. The sun baked the moisture from my skin. I dug my toes into the fine granules until I felt grounded. At least with sand, I knew what to expect.

Divinius sat beside me.

Below my feet, out of my sight, Astra's remaining men unloaded the barrels and hauled their dinghy onto the beach. The waves lapped at their heels as if they still sought to claim us.

My stomach cramped, either from swallowing all the sea water or because it had been far too long since I'd eaten. A handful of minutes passed before I turned to Divinius. "I don't suppose you can conjure something up for dinner?"

He gave me an odd look, studying my face as though searching for a hidden meaning.

I raised my eyebrows and stared back. "What?" It was a simple question.

After several heartbeats, he sighed and focused his attention back on the horizon. "Conjuring is illegal."

So was assassinating people. What did that have to do with anything? "Yes, but that doesn't mean you can't do it." I glanced at the bedraggled group of sailors scattered around our sliver of sand. "Besides, who would tell?"

Black cliffs towered to either side of us, reaching as though they could scratch the sky itself. They seemed to be constructed of an interlocking pattern of six-sided columns that I'd never seen before. Between them, luscious greenery akin to the jungle we'd traveled through to get to Tenara beckoned. Leaves and plants in different sizes and shades of emerald and jade fluttered in the breeze.

I blinked in dismay. I'd never seen so much green in one place.

Astra heaved to his feet. "Alright, you lot. Let's get organized and decide what we're going to do. I need volunteers to go find water and food. The rest of us will build a shelter and figure out what we're going to do from here."

Well, if our resident mage wouldn't provide dinner, at least Astra was handling it.

A few minutes later, half the men disappeared into the jungle as the remainder scrambled over the sand like a bunch of ants.

I pulled my blade out and polished the crusted salt away before laying the scabbard in the sun to dry. My whip was another issue. Removing it from my belt, I studied the leather. If it dried as-is, my primary weapon would be ruined.

Hoisting myself to my feet, I tottered toward the sailors on unsteady steps. I cursed my weakness, uncertain if it was from the terror of nearly drowning or the frantic kicking.

Behind me, Divinius mentioned something about getting my land legs back, but that made no sense so I didn't bother to respond. Clenching my jaw, I shook my head and growled, "Astra?"

He turned from where he was supervising the digging of a fire pit. "Yes?"

"Did any of those barrels you rescued contain oil?"

"Most of them, actually." He paused, frowning. "Why do you ask?"

I gestured to my vest and whip. "Do you mind if I open one and recondition the leather before it's ruined?"

He eyed me up and down then shrugged. "Why not? Someone may as well get some use out of them."

I picked the nearest barrel and carefully muscled the lid off with help from my sword. Red liquid with a faint berry scent greeted me. Sand demon spit.

"Oh, praise the mages!" Divinius came up behind me and, cupping his hands, drank several deep swallows.

Royals. I sighed, shook my head, and moved on to the next cask. The last thing we needed was a mage drunk on elven wine. He'd better not be a drunkard like Roland.

"Gin, stop."

Divinius' voice froze me in my tracks. Heart leaping into my throat, I glanced around, searching for the threat as I brandished my sword. "What?"

He pointed to the label. "Don't open that one. It's wine, too."

I frowned at the paper, which contained a flowy script with characters I'd never seen before. "How can you tell?"

He smiled between gulps. "It's Elven. I can read it." Nodding at a group of barrels further down the line he turned back to the alcohol. "Those have the oil."

I scowled, my hands curling into fists at my side. "You knew the whole time I was opening the wrong one?"

Divinius shrugged. "Yes, but I wanted wine."

I clenched my jaw so hard, I was surprised my molars didn't crack. Stupid, self-absorbed crown prince—

"Hey, elf!"

Divinius glanced up as Astra stormed over and slammed the lid back on the cask. "This trip is enough of a loss already. I don't need you drinking up our profits." He spun on me. "And I gave permission for a barrel of oil, not the other!"

My fingers went white around my whip's handle. I ground my teeth as I resisted the urge to drag the edge of my sword across Astra's throat.

Divinius studied my face for a heartbeat before stepping between us, forcing the merchant to step back. "Astra, calm down." Then he glanced over his shoulder at me, looking like he expected me to fly into a murderous rage and skewer them both with my blade.

A very reasonable fear.

I took a steadying breath and relaxed my grip on my weapon. Divinius couldn't die. At least, not until he'd helped me claim my revenge and freedom. My mission was more important than ever now.

Seeing the subtle change in my posture, Divinius turned back to Astra. "Not everyone can read High Elven. If you wanted a certain barrel opened, you should have specified which one."

I blinked. He was defending me. It had been a long time since anyone had done so. I stood there, blinking like an idiot, my jaw slack for far too many heartbeats before Astra cleared his throat.

With a sigh, he dragged a hand down his face. "I'm sorry. You're correct. It's been a trying day." He spun on his heel, heading back to the remaining members of his crew. With a quick glance over his shoulder at us, he called, "I suggest you two get some rest. You're on watch tonight."

I studied Astra as he rejoined the sailors. "You realize," I murmured to Divinius, "we're no longer getting paid for this trip, right?"

He nodded. "I know. But it's not like we were doing it for the paycheck."

I snapped my head around to face him so quickly I risked whiplash. "You're not, maybe." It must be nice, to not go through life worrying about basic necessities like coin.

He scoffed. "We're taking me home. Not everything is about money."

"Spoken like someone who's never had to worry about such things."

Divinius flinched, as though I'd actually struck a nerve. "If you're so worried, why don't you just go take over another assassin's guild and rob their treasury, then?"

I pressed my lips into a thin line. It wasn't like I could carry it all by foot across the world. "Shut up." I pointedly turned my attention away, studying the sailors. None were within hearing range.

Divinius plopped onto the hard-packed sand and rolled to his back, placing his hands behind his head. "Get me to Elysia, Gin, and I'll make sure you get your funds, if that's all you want."

I didn't want his coin—I needed his army. Ugh! I wanted to scream and rip my hair out by its roots.

"Wake me up when they come back with food, will you?" Divinius settled, one arm thrown casually over his eyes as if there were no threats here to be concerned with.

With a low rumble in my throat, I turned my attention to the barrel Divinius had indicated held the oil. After several minutes of grunting and a few screeches as the nails protested their separation from the wood, I pried the top off.

The unmistakable smell of olives greeted my nose. I scrunched my face and frowned. Olive oil wasn't the best for leather, but hopefully it was better than nothing.

I glanced at Divinius. His eyes were closed, his breathing deep and even. It must be one of the benefits of being royalty—the security to be able to sleep through anything.

Dipping my hand into the liquid, I collapsed to the ground, the barrel at my back as I massaged the lubricant into my whip.

I shouldn't have compared Divinius to Roland. His Royalness apparently had some mild concept of loyalty, and he was no drunkard. Divinius also had none of the telltale signs of alcoholism. His eyes weren't red and puffy, and his skin wasn't covered in little bumps. Despite Orion still haunting my dreams on almost a nightly basis, I hadn't thought of Roland and his betrayal for the better part of the week we'd been at sea.

An invisible knife of ice slammed through my back into my heart as my memory crashed to the forefront of my thoughts. Combined with the recent terror of nearly drowning, it was too much. I gasped and pressed my hand against my chest in a futile attempt to relieve the pain.

My throat turned thick as my eyes burned. Water obscured my vision as the tears threatened to spill down my cheeks. At least with the sailors occupied and Divinius asleep, there was no one around to witness my vulnerability.

This would pass faster if I kept busy and didn't give my mind a chance to dwell on everything.

Finished with oiling the whip, I shrugged off my vest, re-loaded my hand with oil and moved on the garment.

I sniffled as my nose started to run. With a surreptitious glance at Divinius to make sure he was still sleeping, I wiped my sleeve across my eyes, hating myself for the weakness.

Being alone sucked.

Through eyelashes heavy with unshed tears, I studied Divinius. He'd been deposed, transported hundreds of leagues away from home, and both of his parents were most likely dead. He was so unflappable, able to roll with all the punches life threw at him and looking darn good doing it. It must be that royal poise I'd heard so much about growing up.

Poise I'd never acquired. I kicked my heel into the sand, digging out a small hole. Not like it mattered. I certainly wasn't royal, not anymore. And I had no desire to be.

I glanced at the sleeping mage one more time. Being queen would be nice in that no one would be able to tell me what to do. I'd be in control, have rights again, a say in my own destiny. And I'd have the power to make sure that men like Warlord Akre and Orion couldn't hurt anyone else.

But then I'd spend the rest of my life watching my back, and those of the people I cared about. And I'd probably get betrayed just the same.

The phantom press of rose petals across my lips was the final straw.

The vest fell from my fingers. I pulled my knees close and buried my forehead against them as silent sobs heaved from my chest. I bit my cheeks hard enough to bleed, forcing the emotions back inside.

The last thing I needed was to show vulnerability to Astra. Or Divinius.

Wiping the tears from my eyes several minutes later, I pushed my feelings away and slipped the mask of the unshakeable Desert Rose back in place. Then I finished oiling down my vest and set it against the barrel to dry.

The sun beat down on my shoulders as I rested my forehead on my knees once more. Letting the heat lull my eyes closed, I allowed the strain of the day to pull me under.

At least Divinius had passed out before I'd started crying.

Chapter 13
Divinius

I peeked between my slitted eyelids as I did my best to ignore the headache that pounded silver spikes into my temples and the sand that seemed to get everywhere. Who knew? Beneath the exterior of anger and brazenness, there was a young woman who felt enough emotion to cry. Over what, I had no idea. Surely not at Astra's mild reprimand for opening the wrong barrel.

From the look on Gin's face, Astra had had no clue how close he'd come to being gutted. And after using so much magic battling the sea dragon myself, I'd been in no shape to fight her off, had she decided to attack him.

I groaned. Throwing an arm over my eyes, I turned my face away from the relentless sun. I wouldn't be up to much of anything for at least the next few days. Hopefully the alcohol I'd consumed would kick in any minute now and dull the migraine.

But I hadn't been able to resist the urge to send a small tendril of magic toward Gin when I'd noticed the tear trails down her cheeks.

Being alone sucked.

Her thought ricocheted around my skull as clearly as if she'd been screaming at me. I knew all too well what it felt like to be surrounded by people and yet be lonely.

But she wasn't alone, even if she didn't know it. Not since she'd rescued me from those assassins-turned-kidnappers.

Voices lifted from the sailors on the other side of the barrels. Their cacophony mixed with the screams of the few seagulls that soared overhead. I squinted as I studied Gin. She didn't stir.

My head pounded from the racket. I glanced across the beach to Astra. Gin's thoughts were as easy to read as breathing. All I needed to do was focus. The merchant's however, were hidden behind a shield that may as well have been antimonite—the one material known to devour magic. Every time I tried to reach out to his mind, my power touched an ethereal white wall and crumbled to dust. I'd never met anyone—mage or human—who'd had a similar mental block, and I couldn't help but wonder exactly what Astra was.

More shouts echoed across the beach. If only they'd be quiet and let the gentle lapping of the waves lull me to sleep.

The only way to shut the sailors up would be to figure out what they were so excited about. With a groan, I pushed onto my feet and strolled over to the cluster of humans.

My shoes sunk deep into the loose sand as I approached where they stood around a pile of small balls larger than my head. Some were brown and hairy while others were green and smooth.

"What's this?" I asked.

"We found some coconuts," one of the crew answered.

It had been a long time since I'd eaten coconut, and it had never been fresh. These looked nothing like the shredded white strands I was familiar with. Grabbing one of each type, I headed back to Gin.

She stirred at my approach and blinked, her eyes bleary and puffy. Fortunately for her, that could be chalked up to irritation from salt water rather than tears.

I held up my prizes. "Which one do you want?"

Her eyebrows furrowed as she glanced back and forth between the two coconuts. "What are they?"

It was good to know I wasn't the only one unfamiliar with them. I tossed her the brown one. "Food."

She studied the hairy shell in her hands and shook it. Liquid sloshed inside. She stared at it for several heartbeats before breaking into a grin. Setting it on the ground, she jabbed one of the eyes with her dagger.

She evaluated the hole for a heartbeat, then held it up and poured the water into her mouth. Swallowing, she nodded. "It tastes weird, but it's still better than what we have in Obron."

I held back a snort. From her description, even the elven ale at the cheapest inn would be finer than the slop they had in her country.

Her coconut's liquid gone, she put the shell back on the ground and slammed her sword into it. The ball snapped in half, revealing hard white flesh inside. She scraped some off with the tip of her blade and popped it into her mouth. "Mmm. It's good," she said around bites.

I tossed my coconut to her. After all, my weapon had gone down with the ship. She stabbed it and I drank the milk in the same manner she had, holding back a grimace.

Yuck. "If this tastes better than the water in Obron, remind me never to go there."

She raised an eyebrow. "There's a reason most people drink arak."

Reaching for my fruit, she waved her hand at me impatiently. I handed over the green globe and she sliced it in half for me. The flesh of my fruit was softer than hers, and I was able to peel it out with my bare fingers. It wasn't the best I'd had, but at least it did fill the developing hole in my stomach.

And my headache from the magic hangover was beginning to abate.

I turned to face her and reached out with my free hand. "Gin, I—"

She peered at me over the rim of her coconut. The wariness in her eyes and the hard line of her lips had me rethinking what I'd been planning to say.

"Thank you." I dropped my hand and held up my dinner.

She nodded, tossing her now-empty shell to the ground and glancing at the sky. The sun was well on its way toward the horizon. "Did we sleep so long?"

"We were quite tired." Engaging in a battle, surviving a shipwreck and laying in the heat on the beach would do that. One side of my mouth twitched. Though now that I thought about it, she'd probably change her mind about learning how to swim after today's misadventure. Which would be a shame because I bet she'd look great in swimming attire.

She stretched her legs out and leaned back against her barrel. "Now what are we going to do?"

I shrugged. "For tonight? It looks like we'll stay here." It wasn't like there was anywhere more advantageous to go in the few hours before we lost the sun. I nodded at the far section of the beach, out of her view. "They've turned the dinghy on its side and propped it up. I don't know that it'll provide anything in the way of shelter unless it rains." With a pointed glance at the cloudless sky, I continued, "But I suppose it gave the men something to do, which in situations like this, is a sign they have a good leader."

She scoffed. "Good leader. Sure."

"Don't be that way just because he yelled at you when he shouldn't have. He's under quite a bit of stress." I honestly couldn't say I'd deal with the situation with as much grace, were our positions reversed. Not that I would admit that out loud.

She opened her mouth, froze, then opened it again.

"Astra's in a rough spot," I said, "and is likely scrambling for how to handle things."

Speaking of Astra, the merchant was making his way over to us. I raised my eyebrow as he approached, bracing myself.

"Divinius," he said as he leaned against the now-closed wine barrel. "Do you have a way to send a message? Magically, I mean."

I shook my head and frowned. Normals always assumed magic would solve all their problems. But that was no reason to snap at the man, as I'd just been telling Gin. "Unfortunately, I don't. The closest thing I can do is project my voice in a loud room. But to be heard miles away? No."

He stepped forward. "Can you summon an animal, a carrier pigeon, perhaps, and instruct it to deliver a dispatch?"

My hackles raised as I fought the urge to grind my teeth. Instead, I forced cheer into my words. "Even if I could, I'd be unlikely to get blind obedience from a wild creature."

Astra narrowed his eyes and turned a hard gaze on me, almost like he thought I was lying. Which was stupid because why would I do such a thing? "You can't summon something, anything, to carry a letter?"

My expression went flat. I was so tired of everyone assuming my magic could fix all their problems. Especially when that always seemed to involve them asking me to conjure. Forget being polite. "Summoning something to this plane is illegal in every country." Shaking my head, I took a dramatic breath. "I'm sorry, I've never learned how to," I lied.

Astra's shoulders deflated as he sighed. "I suppose it was a faint hope, anyway, as I'm sure you'd have said something earlier if you had been able."

I nodded, pressing my lips into a thin line. And I would have, assuming I was willing to break the most sacred of magical laws and get myself excommunicated from The Mage College. Which I wasn't.

"As near as I can tell," Astra continued, "we have two options. We can re-load the cargo onto the dinghy and swim with it along the coast. The other option is to leave it here," he shuddered, "under guard, and make our way on foot until we reach a port where we can send a vessel back for it."

Gin studied the tangle of plants to our right, and the open water on our left. Her complexion went pale as she stared out over the ocean.

I chewed the inside of my cheek. Both options housed all sorts of unimaginable dangers she and I would be expected to protect Astra's people against. But at least the jungle route would prevent those threats from swimming up at us from below.

"I vote by land," Gin said a little too quickly.

I turned back to Astra. "Which is closer? Tenara or Elysia?"

He shrugged. "We're somewhere in the middle. It's hard to say which would be faster, though the bulk of my fleet is based out of Tenara."

I frowned. While enough coin might buy the Tenaran port master's forgiveness for our aggressive departure, my time was much more valuable than that gamble. "We're heading to Elysia, and I would rather continue in that direction. Come with us. I—" I caught the warning glare Gin sent me and wrinkled my nose at her. I'd learned my lesson about revealing my name. "I know the port master in Elysia's capital well. If one of your ships is not available, he'll find you one that is."

Astra chewed the inside of his cheek as his gaze lost focus.

"I give you my word as a mage," I said.

After several heartbeats, he nodded. "Very well. We are more likely to survive an overland journey unscathed with you two beside us." He glanced over his shoulder at the dense foliage. "We'd best get some rest. Traversing that mess tomorrow will not be fun."

As the other man headed back to his sailors, Gin faced me. "How many do you think will be coming with us versus staying here to watch the shipment?"

I shrugged and turned away, laying on my spot in the sand. "I don't know. That's not our problem." Throwing my arm back over my eyes, I focused on ignoring my headache.

"Hopefully he'll leave most of them here," she mumbled.

"Why do you say that?"

"Fewer to guard, of course."

I held back a snort. Knowing Desert Rose, it was less bodies to get rid of if something went wrong.

Chapter 14

Gin

I worked the point of my dagger underneath my fingernails, clearing out the intrusive grit that got everywhere. To my right, Divinius lounged against the overturned boat, staring out to sea.

The reflection of the moon on the ocean was stunning. I'd never imagined such a scene existed. The rasp of water over sand lured some of the tension from between my shoulder blades. It reminded me of the desert wisteria vines...beautiful to gaze at, but deadly to touch.

If only I could forget the terror living beneath the waves, or how much I hated having my head submerged.

The breeze smelled of seaweed and raised goosebumps on my arms. I rubbed my hands over them to warm myself. For as pretty as it was, the coast sure was chilly.

"What are you thinking?" Divinius' whisper made me jump.

I glanced at him. He was studying me with too-keen eyes and one lifted eyebrow.

Turning my focus back to the water, I gestured to it with my chin. "For something so deadly, it's captivating."

"There are a lot of beautiful but deadly things in the world," he said.

Yeah, like Orion. And every magic wielder out there, even if they weren't warlords. Replaying his words in my mind, I peeked at him from the corner of my vision. He was staring at me far too intently for comfort. I blinked, keeping my expression blank and resisting the urge to shift my weight. Surely that hadn't been some sort of attempted compliment? I shook my head and rolled my eyes so hard I was surprised they didn't get stuck. His Royalness would hardly go to the effort for someone who wasn't himself.

With an internal sigh, I turned my focus back to the wall of green stretching between the two cliffs behind us. There would no doubt be several things that could kill us once we started bushwhacking through the jungle. "Are you at all familiar with this area?"

I caught the shake of his head in my peripheral vision. "Nope. I never traveled internationally before this."

I sighed. So much for any intel from him. I'd have to ask Astra in the morning if he had any insights. I shivered as another breeze drove a few loose strands of hair in front of my face. "Did it seem like he agreed to continue to Elysia a little too easily? Astra, I mean."

Divinius went still and narrowed his gaze. "I didn't think so," he said, dragging each word out. "You and I are going in that direction, and he has the resources he needs to recoup this mess once we arrive. If he wants protection while he travels, it makes sense for him to accompany us."

Maybe. But Divinius was also a crown prince, used to getting his way without any effort or thought. "But if we're equidistant from both ports, and his main support base is back at Tenara, I'd have expected him to push to return there." Even if it meant facing a whole port full of angry guards. Though they were more upset with me than him.

"Perhaps. He is a merchant, though. The successful ones maintain networks at all the major trading centers. Otherwise, they aren't likely to keep their fleet employed."

I nodded. That made sense. Maybe I was being too paranoid. After all, it wasn't like Astra was a warlord or something. According to Divinius, the man didn't have a single drop of mage blood in him.

Divinius shrugged out of his robes. The moonlight cast shadows over the planes of his chest that were much better defined than those of someone who relied on magic rather than a sword should be. It really was not fair. "Here."

"Here what?" I blinked and frowned as he held them out for me.

"Any idiot can see you're shivering. Take it."

I stared at the garment and the warmth it offered, resisting the urge to accept them. To be in his debt. "But won't you be cold?"

He watched me like I'd grown a third eye. "Where I'm from, this is a perfect spring evening."

I eyed the offering as I struggled to ascertain his motives. A thick, lumpy scar crossed his left shoulder blade and headed for his spine. It reminded me of a lash.

I held back a flinch at the remembered pain from my own lashings. But I'd been a lowly slave.

Surely, no one would dare whip a crown prince.

I studied him, my lips pressed together. There was more to Divinius than the spoiled, pompous nobleman he showed the world. Perhaps that was as much a shield he hid behind as Desert Rose was for me.

A corner of his mouth quirked up, flashing that irritating dimple. "The clothes aren't going to bite," he said with a chuckle. "I promise."

And yet I couldn't help but wonder what expectation I was setting myself up for by accepting.

A sharp breeze drove blades of ice against my skin.

Screw it. I shrugged into the robes. They were stiff with sea salt, but still warm from his body heat. The smell of mint baking in the sun tickled my nostrils. "Thank you." I took a deep breath. "How did you get the scar?"

He turned, shielding the imperfection from view as his expression closed off. "I angered someone I shouldn't have."

I opened my mouth but thought better of it since the garment was so toasty. I pulled the cloth tight around my shoulders, uncomfortable with the sudden weight pressing on my chest at his reaction. "Sorry. I didn't mean to pry."

"Don't worry about it. It happened a long time ago." He nodded with forced casualness and waved the fingers of one hand in front of him. "Aga."

I flinched as a small flame manifested a few feet away, burning merrily on the sand. The wind blew a gust of its heat in my direction.

That sure was handy. Maybe not all magic was bad, if it wasn't being used by an evil person. "Divinius?"

"Yes?"

"Tell me about magic. How does it work?" Were there any more weaknesses I could use against Orion and Akre? Not like I could flat-out ask him, but a girl could hope he'd let something slip.

His eyebrows furrowed as he tilted his head. "What do you mean?"

I gestured to the fire. "Every time I've seen you summon your power, you've always said something to trigger it." Like Orion had. "But Warlord Akre rarely says anything at all when he uses his." I shifted my weight to hide an involuntary shudder.

"Ah, yes." He paused, taking a deep breath. "There are two types, passive and active. Passive magic is more innate and applies to sensing the environment or world around us. Most mages figure out how to do that by instinct when they're very young."

He cleared his throat. "In contrast, active magecraft deals with manipulating one's surroundings. It requires a precise combination of words and gestures to summon. The active variety is considered stronger and takes many years of studying to master." He stared at me. "If Warlord Akre only has access to passive power, he shouldn't be too formidable of an enemy from a tactical standpoint."

I shook my head. If only it would be that easy. "I said 'rarely,' not never. The man can cast lighting bolts and magically torture people with the best. He just prefers to," I paused, hunting for the right word, "outsource his dirty work, whenever possible." Except when it came to me. I was special that way. Lucky me.

Divinius' eyes bored into mine with an intensity that flayed my skin from my bones, leaving me vulnerable and exposed. I pulled his robes tighter and looked away as the silence stretched.

He must've picked up on something in my tone to kill the conversation. I replayed the words over in my head. No... I hadn't let anything too personal or revealing slip.

"Why are you so afraid of water?"

His quiet voice raised the fine hairs on the back of my neck.

Staring at where the waves lapped against the beach, I tugged his robes closer around my shoulders until the stitches were at risk of splitting. "That's a random question."

"I would've assumed it was just a reaction to being shoved off a sinking vessel," he murmured, keeping his words low enough they wouldn't carry. "But I saw your expression when you almost fell off the dock in Tenara. And then you asked me to teach you how to swim."

I clenched my teeth. My jaw creaked. Sand demon spit. We were so not having this conversation. I would not give him more opportunities to mock me for my weakness. "No reason. Just like there's no cost to your magic." I didn't know why I said the last part, but he couldn't expect me to share my secrets if he wouldn't be open about his. He recoiled at the sting in my tone, just as I'd hoped.

I swallowed as lead settled in my gut. Wiggling deeper into the warm robes that still smelled of sun-banked mint despite their dip in the ocean, I sighed. Lashing out at him wasn't any more fair than it had been with Astra. I opened my mouth to apologize but the words dried on my lips. I cleared my throat. "So, what do you think we'll find in the jungle?"

"I don't have any idea." He relaxed, like he was glad for the change in topic. "I've never hiked anywhere before, much less bushwhacked my way through the wilds." Winking at me, he threw a lopsided grin my way. "But there's a first time for everything and at least the scenery will be worthwhile."

I chewed the inside of my lip as I glanced over my shoulder at the wall of greenery. In the shadows, it was so dark it was almost black. Frowning, I rolled my eyes. The so-called scenery didn't look very promising to me, but whatever. I shivered as a wave of foreboding crawled over my skin. "I think it might be wise to have one of us in front and the other in the back."

"But if we get into trouble at either end, that leaves you and me separated by however many people Astra brings along. We'll have no backup."

"True, but if we're both leading, there will be no one to protect the rear, and vice versa. I vote you go first, so you can magic a trail through the underbrush for us."

Divinius narrowed his eyes and studied me for several heartbeats. Behind us, some sort of bird called out from the tangle of green and gloom.

The silence stretched again. I couldn't stand it. "What?"

"I'm trying to decide if you're serious or making a bad joke."

I blinked and scratched my head. "What makes you think I'd be joking?" If magical ability wasn't only used to torture and kill people, then the least it could do was be helpful for a change.

He sighed. "Remember when we talked about the cost of performing magic?" He waited until I nodded. "I could do it, but it would burn me out and I'd be no good should we be attacked."

Oh. "I see." So, Divinius did have a price to his magecraft, after all. Just not one he was willing to share. I eyed him. "You don't seem to be any worse for wear after the fight with the sea demon."

He mumbled something.

I leaned toward him. "What?"

"I said, shows what you know," he repeated, his words louder than necessary.

"Hey, quiet on the watch!" someone called from inside the dinghy.

I sighed. A convenient excuse. So, the crown prince expected me to be the one clearing the trail for them. As if my arms would be any use in a skirmish, either, after a day or two of that.

I pulled my knees to my chest, rested my chin on them and stared out to sea. It would still be better than being back in the water, where I could drown at any moment. My vision went blurry, so I closed my eyes before the wetness could fall to my cheeks and betray me.

That night, I was back on the balcony overlooking Kadena at sunrise. Except this time, instead of shadows and black roses, I was surrounded by the scent of baked mint and mage robes.

Way too early the next morning, I studied the lush tangle of green in front of us as I peeled the last of the flesh from my morning coconut. The tip of the sun was about to peek over the cliff and blast us with light. Multiple bird calls mingled, their energy far too high for the pre-dawn hours. In the distance, hidden behind this wall of vegetation, animals whooped and cackled.

Hopefully, some of them would be edible. A diet of only coconuts was going to get old.

"You'd think there'd be a game trail somewhere we could use instead of creating our own," Astra said.

Divinius glanced around the sandy beach. "Why would they bother, if there's nothing to eat or drink here?"

"We may as well start with the path cut by the men you sent to find food yesterday," I said. "Where is it?"

Astra stared at the jungle wall, then over his shoulder at the sailors congregated near the dinghy. "Would you believe they said they couldn't remember?" He shook his head. "Cowards, the lot of them."

I froze at the vehemence in his words, at the unexpected rage in his tone. After a few heartbeats, I peeked behind me. A spark of hope burned in my chest. "No one's coming with us?"

Astra glowered. "No. And once the shipment is picked up and delivered to port, none of them will have jobs anymore, either."

I grunted and considered offering him Desert Rose's services. With such a massive loss on this trip, it was unlikely Astra had the funds to cover my fees, especially for the entire remaining crew. Best to keep my identity secret for now. "Which way are we going, then?"

Astra met my gaze with an apologetic smile. "Without a map, it's hard to say. Elysia is to the north and west, so if we make sure the sun's at our backs until we find a road or settlement, we'll at least be heading in the right general direction."

I opened my mouth, but from behind the merchant, Divinius shook his head. With an eye roll, I bit back my words and resumed studying the wall with a shrug. If no one else was coming, all the fewer people for me to worry about. Spinning my sword to warm up my wrist, I sliced through a thick vine. "Well, what are we waiting around here for? Let's get going."

I stepped through the opening I'd cut and was rewarded with a shower of dew. "Great." Although there was probably no saving my leather from its dunk in the ocean, even with the oil from last night, hiking in wet gear only added one more layer of discomfort.

Divinius smothered a chuckle as he ushered Astra along behind me.

I growled deep in my throat. Stupid royals. Fixing an image of Orion in my mind, accompanied by the satisfying glide of what my blade would feel like as it slid between his ribs, I swiped my sword in front of me as I stalked into the jungle.

It took us over two hours to find a game trail, and another until the day's heat melted away all the dew. I squeezed the excess water out of my hair and into the packed dirt ground before scratching at one of the larger red welts on my arm.

"What are these things called again?"

"Mosquitoes," Astra said. "We'll make a fire tonight when it cools down enough. The smoke will drive them away."

"I hate them." I clawed at the skin until it felt like it would peel off beneath my fingernails. The itching persisted.

"You're not alone," Astra said with a sigh.

"But if that's all we have to contend with," Divinius said, his voice annoyingly cheery, "we can count ourselves lucky."

I glared at him. "Yeah, says the one who didn't get a single bug bite."

He shrugged. "Perhaps they don't like the magic in my blood."

Astra chuckled as I tucked my sword back at my waist and marched down the trail, keeping the sun at my back.

"Hey, wait up!" Divinius jogged to catch me. "Why the rush?"

"The faster we go, the less chance they have to bite me." And, all the weird noises from the animals and insects I couldn't see unnerved me. At least in Obron, the deserts in between the towering sandstone formations were open and exposed. One could see for miles in any direction from the right vantage point. Plus, there was no humidity. Here, the jungle pushed in, like it was a living presence breathing down my back, along with tracks of sweat. I glanced at Divinius. "What? Don't tell me you're getting tired already?"

He huffed, the exaggerated offense on his face would've been comical if I wasn't so uncomfortable. "Of course not. I'm only concerned for Astra's ability to keep up."

The merchant in question raised his eyebrow. "Me? You're worried about me? For some reason, I find that hard to believe." He checked the sun's position over his shoulder. "Though now that you mention it, I think it is a good time to stop for food."

Ugh. The more breaks we took, the longer we'd be in this oppressive place. "Can't you eat while we walk?" I asked.

Astra shook his head. "If we maintain this pace, we'll burn out long before we reach our destination." He glanced at Divinius. "Besides, I'm still your employer, and I say we break here for lunch."

He flopped down in the middle of the narrow deer trail and stared up at me.

I bit back a retort that would have flayed his flesh from bone. An employer had the means to compensate their employees. With the losses on this trip, Divinius and I wouldn't see a single copper coin. But the last thing I needed was the merchant racing off into the jungle in a huff and causing us to lose time chasing him down. "Fine." I spun on my heel and strode back to him. I cocked my hip, crossed my arms and tapped a foot.

Astra nodded into the canopy overhead. "Divinius, would you be so kind?"

I followed his gaze to the bunches of coconuts.

Divinius elbowed me. "Well, at least he picked somewhere with food, right?"

I glowered back. "I'd kill for some fresh-baked bread with non-coconut-flavored water to wash it down." Heck, at this point, I'd welcome Roland's week-old arak, and wasn't that a sad state of affairs?

Divinius chuckled before turning his attention to the foliage above. "Aga." He flicked his wrist and a small arrow of flame shot toward the trees. Four of the fruits tumbled to the ground at our feet.

I glanced at where they'd come from and where they'd landed. "You could've clobbered us."

Divinius winked. "I would never make such a miscalculation!"

I popped eyes out of three coconuts and passed them around, holding back what would have been a truly dramatic sigh. The fourth fruit I slipped into my backpack for later.

I rubbed the tattoo on my cheek absentmindedly. It hadn't itched or burned at all since the fight with Orion, four days ago. That was unusual, as Akre always made a point to check up on me several times a day. He didn't trust me, and with good reason. I didn't know anything about the ink or the magic involved, but Orion had to have done something to it when he'd slammed me in the face with his lightning.

It had hurt so badly, I'd thought I was dying. Perhaps the magical blow-back had injured Akre enough he couldn't use the tattoo anymore? Or maybe it was a distance thing, and as long as I stayed as far away from Akre as possible, he wouldn't be able to track me.

I shook my head. As much as those fantasies made for pretty dreams of freedom, it was more likely Orion had damaged the nerves in my face until they couldn't feel when Akre was using it. While I wasn't at all upset about not having to deal with the constant discomfort, I missed the early warning system the mark had become. With no idea when Akre was watching me, he could jump out of the shadows and catch me unawares.

I examined the vegetation surrounding us, my eyes narrowed in suspicion. Nothing moved, beyond Astra's rubbing the back of his hand against his mouth as he finished drinking his coconut water.

Who was I kidding? Akre wouldn't come track me down himself. No... he'd send someone else to do it. A person I wouldn't suspect.

I studied Divinius, but him being the traitor made no sense. He hadn't once mentioned taking me back to Obron and into Akre's clutches. He was entirely motivated to go the opposite direction, in fact, and to get on with his own life in Elysia. And what could an Obronian warlord have to entice an elven crown prince who was already a mage in his own right?

My attention turned to Astra. Now, here was a much more distinct possibility. The merchant had shown up out of nowhere, and, despite what Divinius insisted, I still thought he had some sort of magic relating to fire. The laws of nature just didn't allow for explosions to flow around an object like it had when we'd been escaping Tenara. But he hadn't tried to take me back to Obron, either. The easiest way to get me back to Akre would've been to let the Tenaran guards have me, and he'd risked his ship to prevent that.

Divinius raised an eyebrow at me. "Are you going to eat?"

I blinked, focusing on the coconut I still held in my hand. Tilting it to my lips, I poured the watery contents down my throat. Swallowing the too-sweet liquid, I ground my teeth. As much as my instincts screamed otherwise, it didn't seem like Astra or Divinius were working for Akre. But someone had given Roland the knowledge and ability to teleport me. If it wasn't Akre, the next most likely candidate was Orion.

An invisible fist clenched in my chest at the thought of my ex-fiancée. Seven years ago, I'd thought I knew exactly what Orion wanted—me, and to rule Obron by my side. But discovering he'd become a warlord had only served to prove I'd had no idea who he was, or what his motivations were. Every memory I had of him was now tainted with the knowledge that it had all been a ruse, and a reminder I couldn't trust my judgement when it came to people. Orion could want me back in Kadena to kill me himself, or he could want me out of the way for when he made his move against Akre.

Based on where I was now, I would be willing to bet it was the latter instead of the former. Orion had always been intelligent and cunning, a brilliant tactician who understood his allies as well as his enemies. I couldn't rule out either Divinius or Astra when it came to working with him—Orion would find something to offer anyone whose alliance he needed to reach his goals. I'd have to be on my guard with both Astra and Divinius, so when the inevitable betrayal came, I would be prepared.

It was pretty obvious Roland wasn't allied with Akre—he'd saved me from Akre's guards by teleporting me out of there. I probably owed him a thank you, but it would be much more satisfying to fillet the skin from his bones for drugging me in the first place.

"Are you going to finish that?" Astra asked, gesturing to the coconut still in my hands.

My stomach lurched at the prospect of food. It twisted with the revelation that I was likely playing right into Orion's plans. "No. I'm not hungry." Slipping my pack off my shoulders, I went to stash the fruit.

"If you don't eat, you won't be able to keep your strength up. We'll have to stop again in a few hours," Astra said, his shrewd eyes fixed at whatever they saw in my face.

He had a point. The last thing I wanted was to be stuck in this jungle longer than we needed to be. I shrugged my backpack into place and spun the coconut in my palm. Fine. "I'll eat while we walk."

I held out a hand to pull each of them to their feet and glanced at the sun. With plenty of daylight left, we should be able to cover another three leagues or so before we had to stop for the evening.

I took another step and pulled a stick from beneath the ferns. We'd barely covered half my estimated distance today and were never going to get out of the jungle at this rate. I shook the piece of wood, splattering drops of liquid across the leaves. This kindling was too wet to make a fire.

Apparently, His Royalness scoffed at physical laws that said damp objects didn't burn. One of the bonuses to being a mage, no doubt.

I added the small branch to the pile I carried. The air hung heavy, making it hard to breathe. My garments clung to my skin.

I wiped the back of my hand over my forehead. Where was all this water coming from? It wasn't nearly hot enough to justify so much sweating.

Another of the ubiquitous oversized crickets chirped a few feet away. They were at least three times bigger than the ones in Obron, and far more prevalent.

One of my sticks slipped and tumbled to the ground.

I frowned, debating whether it would be worth shifting the firewood in my arms to pick it up. I twisted to do just that but paused. My biceps were starting to get sore from cutting our way through the jungle. Screw it. What I had would be sufficient.

I pivoted on the balls of my feet and headed back to camp.

Astra and Divinius' voices drifted through the foliage over the din of the strange furry creatures Astra said were monkeys. I slowed my pace as I approached, pausing just out of view.

"It's been a while since anyone from the Elysian court graced Tenara with their presence." Astra leaned back against one of the boulders that lined the clearing we'd selected as a campsite for the evening.

My gut twisted, cutting off my breath. Astra knew who Divinius was. I hadn't considered the possibility the two of them were working for Orion, but I should have. Orion Lyncis would never hang all his plans on one person when he could have multiple contingencies. Sand demon spit. If they were both in on it, then I truly was on my own.

Something suspiciously close to my heart cracked in my chest. I'd have expected a little more loyalty from His Royalness after I'd saved his pompous ass from the assassins. You'd think I'd learn by now that anyone could and would double-cross me.

No, that didn't make sense. Divinius was obsessed with returning to Elysia and getting his parents back. He didn't care about helping some Obronian warlord. And in payment for me rescuing him, he'd threatened Astra to force the merchant to save me in Tenara after my disastrous rescue attempt of the slaves.

I wrestled my insecurity to the back of my mind. No, Div wasn't allied with Orion. He wouldn't betray me. He had no motive. Without me, he had little chance of making it back home and finding out what had happened to his mother and country. Astra, however... the merchant could be working for Orion, or one of Divinius' enemies, or both.

I studied the thick undergrowth surrounding the camp, scouring what I could see in the fading light for any signs of movement. If Astra chose to jump us now, I would be next to useless in fighting off his crew or anyone else he had waiting to ambush us.

"Indeed," Divinius said, sorting through his pack with a forced causal affect, pulling out the coconuts that would no doubt be tonight's dinner. "I didn't realize you'd recognized me." He glanced in the direction I'd headed when I left, almost like he was hoping I'd come back soon.

I couldn't help the one corner of my mouth that tugged upward. Div was missing me, though it was probably just for my skill with a blade. Despite his brashness, he was smart enough to understand what Astra's revelation meant.

Astra's gaze followed Divinius,' tracing my path. "You give your slave a lot of freedom. What's to keep her from running away?"

No...

I froze, my blood turning to ice as a steel band wrapped around my chest and squeezed. The memory of Divinius' confusion over why I would waste my time on "those wretches" back in Tenara slammed into me with the same impact as the initial blow.

Divinius turned to Astra and stammered, "Who—What are you talking about?"

The merchant sat back, as what might have been a self-satisfied smile twitched across his face before he schooled his expression. "Oh, I apologize." He gestured to his cheek. "I assumed, what with the slave tattoo and all."

Astra pursed his lips and stared off into the distance. "I thought it odd, considering the elves aren't known for keeping slaves. But members of the royal house can do as they please."

The sticks stumbled from my numb arms as the truth of Astra's revelation settled on Divinius' face.

Nausea curdled my stomach as my entire body trembled. Divinius knew. He knew what I was. Property, not a person. I had no rights, and no protection against anything the world chose to throw at me. I would never be able to look him in the eyes again.

The firewood crashed to the ground.

"Gin?" Divinius' head spun in my direction.

I turned and sprinted into the jungle.

"Gin, wait!"

The last thing I was going to do was stand there and let him catch up so he could judge me to my face.

His boots pounded behind me, with the occasional curse and sound of ripping cloth. Overhead, the elusive monkeys roared and cheered, egged on by the action below.

I redoubled my efforts, and soon his steps faded into the distance.

My lungs burned, my attention was so focused on trying to breathe I nearly sprinted right into the river. Flinging myself to the ground, I hit the bank hard as the soft mud absorbed the force of my momentum. A sob tore from my throat.

I plunged my stinging hands into the silt and splashed cool water on my face.

It didn't work. The flush of shame and embarrassment still lingered and probably would until the day I died. I could imagine the disdain on Divinius' face, the contempt evidenced by the curl of his too-perfect lips. At least I'd lost him and wouldn't have to witness the expression in person. Maybe the gods would at last take pity on me and the mud lining the bank would split open, swallowing me whole.

When that didn't happen after several heaving breaths, I sighed. Pushing myself into a sitting position, I stripped off my waterlogged sandals and plunged my feet into the river. The cool water soothed my soles, taking away the sting of running. After a few minutes, I pulled my legs to my chest, wrapped my arms around them and rested my chin on my knees.

This couldn't get any worse. How could I face Divinius now that he knew? The truth was, I could no more face him than I could Orion without the flames of my rage to give me courage. Div hadn't done anything—lately—to irritate me, and if I didn't have my anger to drive me, I was a coward at heart.

A different heat sparked in my core, one that would burn for a long while. I latched onto it with all my strength. How slowly would I kill Astra if he was working for Orion?

If only I still had my obsidian stilettos. But that was a useless wish—they were back at Orion's house in Obron. The serrated blades had a wicked curve that had made more than one man wet themselves when they'd beheld them. There was a reason they'd been my favorites.

Footsteps sounded behind me. "Gin?"

Sand demon spit. "Go away, Divinius. Please." I squeezed my eyes closed, silently begging him to just do what I asked for once.

His robes rustled as he sat on the bank next to me, heedless of the river mud leaching into his clothes. "I'm not leaving. We need to talk."

Cursed elves. There was nothing to talk about.

I turned away, keeping the tattoo well out of his sight.

We were both silent for several minutes. Maybe he wouldn't say anything and after he realized I wanted to be alone, he'd go away.

He took a breath.

Damnit.

"Is it true, what Astra said?" he asked.

Fates, as much as I wished it wasn't... "What do you think?" The words dragged themselves out of my raspy throat. I tried to keep the bitterness out of my voice, but failed.

"I'm sorry, Gin. I had no idea. I thought..." He drifted off. He swallowed hard before continuing. "I assumed it marked you as an assassin or something."

"Yeah, well. Now you know." The water trickled past my knees on its way to the ocean.

He shifted his weight, nudging my arm in the process. "I don't think any less of you, you know."

Well, that was a blatant lie. "Like you cared so much about the slaves in Tenara?" I snapped. "You have no right to judge me."

"There's the Gin I know and love." I almost missed the hint of wry sarcasm in his words before his hand landed on my shoulder. "Come on, partner. Look at me."

I shrugged his grip off. "Go pick a fight with a sand demon."

He backed away. "I have no idea what a sand demon is, but based on our experience with the sea monster, it doesn't sound like a fun way to spend my time." With a sigh, he shoved himself to his feet.

Water splashed as he marched into the river and knelt in front of me, so we were nose-to-nose.

I squeezed my eyes closed and burrowed my face between my knees.

"Come on. I'm getting soaked here. Will you please look at me?"

"If I do, will you go away?"

He chuckled. "Yeah. Sure."

I squinted and peeked at him. "Why don't I believe you?"

"Were you born a slave?"

I forgot to keep my face averted. "What? No, of course not!"

"Well, how would I know if you don't tell me?" He jutted his chin toward me. "How did you get the tattoo?"

I shrugged and looked away. "I suppose Warlord Akre got his rocks off keeping the daughter of his rival alive." Honestly, I didn't know if Akre knew who I was or not. He was smart, and any intelligent tyrant knew their first priority was to kill all potential contenders for the throne. As I wasn't dead, that was a solid indicator Akre had no clue.

"I see," Divnius said. "How old were you?"

I studied him and was astonished to see no judgement or pity in his expression, only curiosity. "Seventeen."

His brow furrowed. "What happened?"

I frowned, swallowing past the lump in my throat. "The warlords overthrew the ruling monarchs, then over the next few weeks, carved bloody pieces of Obron up for themselves." So many people had died in the aftermath of the coup, the streets of Kadena had run red for months. "Warlord Akre found me after I'd killed a teenager almost twice my size over a bit of food I'd gotten from a local priory. He decided he liked what he saw and could capitalize on my skills."

Divinius wrinkled his nose, tilting his head. "And how did you end up in that clearing with me, before we entered Tenara?"

Of all the questions he could ask, he chose that? I opened my mouth to tell him to go ride a sand demon, but paused. Fates. Why not tell him? It wasn't any worse than what he already knew. My insides were exposed and shredded to tiny bits, one more truth wouldn't make a difference. "Akre sent me after another warlord. It turns out that person was someone I used to care about. To love." What a naïve fool I'd been. I took a deep breath, shoving the icy dagger of Orion's betrayal back into the lock box in the darkest corner of my mind where it belonged. "But that was another life, before Akre blew in and destroyed everything. Anyway, with Orion...it messed me up, threw me off my game. My childhood best friend and former betrothed is one of the bad guys. I still can't wrap my brain around it—the person I thought I knew so well, was willing to tie my life to, betrayed Obron, betrayed me, and now he's one of them. A Warlord." Shaking my head, I tucked a stray lock of hair behind my ear. "I barely escaped and ran to a friend's safe house, only to have him drug me. The next thing I knew, I was in the clearing with you."

I caught the tilt of Divinius' head from the corner of my eye as he studied me. "But you didn't assassinate him? Your former friend?"

Friend was the weakest possible descriptor of what we'd been, but now, even that no longer applied. "No. But not for lack of trying." I stared at the water as it trickled past us. "He almost murdered me in the process."

"Hmm. But you would kill Akre?"

I nodded, my throat so thick I had to force the words out. "And all the warlords, even...him. In a heartbeat, if I was good enough." Which

I wasn't. Not on my own. I clenched my fingers into fists, around the phantom hilts of my obsidian blades.

Divinius glanced at my hands and pressed his lips into a thin line. Placing a finger beneath my chin, he nudged it up and to the side.

I flinched but let him turn my face to display the tattoo. He'd already seen it plenty of times, but I felt so much more exposed now that he understood the meaning behind it.

He stared at it for several heartbeats. I fought not to shift my weight as the ink itched under his scrutiny.

"You know," he finally said, "I think I could get rid of this, if you want?"

I jerked out of his grip and barked a laugh, slapping his hand away. "It's illegal to remove one if the contract isn't officially dissolved. The punishment for doing so is death."

The edges of his mouth hardened. "Maybe in Obron, but in Elysia, slavery is against the law and also carries the death penalty."

I peeked at his face from between my eyelashes and caught my breath. Divinius had a mischievous glint in his eyes I'd never seen before.

One corner of his lips turned up, flashing that dimple. "I don't know about Tenara's laws, but I say screw Warlord Akre. What about you?"

I almost chuckled. Maybe there was a small chance he wouldn't see me any differently now that he knew what I was. "Who would've known the crown prince of Elysia had a rebellious streak when it came to authority?" I curled my toes. "I'm always down for throwing a kink in Akre's plans." Especially since it guaranteed he wouldn't be able to track me or look in on me.

Divinius wiped tear tracks from my cheek with his thumb and rested his palm against the markings. "You'd be surprised about my rebellious side, I think. Now, try to relax. This might get a little uncomfortable, but don't move or I might botch it."

My eyes flew open. "How so?" The last thing I needed was a scar and the tattoo. The image of me with raised, lumpy skin covered by ink that had bled until the design was indecipherable flashed through my thoughts.

He shook his head. "Do as I say, and it won't be an issue."

A little bit of risk was worth it for a big payoff, assuming he could do what he claimed. Which I doubted, but I wasn't going to say anything, just in case. I took a deep breath and settled into position. I closed my eyes as the warmth from his hand sank into my cheek.

"Suda Karana," Divinius whispered.

It started slowly, an effervescent tingling like bubbles across my skin. The sensation intensified to stabbing needles akin to having an arm or leg fall asleep. I clenched my jaw against the discomfort.

Tattoo gone, tattoo gone, tattoo gone. My mind repeated the words in conjunction with my heartbeats.

Divinius' low voice washed through my thoughts, blunting the pain. "Relax. You're tensing up."

I swallowed and forced my muscles to release.

The energy spread throughout my face until it felt like my teeth were trying to leap from their sockets.

"Halfway done."

My heart leaped into my throat. Did that mean he was succeeding? Was this really happening at last? My freedom, within reach after all these years?

I squeezed my eyelids together as a fresh wave of motivation swept through me, steeling my spine and giving strength to my muscles. I'd been through worse; I could get through this. At least here there was no water wheel.

After an eternity, the magic faded and Divinius sat back, panting.

My cheek felt cool as I brushed it with my fingers. Everything seemed intact. I leaned over to stare at my reflection. The image blurred as my eyes burned, tears threatening to overflow. There wasn't a hint of where the ink had been. The princess of Obron stared back at me, complete with her lack of emotional baggage and entanglements. My knees and arms went weak, nearly dumping me into the river, but I didn't care. The last seven years fell away like a backpack stuffed with rocks. "This is amazing," I whispered. "It's like it never existed." The master surgeons back home couldn't do such work. I met Divinius' eyes and took my first breath as a free woman. I wrapped my arms around his neck and buried my face in his shoulder as my eyes started to burn. "Thank you." Even my voice sounded lighter.

His arms tightened around me, and we stayed that way for several minutes.

Eventually, he pulled back, dabbing the sweat from his brow with the edge of his robe. His eyes warmed at whatever he saw in my face. "You're welcome. Consider it payback for the daring rescue in Tenara."

Nodding, I swallowed past the thickness in my throat. I could live with that. Perhaps not all magic users were evil bastards, after all.

The heat in his gaze had a matching sensation uncurling deep in my stomach. I laughed awkwardly, wrenching my attention away from his lips and startling several birds from the branches above. "If all it takes to earn a favor from you is fighting off a few thugs and second-rate assassins, I think you're going to owe me many more before we're done." Speaking of thugs... I dropped the smile and fixed him with a hard stare. "How did Astra find out who you were?"

Divinius paused at the sudden change in topic. He took a deep breath and exhaled while he ran a hand through his unnaturally lustrous hair. Really, it wasn't at all fair how perfect it remained after everything we'd been through. I certainly looked no better than a bedraggled rat. Shaking my head, I sighed. Elves.

"I'm not sure," Divinius said. "He's the one who brought it up and didn't even bother to have me to confirm it."

I frowned as I chewed the inside of my cheek. A cool sense of warning washed over my skin. "That doesn't bode well." I'd been right to be suspicious. There was more to the merchant than met the eye.

"No," Divinius agreed as he gazed into the river, his attention elsewhere. "It doesn't."

Chapter 15

Gin

I strode into the clearing. Overhead, the sand-blasted monkeys swung through the trees, chittering and screeching at my appearance.

Astra jumped. His eyes widened as his gaze snapped to the tip of my falchion pointed at his throat, then drifted to my now-unmarred cheek. "Ah. Gin." He licked his lips. "Nice to see you." Meeting my eyes for a heartbeat, he scrambled back and turned to flee, only to find an angry mage blocking his escape.

Divinius uncrossed his arms and spread them as he did in preparation for calling his magic. "You've got some explaining to do. Have a seat."

Astra gulped before sitting in the dirt next to the empty fire pit.

I removed my belt and tied his wrists behind his back. "Start talking," I growled. "Who are you working for?"

"I'm a merchant. I work for myself," he sputtered, peeking at his backpack several paces away.

I glanced at the satchel. It didn't look big enough to carry a weapon of any decent size.

Divinius took a step closer, kicking a few loose rocks out of his path. "How did you know who we were?"

"Please." Astra eyed him up and down. "You were literally announcing yourself all over Tenara."

Well, I couldn't fault that line of reasoning. I crossed my arms and studied Divinius as I chewed the inside of my cheek. His Royalness had the good grace to flinch and flash me a chagrined smile.

Rolling my eyes, I turned my focus back to Astra. While Divinius had been making a scene about his precious elven red, Astra had swooped in. "You must have known who we were, to have gotten my ring back from the bartender and approached us as quickly as you did." I flashed my hand at him, wiggling the finger with the gold and onyx band. "It was almost like you had a plan."

Astra shrugged. "I'm a merchant. I pay well to be informed of noteworthy events in the ports I frequent. An unofficial visit by a foreign royal is noteworthy." Turning his attention to me, he continued, "Plus, I saw a young—" he cleared his throat— "lady being taken advantage of, as well as the opportunity to make an easy profit with a quick currency exchange."

Divinius' expression softened. Recognizing the signs of imminent breakdown, I furrowed my brow. Glaring at him, I shook my head. We couldn't let Astra off that easily. Not if we didn't want to wake up one morning and find his knives in our backs.

Overhead, a noisy monkey screamed. I clenched my teeth, fighting the urge to hurl a dagger at it. If I hit, not only would it shut up, but we could eat something other than coconuts for dinner tonight.

As though it could read my thoughts, the animal went silent.

"What was really in it for you?" I asked, turning my attention back to Astra.

The merchant's too-innocent expression rankled. My fingers tightened around the hilt of my falchion, itching for the smooth sensation of the blade cleaving through flesh. But I couldn't kill him, not until we figured out his angle.

"Even if you did pay the bartender a quarter of fair market value for my ring, there's no way you made your investment back on that thirty percent cut on our currency exchange. No successful merchant makes a deal they'll lose money on." I paused. Unless there was an alternative revenue stream of some sort, like someone was paying him to watch us.

Divinius turned his attention to me as his eyebrows crawled up beneath the locks of hair that hung over his forehead.

"Oh, please, as if you didn't realize that, too," I snapped at him.

"I didn't," Divinius said. "I'm not in the habit of appraising jewelry."

"Hmm." I studied him, keeping most of my focus on Astra from the corner of my eyes.

When no great revelations presented themselves, I turned back to my ring. Had Astra managed to do something magical to it before returning it to me? Akre had been able to keep track of me through my slave tattoo, so it made sense that inanimate objects could be used in the same manner. I'd have to ask Divinius when we were done with this. Certainly he'd have checked and told me if the band had been tampered with?

Divinius mulled over some private thought for a few heartbeats before turning to Astra. "You were waiting for us. Why?"

The clearing was suddenly far too silent. I flicked my eyes to the canopy overhead, but there was no movement. It was like the monkeys had disappeared, along with the rest of the insects and everything else that made the jungle their home. We were alone. There wasn't even the slightest breeze to rustle through the leaves.

Astra raised an eyebrow. "I'm always looking for the chance to network, and making a connection with the Elysian royal court was worth the investment."

I chewed the inside of my cheek and met Divinius' gaze. He nodded, as though he agreed with Astra. On impulse, I grabbed the merchant's pack and upended it.

"Hey, what are you doing!" Astra lunged toward me but scrambled back as I pointed my sword at his torso.

I scattered the contents with my foot. Interspersed with the expected items were several coins. "There's somewhere between fifty and a hundred Obronian marks here." The humid atmosphere became oppressive, weighing down on me like I'd been shoved underwater.

Astra shrugged, unaffected by the change in tension. "So? I'm a merchant."

I narrowed my eyes, as if my glare could burrow down and see into his soul. The fine hairs on the back of my neck raised. Resisting the urge to rub the sensation away, I cocked my hip to one side. "That's way more than I gave you. And we're nowhere near Obron for you to get more."

Divinius held his palms forward as though ready to cast his magic. "Where did you get the money?"

A trickle of sweat worked its way down Astra's temple as he pressed his lips together and swallowed. "All successful merchants carry coin in various denominations. It's good business."

I scattered the metal discs with my toes. "There's hardly any Tenaran shivs here." I raised my eyebrow. "How were you planning to pay us? Or your crew?"

Divinius' forehead furrowed. "And no Elysian dalasi, either. Which I find doubly odd, as we were headed for Elysia." He narrowed his eyes. "In theory."

Meeting Divinius' gaze to make sure he had Astra under control, I bent and rummaged through the bag's contents. I pulled a crinkled square of paper from the pile, lead pooling in my gut. The red drop of wax was unstamped, leaving the sender anonymous. "What's this?" I slid my finger beneath the already broken seal and opened it.

My attention zeroed in on handwriting that was as familiar as my own. Muscles locking, my vision went white, my heart pounding against my ribs as though fighting to escape.

"Gin?" Divinius' voice sounded as if it came from miles away over the thudding in my ears. "Gin! What's wrong? Pharo!"

Somewhere off to the side, Astra cried out. I couldn't tear my gaze away from the letter to see what Divinius had done.

Footsteps crunched over dirt and gravel, followed by soft fingers as they disengaged the paper from my numb hands.

"Master Astra," Divinius said from beside me, reading aloud. "Enclosed please find the down payment to keep Desert Rose alive and away from Obron for the next month, as we discussed. I'll throw in an extra ten percent for every week you are successful beyond that. Turn this missive over to the branch manager at the Royal Bank of Elysia or the one in Tenara, as appropriate, at the end of the term and you will be compensated the balance due. Warlord Byre." He paused, turning to face me. "Gin?"

I blinked, his voice a tether pulling me back to the present. I stepped backward as his face came into focus inches from mine. My thoughts were sluggish. I was as stunned as I'd been to find Orion as my target back in Kadena. "Orion Lyncis," I croaked, "is the warlord I told you about. The one I couldn't kill. That's his handwriting." I'd been right—he was using an alias. Warlord Byre.

Byre was one of the seven warlords. He controlled the territory north of Akre, and had a reputation for being even more ruthless.

Orion had moved quickly, arranging for someone in Tenara to keep me out of the way mere hours after I'd tried to assassinate him. As if he'd known where I'd be. I shoved that thought aside for examination later.

If Orion wanted me away from Obron, then Obron was where I needed to be.

Divinius' head turned toward Astra with predatory intent. "How interesting." He stalked over to the other man.

Astra leaned against a tree, his arms stretched above his head. An azure ring of energy encircled his wrists and bound them to the broad trunk. Divinius moved out of the way, revealing the merchant's ankles surrounded with the same magic.

My throat burned as my vision went red. Astra was in league with a warlord, and I hadn't been smart enough to see it. My fingers twitched. I was never going to be able to foresee every betrayal, but I also didn't want to have to spend the rest of my life always looking over my shoulder, waiting for the next person to double-cross me.

A heavy weight settled on me. Perhaps this was what I had to look forward to—a lifetime of treachery and treason from those closest to me.

Divinius' voice took on a deeper, more threatening tone that vibrated through my bones as he turned to Astra. "Start talking."

Maybe I should just go 'scorched earth' and kill everyone. That would solve the constant betrayal issue.

"It'll get awfully lonely once everyone else is dead," Divinius said. "Is that better than being betrayed?"

I froze. "What?"

He rolled his eyes. "I said, it'll get awfully—"

I shook my head, cutting him off. "I heard you the first time. How did you know what I was thinking?" I was positive I hadn't said that out loud. My heart skipped a beat. Sand demon spit. "Can you read minds?" My throat dried at the thought.

He tilted his head and studied me. "Well, not everyone's. And not simultaneously."

Fates. He'd likely had his fingers all over my mind since we'd first met. My breath stuttered at the invasion. I suppressed a shudder and glared at him. "Get your grubby magic out of my head this instant!" The violation sent an invisible hoard of sand spiders crawling over my skin.

Divinius gasped, staggering backward. His hands slammed over his chest as though I'd stabbed him. "Grubby? My magic? How dare you!"

I bared my teeth. "Everyone deserves the right to keep their thoughts private!"

His mask shattered, frustration flashing across his face. "What's the matter? Afraid I'm going to find out that underneath the confident, swaggering façade you're a regular person like the rest of us with all the normal hopes, fears and," he wheezed, lifting the back of his hand to his forehead like he was some noblewoman about to faint, "weaknesses?"

I stumbled backward, resting my hand against a tree trunk as my knees threatened to give out. I leaned into it, glad for its support. The rough texture of the wood grounded me, giving me something to focus on. "What gives you the right to casually invade my privacy? God's teeth—I can't think anything anymore!" What had he seen? What did he know and how would he use that knowledge?

"By the mages!" Divinius threw his arms in the air and turned away from me. Taking a few steps, he spun on his heels and marched back. "Do you think I want to spend all my time in your mind?" He shuddered. "Not to mention the vast expense of power that would waste, why in the realms would I want to submerse myself in that raging lake of toxic fury more than necessary?"

I froze. "What?" Toxic fury?

He deflated, as though all the fight had fled his body. "It takes a lot of effort and focus to detect someone's thoughts. It's not something casually done. By Helani." He shook his head. "You can hardly blame me for caring about your state of mind on occasion."

He muttered something under his breath.

I shoved away from the tree, relieved my knees supported my weight. My hands cracked as I squeezed the hilt of my falchion. "Don't ever do that to me again." I felt like screaming, like those monkeys had when I first appeared.

He ran his fingers through his hair, pulling it off his face. "I apologize. In retrospect, it was probably not the ideal option, but it's not like you're a bubbling font of honesty when it comes to what you're thinking or feeling."

I blinked, my mouth opened once before I slammed it shut. "No. Well, yes, of course it was wrong." A small corner of my mind was surprised he'd apologized. Most royals, including my parents, wouldn't have bothered.

He stared at me for a few heartbeats. "Has it ever occurred to you that killing is not the best way to solve your problems?" A burst of wind blasted through the clearing to punctuate his words, rustling the leaves and blowing swirls of dust into the air.

I took a step toward him before my brain processed what he'd said. My knees locked. Of course, but some things, like the warlords, were so big that the only way to fix them was the permanent solution death offered. I scoffed. "I'm an assassin. Killing is what I do, and it *is* a good way to solve some problems. Permanently." Besides, if I left Akre, Orion, or any of the others alive, not only would it dishonor my parents and everything they'd worked for, it would leave Obron open to another invasion or coup, and result in the deaths of more innocents. Not that I thought I had a sand demon's chance in winter of surviving any attempts to assassinate a warlord. Much less all seven.

I flashed my teeth at the bewildered expression on his face. "Don't tell me you've never wished an inconvenient political rival would just—" I waved my fingers— "go away."

"Of course not!" he stammered. "If my father killed someone in the Mage College every time they disagreed, there would be no magic users left."

"Perhaps that wouldn't be such a bad thing," I said. Especially if the warlords disappeared with the rest of them.

Divinius stepped toward me even as he flinched at the barb in my words. "On the contrary. The mages bring a wealth of talent, knowledge, and wisdom Elysia would otherwise not have; another point of view. Wise leaders consider all options, all perspectives, before making a decision."

He dared another step. "Wouldn't you rather know why this Warlord Byre wanted you out of the way? Or why Roland betrayed you? Or are you so blinded by revenge that you'd deprive yourself of that information, and the advantage over your enemies?"

I could feel the ground tremble beneath my feet, as though responding to his anger. That was probably just my weak knees. No magic user was strong enough that his mood swings shifted the earth.

Divinius crossed his arms, his glare spearing me straight to my soul. "It seems Roland and this Warlord Byre may have done you a favor. They both got you out of a bad situation, and now you have a real chance of starting over, but you're so blinded by rage, grief, and whatever else, you can't see it."

I blinked as the dirt plummeted from beneath my feet.

No. No, no, no. The warlords were evil incarnate. I'd spent the last seven years of my life living with that as my core tenet. If the warlords had the capacity for shades of gray mixed in with the black that stained their souls, it would upend my entire world view and send me careening into the void of uncertainty. Something deep inside my chest shattered. I collapsed, not feeling the impact on my knees. I braced both hands in the dirt as I wobbled, practically tipping over as the ground dipped to one side.

One hand flew to my sternum as I gasped, forcing wheezing breaths into my lungs. Divinius was right—there was the slightest possibility Roland, and Orion, had done what they did to keep me away from Akre. Whether it was for their benefit or mine, I didn't know, but by refusing to consider the idea, in not looking at every possible angle, I'd limited my information. It was a weak attempt to protect my own emotions, my own heart, and in so doing, I'd made it likely I'd draw the wrong conclusion and had betrayed myself.

My knees stung as they slammed into the dirt as I collapsed. My palms splayed across the ground, catching my weight as sharp bits of gravel cut into my skin.

The back of my eyes burned. I blinked several times, as though I could clear my worldview by strength of will alone.

Divinius knelt beside me. One hand settled on my shoulder, steadying me. "You could stay in Tenara, with the assassins. Or without them. You'd also be welcome in Elysia. You could go anywhere, settle wherever you wanted. Start over."

Could I?

Now that I didn't have the slave tattoo, I could. But that would allow Akre to remain in power, the man who had murdered my family, destroyed everything I knew. And the rest of the warlords with him.

There was no way I could retire and live with myself if I didn't do something. I couldn't abandon Obron. But I would have to do some serious thinking about how to deal with Orion, with the lines blurred so badly between us.

Divinius' face hovered inches in front of mine.

"I can't," I whispered. Swallowing, I tried again. This time, my voice came out stronger. "I can't leave my home under warlord control."

Divinius stared into my eyes for several heartbeats before nodding. Reaching a hand down, he pulled me to my feet. "Fair enough. If our situations were reversed, I couldn't abandon Elysia, either. But rather than storming over there with no plans beyond an anger-fueled barrage, take the time to develop a strategy. Collect your allies, including the assassins in Tenara, and come up with a plan that actually has a chance of succeeding."

I took a deep breath and nodded. He was right. I stood much better odds of surviving my return if I knew what Orion's motives were. Then I could strategize.

Brushing my dirty palms on my pants, I tucked a loose strand of hair behind my ear and sighed. Sand demon's spit, this day sucked.

"Okay, say you have a point," I said, willing to concede his logic. I leaned my weight on one hip and pointed at Astra. "Then get him to talk, or I'll do it my way." I turned my best glare on the merchant, who paled and swallowed.

Turning my attention away from the men, I bent down and began picking the merchant's coins off the ground and slipping them into my purse.

Divinius focused on Astra. "You heard her." He kicked dust at the man cowering against the tree. "Start talking. Why does Warlord Byre want Gin out of Obron?" He sneered. "And remember, I can read your mind, so don't bother lying."

I blinked, freezing in the middle of pocketing another fistful of Astra's money. Why hadn't Divinius done that with the bartender back in Tenara? I rolled my eyes. Elves and their stupid secrets.

"I—I don't know why," Astra said. "Not exactly."

I spun on him with a grimace, my hand curled around the hilt of my sword.

His eyes widened at whatever he saw in my face. "But I can guess!"

"By all means, do," Divinius said, his voice unusually deep.

I glanced at Divinius' face. My heart skipped a beat at the hardness of the lines there. It reminded me of how Akre looked when I'd failed or upset him, right before I was about to be dragged down to the water wheel. I'd need to remember to not anger Divinius—he was scary when enraged.

Astra's throat bobbed. "I think Warlord Byre wanted her out of the way because he was worried she'd interfere with his plans."

I stood, stepping closer. "What plans?"

Astra raised an eyebrow and studied me as though I was the village idiot. "Overthrowing Akre, of course." He shrugged, as much as anyone anchored to a tree could. "The other warlords, too, I'm sure, but none of them have such a deadly tool in their arsenals."

My blood pounded in my ears. "He wants to reunite Obron?" Fates. The geopolitical ramifications... all of Obron, under one despot.

There would be no stopping Orion then. With all the other magic users dead, he'd be more powerful than my parents had been when they ruled.

"There's got to be more to it," Divinius said. "After all, I was banished, too. My father was assassinated."

Astra studied him. "Indeed. And your mother? Did she survive?"

Divinius exhaled hard enough his robes trembled. "I don't know."

Astra pursed his lips and raised his eyebrow, unimpressed with the two of us. "Perhaps you should find out, elf."

"I do not practice Divination!" Divinius threw his arms wide. "Why does everyone assume I do?" The trees rustled overhead as a blast of hot air slammed over us.

Astra stared into Divinius' eyes. His words were slow and precise. "I merely meant that once you figure out who is behind the coup and your banishment, you will know who the warlord's allies are."

The light of realization practically flashed above Divinius' head, and I had to bite back a chuckle. It was nice to not be the only one losing their mental balance today.

"I see." Divinius stroked his chin with a finger, his focus directed inward.

"What are you thinking?" I asked. If Orion had allied with Elysia, there was a good chance he had other rulers supporting him, as well. It may well be too late to stop him.

"It seems to me," Divinius said, "if my mother lives, she is the most likely candidate for an alliance with this upstart warlord. Though what she would gain by unseating my father when she was already so skilled at bending his ear, I have no idea."

"And if it isn't your mother?" I asked.

He sighed. "Another possibility, as much as I hate to say it, is the Mage College. I'm sure they'd love nothing more than to have magic users sitting on the thrones in all the countries of the realm." He flicked his eyes to mine for half a heartbeat. "Even if one of those is a warlord."

I waved at the clearing around us, the shadows stretching long as the sun headed toward the horizon. A few brave insects buzzed. "Well, there we go."

"Not so fast," Divinius said. "My mother had power, influence and the ability to arrange for a mage to illegally conjure me away from court. However, she was so focused on my impending nuptials, to the exclusion of everything else. I have a hard time believing it could be her."

"What?" I asked before I could stop myself. He was betrothed?

I don't know why I was so surprised. He was a crown prince, after all. And he certainly was attractive. The next in line for Elysia's throne would be a good catch and no doubt had an army of equally worthy women beating down his door.

"I am, in fact, Elysia's most eligible bachelor." Divinius winked, the levity in his tone feeling a little too forced. "What's the matter, partner? Jealous?"

"Of course not!" I scoffed, then turned away to hide the faint tint of heat that rose to my cheeks. A mosquito buzzed in front of my face, and I swatted it with more force than necessary.

"The night of the coup," Divinius said, "my mother gave me a list of names from appropriate families in the court and ordered me to pick one for a wife. Then she sent me out to dance with the wolves."

I almost missed his shudder. Something tight in my core relaxed. The bitter aftertaste in the back of my throat receded.

"I wonder if any of them survived?" he mumbled to himself.

Astra shifted. "Excuse me? Not to interrupt this enlightening conversation, but as I've told you everything I know, perhaps your highness would consider releasing me now?"

Divinius crossed his arms and glared. "Not so fast. Why bother outing Gin as a slave? You knew who she was beforehand. And you knew me. What was the point?"

I perked up and peered at Astra. I hadn't expected Divinius to ask a question not centered around him, but my heart skipped a beat. Our surroundings faded as I focused on Astra's face and waited for the answer.

At least the merchant had the decency to look uncomfortable. "You were so baffled by her reaction to the slaves at the Tenaran docks. I suspected you didn't know what she was."

Divinius glanced at me, understanding flashing in his eyes before turning his attention back to the merchant. "And? You expect me to believe you did that out of the goodness of your heart? As a favor to me?"

Astra nodded. "Of course."

Divinius glared and tapped his temple.

His shoulders deflating, the other man sighed. "No... I had to think of a way to separate the two of you."

"Why?" My too-loud voice echoed around the clearing.

Astra shrugged. "If you're half as intelligent as Warlord Byre thinks you are, you can figure it out."

I pressed my lips together as I raised my falchion to line it up with the merchant's neck. "Cut number one, coming right up."

The corners of Divinius' mouth tightened. "You can't just kill anyone who annoys you, Gin. That's not how the real world works."

I narrowed my eyes and turned the full force of my fury on him.

"Astra's sworn to secrecy to withhold...something," Divinius said. "I don't know what, but the magic prevents him from saying more. We can either turn him over to the local port authority at whatever township we first encounter, or we can take him back to Elysia and assure he gets a proper trial as a traitor." Divinius paused. "It will take more effort, but if we bring him to Elysia, we can extract any additional information from him, then I can guarantee an appropriate punishment."

I flashed my teeth. "There's only one penalty for treason." And from the standpoint of Elysia's royal family, conspiring to overthrow the king qualified.

"Perhaps," Divinius agreed, the corners of his eyes tightening as his lips pressed into a thin line. "But I'm positive that between you, me, and my father's Tormentor, we can come up with something more creative."

I raised my eyebrow. "Tormentor?"

Divinius nodded, his face solemn. "He's better at extracting information than you will ever be."

I wasn't quite sure about that. I could sink pretty low if I needed to, especially where the warlords were concerned.

"The man is sadistic. Until now, I'd never understood why my father kept him around. In fact, I'd planned to eliminate the position as soon as I took the throne. In light of recent events, however..." He brushed his fingers through his hair, pulling it away from his face.

"Interesting," I muttered. It sounded like Elysia had its own version of a warlord in this tormentor. I had no desire to ever meet them. I returned my focus to Astra. The man's face was pale, the dragon scale tattoos up both sides of his face stood out in sharp relief. "Okay. I'll help you keep the traitor alive, if only to find out what else he knows." I slanted a glance at Divinius. "Assuming you can't pick it out of his mind right now and save us the trouble?"

Divinius shook his head. "To strip a person's thoughts to the core and filter through the results, you need someone as depraved as a tormentor."

Something snapped that reverberated through me as though a giant had fractured a bone. White light flashed through the area followed by a concussion wave that threw me to the ground.

Where Astra had stood was a large lizard with iridescent blue-green scales. Long membranous wings twice the length of a man stretched behind it.

I stumbled backward, barely managing to keep my balance.

"Valek!" Divinius rolled onto his back from where the force of the explosion had tossed him into the dirt.

With baleful eyes, the dragon glared at us. It beat its wings, the gust of wind blowing all sorts of debris over us as it rose through the tangled canopy and into the sky.

Astra was a dragon.

I blinked, my jaw hanging open like a moron as the realization settled over me like a net.

Somehow, Orion had hired a dragon—a freaking dragon!—to keep me out of Obron for a month.

I met Divinius' wide-eyed gaze. We were in so far over our heads, neither one of us was likely to make it out of this mess alive.

I don't know how long we lay there, catching our breath. My thoughts churned over everything Astra had done since we'd first encountered him. Anything that may have clued me in to his motivations, or what Orion was planning.

Astra was a dragon. A younger one, based on his size, but one who had let a sea dragon crush his ship, drown most of his crew and destroy his cargo, all to extend my time away from Obron.

"Well." Divinius pushed to his feet, brushing the dirt from his palms. "We can either waste more time here, or we can continue, and focus on the priority at hand."

"Oh? And what priority is that, princeling?" My words came out sharper than expected, but I could hardly be blamed, as scattered as my thoughts were at the moment.

Divinius studied me as if I'd grown a second head. "Why, restoring me to my rightful throne, of course."

"Uh, huh." Then I could get myself back to Obron at the head of the Elysian fleet. I braced my free hand on my hip and slid my falchion into its sheath as I clambered to my feet. "Don't worry—I know how you can repay me."

He furrowed his brows. "Other than with my gratitude?"

I snorted. "Don't get me wrong. A royal favor is nice, but I already know how I want to call it in."

"Oh?" He tilted his head and studied me like a raptor studying its prey. One side of his lip curled up, revealing that infuriating dimple. His eyes sparkled as he opened his mouth.

I spoke the words in a rush, cutting off whatever he'd been about to say. "Once you're settled, lend me your army so I can use it to eliminate the warlords."

He froze. "Wait, what?"

"Yes." I steeled my spine and met his gaze. "This is the favor I want, in exchange for putting you back on your throne."

"No." He shook his head. "I promised to help you. I'll provide you with any and all supplies you could want and the fastest ship of my fleet to take you home."

Heat flushed my face as I glared at him. "So, you'd drop me off at the port, wish me well, and leave me to take on the warlords by myself?"

He splayed his hands to either side and shrugged. "What are you so upset about? I've seen you fight. You're better than everybody in my father's Royal Guard." He swallowed. "Well, my guards now. If anyone could do it, it's you."

I couldn't believe what I was hearing. Divinius truly did live in a different reality than the rest of the world. Something snapped inside of me, a shattering of the last core of strength keeping me on my upright. "You think one person, no matter how skilled, stands a chance against two armies, each headed by a mage?" The rasp in my voice surprised me, but at least my words sounded angry rather than broken or betrayed. "You're more of an idiot than I realized." I turned away, shaking my head.

His hand rested on my shoulder. "Hey, partner."

I jerked out of reach, keeping my face averted lest the stinging wetness in my eyes spill over and betray me. "Don't." I sniffed and swallowed. "Everyone I let close betrays me, lets me down. I don't know why I expected you to be any different." I took off down the trail, walking so fast I was practically jogging. I didn't care where I was going, so long as it was away from him and this stupid, stupid jungle.

"Gin, wait! What are you talking about?" He rushed after me. "Don't you think you're being a little dramatic?"

I didn't bother responding to that sand-drivel.

He grabbed my arm hard enough I couldn't pull away and turned me toward him. Deep blue eyes met mine. "I'm sorry. I suppose I didn't think the situation through. It's just...you're so talented and I didn't realize what you were up against. But, if I send the—my army to Obron, that opens political doors my country and people may not be ready for."

I glared at him through the thick layer of water that threatened to overflow and course down my cheeks. "I think it's long past time for the elves to take a stand and do something. You've had the luxury of being elevated above everything, so much better than the rest of us, so uninvolved." I jerked out of his grip and took a step back. "Has it ever occurred to you that you could help make the world a better place? Not just for Obron, but for everyone, including yourselves?"

He wrinkled his forehead. "How would involving ourselves in another's war benefit us?"

I spat out a laugh. "Trade agreements, for one. Obronians would pay a fortune for Elysian water, if it tastes anything like it does in Tenara. Probably other things, too. Obron must have some goods or resources Elysians desire." I wiped the back of my hand over each eye, wiping away the tears. "If you're going to be king, you need to consider the long-term consequences of inaction, not just the immediate ones."

He gasped like I'd insulted him. "Don't lecture me on what I have to do for my people." He stepped toward me, using his superior height to its best advantage.

I refused to back down, to give him one bit of ground.

"You have no idea what it means to be royal," he continued. "The decisions we have to weigh every single day. My kingdom will always take priority over what I want."

I opened my mouth then slammed it shut with a snap. He wanted to pull that card? Two could play that game. "Fine. Then you need to act like it. You have a responsibility not just to Elysia, but to the entire realm. Because once the warlords sort themselves out, the victor will be coming for you, and everyone else."

Several emotions flashed across his face, and I would kill almost anyone to know what he was thinking. The warlords of Obron were a ruthless, power-hungry lot. Up to this point, however, they'd been content with their own little piece of the pie. But that was changing, and at least one of them was clawing for something more.

"Someone has to stand up to them. Whether they form an alliance or destroy each other until there is only one left, eventually they will come for Elysia and the rest of the world. When that happens, your precious kingdom will be destroyed, just like Obron. Will you be able to live with yourself?"

Divinius inhaled slowly as I waited, his gaze unfocusing as he stared into the distance. After several heartbeats, he nodded. "Okay, you're right."

I raised an eyebrow and froze, holding my breath, not certain I'd heard him correctly. In the weeks I'd known Divinius, he'd never admitted to being wrong.

He held out his hand. "Help me regain my throne, and my army and I will accompany you to Obron."

I studied his hand as the atmosphere turned oppressive. A drop of sweat rolled down my back as I processed his words. A smile exploded over my face and I leaped at him, disregarding the extended arm as I wrapped both of mine around his neck in a crushing embrace. "Thank you, partner."

He froze at my touch. I'd taken him by surprise, but I didn't care as long as I got to march on Obron with an army to back me up. After a few heartbeats, his arms circled me as he patted me awkwardly. "Be careful," he murmured, his light, teasing tone contrasting the emotions careening inside my chest. "With all these random displays of affection, I might get used to having you in my debt."

His wink stirred a pool of heat low in my core that had me wanting to pull him closer. Instead, I released him and scrambled backward, a blush creeping across my cheeks as I turned away, coughing.

He cleared his throat as whatever had been building between us faded. "Let's see if we can cover enough ground to maybe sleep in a hotel tonight."

The change in topic snapped the tension as if I'd sliced it with my whip.

An inn would be perfect. One with a bath.

Chapter 16
Gin

Divinius was silent for several minutes as we hiked down the trail, which was for the best because my thoughts were a tangled mess. Orion. Akre. Astra. Whatever-this-was building between Div and me—something that could never be on account of his long line of suitors awaiting his return. After all, he was the most eligible bachelor, by his own admission. I needed to harden my heart, to put the walls back up, otherwise I was just going to get hurt again when we finally arrived in Elysia.

Somewhere off in the distance, a bird screeched. It sounded like a mix of seagulls and a sandpiper, but much louder. And bigger. If I never hiked through a jungle again, it'd be too soon.

Divinius spoke, breaking the silence. "The day we ended up together in Tenara, I'd been at court when a mage I didn't recognize conjured something that transported me to where I met you. Just before that, when I was trying to counter his spell, cries rang throughout the castle that my father was dead." He took a deep breath. "I never heard anything about my mother."

I furrowed my brow as I turned to face him, walking backward up the trail. Other than the connection with both of our parents losing their lives in a revolt, I wasn't following where this was coming from.

He glanced at me once then continued, "The only mages in Elysia belong to the Mage College. The College and my father constantly butted heads, but as a magic user myself, I typically sided with them on political matters. A member being involved in the coup is tantamount to the whole lot of them betraying me." He ran his hand through his hair, pulling the damp strands from his neck. "I'm not sure if my mother was part of it, or another victim."

My gut twisted for him and his mother's possible betrayal. Thanks to Orion, I knew that pain well. "I suppose we'll find out once we get to Elysia and learn if she lives." I hoped she did. Regardless of the implications for the Mage College, losing a parent was a wound most never recovered from. And Divinius didn't need his mother's treachery weighing on his shoulders.

"True," he said. "I haven't yet decided which outcome I would prefer."

I smiled in sympathy. "I understand. When I snuck into Orion's stronghold to assassinate him, I was elated to discover my best friend still alive with one breath and devastated the next when he tried to kill me, as I realized he was a warlord." I grabbed his hand and squeezed.

He met my gaze, his blue eyes locking with mine. "The truth is, I have no idea what we'll find in Elysia. Or who we can trust."

I flashed my teeth in a dangerous smile. If the queen lived, she would almost certainly be our enemy. "When in doubt, prince, rely on the underground. I'll learn what happened with your parents, and we can go from there."

He studied me, his eyes traveling down to lock onto my mouth. "I don't want to know, do I?"

I shook my head with a smirk, ignoring the heat and tension crackling between us. Acknowledging it would accomplish nothing beyond messing me up even more, and I'd made more than enough bad decisions when it came to men. I wrenched my attention back to our conversation. "Not if you want plausible deniability."

We stepped around a sharp corner in the path and I froze. The trail emerged above a cliff with a sheer drop-off at the edge of the too-narrow route that zig-zagged down the rock face. A valley spread below us, abutting the surf. The chittering of monkeys and crickets behind us was replaced with the faint taste of salt and the call of seagulls. Minuscule boats, like child's toys, dotted the lagoon.

I sighed as the crisp breeze blew the final remnants of the jungle's humidity from my skin. "I never thought I'd be so happy to see the ocean again." Even with its impenetrable depths and sea demons.

Divinius grinned. "Nor I."

I had little time to get the lay of the town, as focused as I was on not tumbling from the precipice. Fortunately, we didn't encounter anyone going the opposite direction. I paused at the last switchback and glanced above us. "I am never hiking back up that."

"Even if it means getting on a boat again?"

Sand demon spit. I froze and glared at him, frowning at the teasing glint in his eyes. Conflicting emotions warred in my gut. I slammed the icy terror into a small box and stomped on it for good measure before shoving it into the dark recesses of my mind. Besides, going back would only lead us in the wrong direction. The faster we got to Elysia, the sooner I could get back to Obron. "Hopefully we can find one that will stick close enough to the coast that sea creatures won't be a concern." And maybe I could tackle my fear and learn the basics of swimming before we left.

Divinius shrugged. "Fingers crossed."

I frowned. For some reason, he didn't sound too hopeful.

We located an inn on the edge of the docks that reminded me of The Golden Gosling, with the exception that it was crammed to the brim with sailors from all corners of the realms. I steered Divinius to an overlooked table in the back, where I could face the room.

A barmaid set two bowls in front of us.

Divinius sighed. "Praise the mages. Actual food!"

It looked like I wasn't the only one sick of eating coconuts. I poked at the concoction with a spoon. The hard bread on the side dripped with butter, the stew was thick and steamed. I ate a mouthful. An explosion of spices and salt greeted me as the meat and broth slid down my throat. "Hey, it's good!" I fought to hold back the slack-jawed expression threatening to overtake my face. Fare at The Golden Gosling had been flavorless, but it had filled the stomach well enough. Compared to that, this was divine.

Touching the spoon with two fingers as though it would pollute him, Divinius lifted a chunk of beef from his bowl. His eyes sparkled as the edges of his lips turned up. "Delicious! All this needs now is a glass of red."

Sand demon spit. I glared at him, jabbing my utensil at his chest. "Don't start that again. Remember how poorly it went last time."

He glowered but shoved a bite of the stew into his mouth without further complaint.

The food was gone too quickly. I flagged the harried barmaid to our table.

"What'cha need, love?" she asked me.

I blinked at the overly familiar pet name, nonplussed. Amusement sparkled in Divinius' eyes as I pursed my lips and cleared my throat.

Turning my attention back to the hassled woman, I said, "We're looking to book passage to Elysia's capital." I held up two silver shivs and placed them in her hand. "Help us get word to the right people?"

She nodded, the two coins disappearing as she sidestepped into the crowd.

It took the barmaid longer than I expected to send someone our way. The sunlight turned gold and the shadows grew long before a man approached our table. Dark hair with streaks of gray hung in coarse strands down to his shoulders. A matching beard that had been recently trimmed covered his strong chin. Amber eyes flashed in the evening light. He grabbed an empty chair, spun it around, and straddled it as he settled between us. He scrutinized me and Divinius, his eyes settling on the elf's pointed ears. "Rumor has it you're looking for passage to Elysia."

Divinius nodded. "The rumor is true. Hopefully something departing sooner rather than later."

The sailor frowned. "Trouble with the law?"

"Oh, no!" Divinius' hand splayed across his chest as if the question was offensive.

I had to bite back a laugh at the astonishment on his face.

Divinius mastered his reaction. "Nothing of the sort, my good man, I assure you. We're running late for an engagement and would like to minimize our tardiness."

The newcomer studied Divinius as he chewed the inside of his cheek. "Been quite a bit of political upset in the capital lately."

Divinius opened his mouth, but I kicked him beneath the table. "So we hear," I said. "Nonetheless, we are expected and need to make haste." Well, we weren't exactly expected, but at least the second half of the sentence was the truth.

"Mmmm." He eyed us again.

I did my best to fix him with what I hoped was a neutral, non-threatening stare.

He cleared his throat and said, "My ship, *The Siren's Revenge*, is heading to Elysia. We sail tomorrow morning with the tide. Passengers are twenty dalasi each."

I glanced at Divinius. I had no idea if the rate was reasonable or not. Divinius nodded. "Done!"

"Excellent. We're on pier seventeen. Be there by sunup and bring the coin." He stood and, with a final nod, disappeared into the crowd.

"Divinius," I whispered, leaning close. "How outrageous are his prices?"

He shrugged. "It's a bit pricier than standard, but he is bringing us into a conflict zone, so..."

"Do you have forty dalasi on you?"

He scoffed. "No, of course not. I told you before, I didn't have my purse on me when I was exiled." His eyes trailed down, as if they could see my bottom half beneath the table. "But you did take all of Astra's coin."

I sighed. Of course he assumed I'd pay. At least all good port districts had money changers. "Come on." I stood, pulling him to his feet. "We need to find somewhere to exchange our funds." I slanted a glance at him. "And you're reimbursing me when we get to Elysia."

He waved me away. "Of course. Then, we have to locate an inn. I'm dying for a good bath and a decent night's sleep."

Chapter 17

Gin

I stood at the foot of the boat moored at Pier Seventeen. *The Siren's Revenge* was average, as far as merchant vessels went, judging from my limited experience. The hull was olive green with long, fresh scratches through the paint.

"It's sleek," Divinius said. "We'll have speed on our side. And look," he waved to a deep gouge, "recently scraped for barnacles. At least we know they maintain their ship."

I licked my lips and swallowed. Why gashes on the bow indicated care for one's vessel was a mystery to me. Not like I'd ever admit such a thing out loud. For all I knew, they were from sea demon claws. "As we don't know what to expect when we arrive, you should give the crew a false name," I muttered.

He glanced at me with wide eyes for several heartbeats before nodding. "I hadn't thought about that, but you're probably right. Hmm." Divinius stroked his chin with his finger and thumb. "I'll be Marvin."

I swallowed a guffaw. "Marvin?" Like I was supposed to call him that with a straight face.

"Yes, Marvin. I like it." He turned to me. "And who will you be?"

I shook my head. "I'm not royalty, so no one will care who I am." I narrowed my eyes. "Unless you start referring to me as Desert Rose in public."

He placed his hand over his sternum, a serious expression painted on his face that was only belied by the sparkle in his eyes. "I would never. Gin it is, then."

I bit down on the corners of my lips to control the smile that threatened to explode across my face. "Very well... Marvin."

"What?" His grin hardened as he crossed his arms. "You're going to give us away if you have to fight not to laugh when you say my name."

I took a deep breath and exhaled. "You're right, sorry. I'll just have to think of something very un-funny every time I say it." Like being attacked by a sea demon. Or Orion, paying a dragon shifter to make sure I stayed out of the way. My facial muscles tightened as my mirth drained.

In control of my emotions once more, I nodded at the gangplank. "Okay, let's go. Marvin."

He bowed and waved me forward. "After you, my lady."

I raised an eyebrow.

He winked.

I refused to acknowledge how unreasonably attractive he looked when he was smiling. The last thing His Royalness needed was yet another boost to his ego. Shaking my head with a dramatic sigh and an eye roll, I shuffled onto the narrow board. The wood flexed beneath my feet as I climbed onto the ship. I grabbed the railing as soon as it was within reach. Even tied to the dock, the vessel rocked.

The man from yesterday's tavern glanced up as we stepped up to the deck. He jutted his chin in my direction in acknowledgement as he and three others finished tying off a line.

He approached, dusting his palms on his trousers as Divinius pulled himself up behind me.

"Welcome to *The Siren's Revenge!*" The sailor's voice boomed as he extended his hand to me, then Divinius. "I neglected to introduce myself when we met. Name's Simon." He gestured at the crew as they hoisted the final few trunks into the hold. "We'll be shoving off as soon as these lazy louts finish securing our cargo." He scrutinized Divinius then turned to me. "Did you bring the coin?"

I freed a cloth satchel from my waist and tossed it to him.

Simon hefted the purse before opening it and smiling. "Excellent. Come right this way, please. Passenger quarters are downstairs." He pierced us with a keen stare. "All guests will stay below deck until we're out of the lagoon."

I shrugged. That made sense. "Fine by us."

He led us down a flight of stairs into a well-lit hallway with several doors branching off.

I came to a stop in front of one of the sconces. "What's this?" An opaque crystal sat in an iron holder in lieu of a candle, casting an unwavering glow through the area.

"Light crystals," Simon said with a raised eyebrow. He peeked at Divinius. "Surely you've seen them before?"

I shook my head, my eyes widening. My fingers itched to touch one, just to see if it gave off any heat. I was making a spectacle of myself but couldn't care in the face of such an intriguing object.

"Go ahead," Divinius said with a quick glance toward our host. "They're quite safe."

It was cool and smooth. When I pulled at it, the shard lifted away. It glittered like an opaque diamond in my hand, and I could imagine it fashioned into a pendant that dangled from some noblewoman's neck.

"Rub it between your palms," Divinius said as he imitated rubbing his hands as if they were cold.

Following his instructions, I rolled it vigorously. Dazzling light blasted down the hallway.

"Careful," Simon said with a chuckle as he shielded his eyes against the glow that radiated as bright as the sun. He winked at me.

Heat flooded my body, rushing to my face. My exuberance had revealed my ignorance, and the last thing I needed was strangers thinking I was naïve or easily taken advantage of due to inexperience. "Sorry." I set the crystal back in the sconce and turned to the two men. I had to get myself one of those, for the novelty alone if nothing else. I'd never seen anything like them, and it would make certain illicit night activities easier to have a ready source of light available with a rub of my fingers.

Simon was staring at me with far too much interest. It felt like his gaze was peeling back each layer of me until he could see straight into my core.

I banged a fist against my hip a couple times to stem the urge to punch him in the face and shifted my weight from side to side. I shouldn't have let myself get so enamored with what was obviously a common object in Simon's presence. Especially when Divinius would be all too happy to tell me everything about them the instant we were alone.

Divinius crossed his arms and cleared his throat. Taking a half step in front of me, he glared at Simon.

The sailor glanced between us for several heartbeats before he shrugged and spun, waving us down the hall.

He showed us into a cabin—with two beds, thank the fates—and excused himself, closing the door on his way out. I turned to Divinius. He was staring off into the distance as he licked his lips.

"Marvin?" I waved my hand in front of his face with no response. "Marvin? Marv?" I snapped my fingers. "Hey, Divinius!"

He blinked and shook his head. "Sorry. I was just thinking how odd it was for a merchant supply ship to bother with the luxury of light crystals."

Liar. The captain had done something to piss Divinius off, but for the life of me, I couldn't figure out what as I replayed his actions in my mind. "Are they that uncommon?" I asked, glancing at the one mounted in the wall near our door.

"No," he said, "but they aren't cheap, either. They're mostly used in noble houses. If any of the lower classes have them, they'd likely be considered family heirlooms."

"Well, perhaps he appreciates being able to see below deck?" Unlike Astra's ship, where we'd been in the dark—both literally and figuratively—the whole time. A burst of rage sliced through my chest at the thought of the dragon shifter, but I shoved that away for later. There wasn't anything I could do about Astra, or Orion, right now. "And no one wants to bring fire on a boat."

Divinius nodded. "True. It's still an extraordinary expense, though. And not one most regular merchants will waste funds on."

"I wonder what they're transporting," I mused. "Into a conflict zone." Something that turned enough profit to make such a luxury as light crystals feasible. Or, maybe the cargo was so dangerous they were needed to reduce the liability of someone stumbling on it in the dark?

I licked my lips as my stomach did a flip-flop.

Divinius met my gaze with a mischievous one of his own. "I bet, if we're sneaky, we can find out."

I flashed my teeth. "Glad you're finally starting to see things my way." Later tonight, when most of the sailors were asleep, we'd have a better chance of getting a closer look at the hold.

I wandered over to the door and snagged the crystal mounted there before sitting on one of the beds. "If no one rubs them, do they go out?"

"Of course. Otherwise, they'd have to be constantly recharged."

Interesting. So, in addition to being rubbed, their power had to be refilled. I turned the shard in my fingers, squinting as though I could see past the surface into its core. I couldn't help but wonder if the device would work in Obron, where all magic except that belonging to the warlords had been eliminated.

"Can you recharge them?" I asked.

Divinius held his palm out and I dropped the glowing stone into it. He studied the object for several breaths. "Most likely. I don't know the proper word, however, so it would require access to my library and some light research. Rubbing them is easier."

I rolled my eyes. "Ha ha, very punny."

He tilted his head. "I'm sorry?"

"Some *light* research?" I shook my head at the blank stare I received. "Nevermind. Hey, do you think they'd let us keep one of these if we asked?"

He shrugged. "Well, they are merchants. Everything can be had for the right price."

I chewed on the inside of my cheek, fighting the urge to slip the small object into my pocket. "What's reasonable?"

Raising an eyebrow, he glanced at me. "Between three and four hundred dalasi."

I counted on my fingers as I worked through the currency conversion. I didn't have that many marks, even after plundering the Assassin's Guild and reclaiming Astra's coins. Oh, well. I'd just have to make sure no one noticed one was gone before we departed.

I put the crystal back where it belonged and flopped on the bed. "Now what do we do?"

He nodded toward the tiny round window in the wall. "You could watch as we leave port."

I glanced at the blue expanse outside. My gut twisted as memories of us exploding out of Tenara flooded my thoughts. I swallowed, trying to keep the sudden roiling nausea at bay. "No, thanks. I think I'll just lay here and pretend the rocking is an earthquake. I'm going to forget we're sailing back into the sea demon's maw in case it didn't get enough to eat on the first go-around."

"You're being a tad bit overdramatic, don't you think?" He settled into the other bed. "The ocean's a big place. The chances of us running into another one of them is incrementally low."

I glared at him. "But still possible."

He sighed. "Gin, if even half the ships encountered a sea demon once in their careers, people would stay away from the water. Sea monsters just aren't common."

I scoffed, ignoring the fact he'd grown up on the coast rather than in the middle of the desert, and thus knew a lot more about the comings and goings of the ocean than I did. "Did they teach you that when you were studying to be king?"

He flinched and looked away.

My gut twisted. I hadn't intended the barb to be sharp.

"I was just trying to be helpful. There was no need to bite my head off."

I opened my mouth but froze before any words escaped. Snapping it closed, I sighed. He was right—that had been uncalled for. "I'm sorry. My nerves are making me cranky." I rolled so my back was to him, burrowing into the surprisingly comfy mattress. "I think I'll take a nap, since we had to get up so early."

"That's not a bad idea," he murmured. His bed shifted as he settled into place, too.

I peeked over my shoulder. He was facing the ceiling with one arm thrown over his eyes. I took the opportunity to admire the definition in his muscles and how his robes always hung just right to accentuate his perfect torso. He seemed incredibly relaxed, all things considered. But then, he was certain we wouldn't be attacked by another sea demon. And if by some chance we were, he knew how to swim.

I should quit ogling him like some creep. The last thing I needed was for him to catch me undressing him with my eyes. Ugh. Turning away, I stared at the wall as his breathing deepened.

Oh, to be able to fall asleep so easily... I heaved a deep breath out my nose, half afraid if I did manage to nap, I'd awaken again to the phantom touch of rose petals on my skin.

At least these accommodations were more comfortable than those aboard Astra's doomed ship. Hopefully they lasted longer, too.

I slipped the crystal from our room into my pocket. The moonlight reflected off the ocean outside, casting an eerie white light across the room.

"Gin, what are you doing?"

"Shhh!" I turned to Divinius. "I thought you were sleeping like everyone else, so I figured now would be a good time to go check out what's in the hold."

Blankets rustled as he hoisted himself out of bed. "If that's where you're going, I'm coming with you."

I bit back a sigh. "One person is less likely to be spotted by the night shift than two." Plus, I had a lot more experience sneaking around shadowy corridors than he did. "You should stay here."

"Please." He scoffed. "As if I'd let you explore without me."

I glared at him. He met my gaze with a hard one of his own. The corners of his lips tightened as they turned down.

I recognized that stubborn expression. All royals mastered it by puberty. I sighed. "Fine. You'll make less noise coming with me than standing here arguing about it."

His teeth flashed in the moonlight as the dimple in his left cheek made an appearance. "Glad you're finally starting to see things my way," he quoted back at me.

I rolled my eyes. "Smartass elf. Come on, but stay behind me."

I twisted the knob. The latch stuck. I jostled it again. "I think we're locked in."

His breath tickled my ear as he leaned over my shoulder to stare at the door. "That's a safety concern if the ship sinks. When did they lock it?"

I thought back. "The last person through the door was the one who picked up our dinner plates."

He glowered. "Room service here leaves something to be desired. I'll have to write a sternly worded letter."

I whirled to face him, at a loss for words. "What?" Was he serious right now?

"What?" He stood tall, his shoulders square. "I'm the king of Elysia. How dare they lock me in my room like a prisoner!"

I smacked him in the chest. "Keep your voice down. These walls are thin. Do you want the entire ship to know who you are, Marvin?" I pulled two strips of metal from my belt and flashed him a toothy smile. "And Your Highness-ness can relax. If they don't want us getting into their business, we're going to do just that." I winked as I inserted the two picks and went to work.

"For the safety of the realm?" he asked, dryly.

I blinked, giving him my most innocent expression. "Of course." And for my own morbid curiosity.

Far too many heartbeats later, I squirreled the tools back where they belonged.

Only four pins. My lips curled into a half-grin. Nice try, Simon.

"There, see? Problem fixed." I cracked the door to our room. The light crystals were dimmer than they'd been earlier in the day, but they were still brighter than I'd hoped. "There's going to be no cover out there, so we'll have to move fast," I whispered.

Footsteps sounded from the end of the hall. I nudged the door shut until the sailor passed and was up the stairs.

"Okay. Now's our shot." I slid out the door. Divinius followed, pulling it closed with a click.

"Do you think we should relock it?" he asked.

I glanced at the latch. On this side, it was a simple deadbolt. How had I missed it when we'd first entered? That was an embarrassing oversight.

Oh, right. I'd been struck dumb with amazement at the light crystals, like a child given some tasty sweet.

"Good idea," I said. The real trick would be locking it again once we returned. But that was a problem for later.

Divinius threw the bolt into place with a click and followed me down the corridor.

We met no resistance by the time we reached the first set of steps into the belly of the ship. I held up a hand for Divinius to stop as I listened.

Voices drifted from somewhere nearby, but in the enclosed space it was impossible to determine where they came from.

"Step carefully, and away from the center, so the stairs don't creak beneath your feet," I whispered.

Divinius imitated my example, transferring his weight from side to side, making sure he only stepped on the outer edge.

I made it to the end of the flight and turned, only to have to bite back a laugh. "I never thought I'd see an elf doing the splits walking down the stairs." I locked the image of him awkwardly traversing the steps in my brain for whenever he next annoyed me.

He glowered. "You're the one who told me to not step in the middle."

"Hey, what's that?" The words came from below.

"Go check. Make sure the passengers are where they belong."

I winced. In my amusement, I'd neglected to keep my voice down.

Sand demon spit.

I glanced around and grabbed Divinius' arm. "Come on." I tugged him into the dark on the other side of two water barrels sitting on the landing.

We ducked behind the cover as two sailors came charging by, their cutlasses flashing in the light. I was beyond glad we'd decided to lock our door after leaving.

Rubbing my hands together, I turned my focus to the darkness below. People didn't guard holds with boring cargo, for sure. This was about to get good.

"Stay here," I whispered. "I'm going to scout ahead." Divinius opened his mouth but I cut him off with a wave of my hand. "There's more where they came from, and I'll draw less attention." I eyed him. "Unless you can magic shadows to hide us?"

He raised an eyebrow and stared at me as if I'd asked him to turn the sky purple. With a sigh, he scrunched further back into the gloom.

Well, wasn't that disappointing? Not like the ability to bend darkness to one's will was arousing, or anything. It wasn't. Really. The only reason I asked was because it would be helpful in certain situations...like this one. And Divinius didn't need to be more attractive than he already was. I squeezed my eyes shut and winced. That didn't even sound believable in my head. Hopefully His Royalness wasn't listening to my thoughts right now, otherwise I'd never hear the end of it.

With a quick glance in the direction the two sailors had gone, I ducked around the barrels and slid forward. Distributing my weight across several planks, I crawled until I could peek over the side of the landing into the hold below.

Three more crew members encircled a large barrel, playing cards. Each had a mug of ale and a small pile of coins in various denominations. Some I recognized, like the Obronian marks, and others, like the five-edged white coin with the purplish sheen, I didn't.

Fates. I couldn't take all the men on by myself, not if I wanted to be quiet. Especially if there was volatile cargo about. And the other two could return any minute.

I scuttled back to Divinius.

Putting my lips near his pointed ear, I whispered, "There's three more below. They look pretty deep into their cups, but I can't take them all quickly enough to not bring everyone else down on our heads. We need a distraction of some sort. Any ideas?"

His eyes sparkled as he turned to meet my gaze. He was loving this as much as I was, the miscreant. "Oh, plenty. Can you be more specific about what you want, exactly?"

"I don't know." I waved my hand around in a circle as I willed something to come to mind. "Something to make them leave while we search the hold."

He chewed on the inside of his cheek for a few heartbeats. "I think I have an idea. How about the sails catching on fire?"

I blinked like an idiot. "You can do that?"

He gaped at me, a hand covering his chest. "You wound me. Would I have offered if I couldn't?"

Shaking my head, I swallowed. "No, I didn't mean it like that. I meant can you make it big enough it draws everybody away, even the three below us, but still keep it small so it won't leave us adrift?" Or burn up the entire ship. I shuddered—the last thing we needed was another vessel sinking out from beneath us.

I would never get on another boat as long as I lived.

"Of course. I wasn't going to have them spontaneously combust or anything. By Helani." His forehead wrinkled. "Have a little faith." He threw me a crooked smile, showing off that blasted dimple as he braced one hand on the ship's hull and grabbed the water barrel with the other. "Brace yourself."

A tendril of chilled unease unfurled in my stomach. Following his lead, I wedged my back against the wall, praying to the fates I wouldn't regret this. "If this ship sinks, I'll murder you myself," I whispered.

"Bharama," Divinius muttered. He closed his eyes and grunted.

High above, something cracked, sending reverberations through the floor.

My eyes bulged. With his arrogance and rather flippant attitude toward life, I'd forgotten how powerful he was. I was grateful for the support of the wooden slats at my back as my knees buckled.

One of the crew called from below, "What was that?"

"Fire in the sails!" several cries echoed. "All hands! Fire!"

Wood crashed as the three sailors dropped their cards, leaped to their feet and scrambled up the stairs. I gave them a count of ten before emerging from my shelter. Not caring if my steps caused the wooden planks to creak, I bolted into the hold. The air was ripe with the smell of chewing tobacco, ale and sweat. It reminded me of the taverns back home, and what had once been a haven until Roland had drugged me.

The chairs lay scattered on the floor, along with spilled drinks and playing cards.

I grinned. And all their forgotten money.

Divinius followed me. "Gin! Leave it or they'll know someone's been down here."

I froze, my hand halfway toward the first pile of coins. Fates, he was right. Blast it.

I glanced one last time at the shiny circles and turned away with a sigh.

The hold was packed on one side with barrels labeled in the same flowing Elysian script that Astra's had been. The other half of the space was taken up by rectangular wooden crates with no label or instructions.

"What do they say?" I asked.

Divinius frowned, standing still in the middle of the room. "Black powder." He pivoted toward me. "What's black powder?"

I raised an eyebrow. "You mean, besides the obvious?"

His flat stare met mine, all excitement for our midnight escapade gone.

I shrugged and returned my focus to the boxes. "I don't know. Can you get one open?"

He shook his head, gaze staring off into the distance. "Not if I want to maintain the illusion above."

"What?"

He furrowed his brows. "It takes a lot of concentration, especially since I can't see what I'm casting it on. Now, please be quiet so I can focus."

Rolling my eyes, I sighed. Why did I always have to do the heavy lifting in this relationship?

I marched over to the closest trunk and jammed my sword below the lid, jostling it.

The wood creaked, followed by a screeching of nails that sent icy shivers up every nerve in my body. I glanced over my shoulder at the stairs. Hopefully whatever Divinius was doing above would cover the noise.

I freed my blade and shoved it into the same seam, several hand widths away, repeating the motion multiple times before the top popped off. I flipped it open with a gasp.

Stacks of fancy crossbows were crammed into the container, cushioned by coarse wood shards that tickled my nose with a soft, camphoraceous scent that prickled and cooled my sinuses.

"I smell cedar," Divinius said behind me.

"I found weapons." I hoisted one from the trove and aimed it at the stairs. The workmanship was extraordinary. There was some sort of latching mechanism I'd never seen before. Dwarven, perhaps?

But I'd figure it out.

This would make a worthy addition to Desert Rose's armory, especially if it came with a convenient carrying case.

As an afterthought, I grabbed a canister of quarrels crammed into the corner of the trunk and slammed the lid back into place.

"Shipping munitions into Elysia without the proper permits is illegal," Divinius said, his voice echoing as if from far away.

I glanced at him. His face was furrowed in concentration, his focus a million leagues from here.

Strapping the high-tech crossbow across my back, I marched over to the black powder barrels. Hopefully, these had something as equally intriguing as the crossbows.

Fortunately, these lids had handles. A quick ninety-degree turn, and the top popped right off like the jack-in-the-box I'd had as a child.

The reek of rotten eggs assaulted my nose. I bent at the waist, retching.

"What is that stench?" Divinius growled.

Swallowing hard, I forced the nausea down. Breathing from my mouth did little good, as the scent coated my tongue and the back of my throat. I ran my fingers through the barrel's contents.

"Black powder, like it said." The coarse granules rolled off my skin like sand on a hot day. "There's nothing else in here."

Whatever was this stuff for? Was it worth anything?

That was a stupid question. Merchants and smugglers didn't fill half their ship's hold with worthless merchandise.

I studied the barrels. There must be at least fifty of them here.

As I glanced around the space, nothing stood out as a feasible container to carry a sample of the substance back to our room for further study. Besides, who wanted this smell in their quarters? It would give us away.

With a sigh, I screwed the lid back into place.

"Come on, Div. There's nothing else here, time to go."

He didn't move.

Clutching the pilfered quarrels in one hand, I grabbed his arm with the other. "Come on." I pulled him toward the stairs. He followed with surprisingly little resistance.

I settled him on the bed back in our room, tossed the crossbow and bolts onto my sheets, and slid my lock picks back into the latch on our door. I fiddled with them for several minutes. Blood whooshed through my ears in time to my pounding heart.

It was good the fire wasn't real, and that we weren't normal passengers. I shouldn't be surprised weapon smugglers would trap people below deck, but if they were so concerned, why take on travelers at all? A stab of hot anger sliced through my chest, pushing a sour taste up the back of my throat. Now we had to figure out a way to discover who they were destined for. The last thing I needed was Elysia breaking out in a civil war. Divinius' army had to go to Obron with me, and they couldn't do that if their own country was tearing itself to shreds.

"Hurry, Gin." Divinius' voice was strained, cracking on my name.

I glanced over my shoulder. His face was pallid, sweat dripping down his forehead. He rocked side to side, as though the motion of the waves might tip him over at any moment.

Sand demon spit. He hadn't looked so bad since his abduction by the Tenaran assassin's guild.

Turning back to the door, I took a deep breath and hissed through my teeth, "I'm going as fast as I can. It's a lot harder to lock something when all you ever learned to do was unlock it."

After far too long, the final pin dropped into place.

Thank the fates.

I rolled backward, collapsing on the floor. The ceiling rocked above me.

"Okay, Div. Go ahead and end it."

Moments later, he collapsed onto the bed with a gasp. "The next time I offer to do a remote illusion, smack me upside the back of the head for being such an idiot."

I held back a snort. "Gladly."

After several minutes, a horde of boots pounded by our door on their way back to the hold.

As soon as my heart quit pounding, I pushed myself into a sitting position and scooted over to the edge of my mattress. Picking up my pilfered crossbow, I ran my fingers over it. The limbs were smooth and alternated between fine layers of wood and horn, covered by a shiny finish. The cocking stirrup was in the back instead of the front as usual and was attached to a round barrel with several openings in it.

I pulled the mechanism into place, aimed at the door then squeezed the trigger. The latch clicked with a release of pressure. The barrel rotated a few degrees. The string remained taught.

I frowned. What manner of magic was this? The stirrup was still in place. With a shrug, I squeezed the trigger again. The apparatus discharged, and the process repeated until the barrel had spun a full circle and the stirrup released with a click.

I sat the weapon back on my bed and studied the rotating barrel. "Hey, Divinius. I think this crossbow may be able to shoot multiple bolts at the same time."

"Don't be ridiculous," he said from where he lay with his arm flung over his eyes. "Repeating crossbows don't exist."

The corners of my mouth hardened. "This begs to differ." And my fingers itched to try it out. If we could outfit his army with these before I returned to Obron, it could go a great way toward leveling the playing fields against the warlords' armies. Especially if there were a few mages mixed in with the elven troops.

Divinius groaned. "Have you given any thought to how you're going to smuggle that off the ship? It's too big to fit in your backpack."

No. That was a problem for tomorrow.

Unfortunately, so was trying out the weapon. The only way I could use it now would be to go above deck and start shooting things. The crew wouldn't likely take kindly to me stealing their merchandise.

Patience.

I rolled my eyes and clenched my jaw. Patience was not my virtue. I was more of a vengeance and retribution type.

I slid a bolt into each opening in the barrel and re-cocked the stirrup.

I should've grabbed two canisters of ammunition.

"The next question for you, Divinius, is if we're smuggling these into Elysia, who are they going to?"

"I think it's safe to say it's not the mages," he mumbled. "They have plenty of power and thus don't need weapons. But as for exactly who the other side of the conflict is, your guess is as good as mine."

I doubted that. Of the two of us, he had the political experience in Elysia's court and knew all the players, along with who was likely to resist the magic users. But when I opened my mouth to say so, the tenseness in his face and posture stopped me. I would bet anything the way he was acting—like he had a migraine—had something to do with the cost of his magecraft that he refused to discuss. But that wasn't what was most important right now. "Then I suppose you'll have to follow the shipment to its buyers."

Divinius heaved himself partway up, until he was braced on his elbows. "And what will you be doing?"

I flashed my teeth with a dark smile as I brandished the crossbow. "Making friends in low places. Getting us information."

I stood on the balcony overlooking Kadena as the sun rose, the hard press of a muscular chest behind me. Leaning back, I let Orion support my weight as his body heat counteracted the last cool kiss of the desert night.

Closing my eyes, I took a deep breath, enjoying the faint scent of mint and spices that floated up from the bazaar below. There was something wrong with this, a reason I shouldn't be here, or something I needed to attend to, but for the life of me I couldn't remember what it was.

Something soft rubbed up and down my arm, raising goosebumps and stoking the slow fire that was brewing inside me. The gentle scrape of calloused fingertips over my skin changed to silk and velvet.

Like rose petals.

Unease coiled in my chest, sending icy shivers down my spine.

Opening my eyes in a lust-filled haze, I glanced down, expecting to see the obsidian bloom as the sensation brushed the curve of my shoulder and along my collar bone.

But there was no flower. Instead, elegant fingers, too perfect to be human, wrapped in navy blue robes with silver runes shifted over me as Divinius leaned forward. The press of his cheek against my throat sent a wave of heat through me that centered below my navel.

"Stay with me in Elysia."

His breath tickled the fine hairs on my neck, sending pleasant shivers down to my toes.

And that was ridiculous, because Divinius would never ask such a thing.

My eyes flew open. I stared at the dark wooden beams of the underside of the deck of *The Siren's Revenge* and listened to Divinius' deep, even breathing as the flush of arousal faded far too slowly.

Fates. Closing my eyes, I covered my face with both hands. There was no way I was developing feelings for His Royalness.

Absolutely no chance.

Chapter 18
Gin

I sighed in relief as *The Siren's Revenge* came to rest against the pier. In front of me, Divinius shifted his weight, uncomfortable with the bulk of the crossbow tied on his back beneath his robes.

I took a step closer and put my hands on his shoulders. "Quit fidgeting, Marvin." If he kept moving like that, it would raise suspicions and the last thing we needed was some overly cautious sailor deciding to pat us down before letting us onto the docks.

Simon settled the gangplank into place and gestured for us to disembark.

With our feet firmly on the dock, I glanced up at the railing. "Did that seem a little too easy to you?"

Divinius whirled to face me. "You call the other night's debacle easy?"

I blinked as we strode down the pier. "I'd be a little more sympathetic if you'd be less closed-lipped when it comes to the cost of your magic."

He pressed his lips together into a thin line. A muscle in his jaw ticked.

I shrugged. No one could expect me to feel bad about something he refused to trust me enough to discuss.

A column of soldiers, complete with crossbows and longswords marched past, eyeing the crew coming and going as they approached our ship and started rifling through the cargo manifest the captain handed over. I furrowed my brow. I was no expert on ports, but Tenara had been busier than this, with only a few squads of sentries patrolling. Elysia's, in contrast, had more guards than sailors. It looked like half the army was stationed here, and those troops were bristling for a confrontation.

A cold lump settled in my gut as I studied our surroundings, taking in the details I'd been too distracted to notice before. Part of a dock opposite of us was missing, another patch of wooden planking was scorched, as if it had caught fire. Several of the structures had busted windows and other damage that reminded me of Kadena after the warlords had attacked.

There'd been a recent battle here. My fingers itched for my new weapon.

As we arrived at the end of the docks, I pulled Divinius into a narrow alley with the eagerness of a child on solstice. "Okay, give me my crossbow."

"Gladly!" He reached beneath his robes and released the knots. The crossbow dropped.

"Careful!" I lunged, snatching it right before it crashed to the ground. "This baby is priceless!"

He shot me a wry glance. "As 'priceless' as the light crystal in your pocket?"

I winced. I'd been hoping he hadn't noticed me snatch it, but he was too observant. And he did have a point—everything I stole was technically without price.

I shrugged. "What? I doubt I'll see you complaining if it comes in handy when you retake your throne, Marvin." Slinging the crossbow over my back, I adjusted it so it wouldn't interfere with my ability to draw my blades or whip.

"Stealing is wrong, Gin."

I glanced at him as though he'd said the sky was green. After all we'd been through together? "Even from weapon traffickers?" Speaking of...

I nudged Divinius to the edge of the alley, where we could stay in the shadows but keep an eye on the crew as they unloaded. "We need to keep close watch, or we'll miss the buyers."

Divinius harumphed but didn't deign to respond.

The sun had moved three finger widths before the sailors finished unloading the cargo into several horse-drawn carts.

As the driver tied the tarp to cover the final load, I grabbed Divinius' arm. "Come on! Now's our chance." I ducked out of the alley and shimmied beneath the cart, grabbing a couple of boards and tucking my legs up over the rear axle.

"Oh, no way," Divinius said, rolling in beside me. "We'll get all dirty under here."

As if we weren't already filthy. Five days on a ship without a bath would do that. "It's just a little bit of dust, Your Highness-ness," I whispered. "Hurry and grab on, or you'll be left behind."

He growled and shrugged out of his robes. Balling them up and smashing them between his thighs, he copied my position. "At least this way, my clothes will be clean."

I raised my eyebrow and almost pointed out the rest of him wouldn't be. Fortunately, my brain caught up with my mouth before I said anything. Besides, a shirtless Divinius definitely improved the scenery.

The cart jerked into motion.

I clenched my eyes and curled my head to my chest to reduce the amount of dust I breathed in.

My arms were trembling from the strain by the time we rolled to a stop. As soon as the driver's boots hit the ground, I dropped, careful to keep the sound in time with his footsteps as he walked away.

Divinius tumbled into the dirt beside me. He coughed. "Why I let you continue to get me into these situations is beyond me."

I turned my head toward him. As if any of this was my fault! "This is your bloody kingdom," I hissed. "Not mine."

Something wet landed in the dirt a few feet away, and a putrid stench assaulted my nostrils.

I looked up to find a pile of green muck behind the horse, far too near my head. "Whew, that was close."

"Ugh!" Divinius held his nose and looked away, unrolling his robes and shrugging them back into place.

A tendril of disappointment snaked its way through my stomach as his muscular torso disappeared behind folds of fabric.

"Wuss. It could've been worse." I rolled onto my front and peeked out from underneath the cart. Several workers unloaded the back, but no one watched the front. "Come on." I tugged on his arm. "Time to get out of here."

We scrambled from beneath the wagon and past a pile of the black powder barrels. I glanced around. This area seemed secure, at least for the time being.

"Can you stay here for a little bit, and watch for the buyer?" I asked. Divinius nodded. "Of course."

I stared at him until I had his full attention. "Don't engage, just note who they are, and if you have to, follow them." Hopefully we'd get lucky and he'd recognize the noble or merchant and tailing them wouldn't be necessary. "I'll return before sunset. If you have to leave, be back by then, too, or I'll have no way to find you again."

He waved me away, as though I were a fly buzzing in his face. "No need to speak to me like I'm a child. Just make sure you're here in time for dinner."

Royals. I rolled my eyes and slunk out of the bustling warehouse.

Chapter 19
Divinius

I watched Gin disappear. Not that I'd ever admit it out loud, but the ease with which she slipped from shadow to shadow made me the tiniest bit jealous. Of course, when I tried to imagine her center stage, holding court like my mother, the image never quite materialized. Gin was not built for public spectacles. She would, however, make an excellent minister who could handle my less... tasteful jobs.

I'd have to make a mental note to offer her the position after I'd reversed the coup and reclaimed my throne. She'd be happy to accept. It was an honor to serve the Morganis household.

The workers hoisted the final crate from the cart and piled it beside the rest of the load. The driver climbed back into his seat, cracked his whip, and the wagon jostled out of view.

"Come on," one of the laborers said, slapping another man on the back. "*The Sunfish* got into port early, and the captain's giving the boss a hard time about not unloading it fast enough."

"Best get on with it then, if we don't want a crabby foreman when it comes time to collect our pay."

The two men wandered off.

I stared at the containers labeled 'Black Powder.' What was the point of being such a talented mage if I had to miss out on limited-time research opportunities when they presented themselves?

I glanced left and right.

No one was around.

I took a deep breath, stepped up to the closest barrel and, following the directions, unscrewed the top.

The stench of sulfur and rotten eggs clogged my nostrils. At least here, in the open air, the smell wasn't quite as cloying as it had been on board. I scooped up a decent sample in my palm, secured the lid, and ducked back into hiding.

Gin was right. The fine granules reminded me of blackened salt, similar to what the ladies at court used to exfoliate. Of course, no one would use such a stinky concoction like this on their skin.

So, what could it be for?

I squinted and rubbed the grit between my fingers.

Nothing.

Taking a deep breath and centering myself, I whispered, "Darasana."

The black powder remained inert.

Well, at least it wasn't magical in nature. I'd need the court's alchemist to determine its chemical properties, then.

If only I had a small container with which to pocket the sample. It would hardly do to put the loose grains in my pockets. My robes would stink for weeks.

I tossed the particles toward the loading dock and brushed the remnants from my palms.

As I settled back into place, another wagon clacked into view, pulled by four horses.

Their hooves clattered through the thin layer of powder. A wave of pressure assailed my ears as a fireball erupted at the steeds' feet. Smoke obscured their legs. The animals reared. With a crack, the cart tipped over. The reins snapped as they bolted.

Screams and curses sounded from all around. My jaw hit the ground as I scrambled back behind the barrels.

A non-magical way to create fire!

The possibilities were... well, endless, and few of them good. It seemed the Mage College was in for a surprise.

Workers converged like angry wasps protecting their nest. Profanity in multiple languages polluted the air. City guards brandishing swords and crossbows charged into the fray, screaming for the magic user that attacked the unfortunate laborers to show themselves. I crawled further back into the shadows amidst the sea of fae. There was no way I was going to surrender to the soldiers, not until I knew who the players were in the current political climate.

Now I definitely needed to obtain a sample of the black powder. For research purposes, of course.

Assuming it wouldn't explode as I carried it.

The substance had been stable during shipping, and when I'd rubbed it on my palm. By Helani—I could've lost both hands! I sighed as a trembling heat spread through my chest. A king without the ability to sign his name was hardly an acceptable ruler. I had to be more careful going forward.

I shook my head, forcing myself to shove my concerns aside and study the problem as one of our scholars would. Perhaps it was pressure that triggered the powder's explosion? Or some feature of the packed dirt floor?

If I was patient and sneaky enough, I might find a suitable container in the warehouse office. With limited money and a need to keep my identity quiet, going to the market for one was out of the question.

I settled back to wait for the crowd of bodies to clear.

Chapter 20
Gin

I planted myself on top of the roof of the building opposite the roughest tavern I could find in the dock district. Crossing my legs, I settled in for some surveillance.

The shadows turned long. Most of the ruffians who entered and exited were too deep into their cups or didn't move right for someone with the type of skills I was looking for.

When the sun hovered a mere three-fingers width from the horizon, the man I'd been waiting for emerged. He moved with the confidence of one who could take care of himself, but without the need to prove it to those he encountered. Sticking to the shadows, he navigated the pre-dinner crowd with the ease of one skilled at blending in.

I smiled.

Hello, assassin.

Slipping from my post, I made sure to stay at least a half block away from my target. I tailed him for a solid ten minutes before he ducked into an alley.

My heart skipped a beat at the prospect of losing the lead I'd waited all day for.

I jogged to the edge of the building and peeked around the corner, just in time to see the man glance over his shoulder and disappear behind a door hidden by a stack of refuse.

Wrinkling my nose, I shook my head. Of all the places for the assassins of this community to claim as their safehouse, why did it have to be a back alley filled with garbage?

I much preferred the upscale mansion in Tenara.

Settling myself in for another vigil, I encountered five more people with similar qualities, but lesser skill levels, as they entered or exited.

This was definitely the right place.

Moving to the back of the building, I descended the wall, dropping into a puddle of what looked like water but smelled like piss.

I frowned. Gross.

His Highness-ness owed me a new pair of boots.

I drew my high-tech crossbow, stalked down the alley and threw the door to the safehouse wide open like I owned the whole block. "Who's in charge here?"

Five startled elves—three men, two women—stared at me with blank expressions from where they sat around a table.

A male with greasy brown hair that did nothing to hide the pointed tips of his ears reached for a blade at his hip as he stood. His chair tumbled to the floor behind him. "You just made your last mistake, human," he growled.

I buried two quarrels in his torso and swung the crossbow to point at the middle of the remaining four. "Anyone want to see how many more shots I have before I need to reload?" Unexpected warmth unfurled in my stomach, bringing the ghost of a smile to my lips. This weapon was... power. Pure and simple, and I reveled in it.

The elf collapsed to the ground with a wet gurgle.

A woman with dark skin and silver hair who was halfway to standing froze and sat back down. She nodded and the other three relaxed, though they continued to clench their hands around various weapons beneath the table.

"What do you want?" she asked.

I strode forward. "Are you in charge here?"

She dipped her chin. The elven female had the same dignified bearing my mother had, before she was murdered. Something softened uncomfortably in my chest at the wisdom in her eyes. "My name is Sana," she said. "What do you want?"

I tossed a leather pouch to them. One of the younger boys grabbed it and upended its contents for all to see. The remaining dalasi we'd recovered from Astra flashed in the light. "Information."

Sana blinked twice. "You can buy that in the taverns."

I met her molten gaze with one of my own. "They don't have the info I need."

Something sparkled in her eyes as she studied me with more regard. "I see. And what sort is that?"

"Political. The situation at the palace. And," I paused, "the best ways to sneak inside."

Sana squinted at me and tilted her head. "Who are you? Your accent is Obronian."

I speared the female with a glare. "You know who I am. And until I leave, this guild is mine."

"Now wait a minute!" The younger boy who'd emptied the coins from my purse earlier stood up. "You can't just come in here and—"

"Caeda!" Sana kicked his shin.

Was that his name, or an order? I sighed to myself. I should've spent more time trying to learn Elven from Divinius. Not that I'd ever need it again, after I put him back on his throne and left to purge Obron of its warlords.

I snatched my whip with my off hand and flicked it at the youth, wrapping it around his neck. "I think you'll find I can." I jerked the leather again, releasing its hold before it could do any damage.

The lash dropped, leaving a thin red band circling his throat. Part of me felt bad about that, but the welt would heal within a day, and these people would only respond to a show of force.

"Cooperate, and I won't have to kill each and every one of you." Footsteps rasped over stone in the next room. I glanced at the door behind Sana. "Including the two in the back."

She blinked, taking a deep breath. "Very well. We will assist you... Desert Rose. We don't want a repeat of what happened in Tenara."

I nodded. I'd hoped word would precede me and smooth the way. "Good." I curled my whip and settled it at my waist. Putting one foot on the closest chair, I leaned forward, bracing my elbow against my knee. "Now, tell me everything I need to know to depose whoever's occupying the throne."

Chapter 21

Divinius

I started at the sharp rasp of wood against stone just a few feet away. I rubbed my eyes and stifled a yawn. Good thing Gin hadn't caught me napping, or I'd never hear the end of it.

An arm's length away, two men in dark cloaks stowed the black powder barrels under a tarp in a small handcart. I slid further back into the shadows.

The cart wasn't hooked up to any sort of beast of burden. Surely the two didn't intend to haul the entire load themselves?

Cramming a sixth barrel into the wagon, they secured the cover and each took a handle. With a groan, they jostled forward.

I glanced between the remaining casks and the chests of crossbows stacked next to the wall. What if someone else came for the munitions while I was following the black powder?

Not even Gin could be ridiculous enough to expect me to be in two places at once. And the owners of the weapons may take hours or days yet to claim their property. If I didn't go now, I risked losing these two.

I pulled my robes tighter against my shoulders and took a deep breath. "Bharama." The light flowed around me as the magic settled into place.

My majestic, if a little worse for wear garments disappeared, replaced by nondescript trousers and a tunic in mismatched shades of tan. My normally coiffed hair hung in tangled strands down to my collarbone. No one would identify the heir to the throne looking like this.

I smiled, betting Gin wouldn't recognize me, either.

Stepping from the shadows and glancing in each direction to confirm no one was taking interest in my doings, I followed the men.

I tailed them down the main street, scowling every time I caught my feet on the cobblestones as I focused my attention on my targets. This was ridiculous. I had no idea how to follow someone. No one had ever taught me how far to stay behind a target to avoid detection but not lose sight of my quarry.

Gin would be better at this than I was. I should've spent a few of the days we'd had on the ship learning as much as I could about this sort of thing. If only I'd had the common sense enough to realize what I'd be facing upon my return.

I jogged to catch up as the cart disappeared around a corner.

I rounded the bend just as a fist sank into my gut. I doubled over as my breath exploded from my lungs with a whoosh. My ribs burned.

Fingers tangled in my hair and yanked my head back. The cold chill of a blade pressed against my throat.

"Who are you," a deep voice rasped, "and why are you following us?"

My vision sparkled at the edges as I fought to drag air back into my chest. I opened my mouth and gasped.

The grip on my scalp tightened. "Answer me!"

The man would rue the day he was born. "Darasana," I whispered, feeling the power surge to my call. It crawled over my skin like a warm blanket on a cool fall night.

My captor's hold wavered as my mage robes reappeared. The blade still kissed my throat, however.

"How dare you assault me. I am Divinius Morganis III, Crown Prince of the Fae Realm and Holder of the Seven Orbs of Femora. You will unhand me this instant!"

The knife disappeared and my assailant released my hair. "Your Highness?" The man dropped to one knee. "Forgive me. I didn't recognize…" His voice drifted off as he swallowed. "You're supposed to be dead."

I glowered at the tawny waves parted sharply in the middle of the man's head. That was more like it. "As you can see, I am not." Brushing my hands down my robe to smooth the disheveled wrinkles, I pierced him with my gaze. "Now, you may rise and tell me where you're taking these barrels."

The man stood as he scurried several steps backward, keeping his attention on the ground. "Apologies, Your Highness. I cannot." He glanced over his shoulder at his companion standing next to the cart. "With all due respect, many mages in the College are skilled enough to impersonate you."

A muscle ticked in my jaw as I clenched my hands. I waved my ring in the worker's face. "Can they also imitate the signet of House Morganis?" It was the one object the royal family had convinced the head mage to enchant to prevent duplication—the copies would always be obviously flawed or fake. Not that my parents had made that tidbit of information known. These common laborers would not likely see it as the proof it was.

The man's Adam's Apple moved. "I don't know, Your Highness. I am no magic user."

I sighed. That sad fact was obvious enough. "That is circular logic and conveniently provides me with no way to prove myself to you."

The worker nodded, his throat bobbing with a hard swallow. "We do seem to be at an impasse, m'lord."

I reached out and skimmed the surface of his thoughts. I jerked my head back and gave a bark of laughter. "Taeral?" My mother's steward was here with these illicit weapons?

The man's jaw flapped open and closed a few times as his skin went pale. He lifted his gaze to mine. His hair was different—cropped much shorter than his usual fashion. His attire was designed to blend in on the streets. With all the changes in his physical appearance, I hadn't recognized him.

"Oh, no need to panic, old man. I won't tell my mother you assaulted me." I wrinkled my forehead. What would Gin do here? "That is, of course, if you give me news of my parents and the current situation in the castle."

Taeral studied me for several heartbeats. "Can Your Highness prove your identity by telling me the last words you spoke to me?"

I thought back. It seemed like a lifetime ago, though it hadn't even been two weeks. "You came to summon me to my birthday party. I told you to inform my mother I would be there within half an hour, once I was properly attired." Or something to that effect.

Taeral shrugged. "Close enough." He glanced over his shoulder at his companion and nodded.

The other man came forward, removed his hat and held it over his heart. "Your Highness. I regret to report your father has been assassinated in a plot orchestrated by the Mage College. Your mother holds the castle, but the magic users have the advantage. She will be hard-pressed to hold power much longer."

The ground wobbled beneath my feet. My mother lived.

I didn't know if I should laugh or cry. Warring emotions did gymnastics through my insides, making me nauseous.

Taeral gestured at the cart, a righteous glimmer in his eyes. "This fire powder will go a long way toward helping to even the odds. With you fighting with us, we can curb their progress and eliminate them!"

I chewed the inside of my cheek. Before I chose sides, I would need to get the Mage College's version of events. For them to so brazenly assassinate my father, without consulting me first, was beyond comprehension.

I tilted my chin to the wagon. "These barrels are destined for the castle, then?"

Taeral nodded. "We have some new weapons, too. Dwarven-made. Came in on the same ship as the powder." He peeked down the street, then leaned closer and dropped his voice. "We've got until sunrise to get the supplies inside. Then we launch our offensive at dawn."

I swallowed past the lump in my throat. That didn't give me much time with the mages, or to find Gin.

"Come, Your Highness." Taeral waved to me as he headed to the cart and the two men shouldered their burdens. "We'll escort you into the palace so you won't be seen and reunite you with your mother."

Assuming, of course, my dearest mother wasn't the one responsible for my banishment. I should speak with Gin and see if I could confirm this information lest I stumble into a trap. "Thank you, Taeral. I will walk with you to the castle to ensure your safety." Learning which access point the man was using was prudent, and something Gin and I would need later. "But I have a colleague in the city I have to collect before I can meet with my mother." I paused for a moment. It wouldn't do to tip my hand quite yet. "I would appreciate it if you didn't inform the queen of my presence." I winked. "I'd like to see her face for myself when I surprise her."

Taeral frowned and blinked a few times as he studied me as though trying to read beneath my words. The man probably was attempting just that, but he was far from the most intelligent in my mother's employ, so I wasn't too concerned. "Very well, Highness, if that's your wish. We would be grateful for the protection." His tone was less than sincere, but as long as he was capitulating, I didn't care.

I worried my lower lip with my teeth as I followed the men down the street. It didn't sound like Taeral bought my excuse. Apparently, I wasn't as good at improvisation as I'd hoped. Either that, or the man was smarter than I'd given him credit for. But the alternative was killing my mother's favorite servant, and while the man was annoying at times, he hadn't done anything to deserve being murdered. Although Gin might argue otherwise.

I held back a chuckle.

Taeral and his companion led me through the crowded streets to the market that abutted the castle walls. The bustle of the bazaar and the press of the crowd that scuttled through the shops before disappearing into the bowels of the city had me keeping my head low as I tried to imitate Gin's gait—the one that allowed her to blend into the background so easily. No matter how hard I tried, though, people kept glancing at my robes and giving me a wide berth.

From the stall ahead, the scent of sizzling pine boar covered with melted garlic butter tantalized my nose. My stomach growled and twisted in knots. "Excuse me, gentlemen," I said, stepping away from the cart. "I'll be but a moment."

I rejoined Taeral a few minutes later, licking the last bit of seasoning from my fingers in a decidedly peasant-like fashion.

With my stomach ache assuaged with something other than ship fare, I sighed. It was good to be home.

"Your Highness," Taeral said, "we have sufficient stores in the castle. There's no need for you to stoop to street fair food. Especially when the market is so empty, and the meat's likely been on the spit for hours."

I eyed the man. Clearly he'd never subsisted on sailor rations, backwater taverns and coconuts. Taeral would not survive the real world if the nobility should fall. As much as I loathed to admit it, I'd have to say the same for myself before I met Gin. "You have no idea what I've had to make do with for the past two weeks, Taeral. I'll eat as I please, when I please."

He nodded as the cart pulled up to an empty stall, hidden in the darkness of an alley. "Very well, Your Highness."

I sighed. Based on his tone, I could likely expect a lecture from my mother on my eating habits when we reunited.

Taeral's companion unloaded one of the barrels and rolled it into the abandoned space. He glanced both ways before lifting the heavy carpet on the floor, revealing a trap door.

"What's this?" I asked. I'd had no idea this was here, and I'd spent my entire life in the castle.

"The secret bolt-hole, in the event of an invasion, of course," Taeral said. "Known only by the King and Queen...until this week." A slice of ice flashed through my veins with the knowledge that neither of my parents had trusted me with this potentially lifesaving information. "Now that we've reclaimed the port from the mages, it's allowed us to resupply, and why everyone at court hasn't starved these last two weeks. But we have to move, because the mages could attack and retake the docks at any minute."

We'd been more fortunate in the timing of our arrival than I'd expected, it seemed. "Interesting."

"Most of the conflict takes place at the main and east gates. For some reason, the magic-users don't seem too interested in the south portion of the grounds."

"Of course not," I said. "There's not supposed to be any entrances back here, and the fighting would disrupt the market. They want to starve out the nobility, not the city. If you interfere with the populace's food source, you lose the support of the people." Something neither side could afford, if they wanted to maintain control in the end. "If the College bombs the bazaar, the people won't forget."

Just like they wouldn't forget my mother failing to protect it.

Taeral nodded. "That was your mother's assessment as well, High-ness." He unloaded another barrel, which disappeared below as quickly as the first. "Thank you for your assistance. We will leave a man stationed here to watch for when you come back with your...colleague. The way is full of twists and turns. Your mother would hate for you to become lost."

Of course she would. I rolled my shoulders. "Very well. I will return by sunrise."

Taeral bowed. "We await you."

I sent a tendril of magic toward Taeral but found the man's mind care-fully blank. As though the servant knew I could detect surface thoughts.

Fates. Was my mother telling everyone about my abilities, now?

I turned away with a sigh and glanced at the sun. Gin would expect me back at the warehouse in a little over an hour. There was plenty of time to snag some more food from the market before I headed back.

"Bharama." The nondescript tan outfit and tangled hair illusion set-tled into place over me once again. I peered over my shoulder as I ducked out of the alley. Taeral had the last two barrels off the cart.

I may well regret leaving the small man alive to inform my mother of my return. Gin would berate me for it.

If she ever found out.

Chapter 22
Gin

I examined my clothes for flecks of dust before I ducked into the warehouse where I'd parted from Divinius hours ago. I was lucky Elysia's Assassin's Guild was much more reasonable, and more easily cowed, than Tenara's.

What was the point of having a notorious reputation if it didn't pay off on occasion?

Divinius was right where I'd left him, though two-thirds of the black powder barrels and a little less than half the weapon crates were gone.

"Divinius!" If he'd fallen asleep, or let the buyers get away without any information, I'd... well, I wasn't sure what I'd do. Something that hurt, but wouldn't damage him permanently. I still needed his help, after all.

"Ah, Gin." He waved to a large leaf with two hunks of meat that smelled of garlic. "I brought you some dinner." His gaze pierced mine. "I assume you haven't eaten?"

My stomach did a joyful backflip at the sight of something other than coconuts or hard tack. But if he had the opportunity to acquire something to eat, he wasn't focused on where the weapons were going. My brows furrowed as heat spread through my chest. Once again, I had to do everything myself. "Food? Is that all you can think about at a time like this?"

He flinched, biting the lower part of his lip. "Of course not. I apologize for trying to be courteous. It won't happen again."

I tucked an errant strand of hair behind my ear with a sigh. What could I expect? He was a spoiled princeling, used to having everything handed to him. That was only partially his fault. Much of the blame lay at his parents' feet. "I'm sorry to snap at you. I didn't mean to. It's just...I have some bad news about your mother." I scooped up the leaves and took a bite of the larger piece of meat. Lukewarm juices, butter and garlic exploded in my mouth. I bit back a groan of ecstasy.

"Oh?" The wounded puppy dog eyes disappeared, replaced by a piercing gaze and raised eyebrow. "And I have some information about the buyer of the powder and crossbows."

I nodded. Perhaps I'd been too quick to assume he hadn't done his job. The sharp sting of shame spread through me, cooling the burgeoning anger. My cheeks flushed with unwelcome heat. "Come on, walk with me. It's not safe to talk here with all the soldiers."

Divinius followed me out of the warehouse. I glanced around. Where could we have some privacy?

I smiled. Sana's safehouse had that extra room in the back. We could speak there.

Less than twenty minutes later, I stepped into the Assassin's Guild headquarters, with Divinius trailing behind me. "We need the back room," I announced.

Sana and two young boys looked up from mixing powders on a table. The older woman studied Divinius before nodding. The three ducked out, leaving us alone.

"By Naraka, Gin. My father would be impressed with your commanding presence."

I winked, ignoring the warmth unfurling in my gut at the compliment, and headed into the back. A large butcher block dominated the space, along with a sink, several shelves for crockery, and a pantry.

A kitchen. I smiled. Grabbing an oversized pot, I set it in the hearth. "Divinius, if you please?"

He gave me a blank stare. "What?"

"Start the fire. I feel like stew. Your appetizer made me hungry." There must be enough here to make something passable to fill the remaining crevasses in my stomach. Maybe even some bread to go with it.

He took a deep breath and exhaled. "Gin, magic is not for such mundane tasks. It's reserved for—"

"Div, I'm starved. I'm sure you are, too. Unless you want to wait until after whatever's going to happen tonight to have a good meal, light the sand-blasted fire already."

"Fine." He pouted. "Aga." A burst of flame engulfed the pot before settling down and chewing away on the wood below it.

I reached into the cabinet and pulled out starch, a jar of something that smelled like beef stock and a few vegetables. "The Assassin's Guild says your mother staged the coup," I said as I threw the items into the cauldron. "That she orchestrated your father's assassination and your banishment. The Mage College has been trying to remove her, but so far, she's successfully foiled their attempts."

"Indeed." One corner of his lips creeped up. "My mother claims the Mage College planned the revolt and assassinated my father."

"What?" I whirled around to face him. "You spoke to her?" At least he hadn't been waiting in the warehouse all day, but to go into the castle... he may never have come back out. Stupid male.

He waved his hand in my direction as he inspected the pantry. "Of course not, don't be absurd. As if I'd enter the grounds before being certain she wasn't the mastermind behind my banishment." Divinius took a deep breath. "My mother is the one importing the munitions. The stinky black powder creates fireballs without using magic. It's quite amazing…" He stroked his chin. "I need to discuss it with the royal alchemist, but its properties could be put to use for an intriguing number of things."

"Including weapons that explode." I peeled several leaves of a ball of cabbage and, placing them on the butcher block, chopped them into thin strips with my blade.

He nodded. "Explosives. She intends to 'even the playing field,' so to speak."

That sounded like mass destruction of the city and a massacre of its civilians. At least, those who hadn't already fled the uprising. Echoes of The Purge and its devastation poured through my mind. "Who did you get this information from?" I tossed the cut greens into the mixture.

"Her steward. He came to pick up the barrels and was all too happy to tell me their plans and show me a back way into the castle."

I froze, spearing him with my stare as my heart skipped a beat. "A back way?"

Divinius met my gaze, flashed his fangs in a smile and wiggled his eyebrows. "That the mages don't know about."

"An unguarded entrance." My focus drifted off as my brain sorted through all the possibilities. "The Assassin's Guild doesn't even know about it."

"Not unguarded," he clarified. "I was assured the way through was a veritable maze, and we'd need an escort. So, my mother stationed a man to wait for us."

I blinked, ripping my attention back to the present. Either a guide, or an assassin. "Just one person?"

He shrugged. "I assume so."

I rubbed my tongue over the front of my teeth. When it came to staging coups, or anything, really, basing plans on assumptions never went well. "Let's plan for more, but if there's only one and he tries something funny, you and I can take him." I chopped up a handful of leeks.

He nodded. "Now that you know what I've been doing, what have you been up to?" He paused, as though bracing himself before glancing around the room. "Taking over another Assassin's Guild, I assume?"

I grinned. "Of course." At least, temporarily. I wasn't going to come back here, and it was hard to maintain control of something when one wasn't present. The heavy weight of disappointment settled over me. Once I used Divinius' army to free Obron, he and I would go our separate ways and probably never cross paths again. I shook my head, wiping the thought from my mind. That was a problem for future Gin. Today had enough issues without borrowing from tomorrow. "What better way to get information?"

His shoulders dropped as he exhaled. "So, you didn't kill anyone?"

"No." Not technically. The man with the two quarrels to the chest would recover, through sheer luck. He'd be out of the fight for the next several days, however.

"You know, partner, I'm not comfortable with this criminal enterprise you're building."

I barked a laugh as I threw a fistful of a spice that smelled like it would be good with soup into the pot. "You think I'm some sort of entrepreneurial evil mastermind?" Who knew? Maybe I was... being able to summon trained killers from all corners of the realm to deal with Akre and Orion might not be such a bad thing. The corner of my mouth ticked up. "Divinius, you're a genius. An army of assassins with me at its head would be incredibly effective." I punched him in the bicep. "Thanks for the idea."

He rolled his eyes and sighed. "And now I regret mentioning it." He added a pinch of something like pepper to the soup.

I winked at him. "Perhaps we'll make a few side trips on our way back to Obron."

He shook his head. "Not in my ships, we won't. However, before we get into that argument, I believe we need to develop a plan for ending this conflict and placing me on the throne."

I lifted an eyebrow. "Even though your mother still lives?" I dumped several chunks of what looked like chicken leftover from today's lunch into the mixture.

"I'm not convinced of her innocence. If she is, and this was all the Mage College's doing, then yes, she will remain the queen." Something halfway between regret and disgust flashed across his face. "And I'll be back to selecting brides from her pre-approved list."

My heart plummeted to the ground, despite the fact that it had no reason to do so. Of course, he would marry some elven beauty who would dutifully produce several glorious fae babies as future heirs. He'd go back to his castle and move on with his life as if our paths had never crossed.

Divinius sighed. "There's something I've been wanting to discuss with you."

The water was starting to steam. Good. "Oh?" I kept my voice neutral as I stirred the pot and brought a spoonful to my mouth to sample. Whatever the guild had eaten for lunch today was delicious.

"Yes. Once this whole matter is settled and the throne stable, Elysia could use someone of your skills." He paused, sweeping his arm to one side. "I'd like to offer you a position in court."

I choked. After several coughs, he slapped me on the back hard enough to dislodge the meat. I swallowed and took a deep breath. "As what, a lady in waiting? The token human?"

He burst out laughing. "A lady in waiting? Of course not! You'd most likely stab anyone you were assigned to serve."

I flinched, my head jerking back at the unexpected sting of his words. My hand itched as I fought the urge to stab *him*. "What, you don't think I could do it?" Not like I wanted to. I needed to go back to Obron and free my country. But to have the tidbit dangled in front of me and then ripped away because I was insufficient... I clenched my jaw, resisting the impulse to draw my sword by blindly grabbing something else from the pantry. I threw it into the pot without bothering to see what it was.

I would throttle his... his self-centered, chauvinist, ego-centric throat.

He shook his head, ignoring the rage roiling beneath my skin. "Oh, no... I have no doubt you could." He chuckled again, flashing that annoying dimple. "I just don't see you being meek enough to restrain yourself from slapping your charge in the back of the head when they do something you disagree with. I also think you lack the appropriate training to avoid offending the nobles."

My hand twitched, sliding toward my waist as the edges of my vision went red. I'd show him appropriate training. I was already planning how I'd kick his legs out from under him and slam his forehead against the counter as I stepped closer to him.

"No," he continued, oblivious to the thin line he was walking. "I was thinking of a position more suited to your strengths." His gaze pierced mine. "Sort of a... minister of underground connections, so-to-speak.

Someone with the skills and knowledge to work behind-the-scenes to make sure the realm runs smoothly."

I blinked twice and fixed him with a hard stare before I turned away, plans for kicking his ass suddenly vaporized by my astonishment. He hadn't really just said that. Had he?

Grabbing another stupid vegetable, I began hacking it into precise squares no thicker than my thumb as my mind reeled. When I was done, I quartered the chunks again as my vision blackened at the edges. My tendons creaked with the pressure from my clenched jaw.

"You want me as your personal assassin." I sliced the bits in half again for good measure, with enough force it left small gouges in the wood underneath.

"Gin, stop." He placed his hand over my wrist and I froze. "You've murdered that squash."

I bared my teeth at him as I slammed the knife point into the table. "Better it than you!" I glanced down, but he was right. The squares were all crooked with irregular angles and edges. I scowled at the unprofessional slices. How dare they be so uneven?

"Besides," he continued, ignoring my threat, "it sounds so trite when you put it that way. I'm certain there'd be very little assassination involved. In addition to a generous monthly stipend, I guarantee you access to all the drinking water you could want."

I opened my mouth but froze before any words came out. All I could want...

I scraped the mush that had apparently formerly been squash into the trash with a violent flick and crossed my arms. "I don't know... I want quite a bit." Especially if it tasted as good as he'd promised.

Something sparkled in Divinius' eyes. Victory. "You'll get it. After all, Elysia has more than it knows what to do with."

That much was true, as evidenced by all the green foliage along the streets and the unaccustomed frizz to my hair. I shook my head. What in sand demon's spit was I doing, letting him buy me off with water?

Clenching my jaw until I was certain I'd break at least a few teeth, I grabbed a jar of something brown that smelled like a cross between cinnamon and nutmeg and upended the entire thing into the soup. Whatever it was, I didn't care. It didn't matter.

He was so stupid. And so was I, for daring to hope he'd be anything better than everyone else in power who had ever sought to use me as a tool to achieve their own ends. Akre, Orion, and now Divinius, too.

So much for having someone who saw me as an equal, a friend. Someone who viewed me as an actual person. It shouldn't sting like it did. I'd been so incredibly foolish and naïve to think that maybe His Royalness would be different, better than the human nobility I'd spent my life with. But it turned out everyone had their own agenda, and that included making me their pawn. This was the payback I got for getting too close, for opening myself up and daring to wish for more.

I spun and blasted him with all the rage I could muster. "Why is it that all those in power are ever interested in is how they can best use me to their advantage? Why do you all only care about what I can do for you?" The back of my eyes burned, but I would not cry here. Not in front of him. I wrinkled my nose in a grimace. "Why doesn't anyone think about me, and what I want?" I kicked the pot, upending the contents over the fire and the floor. "You're no better than Akre and Orion!"

The flames sizzled and disappeared with a puff of smoke.

My vision turned watery as I blinked furiously.

Divinius grabbed my arms, holding them splayed far enough out that I couldn't rotate my wrist to gut him where he stood.

"Gin! Partner, calm down. I'm sorry. I meant the offer as a compliment. An honor." He swallowed. "I didn't think—didn't realize you'd see it that way."

I jerked out of his grip. "Yeah, well, you should've."

His gaze unfocused. The expression on his face would've been comical, if I wasn't so sand-blasted angry. I turned and ripped a bowl from its spot on a shelf and emptied the last remnants of the soup into it.

Eventually, he nodded. "I think I understand. You're upset because I asked you to do for me what Warlord Akre forced you to do for him."

"Congratulations on working that out all by yourself." I flashed my teeth before lifting a spoonful into my mouth.

The hearty tang of beef, seasoned by a dozen different spices burst over my taste buds, overwhelming the heat of my anger.

Fates... it was delicious.

Wait. My mind ground to a halt amidst the flavor explosion. "You were reading my thoughts!" My voice pitched louder, no doubt carrying to wherever the rest of the assassins were lingering in the safehouse. "Stay out of my head!" I balled up my fist and punched him in the solar plexus, throwing the entire strength of my core muscles behind the blow. Two of my knuckles popped, pain shooting up my hand.

Stupid elven mages and their too-muscular physiques.

His breath exploded out as he doubled over. I fought the urge to ram my knee into his face, but I clawed back the tiniest bit of restraint. It would be a crime if that too-perfect nose was made crooked.

Besides, I still needed him, needed his army. "You can take your offer and shove it down a sand demon's maw!"

I turned away, wiping the back of my hand across both cheeks, obliterating the telltale tear tracks lining them. Flopping into a chair at the far end of the butcher block, I shoveled another spoonful of the soup into my mouth.

Divinius wheezed, his breath a reedy whistle as his muscles fought to draw in air. After several moments of harsh silence, he stood, rubbing his abdomen. "I'm sorry. I didn't think."

"No, you did," I said, forcing the words past my too-tight throat. "You just thought of yourself." As royals always did. I swallowed another bite.

He sighed and ran a hand through his hair, dislodging the one wave that always fell so artfully across his forehead. "You're right. And I've already apologized, which is not something I'm in the habit of doing." He paused as the stillness stretched between us and became more oppressive.

I narrowed my eyes and stared into my bowl. The muscles in my jaw ached from being tense for so long.

He cleared his throat. "The appropriate response here would be for you to accept my apology."

"I don't give a sand demon's fangs about propriety."

His gaze drifted down to the soup in my hands. "That smells delicious." He stepped closer to me, apparently forgetting the danger of getting too close to me when I was angry. "Let me try it."

I glared at him and pulled my food against my chest with one hand as I freed my dagger from my belt with my other. I set it on the table, blade toward him.

He took a step back.

Warning received.

"Please? I promise I'm not going to eat it all."

I glanced at the saucer as I consulted my stomach. I was still hungry, but one mouthful wouldn't make a difference. And I had been the one who had kicked most of the batch over the floor. Plus, I still needed his army.

Sand demon spit.

Before I could open my mouth, he swept in with a spoon I hadn't noticed and scooped up a bite for himself, then danced back out of reach of my dagger.

"Mmm. Delicious!" He winked at me, that stupid dimple making an appearance in his right cheek. "You should make angry food more often."

I glowered at him but couldn't keep the frown plastered on my face. I chuckled at the wicked glint in his eyes. "Anger me again, and it'll be your guts that go into the soup."

The corner of his mouth turned up. I really hated that dimple. "You know," he said, "threatening the crown prince could be considered treason."

I snorted as more of my rage drained away at the sparkle in his eyes. "I'll show you treason when we toss your mother off your throne." I met his gaze and froze, his deep blue eyes pulling me in. My breath caught as I fought to swallow. Warmth unfurled low in my gut.

Divinius licked his lips, his eyes molten.

Clearing my throat, I tucked a loose strand of hair behind my ear and turned away before the flush racing to my face betrayed me. "I still have no idea how Orion plays into this." I glanced over my shoulder as I picked the kettle up from where it lay next to the hearth. "But he's got to. There's no way both of us were banished at the same time to the same place otherwise."

Divinius tilted his head and stared at me. "You know, I hadn't thought about that."

Of course not. He really needed to start looking at the world beyond the tip of his nose.

"Now that I think about it," he continued, "it would be a lot easier to perform the transportation spell on two people simultaneously than to cast it separately twice."

I scrunched my forehead. "Can that be done? With us being in two different countries?"

He shrugged. "Sure. All it would take would be for someone to plant a marker on both of us beforehand."

"A marker?"

"Yes. An uncommon substance, usually metal, that the magic can be directed toward. Violet pyrailite is often used."

I'd never heard of such a thing. "What? You're making that up."

He shook his head, his expression intense. "No, I'm not. It's a rare compound that has to be manufactured by the alchemists. Since it doesn't exist in nature, and is expensive and difficult to make, the mage would be almost guaranteed no one else would be marked with it at the time they were casting."

I opened my mouth but froze. I'd had bluish-purple dust of un-explained origins on my shirt after Roland had patted my arm in the Golden Gosling.

I growled deep in my throat.

Absent-mindedly, I brushed my hand down my sleeve, as though I could remove the pyrailite and reverse the effects of the spell.

Divinius rested his hand on mine, stilling it. "I didn't see it, either. And of the two of us, I should have. There was a woman in a green dress who knocked against me, right before the magic took hold. I'd bet my crown she did it." He studied his clothing. "The color of the powder probably blended so seamlessly with my attire, I didn't notice." He spun away, robes flaring. "I'm so stupid!"

"You may be many things, but stupid is hardly one of them." Well, most of the time.

"Of course, I didn't mean it literally." He glanced around the kitchen. "It looks like a tornado came through here.

I shrugged. In a manner of speaking, one had.

"Are you finished?" he asked. "I'd like to go speak with the Mage College tonight, before we confront my mother."

I blinked. "Are you sure? It sounds like they played no small part in your banishment. Well, one of their members did. Are you certain you want to put yourself in that kind of danger?" Being surrounded by an entire building full of mages who were as powerful as the warlords was not something I looked forward to. Especially when at least one of them wanted my only ally dead, and likely me by extension.

Divinius lifted his chin, threw his shoulders back and stuck out his chest. "There will be no risk. I'll ensure no one uses magic to attack us. You'll make sure no one gets close enough to touch us physically."

My eyebrows creeped up my forehead. "Oh, I will, will I?"

He graced me with that infuriating, dazzling smile of his. "Of course, if you want me back on the throne so I can help you with your little warlord problem."

I sputtered. "Little?"

He laughed, and the sound unfurled the last bit of coiled tension in my gut. I really did like his laugh.

Grabbing my arm, he tugged me toward the door as the mirth drained from his eyes. "Come on. No one wants to visit the Mage College after nightfall."

Chapter 23
Divinius

I refused to let my steps falter as we approached the building that housed Elysia's Mage College. As a child, the tall brick structure had reminded me of a library. As an adult, however, the narrow windows crowned with battlements and a single turret in the southwest corner—closest to the castle—took on a more sinister feel.

Beside me, Gin stalked through the streets, her feet moving soundlessly over the cobbles. She was the embodiment of deadly grace. Her eyes darted in every direction, likely evaluating threat levels from objects and people I barely noticed. One hand gripped the handle of her sword, while the other rested within easy reach of her whip. At least she would make sure no one caught us by surprise.

I led her up the marble stairs to the front. The polished white stone with gray and gold veins reflected the sunlight and made the air around the building sparkle.

Of course, that was the effect the mages had been aiming for all along.

We stopped in front of a large entry with no external handle, just a metal plate at shoulder's height. I rested the palm against the device and grabbed Gin's upper arm.

"Hey! Let go of me!" She tried to shake me off.

I tightened my grip. "If you want to be able to enter, we have to be touching when I open the doors."

She quit struggling. "Fine. But warn me next time, or you might lose a hand."

I glanced at her. Every muscle in her body was tense, like she was marching into battle with one of her warlords.

My heart skipped a beat. To her, whose only experience with mages were the warlords, that was probably exactly what this felt like. I was an idiot to miss that connection. By Helani.

"Don't worry, I've got you," I said, dropping my voice in what I hoped was a soothing tone. "It'll be fine."

"There's no way you can promise that," she muttered.

I ignored her, but only because she was right and I didn't have any retort. Turning my focus back to the plate bolted to the wall, I took a deep breath and whispered, "Aga."

A poof of flame encircled my hand before being absorbed by the metal.

A low clank sounded from behind the doors and they rolled open.

Gin gasped.

"Welcome to the Mage College." I stepped inside, tugging her along with me.

Out of the sunlight, the white floors weren't quite so blinding. It took several heartbeats and blinks for my eyes to adjust to the dim illumination.

The soothing scent of ozone magic residue tickled my nose, and I smiled in spite of myself. Long rows of columns lined the entryway leading to the central corridor. Larger versions of the light crystals Gin had been so enamored of on the ship hung from sconces high above, casting a gentle glow throughout the room.

I released her arm once we crossed the warded barrier and glanced around. How rude of the mages to not have an attendant to greet us. In fact, now that I thought about it, I'd never seen the great hall so dead. Our footsteps echoed off the walls in an eerie mockery of the controlled chaos that usually ruled these halls.

A heavy weight pressed on my shoulders and chest. This didn't bode well. "Keep close," I whispered.

She peeked at me from beneath raised eyebrows before I returned to scanning our surroundings. "Is something wrong?"

I nodded. "It's too silent. This place should be bustling with activity. At the bare minimum, they should've dispatched a page to greet us the instant my magic touched the door."

She cast me a wry glance. "Welcome to war."

Indeed. Well, if the mages were so rude as to ignore their crown prince's arrival, I'd be just as impertinent and go find them rather than waiting here politely.

"They're most likely in the conference chamber. Come on. It's up ahead on the left."

We approached the doors to the central meeting room with their elaborately carved twin griffons facing each other. A six-pointed star representing the schools of magic was painted between them. I'd never taken the time to admire the artistry of the carvings before, but the detail in the griffins' manes and eyes was breathtaking. They seemed to move as we did. Pausing just outside to glance at Gin, I asked, "Ready?"

She drew a sword with her right hand and the whip with her left and nodded. "For anything."

"Khula!" I pushed my hands to each side as though parting water.

The doors flung open with a dramatic crash.

The entire Mage Council turned, all twelve startled faces staring at us. At me. The imposing marble table occupied most of the room. It was white, of course, to match the rest of the college's motif, with veins of turquoise, gold and maroon interspersed throughout. Several chairs screeched against the floor as their owners lurched to their feet.

I bit back a satisfied grin. It served them right for ignoring me. Studying each man and woman, I searched for any flicker of anger or other emotion that could tip their hand before they schooled their expressions.

There. A flash of fear.

I bared my fangs as a tidal wave of energy gathered in my gut. This must be what Gin felt every time she imagined getting her revenge on the warlords. Suddenly, I could understand the appeal. "Not expecting to see me, Abram?"

The head of the council bowed. "Of course not, Your Highness. You've been missing for two weeks."

The words were true, but the intent... I sent a cursory tendril of magic toward the other's mind. "The hospitality of the College has lessened since I was last here."

My power slammed into an adamantine wall. I cursed silently. But of course the man would never be so careless as to leave his thoughts unprotected.

Speaking of which... I stretched my own mental protection over Gin, as well.

"Ah, yes." Abram's gaze flicked to her before focusing back on me. "The queen's men damaged the sensor at the front door in their latest assault. We haven't had the chance to fix it."

I nodded, not certain if I believed him or not, but it didn't matter. "I see. I would be happy to assist with that, should you lack the resources yourselves."

Abram rested his hand over his heart. "Your Highness is gracious, but that will not be necessary. The repair was simply not a priority."

I held back a snort. Now I didn't believe anything he'd said. "Of course. Abram, I would speak to you alone." I let my eyes scan across the other council members. "May we have the room, please." I kept my tone firm so there would be no doubt it wasn't a request, despite my wording.

The others paused, their focus shifting to Abram. At his nod, the wooden chair legs scraped against the floor as the other eleven associates stood and filed out the door at the opposite end of the chamber.

I caught Gin's gaze and nodded in their direction. She trailed behind the departing mages, splitting her attention between those she followed and Abram.

The head mage peeked at her from the corner of his eye while doing his best to not act like he was. "Who's your friend, Your Highness?" he asked, when they were out of hearing range.

The unmistakable tingle of power flitted across my awareness as Abram sent a cursory filament toward Gin, likely seeking to pull any host of information from her surface thoughts. I redoubled my efforts, my magic fanning out over the adamantine walls of the other's shields, probing and searching for a crack.

Abram blinked and met my gaze.

Half of my mouth curled up in a vicious grin. That's right, old man. Watch yourself.

"She's no one for you to be concerned with," I said, surprised at the wave of protectiveness that washed over me at the thought of him rifling through Gin's mind. It wasn't like I hadn't done that exact thing a mere hour ago, but unlike him, I had her best interests at heart. Pulling out one of the council's chairs, I plopped into it with what I hoped was casual grace. Nodding to the chair on the opposite side, I continued, "Have a seat."

Abram met my gaze for several heartbeats before he, too, sat. Not in the indicated space, but in the one he'd occupied when we'd first arrived—at the head of the table.

I shrugged to myself. The small act of rebellion was inconsequential beyond confirming the man was not my ally. My ego wasn't so fragile that it couldn't handle one passive-aggressive gesture.

Gin prowled back from the far edge of the room, stationing herself opposite me, where she could face us both at once. She lounged against the marble slab that served as the table top with the grace of one of the lions that roamed the highest peaks of Elysia. Putting one foot on a chair, she rested her sword across her knee in a not-so-subtle warning I couldn't help but appreciate for more than just the tactical maneuver it was.

She was glorious—deadly and beautiful, just like the desert she hailed from.

In fact, she looked very relaxed for a professional killing machine, and she was doing everything she could to keep Abram on edge.

I bit back a smile that would have had my fangs on display. Good girl.

Abram glanced at her and focused back on me.

Gin winked at me and speared Abram with the full power of her glare.

Perhaps I'd underestimated Gin's knowledge and skill when it came to the finer points of political maneuverings.

I turned my attention back to the other mage. "Why did you banish me? On my birthday, nonetheless." I waved my hand, cutting off the other's protests. "Don't bother denying it, we both know you had a hand in it, or it never would've happened. I'm giving you one chance to explain before I go to my mother and help her expel the mages from Elysia."

Abram blinked a few times and swallowed, his gaze flicking between me and Gin. "Your Highness, I know what it must look like to you, but you need to understand. We learned of a plot to assassinate the royal family and had little time. The only way we could think of to save you, our staunchest ally, was to remove you from the scene."

I crossed my arms at the obvious lie. "I see. My father met with representatives from the College just a few hours earlier. You couldn't have warned him and let his ministers deal with the situation?"

Abram shook his head. "As I stated before, Highness, there was no time."

Gin shifted, the rasp of her chair against the floor drew both mine and Abram's attention.

"Right. And about my colleague over there," I nodded to Gin, "who was transported to the same location I was, at the same time?"

Abram turned to Gin and studied her with more interest.

A prickle of unease worked its way up my spine. There was something about the way he was looking at her...

If I hadn't known her so well, I'd have missed the subtle tension that crept into her posture at the other mage's scrutiny. It was in the rigid corners of her lips and the white knuckles of her sword hand. Abram had best be careful or he'd find himself relieved of his head, courtesy of her blade.

I leaned forward, letting the cold of the marble ground me as it sank into my skin. "There are only a handful of mages in the college with the knowledge and ability to pull off a simultaneous teleportation," I said, calling Abram's attention back to me before Gin did something I'd regret. "I want to know who did it, and I want to know why." I paused. "The real reason." I redoubled my attempts to find a weakness in Abram's shield and felt a tickle as the head mage's magic encircled my own mental block.

My heart thumped against my ribs as my stomach hardened. Abram was talented. One didn't become head of the college without being the best. If I didn't get the answers we needed soon, his abilities would overwhelm my own shields, then both Gin and I would be easy pickings.

I glanced at the assassin. How strange this must look to her, with no way to identify the power or know the psychic battle we fought.

Judging by the scowl on her face, she was becoming more than a little impatient.

"Who, and why?" I punctuated the words with two solid thumps against Abram's shields. A drop of sweat rolled down the other male's temple.

"I don't know, Prince," Abram ground out between clenched teeth.

"You lie!" Gin exploded in a flurry of motion that ended with her sword at his neck.

Both he and I blinked in surprise. I wasn't fool enough to waste the opportunity, though. Taking advantage of his distraction, I raked my power down his walls like giant talons. They left deep gouges.

Abram swallowed, the lump in his throat scraping against Gin's blade. "Call off your human dog, Highness," he said, flicking his attention to me.

I barked out a laugh. "You think I can control Desert Rose?"

Abram paled. "Desert Rose is a myth, a bedtime story to scare naughty children into behaving."

I almost missed the flicker of satisfaction that brightened the bedtime story's eyes. It was the same look I'd seen on her face when I first admitted I'd heard of her, back in the jungles outside Tenara.

"You wish," Gin said, pressing the blade hard enough to draw a drop of blood. "Now, answer his question. Who performed the spell, and for what reason?"

Something shifted in Abram's mental shield, and I caught a quick glimpse before the adamantine repaired itself.

The floor disappeared from beneath my feet as I reeled. My jaw dropped. For once, I was grateful to be sitting down, otherwise my tumble would've been embarrassing. I swallowed past the tightness in my throat.

"You did," I choked out. "You did all of this. Why? To kill my father? To give my mother the throne in her own right?"

When Abram didn't respond, Gin glanced at me. "There are two reasons anyone does anything. Love—"

I shuddered at the mental image of Abram with my mother. That would never happen, assuming Lillia Cordelia Morganis had any choice in the matter.

"—or money," Gin finished. She eyed me, her dark eyes full of molten heat. "Orion Byre has a lot of coin."

A sheen of perspiration broke out on Abram's forehead as he turned an intriguing shade of green.

I sat back and crossed my arms. "Is that why, Abram? An Obronian warlord offered you a small fortune for you to commit treason and kill your king?"

"No!" He went to lunge forward but froze at the cold prick of steel as Gin's sword cut just a little deeper. "You have it all wrong. The queen! She was plotting against your father, and you were to be her scapegoat. We only wanted to protect you, and the only way we could do that was to make sure you weren't present when it happened."

Heat rushed through my veins and flooded my face. My nails dug crescent-shaped indents into my palms. "I would have had an alibi—I was in front of the entire court! Hundreds of witnesses who could have attested to my innocence. Instead, you made me disappear in the middle of the whole thing, when I could have prevented, if not my father's death, that of so many others..." I swallowed. By Naraka. I hadn't stopped to wonder what had happened to the innocent bystanders once I was no longer there to hold off whatever the mage had been conjuring.

I took a deep breath. "Pharo!"

A breeze gusted from behind me, blowing loose strands in front of my face. My robes billowed dramatically. A blue ring of solid energy latched itself around Abram's throat and lifted him clear of Gin's blade. The man stood on tip-toe to avoid being strangled, both hands reflexively latching at his neck as he struggled to free himself.

The cold chill of his terror washed over me like I'd jumped into a glacial pool.

Gin scrambled a few steps back, her eyes wide as she pointed her sword at him.

"Relax, Abram." I blinked, surprised to have gotten past the other mage's defenses so suddenly. "You won't suffocate. I just can't have you talking right now." I couldn't risk letting him speak, giving him the ability to call up any active spells.

Warlord Byre showed us proof of the queen's plans. Abram's thoughts echoed through my mind as if he was speaking them out loud. *How it coordinated with your birthday and reaching the age of maturity. The evidence was irrefutable.*

"You could have come to me. I would have brought the information to my father."

The king was not known for valuing input from the Mage College, nor for moving against your mother.

I shook my head, thinking back to the grimoire my father had gifted me the morning of my birthday. "He would have listened to me," I said, ignoring the soreness in my neck and lungs at the loss of the relationship that had only just begun to bloom between us. "My father was coming around."

I apologize for the missteps, Your Highness. But the fact remains that your mother, the queen, did attempt a coup, and your father is dead as a result. You could not have stopped it.

"You didn't even give me a chance to try!" I slashed my hand through the air in a parody of Gin slicing someone's throat. "You are not the ruling family. That decision was not yours to make."

I caught Gin's eye.

She flicked her attention to Abram and shrugged. "Ready for me to gut him yet?" She waved the tip of her blade at his torso. "I can make it quick or slow. Your call."

The seriousness in her voice locked all my muscles. The offer was genuine.

I cleared my throat. "That won't be necessary. He deserves a fair trial before any punishment is meted out."

"A fair trial?" She gestured around the room with her whip. "What do you propose we do with him while we're dealing with your mother and arranging said hearing? Let him go? Throw him in the dungeons your mother controls?"

"Simple. We'll lock him in some antimonite shackles and have the Assassin's Guild watch him." One corner of my mouth twitched, curling into a smile. I was rather proud of that solution.

The final fissure in Abram's mental shields repaired itself and sealed. There would be no more silent communication.

Gin's lips pressed into a thin line. "Sana is an assassin, not a babysitter."

True, but assassins were hired to perform jobs. This one would just be a little lower-risk than usual and hopefully would result in fewer bodies. "I think it's perfect. The shackles will render him susceptible to suggestion and unable to cast magic. He will sit wherever we tell him to and not move until instructed to do otherwise, unless someone comes along and removes the manacles. Which is, of course, why we can't leave him here with the other mages, who may be sympathetic to him."

She leaned toward me and hissed, "Don't you think it'll cause a little bit of a stir if we go parading the head magus through the streets?"

I winked. "Don't worry, I've got it." I turned my attention to Abram. "Now, be a good mage and point me to where the College keeps its collection of antimonite, please?"

Abram flared his nostrils.

Oh, for the love of Helani... "You're starting to turn purple, man. You'll give yourself an apoplectic fit. Once the shackles are on, I'll remove the ring and you'll be able to breathe again."

Abram glared at me and pressed his lips into a thin line.

I sighed. It looked like we'd be doing this the hard way, then. "The alternative, of course, is for me to drag you around the entire building by your throat until we find what we're looking for. Imagine the spectacle that'll make."

With a dramatic sigh that would've outdone Queen Lillia, Gin rolled her eyes and stormed to the door the other council members had exited through. Throwing it wide, she said, "You—take us to where you store the antimonite." Footsteps shuffled just out of my line of sight. "Now!"

She stepped partially out the door and glanced over her shoulder at me. "Come on. Bring him and let's go!"

I couldn't help but admire her efficiency. She gave commands with the same haughtiness as any royal.

Gin turned back to the hallway. "You are responsible for your boss' welfare. Do as we ask, he survives. Try something foolish, he dies, and you'll be next."

I shook my head. She was a little too direct and brash at times. Threatening the Mage College would get a lesser person killed. But she did know how to get things done.

Dragging Abram behind me, we followed the pair of apprentices who were stationed outside the council hall as they led us down two floors into the underground levels. I tried not to gawk like a child, even though I'd never known the building had sublevels. Following the lead of the two Gin had coerced into helping us, I grabbed a light crystal from the small pile at the top of the stairs and trailed after them into the gloom.

The air down here smelled musty, without the characteristic ozone scent that accompanied magic. The weight of the atmosphere and the stone pressed in on me, and I had to fight to keep my shoulders from sagging. The sound of our footsteps echoed down the stairwell.

I glanced at Gin, who marched just in front of me. Her back was ramrod straight, and she still had her sword pointed at the two who led the way. Her head swiveled from side to side, as if committing every detail of our descent to memory.

She was likely assessing the area for threats and traps, like any good assassin or bodyguard would, even though there was very little to see outside the ring of light from the crystal.

Warmth tingled in my limbs. I was lucky she was here, as I wouldn't know a threat if it marched up and hit me in the head. It was also nice to have her unquestioning support. Doing this by myself would've been much harder.

We made a good team.

The pressure eased as we reached the end of the stairs. I held my crystal aloft, illuminating a hallway with a door off to the left. This area was not something intended for outsiders to see. The floor was unpolished and dusty enough it likely hadn't been cleaned in months. The masonry, while still high quality, was a boring gray and still rough rather than polished to the fine sheen like the floors above.

The two mages stopped short at the entrance to the room, their noses wrinkled in disgust. Their faces were pale.

My heart thumped against my chest as the hair on the back of my neck prickled.

"You go first." Gin waved her sword at the two.

Both magic users peered over my shoulder at Abram. I stepped into their line of sight and scowled. "By the order of the House of Morganis, you will proceed. Or you will join Master Abram and be charged with treason."

The two glanced at each other, steeled their spines, and entered.

As soon as I moved into the room, rows of white metal that reminded me of bleached bones met my gaze. Their presence made my stomach roll with nausea and my skin crawl. I braced myself. I was a mage and the crown prince of the realm! I was no coward to flee from an inanimate mineral.

Even if that ore had the power to devour my magic.

Gin marched past me to examine the shelves. She appeared unfazed.

"Here." She tossed me a pair of handcuffs.

I leaped out of the way as the manacles flew by, landing with a crash on the floor behind me. "Hey! Watch it!"

"What?" She studied me, her forehead knitted as she pursed her lips.

"That eats magic!" I said. "I'm not touching it."

"Oh?" She glanced between me and where the cuffs had landed. She raised an eyebrow and gave me a look that couldn't have asked, "Why didn't you say so?" any more clearly than if she'd spoken aloud. After a few heartbeats, she shrugged. "Okay. Sorry, I didn't realize. I'll do it, just give me a moment." She turned back and examined the shelves. "If this stuff absorbs magic, could it be used on the warlords?"

I blinked. "I don't see why not. I've never thought about it, but assuming they access arcane power the same way we do..."

She whirled to face me with a wide grin and sparkling eyes. "This could change everything for Obron."

I cleared my throat, rolling my shoulders as if I could dislodge the millions of pins and needles that were marching their way up my body just from being in such close proximity to the toxic metal. "I understand. However, this room is exceedingly uncomfortable. Can we please do what we came to do and leave?"

She studied the shelves and grabbed two sets of manacles and something that looked like it clamped around the neck. She had them stuffed halfway into her backpack before she froze and glanced up at the two magic users, as though she'd forgotten about them. "I'm sorry. How much do you want for these?"

They stared back at her with round eyes and slack jaws.

When it became obvious they weren't going to answer, she sighed and turned to me. "What's a reasonable price?"

For three items made from the rarest and most dangerous metal in any of the realms? "More than you can afford. Don't worry," I focused on the mages. "The house of Morganis will cover the expense. Please send the bill to my secretary." I blinked. Technically, I may no longer have a secretary. "Best wait a few days before you do so, however."

Gin nodded her thanks and secured the objects in her backpack.

I almost felt bad for the warlords. But then I remembered her tattoo and all the stuff she hadn't admitted to me and, yeah... no. Screw the warlords and the horses they rode in on.

With her lips pressed into a thin line, Gin stalked to the manacles she'd thrown at me and clamped them to Abram's wrists.

The tension drained from the male as his muscles relaxed and became pliant. His face went slack and his mental shields crumbled, revealing a blank slate.

I released the magic holding the ring of power around his neck and Abram gasped. Okay, maybe it had been just a tad bit too tight, but no one could blame me. The man had contributed to my father's assassination and a plot to overthrow the crown. To overthrow me.

After a few minutes, Abram's face lost its alarming purple color.

"Let's go," I said. "Lead the way upstairs and out of here. Don't get too far ahead of us."

The head magus turned and, like a mindless puppet, marched out of the room.

Gin and I followed. I didn't look back to see what the two lesser acolytes were doing. If they were smart, they'd stay below until the three of us left. Then, honestly, I didn't care what they did.

I couldn't believe I'd arrested the head of the Mage College. Of the council. Even if the arrest was lawful—which it was!—the other magic users wouldn't look kindly upon the consequences, or Abram's humiliation. I had no choice but to march him through the building to extradite him for trial. Mages only enjoyed public spectacles of their own making.

As we followed Abram through the halls with tall ceilings and polished surfaces, my chest tightened, spots dancing in my vision. My lungs burned and no matter how many deep breaths I took, the sensation refused to relent.

"What's wrong, partner?" Gin's concerned voice seemed to echo from miles away. "Are the other mages attacking you or something?"

I shook my head. "No. I think my body just realized I've gone and made an enemy of the entire Mage College." And there may be no way to repair the damage.

Chapter 24

Gin

An hour later, I crouched and leaned over the side of the roof as I surveyed the merchant's stall in the alley. Its shingles were rickety, the planks warped by long exposure to the weather and neglect. Even the shadows of twilight couldn't hide the disrepair. Divinius claimed it was the secret way inside the castle. With Abram ensconced in Sana's safehouse, it was time to have a little chat with the queen. Something I was looking forward to even less than being swarmed by sand spiders.

A dry warm breeze danced through the streets, picking up bits of dirt and debris and throwing them against my exposed skin.

I glanced at Divinius. "Are you sure it's safe to just march into the castle? What if your mother—"

He shook his head. "You heard Abram. They were manipulated by Orion. My mother is innocent."

Something nibbled at the back of my mind, raising the fine hairs on my arms. He was a little too certain in that assertion for my liking, but then the queen did deserve the chance to explain. Hopefully. "I still don't like it. Entering through a tunnel is a good way to find yourself in an ambush." I studied the entrance again. Even with the lengthening shadows, no one came and went. If it was a trap, they'd been in place for a while now. At least their attention may be wavering, and we could catch them by surprise. And if my gut was wrong, and everything Divinius said was true, it would be nice to dine in the castle tonight instead of scrounging for food in the market.

"We're expected. If I don't show up, she'll suspect something." He speared me with his gaze. "And you do not want to upset my mother."

I raised my eyebrow. The same could be said for most royals. "Has a temper, does she?"

He nodded. "And she doesn't abide disrespect. Your best bet is to be silent. But if she does speak to you, make sure you answer politely, keep your eyes down, and address her as 'Your Majesty'."

I jerked my head back and furrowed my brow as the muscles in my neck and jaw clenched. "I'm not stupid, you know. It's not like your mother will be the first queen I've ever met."

He flinched at my tone. "I'm sorry." He studied me as though looking for evidence of my claim. "I assumed—"

"Yeah, well," I cut him off, "you were wrong." Typical oblivious prince. I turned my back to him and examined the booth again. I'd probably overreacted. There was no reason to snap at him for thinking something when I'd never given him any cause to assume otherwise. But I couldn't bring myself to apologize.

No one had entered or left the decrepit stall below in the last hour. It appeared the palace had managed to swallow all the weapons and black powder from the warehouse. Who knew what other surprises awaited in its bowels?

I pushed up from my crouch and dusted my palms on my pants. "Well, if we're going to be ambushed, we may as well get it over with, right?"

Divinius blinked and studied me as if I was a wild animal who might bite.

I sighed. "I'm sorry I snapped at you. I'm tired and hungry. I'll try not to do it again." I dangled my legs over the side of the roof, wrapped them around the pipe we'd used to shimmy up and slid to the ground.

Moments later, Divinius joined me. Slapping his hands clean on his robes, he said, "You know, two weeks ago, if you'd have told me I'd be running through the underbelly of my city with a world-renowned assassin, climbing roofs and plotting to invade my own castle, I'd have called you crazy."

I raised one corner of my mouth in a smile. The fact that he considered the market to be the seedy side of town was rather adorable. "Same here, prince."

"Nevertheless, I'm glad to have met you," he continued.

I lifted my eyebrow at the very uncharacteristic statement but held my tongue.

"And whatever happens, know that you have my gratitude."

I wrapped my hand around my sword. In the close confines of the hidden entrance, the whip would be more of a hindrance than a help. "Likewise." And not just because of the promised army. I glanced at him. "I think you'd better go first, in this case, as you're expected and I'm not."

With a nod and an eager sparkle in his eye, he threw me a half-smile that had that darn dimple making yet another appearance. "Agreed." Okay, I didn't always hate his dimples.

He led me to the trapdoor in the bottom of the stall. I rubbed my pilfered light crystal and dropped it into the hole. It landed four or five paces below us, rolling down an embankment.

"Sand demon's spit." If I lost that magic rock, I was going to be very put out.

Divinius leaped into the opening. "Don't worry. The path is steep, but it can't last forever. We'll get your toy back. And if we don't, I'm sure my mother will be happy to replace it." He moved out of view. "Aga!"

The red flicker of Divinius' flames lit the corridor and dimmed as he walked further away.

I climbed into the hole, careful to arrange the rug and door above me so when they shut, the trapdoor would remain hidden. The wood overhead settled into place with a muffled clank. The fresh flow of air cut off, leaving only the dank smell of the underground, with a faint current of mold and that ugly sulfur stench from the black powder. They'd definitely come this way.

I blinked, gathering myself. All I could see was a dim light around a curve ahead. "Hey, wait!" I jogged to catch up to him before I was left in pitch blackness.

Divinius was right. My crystal rested in the middle of the trail some one hundred paces down the way. I picked it up, brushed the dirt off on my trousers, and slid it into my pocket.

I glanced at my pants. Normally an attractive and flattering black, after the adventures I'd had, they were more dusty brown-gray. Not the type of clothing fit for meeting an elven queen. I studied Divinius' robes. If anything, his were in even worse condition, so at least there was that. His mother would likely focus on him and ignore me, anyway. Sometimes there were benefits to being just a token human.

The tunnel surrounding us was earth with occasional roots protruding. But it had been well-used of late. The dirt was packed so hard no footprints or tracks stood out. No cobwebs brushed against our skin in passing. Thank goodness for small favors. But where was our escort?

After several minutes, the passage opened into a cavern. A cool breeze came from somewhere on my right.

A man dressed in dark burgundy stepped from the darkness and bowed to Divinius. "Your Highness. Welcome. Please, follow me. Her majesty awaits."

"Coram?" Divinius frowned. "Why are you wearing scarlet uniforms? Our colors are purple and silver."

The guard scowled, glancing at his tunic. "These are Her Majesty's new colors. The tailors are working to re-attire the staff." He tilted his chin forward and pressed his shoulders back. "I was honored to be one of the first to receive the updated design."

"I see." Divinius rubbed his jaw as the corners of his lips hardened. "Lead the way."

We followed Coram past numerous turns and twists, our footsteps echoing in the empty passages. The third time we passed one intersection, I snorted to myself. The man was trying to confuse us, to keep us off balance. But my sense of direction was not so easily led astray, and he was only succeeding in allowing me to map out more of the underground.

I was about to say something when the tunnel opened into a square room with black stone walls and floors. The ceiling above sparkled with thousands of pinpoint white and yellow lights. A rectangular fountain sat in the middle of the room, dry as the deserts of Obron.

My jaw dropped. "This is stunning!" I could stay here quite happily for the next several hours, admiring the view.

"Erm, yes," Coram said, his glance acknowledging my existence for the first time. "The queen believes it was once a library for the original monarchs." He tilted his head up. "The crystals in the ceiling have remained activated as far back as the records can trace. The magic involved is impressive."

Divinius stopped, causing me to barrel into him. He glanced up. "Magic you say?"

The man bowed. "Indeed, Highness. Perhaps, when this unpleasant series of events is behind us, Her Majesty will consent to your study of this space."

I bit back a smirk. The room made a wonderful carrot to dangle in front of Divinius to ensure his compliance. The queen definitely knew her son.

"Come on. We can come back later." I nudged him. After a few heaves, he allowed himself to be ushered away.

"Do you think you can get us back there?" he mumbled to me as we continued down the hall.

I rolled my eyes. "You doubt me?"

He chuckled. "I should know better than to do that by now. But he's leading us in a rather circuitous route, and I wanted to be certain."

I blinked, surprise flooding through my veins before I remembered how observant Divinius was. Perhaps if I underestimated him because he was the crown prince, everyone else would, too. And that would only be to our advantage.

Coram glanced over his shoulder with a frown.

"Sorry, my good man," Divinius said, waving his hand in a broad gesture. "Please, lead on."

The guard led us through passageways and several chambers used for food storage. I didn't spot the kegs of black powder or the weapon crates, however. It looked like they were smart enough to keep us away from those.

In contrast to the red, orange and tan of the castles in Obron, the floors and walls of this palace were polished marble in shades of white, gray and rose. I winced in empathy with whomever was responsible for buffing all the stone. Silk tapestries and rugs adorned the various hallways and rooms, breaking up what would otherwise be a cold monotony.

The luxurious floor coverings squished beneath my feet, and I avoided looking down to confirm if I was leaving dusty footprints behind. Several alcoves dotted the hall, each displaying a no-doubt priceless piece of art or family history. The impossibly tall ceilings with delicate arches supported chandelier after chandelier. The lavishness was disgusting when there were so many on the streets of Obron who were starving to death.

I fought the urge to sink into myself. I didn't belong here, and it had been years since castles had represented anything other than the opulence and cruelty of the warlords. I rolled my shoulders, but the movement did little to dislodge what felt like dozens of spiders crawling around beneath my clothes.

Divinius glanced over my shoulder.

I shook my head and schooled my expression. Heat rushed to my cheeks. He'd probably expected me to gawk like a child, or like I'd never seen a castle before. And, like a fool, I'd been doing just that. I should've been better prepared for the elven royalty to overdo the grandeur.

We paused in front of a large double door, with more of the burgundy-attired guards stationed on either side. A curly-cue floral design had been carved into the wood at the edges of each door.

Coram peered at Divinius, his gaze skating over me as though I didn't exist. "Ready, Your Highness?"

Divinius nodded, lifted his chin and pushed his shoulders back. He cleared his throat. "Gin, you'll need to leave your weapons here."

I blinked. "What? If that was going to be a problem, you should've said something sooner." Then I would have left them somewhere I'd be certain they'd remain when we returned. I squinted at Coram and the sentries, doing my best to intimidate them into submission.

Divinius stared at me, his gaze penetrating my soul. "Please. The guards will make sure nothing happens to them." He turned to the sentry on his right.

The male nodded and gave a slight bow. "Yes, Your Highness."

Something in his expression shattered my heart. He truly believed his mother was innocent, and there would be no need for swords or any other protection inside. I hoped he was correct, because if not...

I sighed. "Very well." I'd never needed weapons to kill someone. Even a queen.

With exaggerated and precise movements, I unlatched my scabbard and held it out, sword and whip attached. There was no way I was giving up the dagger in my boot, though. Did Divinius even know it existed? I frowned as I thought back. Had I ever used it in front of him? Not that I could remember.

The sentry reached for my belt. I pulled it back a fraction. "I don't need to tell you what will happen to you and yours should any of these get damaged or go missing?"

The male saluted, his face carved from stone. "No, m'lady."

I bit back a bark of laughter. No one had ever dared to call Desert Rose a lady before.

Divinius eyes sparkled as his dimples made an appearance.

I glared at him, as if the heat burning through my chest could wipe the amusement from his gaze.

He cleared his throat and turned to Coram with a nod.

Our escort entered the room and coughed. "I present his Royal Highness, Divinius Morganis III, Crown Prince of the Fae Realm and Holder of the Seven Orbs of Femora...and his companion."

A breeze flared Divinius' robes just as he stepped into the room.

I clenched my jaw as my insides twisted. I didn't even care that the staff didn't bother to announce my name. That phantom wind thing would be a nice trick to have access to at certain times, and by now, I was pretty sure it was something he could do on command. Perhaps he'd be willing to do it for me when I took back Obron.

"Mother." Divinius' voice echoed from halfway across the chamber. His footsteps rang off the marble floor.

Fates, the man could walk fast when he was motivated. Where had that speed been when we were hiking through the jungle? I elongated my steps to catch up.

The room was overly spacious, in my opinion. A wide table meant for strategy sessions loomed in the middle of it. Large tapestries and banners hung on the walls. They rippled in the breeze from the open windows to my right. The faint scent of gardenias tickled my nose.

"My son." The rich voice melted over my skin, and I resisted the urge to close my eyes and enjoy the sensation. "We've been so worried for you."

An elven lady with hair that matched Divinius' perched on a high-backed chair at the end of a long table. Several scrolls and parchments lay spread in front of her.

Divinius approached and bowed. I came to a stop two steps behind him, echoing the movement.

The legs of the seat rasped across the floor as she stood and held her arms out to him. "Divinius, rise."

He obeyed as she enveloped him in a hug. From the tension in his shoulders, he seemed surprised.

After a few heartbeats, the two separated.

"Mother, may I introduce my companion, Gin..." His voice drifted off and he turned to me with a furrowed brow. "I apologize. I never learned your surname."

Getting to my feet, even though I hadn't been given permission to, I glanced at him before returning my focus to his mother. "Trushade."

The queen's wide-eyed gaze spun to me, narrowing. She studied me from my toes to the top of my head and back again.

"Thank you," Divinius said, oblivious to or ignoring his mother's scrutiny. "Mother, this is Gin Trushade, who was instrumental in my safe return and saved my life twice."

Sand demon spit. I flinched. I'd been so distracted, I hadn't paid attention. I'd gone and given my real last name without a thought.

May the Creator of Sand Demons swallow me now.

"Gin," Divinius continued, "may I present Lillia Cordelia Morganis, Queen of the Fae Realm and Heir to the Rings of Reimar."

When I didn't respond, he cleared his throat, snapping me out of my reverie.

I bobbed a quick courtesy as best I could in trousers. "Your Majesty, it's an honor to meet you." Maybe I'd get lucky and my surname would pass the queen by just as it had her son.

"Yes, I suppose it is," Lillia murmured. "We are grateful for the assistance you have afforded Divinius, and for his safe return. You will, of course, be rewarded." She glanced at him.

"Fifty-thousand Obronian marks should cover her troubles," Divinius said.

Wait, what? I schooled my expression before the queen could turn to me. What about the army he'd promised? Fifty-thousand wouldn't buy enough mercenaries to replace that loss, and I no longer needed to pay to have my tattoo removed.

"Indeed." Lillia swiveled her attention back to me. "I don't appreciate being lied to, young lady."

Divinius jerked his head back and gaped. "Mother!"

Her eyes turned hard as they bored into me. "The Trushades were massacred almost eight years ago."

Sand demon spit.

Taking a deep breath that went nowhere, I pursed my lips. My heart skipped several beats. It was too late to back out now. Lead pooled in my gut as I threw Divinius an apologetic glance before I jutted my chin forward and put my hands on my hips. "Not all of us."

"Well." Lillia patted her scalp as though she had flyaways to sweep back into place. "You certainly have a similar bone structure and hair color to the family, but most Obronians look the same. Our physician will verify your claim. If you lie, you'll be executed."

My fingers twitched. I shouldn't have given up my weapons. I glanced around the area for anything I could use to defend myself. There was nothing. Worst case scenario, I could take the queen or Divinius hostage to make my escape. Divinius might even let me, but if I was wrong about that... I shuddered. The last thing I needed was to be blasted with the full force of his fireball.

"Executed!" Divinius stepped between his mother and me. "Mother, I demand to know what's going on. I refuse to allow you to condemn the woman who has single handedly saved my life and returned me home, safe and whole."

Guards appeared from the shadows surrounding the edges of the room, pointing their swords and spears at me. Changing focus from his mother to them, he shifted to head them off.

Lillia turned her blazing stare to Divinius. "You refuse, my son? You bring a con artist here and expect me to pardon her? You are out of line."

Divinius redirected his attention to me. In another situation, the bewilderment on his face would've been hilarious. "Gin, what is she talking about?"

I swallowed, my heart shattering at his expression. "I didn't lie to you. You never asked and it didn't come up." I refocused on the guards, who had spread around him to flank me. Shifting to face them, I put my back to his. The press of his shoulders against mine was comforting. "Before the warlords took over, my parents were the king and queen of Obron."

He slapped a hand over his mouth and barked out a single laugh. "And you never felt the need to mention that tiny detail?"

I risked a glance at him then turned my focus back to the sentries circling us. "And when would I have done that?" I snapped. "In the middle of fighting the sea demon? Or when we were dealing with Astra? How would I have even brought it up?"

"Oh, I don't know." He threw his hands overhead, a gesture I only recognized due to the excessive flapping of his robes. "How about any of the numerous times I pointed out you weren't royalty? Didn't have the requisite training or knowledge?" He spread his arms in a defensive posture, as though ready to summon his fireballs. "Mother, call off your men."

"Maybe I just got sick of arguing with you and decided to let those comments pass," I said.

"You? Sick of arguing?" His laugh was slightly manic. "Since when?"

Lillia cleared her throat. "That's enough, children. Guards, take Miss Trushade to a guest room. See that she stays there until the physician is able to verify her identity." She narrowed her eyes. "My son and I need to talk."

I braced myself for the fight but paused. Proving who I was might be the only way I could convince the queen to lend me the army her son had promised. It may be best to suffer whatever indignity she had planned in the thin hope it would persuade her to work with me.

The guards moved in. One grabbed my upper arm and yanked me away.

"Gin!"

I met his eyes. "Don't worry. I'll be fine." I still had my dagger, after all.

He tilted his head. "I'm less worried about you than I am about them."

I couldn't hold back a chuckle. It was dark, crackling with rage. "They'll live, as long as they don't do anything stupid." But only because it seemed like it was important to Divinius. I glared at the soldier holding me.

"Young lady," the guard said, scowling, "you will address the crown prince as Your Royal Highness."

"I will call him whatever he and I see fit." I jerked out of his grasp and tilted my head to look down my nose at him. Which was impressive, considering he was two hand widths taller than I was. "If you want me to go without making a scene, you will unhand me and provide escort in the fashion a fellow monarch's heir deserves."

There, see? I could act like a spoiled royal when the situation called for it. It took everything in me not to glance toward Divinius to see his response. Instead, I kept my eyes pinned on the person in front of me.

The male glanced at the queen and Divinius for a heartbeat, then nodded.

They herded me away, weapons still pointed at my throat. But at least I had the freedom to walk under my own power. I threw one final look over my shoulder. Divinius stared after me, his face inscrutable. The queen's lips were pressed into a tight, thin line, her hands clenching and unclenching.

Well, I'd botched Divinius' homecoming, all through my carless revelation of my family name. What had I been thinking? Of course, the answer had been that I hadn't been. I dropped my guard for one crucial moment, and now I would pay the price.

I wasn't worried about whatever the physician would decree, whether he told the truth or not. Nor was I concerned about Lillia's promise of execution. I'd gotten out of much tighter situations before. No, the ice dagger in my chest was the loss of Divinius' promised army, because as long as the queen was on the throne, after her chilly reception, I was under no illusions about how unlikely it was she would agree to release her soldiers to me. All my efforts had been for nothing.

The guards led me through several more halls and up two flights of stairs to a small door. They opened it and shoved me inside.

"Behave yourself. The physician will be here in a few hours." The guard winked at his comrade. "If he makes it a priority. With a war going on, it may take a while." They chuckled. "Perhaps we should kill you and save everyone the effort."

I stood in the middle of the room and crossed my arms, leaning my weight into one hip. "Please. You couldn't kill me if you had a hundred years." Assuming, of course, they all lined up and attacked me one at a time, like good little toy soldiers.

The male closest to me smirked. "You don't have that long, human. Even at their best, your kind live less than a century."

He slammed the door, which was followed by the click of a latch sliding into place.

I took a deep breath as the tension drained from my muscles. The room smelled stale and dusty, like it hadn't been used in ages. The space was simple, just a canopy bed with a nightstand to the side. A chair sat next to a cold hearth. The single window in the suite was built into the wall. The only way I'd get it open would be to bust out the thick leaded glass.

I turned away with a sigh. Even if I did shatter it, there was a three story fall beyond. Judging from how smooth the walls had looked from the outside, the chances of finding sufficient handholds to climb down without a tether were minimal. Besides, I still wasn't convinced the queen was innocent, and that Divinius would be safe if I escaped and abandoned him here.

A small bathing room was attached to my prison, complete with a chamber pot and wash basin. A chrome bathtub sat next to the wall, with a pump that looked like a more elegant version of the bilge pumps in the ships we'd traveled on.

I grabbed the handle and cranked it for several seconds. Metal ground against metal before I was rewarded with resistance and the whooshing of gushing liquid. The clear fluid burst from the pipe, pouring into the tub. It swirled down an opening in the bottom as quickly as I pumped it in. A rubber stopper sat on the opposite rim. I snatched it and rammed it into the hole. The remaining water pooled as it should.

I laughed out loud. At least one good thing would come from this. I'd take a nice, long bath. Perhaps two or three for good measure. The physician, whenever he showed up, would just have to wait until I was finished.

Chapter 25

Divinius

As soon as the guards had escorted Gin from the room, I whirled on the queen. "Mother, I demand an explanation." I was so irritated, I forgot to make my cloak billow in the impressive way it always did.

She slanted a shapely eyebrow at me. "Oh, you do, do you?"

Goosebumps crawled up the back of my neck at the coolness in her tone.

She sat and gestured for me to have a seat in the tiny chair on the far side of the table that would put my head lower than hers. I sighed at the too-obvious power play.

"Pray tell, my son, why do you think I owe you an explanation in how I choose to handle potential threats to our family?"

I slid into the indicated spot and shook my head, staring up at her as she towered above me. "While I disagree with how you handled Gin, that wasn't what I was asking about. The Mage College says you planned a coup to overthrow father and claim the throne for yourself."

My mother's twinkling laughter echoed through the empty room. The brand new burgundy banners fluttered in the breeze. "I initiated a coup?" She wiped a tear from her eyes and fanned herself with the nearest parchment. "Please, my son. Why would I do such a thing, when we both know I already had your father wrapped around my little finger?" Her expression turned serious. "Believe me, it's much less work being the puppet master behind the figurehead."

"And," she continued, "I'm hurt you went to the Mage College without first coming to me."

I blinked. "I went to them because I knew a magic user had to have been involved in my disappearance, and wanted to address that," I lied. The silence stretched between us until it became oppressive. "Okay." I gestured noncommittally at the papers scattered on the desk. "Then please tell me what happened. All I know is someone tried to conjure something at my party, then I was teleported to the jungles outside Tenara and left for dead."

She studied me as if deciding to believe me or not. "The mages attacked the castle unprovoked and murdered your father, of course. You know they've always opposed his policies of not giving them freedom to do as they wish, just because they have power over and above the normal populace."

I squinted at her and leaned forward. "Are you sure someone else wasn't involved? A warlord from Obron, by chance? One who goes by the name of Orion Byre?"

She wrinkled her nose. "Work with one of those brutes?" She scoffed. "Please. I know you and I haven't always had the best relationship, but do try to think more of me than that."

I sat back, suddenly tired of the song and dance. "Mother, both you and I know that's only partially true."

She speared me with a glare. "You accuse me of lying?"

I shook my head. "Lying, no." At least, not outright. "Manipulating events to your benefit, however, has never been beneath you."

Mother sighed. "I'm certain I have no idea what you mean."

I bit back a growl as a muscle in my jaw ticked. She was smarter than this. So was I, and she knew it. To continue to insist otherwise was a blatant insult. I sent a tendril of magic toward her and blinked at what I found as I rifled through her thoughts. Reaching for the table, I steadied myself, feeling short of breath. "Why didn't you inform father the dwarven kingdom had collapsed into anarchy? Or the human realm of Estron?" In fact, according to her memories, all the countries surrounding Obron were experiencing a crisis of leadership. It could be no coincidence.

She scoffed, her hand going to her collarbone as if I'd offended her. "The information from my spies was unconfirmed. You know as well as I the dangers of announcing news without vetting its authenticity."

I blinked to hide the eye roll. More likely she'd been taking the proper time to turn it into propaganda. "The timing does seem a little too perfect, doesn't it?"

Mother shrugged. "Of course, in retrospect. We underestimated the Mage College's political clout, and their manipulative abilities."

I tugged on my hair in exasperation. "Mother! Don't you see? The mages and you have both been played. Gin, too. She's just as caught up in the middle of this as we are."

Lillia's eyes narrowed as she pointed a finger at me. "You leave that con artist out of this. Any information she's whispered to you is just as suspicious as anything those blasted magic users claim. I'll deal with all of them." She shook her head, her face relaxing as the anger drained liked someone had blown out a torch. "My poor boy. I'm so sorry you had to return home to this. I know how important the Mage College was to you, and now I must eliminate them for their treason." She reached over and rubbed my arm. "But, once we put this messy business behind us, we will be able to move forward with finding you a wife and setting the realm to rights."

Selecting a bride was going to have to wait if I was going to help Gin reclaim Obron. A thought crossed my mind, causing one half of my mouth to curl into a grin. I should tell my mother Gin was my choice for a spouse, just to see what she'd do.

I studied her expression and suppressed a shudder.

No, that wouldn't do at all. Unless I wanted to add a second scar to my flawless skin and give her another reason to consider executing Gin. I shifted my weight in the chair, sinking lower into its padding.

"Mother, that's going to have to wait. I've confirmed Abram Lastro was the mage responsible for my teleportation, though he had at least two accomplices." One to mark my robes with the violet pyrailite and the other to invoke the conjuring spell I had wasted time tracking that night. "Without his cooperation, however, we'll have a hard time discovering who the other two were."

My mother's eyes pierced my soul. "Abram Lastro? You're certain?"

"I read his mind." Not entirely true, but she didn't need to know that.

Her lips pressed into a thin line. "He'll not last long in the tormentor's care. If we can extract him from their fortress, that is." She zeroed in on me. "You must do this for us, my son."

"I've already arrested him—"

"You have!" she interrupted, glancing around. "Excellent. Well, where is he? Bring him in."

I held up my hand. "I think not. Not until this matter with the mages is settled." And after Gin was free. I doubted the Assassin's Guild would release their prisoner to anyone but her, anyway. "He's safe for now and will remain so until it's time for his trial."

Mother blinked at me several times as her jaw went slack. "What do you mean, you think not? Being away from court for so long has left you with some bad habits." She stood. "I am Lillia Cordelia Morganis, Queen of Elysia, Heir to the Rings of Reimar, and you will do as I've instructed."

I crossed my arms, my thoughts still roiling over the idea that my mother—my own mother—could have been a part of a plot resulting in my father's murder. "I will do so when you start to see reason!"

Her eyes narrowed. "Be careful. Or you'll end up in the dungeons beside the mage."

My knees went weak, and I was grateful I hadn't stood when she did, despite what protocol dictated. "You would clamp your own son in chains? Your heir?" By Helani...

"When he sides with traitors to the crown, yes!" She wiped an imaginary tear away from her eye and settled back into her chair. "Who would've dreamed it would come to this. My own child, siding with traitorous magic users against his own family."

I bit back a sigh. "Mother, it's just you and me here. Dramatics are not necessary. The mages were fed some incorrect information regarding your motivations by an Obronian warlord. I have to assume the other nations falling into chaos at the same time is his doing, as well." I shouldn't have brushed Gin's warlord off quite so readily. If he could arrange the collapse of multiple kingdoms, he was more of a threat than I'd realized. We needed to act before Elysia lost even more. "Why, I don't know, but it seems to suit his interests to have the surrounding countries in upheaval."

"Hoping we'll ignore what's happening in Obron?"

The unsteady floor wobbled beneath my feet once more as lead pooled in my gut. "Exactly what's going on in Obron?"

"I don't know," she said.

The bitter tang of her lie coated the back of my mouth.

"Nor," she continued, "do I care."

I swallowed. Well, that part had been the truth, at least.

She waved her hand dismissively. "The warlords have fractured Obron, and they come and go. They aren't worth maintaining relations with."

Perhaps not, but... "Gin is interested in reestablishing trade. Political alliances, as well."

My mother's bell-like laugh rang through the chamber. "And I suppose, in exchange, she wants us to put aside our own internal conflicts and wade into Obron's mess to set her on her father's throne?"

"Yes, actually." There was more to it, of course, with her obsession on revenge, but that would be the final goal.

"No." Mother gestured to the spread of parchments that adorned the table. "We have our own affairs to attend to. It's not our job to police other countries."

I bit the inside of my cheek. "Mother, think of the benefits to have an ally in Obron. We would no longer need to station so much of the army at the border to guard against a potential incursion by whatever warlord is in power in the area at any given time. Gin has suggested several commodities Obronians would be interested in purchasing from Elysia." Okay, she'd only mentioned water, but once they'd experienced the other fine things we had to offer... If all they had to drink was arak, certainly the population would go crazy for our fine elven wines. "The influx of funds to our coffers would only serve to bolster our long-term goals. Plus, it would allow us a certain level of influence over their policies." I paused, hoping the dramatics would have the desired effect. "Such as slavery." Not that I doubted for one second Gin would put an end to the practice as soon as she ascended the throne, but I knew my mother well enough to know that was an enticing cause for her, too.

My mother brushed her hand in front of her face, as though she was waving away cobwebs. "I don't care at all how the other countries handle their people, free or otherwise. Slaves were always your father's soft spot."

I blinked, frowning as my brain scrambled for another motivator and came up empty. "I see. Will you not consider the possibility, then?"

She shook her head. "I'm far too busy saving this realm from the mages, Divinius. Something you would do well to support me in, if you don't want anyone else to have a date with the tormentor." She glanced through the door Gin had disappeared through.

My blood froze. The threat wasn't lost on me. She wouldn't torture a fellow royal.

I studied the hardness in my mother's eyes, the intention behind the words. She was serious. My mother was not the woman I'd grown up knowing. Not at all.

I sighed, using the gesture to paint a carefree mask over my face as I'd seen her do countless times. I needed to get Gin out of her clutches before my mother did something we would all regret. "Very well. I will bow to your wisdom."

For now.

I swallowed the bitter taste of betrayal from the back of my throat. I'd have to figure out a way to get to Gin.

"Oh, and Divinius?" she asked, almost as an afterthought.

I bit back another sigh, this one real. "Yes, mother?"

"Bring me the mage. I want him in my dungeon within the hour, or I'll wake the tormentor for your friend."

I paused in front of the opening for what Gin had called the safe house for the local Assassin's Guild. My heart thumped against my chest loud enough anyone in speaking distance would surely be able to hear it. The stench of rot, waste and body odor clung to every surface in this part of town. Lifting my robes to avoid dragging them through the multitude of suspicious substances no doubt splattered across the alley, I studied the door.

What was I doing here? The assassins wouldn't listen to the likes of me. They respected the brute strength and raw charisma Gin exuded in spades, not a prince who hadn't stepped two feet outside his castle over the course of his entire life. I wiped my damp palms on my clothes.

"Aga," I mumbled. The fireball manifested above my palm. I may not be as imposing as Gin, but I had my own methods of intimidation.

Throwing my shoulders back, I barged through the door as if I owned it. "I'm here for the mage," I announced.

A vacant living room greeted me. Overstuffed chairs were scattered throughout the space, along with a table and several bar stools off to one side.

I blinked and unclenched my jaw. Where was everyone?

Something rustled in the kitchen, just out of sight. My heart skipped a beat as my skin went clammy. Who was sneaking around the assassin stronghold?

Against my better judgement, I held the fireball aloft and stepped into the room.

My eyes swept over the area—someone had cleaned up the mess Gin and I had left only a few hours ago, though the aroma of the soup still lingered—until they settled on Abram.

The old magic user sat in a chair at the dining table, looking a mix between bored and terrified. No one else seemed to be about. Maybe they were out gathering information at Gin's request.

"I'm sorry it had to come to this," I said as I approached the male. "I had great plans for a time when the Mage College and the Morganis line would rule Elysia together." I shook my head, the dream crumbling to ash that trickled through my fingers. I was uncertain whose feet to lay the blame for that loss on—Gin's warlord Orion, my mother, or the mages themselves. It was probably an equal split of all three. "I wish you'd come to me with your suspicions up front. We could have avoided all this." Even if it meant I would never have met Gin.

Abram studied me. "Would you have listened, prince?"

I opened my mouth, paused, and closed it. No. If I was being honest with myself, I most likely wouldn't have. But that wouldn't have been my call to make. "I would have brought the information to my father's attention and let him address it as he saw fit."

Abram shook his head. "Your father was blinded by his love for Queen Lillia. He couldn't be trusted to act in Elysia's best interests if it meant going against your mother."

I grabbed the male's upper arm and urged him from the chair. "That still wasn't your decision to make."

Abram stood, the calmness in his features likely only due to the anti-monite shackles. "Where are we going?"

"My mother wants you in her dungeon, where she can keep a close eye on you." And interrogate him.

The head mage paled. "And you think that's the correct place for me?"

No, but between him and Gin, there was no question who my choice would be. "What I think doesn't matter. It's what the queen demands." I extinguished my fireball as I steered the older male out of the Assassin's Guild and onto the streets.

Abram turned and studied me. "Can you not see that your mother isn't the best ruler for the realm?"

I shook my head, ignoring the skip in my heartbeat at the treasonous words. "She's the rightful sovereign, and you wouldn't dare speak so freely if you weren't bound for her dungeon."

Abram glared with a surprising amount of vehemence. "My blood froze when I learned your father had died, prince. We may have butted heads more often than not, but at his core, Divinius II was a good man, and his rule was just. Your mother..." Abram glanced at the castle turrets, casting their long shadows across the town. "Your mother will tear down any who oppose her and will lead the rest to ruin. Especially with the likes of Orion Byre barking at our doorstep."

My heart skipped a beat. My mother was ruthless, but enough to destroy Elysia? No. Abram was wrong. "You're speaking treason," I hissed. "You'd be smart to keep quiet."

Abram grabbed my arm and pulled us to a stop in the middle of the dead street.

I froze, my jaw slack. As he was wearing the antimonite cuffs, such an act of rebellion should've been impossible. Abram Lastro had more willpower than I'd given him credit for.

"I'm only telling the truth, my prince." Abram's gaze flickered to my chest and back to my face. "In your heart, you know it, too."

And maybe I did. Or, maybe that was just me recoiling against being forced to choose a wife, and this whole cursed situation.

Abram glanced over his shoulder at the Assassin's Guild as I steered him toward the castle gate. "Don't take too long to come to terms with it, Your Highness, or it'll be too late. For all of us."

Chapter 26
Gin

The latch on my door rattled. I pushed myself into a sitting position from where I lay on the oversized, fluffy bed, and blinked the last remnants of sleep from my eyes. What hit me first was all the yellow—there was far too much of it. The walls, the canopy overhead, even the blankets were all varying shades of the garish color. My eyes ached.

The hinges creaked as the thick door swung open, tearing my focus from the sunny tint of my surroundings. A wizened old elf whose pointed ears drooped with age shuffled in, followed by half a dozen guards.

I went for my sword only to find my belt still missing. Right. I'd given it up before meeting Divinius' mother. I eyed the old man and decided against revealing the location of the dagger in my boot. If I needed a weapon, I'd steal one from the sentries.

"What do you want?" I asked.

The newcomer reached into his pocket and produced a vial of liquid that glowed blue. "My name is Tarred, healer to the Morganis family. Her Majesty the Queen has instructed me to give you this, m'lady."

I fought the instinct to recoil. "What is it?"

The guards fanned out across the room, swords and spears pointed in my direction.

"A truth serum. She wishes to confirm your identity." He waved the potion at me. "This is the least painful way to do so." Tarred paused. "His Royal Highness suggested that, if it could be made to look like water, you would be more likely to drink it."

A burst of heat exploded through my chest, condensing into a ball of flames that churned low in my gut. So, Divinius was in on this, too. I swallowed past a suddenly dry throat.

Maybe I should make my escape after all and leave His Royalness in his mother's hands. It would serve him right if he'd sided with her against me.

If this potion worked the same way as the antimonite handcuffs made someone compliant and open to suggestion, or could compel me to answer all their questions, I'd be completely at their mercy.

It wasn't that I was lying about who I was, but some things were none of their business, from what I'd been doing for the last seven years, to the warlords, to my entangled feelings for Orion and even Divinius. And I had no intention of discussing anything with a queen who might be allied with Orion and might share everything I divulged with him.

"Water doesn't glow blue," I ground out, heat flooding my face at the wobble in my voice.

He nodded. "True. However, it's closer than fluorescent green."

Well, I had to concede that point. But it didn't make me any more inclined to drink the stuff.

Perhaps the color was Divinius' way of letting me know the concoction was safe? Or, it could signal that he'd partnered with his mother and was abandoning me here to rot. But he would know me well enough to at least suspect I'd never take a potion given to me by someone I didn't trust.

The guards must have read something on my face, because they all stepped forward in unison. Spearheads poked between my shoulder blades and waved at the front of my neck.

"Come on, m'lady," Tarred said, his voice low and soothing. "The alternative is a round with the tormentor, and believe me when I tell you, no one wants that."

I raised my eyebrow, certain whatever an elven torturer could throw at me would pale in comparison to the things Akre had come up with. Tensing the muscles in my jaw, I met the healer's eyes. "I'd rather drink a mug of week-old arak some drunkard has pissed in."

Tarred's eyes narrowed as the corners of his lips turned down. "Very well."

Three spear tips dug into the soft tissue beneath my chin from the front to match those digging into my back. A drop of blood leaked down my skin. If I swallowed, I'd likely cut my own throat.

Coming to Elysia with Divinius had been a mistake.

Someone grabbed my hands and jerked them behind my back, heedless of the blades menacing my person. Iron manacles snapped over my wrists. A kick to my hip toppled me to the side. I landed on the bed, scratches burning across my neck where the guards hadn't been quick enough to retract their spears.

I took a deep breath. "At least you managed to not accidentally slit my throat." I spat at the closest guard, earning myself a pommel to the back of my head.

My vision exploded into stars as the sharp pain radiated around my skull to behind my eyes.

Countless pairs of arms pinned me down. One soldier fisted my hair and ripped it backward while pinching my nose shut with his free hand.

I gasped.

Tarred took advantage of the opportunity and poured the entire vial into my mouth before shoving my jaw closed so fast I bit my tongue. I gagged. Feeling akin to when I'd been flailing in the ocean, I swallowed reflexively.

The truth serum tasted like a mix of cinnamon water and warm mud mixed with salty blood from my injured tongue. I coughed, spitting out as much of the vile concoction as I could, staining the pristine comforter blue and red.

"That's enough," Tarred said. "It will kick in soon. She's no longer a threat."

I glared at him from beneath my eyelashes as the last of the sparkly dots faded from my vision. I opened my mouth to tell him he was a dead man, but the words wouldn't come. Tilting my head to the side, I frowned and tried again.

No sound crossed my lips.

How odd. If I'd lost the ability to speak, I should be panicking right now. Why wasn't my heart racing, or the heat of battle flooding through my veins? I was Desert Rose—a fighter, a warrior. I was not someone to stand here like a docile mare.

My thoughts felt as slow as molasses. I blinked through the fog.

Tarred smiled, his worn teeth flashing yellow-white in my dimming vision. "There boys, see? I told you."

The multitude of hands holding me down loosened and released me. Finally. Free.

I tried to roll over, but my muscles didn't respond. And I couldn't feel my feet.

Or my arms.

Sand demon spit.

I groaned. This was definitely not good, and something I should be panicking about.

The healer pulled up a chair and sat across from me, still well out of arm's reach. He crossed one leg over the other.

If he'd moved closer, I could kill him. At least, when my body reappeared.

"Gin, do you know where you are?" he asked.

I took a deep breath and concentrated. "Drugged," I slurred.

He nodded. "Yes. The queen has doubts as to your truthfulness."

"Dead."

"Her Majesty?" He shook his head. "No, she's very much alive. So is the prince, if you'd like to know."

I twisted my face, willing my muscles to work. "No. You... dead," I ground out.

His throat bobbed as he swallowed, his face turning pale. I should be feeling some sort of satisfaction at his reaction. Even delirious, I still inspired fear. But my emotions remained oddly tamped down.

"Drugged to the point of unconsciousness and still threatening people with death." He clicked his tongue. "I think you've got an overdeveloped sense of vengeance, young lady."

I frowned and stared at my feet. They looked like they still existed, even if they didn't feel that way. They didn't even prickle like they did when they fell asleep. They were just gone.

"Gin. Gin!" Tarred snapped his fingers in front of my face. "I know it's hard, but focus on me, please."

I glared at him, which was grueling because he was so blurry.

He cleared his throat. "Who are you?"

"Genevieve Trushade," I said, happy to answer the reasonable question.

"Where are you from?"

"Obron."

He shook his head. "No, I mean specifically. What city?"

"The capital, Kadena."

"I see." He nodded. "Did you have a title?"

I smiled wide, showing my teeth. He could quake in his boots like everyone else who'd met me. "Desert Rose."

He may have paled, a little. "No. One you were born with. Nobility."

"Oh." I frowned as I thought. Hadn't I already told them that? "Princess. My father was the king."

"What happened to you, Genevieve?"

A small spark of the fire that burned in my core exploded. "Don't call me that." The words didn't carry the bite I wanted them to.

He tilted his head. "Genevieve?"

I nodded.

He uncrossed his legs and recrossed them in the opposite direction. "Why don't you want, no, nevermind. What do you want to be called?"

"Desert Rose."

"Why?"

"It's who I am. And who I'll be when I kill you." See? Since he was being reasonable, I could play nice, too, and answer his questions.

"I see." He made a note on a piece of parchment in his lap I hadn't noticed earlier. "What happened to you, Desert Rose? You're supposed to be dead."

I shrugged. "I survived." Obviously. That he would voice such a stupid question had my opinion of his intelligence dropping a little.

He sighed. "You are allowed to give more than two-word replies, you know. It would speed things up."

I didn't respond. There was no need to when he didn't ask anything.

"Desert Rose." His tone was low, and far too patient. "How did you survive?"

My stomach twisted, as though a brood of baby sand demons had hatched and were fighting to claw their way free. That question, I didn't want to reply to, but my mouth moved of its own accord. "Warlord Akre. He found me on the streets, trained me, and turned me into Desert Rose. The best assassin in Obron, and all the realm."

Tarred made a noncommittal sound in the back of his throat. "Does he know who you are?"

I gave him a secretive smile and shook my head. Not even Roland had known who I was. My forehead tightened as my eyebrows pulled together. I should feel a sharp spike of anger at that name for some reason. It didn't matter that I didn't, I suppose. Roland wasn't important right now, and he was so far away...

"Desert Rose, focus on me, please."

I squinted at him, studying the curled tips of his pointed ears. "You're blurry."

"Yes, a side effect of the drugs, I'm afraid. It'll pass, don't worry." He turned to someone behind him. "Your Majesty, do you wish to know anything more?"

I blinked, trying to stare into the fog beyond Tarred. I hadn't noticed anyone since the healer and I had started talking.

"What are your intentions with my son?" The queen's imperious voice filled the room, rattling my eardrums.

I glanced at Tarred, uncertain if I was supposed to answer others' questions or just his.

He nodded.

I took a deep breath. "I need him and his army to invade Obron and overthrow the warlords Akre and Byre." I paused. "Probably the rest of them, too." I stared into the gloom in her direction, but it was too hard to keep looking when there was nothing to see, so I turned away. "He needed to get home and back into power for that to happen. So I promised to help him if he'd do the same for me."

"I see." Lillia's words floated through the room as if from a great distance. "And your intentions for Elysia?"

I frowned. What would I want to do with Divinius' country? "I have none. No, wait." That wasn't true. "I want to open my own bar and import your water, so I can be the only one to sell something other than arak." I licked my lips, imagining the feeling of cool, clear liquid washing down my parched throat. "Your water tastes so good."

"You're not here to take the throne? Or to set my son on it?" Something in the queen's voice wavered. A small part of me would have killed to see her face. Fortunately, that portion was easy to ignore.

I exhaled air through my mouth. "I don't want your country. I don't even want my father's, but I don't want Akre or Orion in charge, either." I took a deep breath and squinted into the fog.

"And who do you want in power?" the queen asked.

I frowned, chewing on her question. "Definitely not you, if you're working with Orion. Divinius is a good man and would be a better king."

Tarred and several guards gasped.

Perhaps I shouldn't have said that? But it was the truth, and she should know where we stand.

"That's it!" Lillia's voice dripped icicles. "Throw her in the dungeon. She'll be tried for treason along with the mage. I'll see her executed."

"Wait, Majesty!" Tarred stood and gestured.

The rough hands of the sentries settled around my upper arms and hauled me to my feet. The world tipped sideways at the sudden change in position. It was a good thing there were lots of them to hold me up. I still couldn't feel my legs.

The healer's face drifted into view a few inches from my own. His breath smelled of herbs and something bitter. "Is Divinius aware of your willingness to dispatch the queen?" He put both palms on either side of my face. "Answer me!"

I barked a laugh. "Divinius doesn't have the stomach to kill anyone, much less his mother." Smiling, I bared my teeth at him. "That's why I'll be the one to do it."

Tarred stepped away with a sigh. His shoulders drooped as tension released from his posture. "Thank Naraka the prince is no traitor," he mumbled.

The guards pulled me from the room and hauled me down several different hallways and flights of stairs. The fog in my head made it too hard to keep track of our path, so I focused instead on the varying textures of marble beneath my feet.

Eventually the polished white, pink and gray flooring disappeared and became dark granite as we moved further down into the foundation of the castle. The air was chilly and damp down here, raising goosebumps on my skin. It smelled like the back alley next to a tavern—stale sweat and piss.

Somewhere to my left a large deadbolt unlatched and a door swung open on hinges that screeched like they'd never seen oil.

My escort shoved me forward. I tripped on the door frame as I flew past and tumbled to the ground, rolling to a stop against a cold stone wall.

Behind me, the door slammed shut, the bolt latching into place. Footsteps retreated until I was alone.

I glanced around. I was in a cell with rock walls on three sides and iron bars with a door on the fourth. Dim light from a crystal in a sconce just out of reach illuminated the area. The chill from the floor sunk through my clothes and into my skin.

Apparently, they were finished asking me things. For now.

At least it was quiet here, even if the poor lighting did make my vision even more blurry than it had been earlier.

One upside to numb appendages was that I wasn't as cold as I could be.

I yawned.

If they were done talking to me, then now seemed like a good time to catch a nap. Maybe when I woke up I'd be able to find my hands and feet again.

I curled up with my back to the door and closed my eyes.

Elysia was just as terrible a place as Obron. The elves were no better than the warlords.

Chapter 27
Gin

My back slammed into something hard, causing vibrations to ricochet through my bones and into my aching head. I pried my sore eyelids open as something cold and metallic clicked around my wrists. Tiny pricks like thorns encircled and dug into them. What in sand demon spit? Light stung my eyes, sending sharp needles of pain through my skull. Rough hands grabbed my ankle and I kicked out in reflex, my heel catching something soft.

With a muffled curse, the grip on my leg tightened, shoving it into place.

Another snap as a band secured first my right calf, then my left.

I tensed, jerking my arms. Shackles bound me.

Clenching my jaw, I forced my eyes open, squinting into the flickering torchlight.

A blur moved in front of me, a splash of darkness against the shadows. I shook my head, making the room spin.

They must've done more than drug me. As dizzy as I was, I probably had a concussion at least, maybe two.

I froze, panting until the world settled. No more moving for the immediate future, then.

I took a deep breath, fighting down the roiling nausea. The smell of mildew, human waste and old blood assaulted my senses. It seemed no matter where I was, all dungeons smelled the same.

An icy wave of water slammed into me.

"Wakey, wakey." The mocking voice echoed off the stone walls.

I sputtered, coughing as cold rivulets ran down my exposed skin. What didn't soak into my clothes dripped onto the floor and made its way down a drain at my toes. The ground was covered in what was likely centuries of dried blood. Layers of it. Clearly I wasn't the first prisoner to be strapped here.

Rusty iron manacles clamped my wrists to a sturdy wooden chair. I threw my weight to the side. The stupid thing didn't even wobble.

"It's bolted down. Trust me, girlie, you ain't going nowhere."

I swallowed past my dry throat. It felt like someone had stuffed my mouth full of sand.

Blinking, I raised my head, suppressing a groan.

The blur in front of me grunted. He was bare from the waist up, his crossed arms serving to enhance what was no doubt an impressive set of pecs and abs if my vision had been clearer. He was almost too muscular, like a blacksmith or lumberjack. His black breeches were oiled to a high polish, likely to make it easier to wash off the blood.

A torturer who planned ahead. Fabulous.

He nudged a table to my left. Several metallic devices sat on top of it. Some, like the tongue tearer and the thumbscrews, I was familiar with. Others, like the tear-shaped gourd about the size of a mouth with a screw on the side, I could only guess.

I clenched my jaw as I glanced around the room. No water wheel and no pool. I didn't know if I would prefer drowning over and over to one of the bloodier implements. The equipment was on full display, no doubt for my perusal to get my imagination running.

Swallowing the bitter taste creeping up the back of my throat, I willed my stomach to settle. If the tormentor was hoping the sight of his trade's tools would set me on edge, well, he'd be correct.

My being here made no sense. I'd told them everything they'd wanted to know, hadn't I? There was nothing more. What did they want from me? Dragging my sluggish thoughts back to my time with the royal physician and guards, I scraped my memories for whatever I could've said to brand myself a traitor. Coming up blank, I opened my eyes. Once again they landed square on the lineup of torture devices.

"It's not often I have the opportunity to work with royalty," the tormentor said.

His voice was deep, rough, like someone had taken a bristle brush and shoved it up and down his throat several times until his vocal cords were destroyed. It sent phantom sand-spiders up my spine.

"I wonder," he said. "Do you bleed red like the rest of us?"

Grabbing a dagger from his belt, he sliced my collarbone. The blade was so sharp I felt nothing until my blood suctioned my shirt to my chest. The sting ramped up, the delay either due to the residual drugs and concussion, or maybe the cut hadn't been as deep as expected.

I glanced down. My flesh gaped, almost to the bone. I winced. It was going to need stitching to heal properly. With visual confirmation of the damage, pain flashed across my torso with a vengeance.

I opened my mouth to say something smart, to let the tormentor know he wouldn't break me so easily, but my gaze locked on the thin strip of metal he'd picked up from the table. It was elongated, like a cross between a stiletto dagger and a lockpick, its tip sharpened to a razor point. I knew exactly what that was for.

I scraped my shoes against the floor, fighting to push myself further back into the chair, as if that sparse bit of distance would delay the inevitable pain. I yanked on my arms, trying to pull them through the shackles that held them mercilessly in place until the spikes on the inside of the metal bands shredded my wrists and my blood dripped down the armrests and trailed its way toward the drain.

"You do bleed like the rest of us. Good to know."

I dragged my focus away from the searing agony scorching its way up my arms and met the tormentor's dark brown gaze. Something malicious sparked there as he towered over me, using the intimidating power of his height and stature to its full advantage.

The realization settled in the back of my mind like a hunk of lead. I wasn't getting out of this, there was no escape. This man, who Divinius had called a sadist, would cut on me until I bled to death.

Sure, I'd threatened others with torture many times, but the end I delivered was always quick and as painless as possible. I was nothing if not a professional. But this man was, too, except his specialty was pain.

Something inside me curdled as I fought against my restraints, the humiliation and helplessness devouring me. After everything I'd done, what I'd become, I deserved this. Karma was coming for me, and I would die exactly where I belonged—in the bowels of a dungeon, covered in my own blood and waste, with no one the wiser. My eyes burned, but I would not cry in front of this man.

I would not allow him to see my fear. This was just like Akre with his water wheel. A small man with an even smaller bit of power, intent on proving his superiority. But I had survived torture before, and I would last as long as I could now, even if the only one who ever knew it was me. Clenching my jaw, I ground out, "Go mate with a sand demon."

He growled, grabbed my left hand and splayed it on the armrest beneath the full force of his weight until my fingers lay flat.

Something in my hand popped, a tendon or bone snapping out of position. A dull pain throbbed up my arm.

Aligning the metal file with the space below my fingernail, he shoved the fine blade between it and my skin.

I screamed, the agony wiping the last of the drug-induced fog from my mind as invisible flames scorched each individual nerve ending, spreading from my finger and across my torso.

Something exploded behind my eyes as the darkness of oblivion rushed to greet me but I blinked, fighting it off. If I lost consciousness now, I'd be letting him win. And I was nothing if not too stubborn to let that happen.

I don't know how much time passed—it could've been seconds or hours—before the metal file withdrew. As the pain faded to the background, I collapsed, heaving deep breaths past my ravaged throat. "Is that all you've got?" I choked out.

His eyes darkened, a grimace flashing across his face. "Human whore!" His fist connected with my jaw hard enough to make me see double.

I opened and closed my mouth, working through the soreness. A coppery tang covered my tongue, and I leaned forward, spitting the blood onto his shoes and too-shiny pants.

The tormentor, it seemed, had a temper. Perhaps I could anger him to the point where he'd finish me quicker than he originally planned. At least that would end this farce with as little suffering as possible on my part.

What would Divinius do when he found out I'd been tortured to death? I wasn't sure his mother would tell him, to be honest. She needed him compliant, at least until the other mages were dealt with.

I squeezed my eyes closed, bringing up Divinius' face in my mind. *Divinius!* I put all my effort into the scream, just on the slim chance he could hear my thoughts long-distance, and was bothering to listen. *Divinius!*

Would he be sad I was dead? Or relieved he didn't have to make good on his promise to help me free Obron?

The tormentor's fist rammed into my solar plexus, driving the air from my lungs with a *whoosh*.

I doubled over, wheezing, trying to inhale past my paralyzed ribs. My vision turned gray as it blackened at the edges. I wrapped my right hand, the one without the injured finger, around the arm of the chair as I fought for oxygen and to stay awake. The world tipped from side to side, spinning like a ship caught in a whirlpool.

The tormentor's heel slammed down on my instep, sending a shock wave ricocheting up my leg.

My lungs finally relaxed and I gasped, hissing in my next breath as the tormentor's dagger sliced against the top of my thigh, narrowly missing the large artery along the inside.

Dang. He'd been so close to making a fatal mistake. It looked like he wasn't angry enough yet.

"Knife-ear scum," I mumbled, my swollen jaw causing the words to slur. "You've got nothing on the warlords." I should've come up with something more witty, more cutting, but my head was still spinning and I didn't have a ton of experience insulting elves. There weren't many in Obron to practice on.

"Wench!"

This time, when he punched me, the world went black.

Chapter 28
Gin

"**G**in! Gin! Wake up."

Divinius' voice cut through the fog of my sleep. The dungeon's chill had sunken into my bones and my muscles were sore from shivering. I was still bound to the chair. At least my brain felt less disconnected and foggy.

The air was filled with the acrid stench of burnt flesh. I gagged at the smell.

Purple robes brushed against the floor in front of me. "Gin?"

My chest tightened at the sound of his voice. A tingling feeling swept over my back and across my face. I ground my teeth and clenched my right hand hard enough my fingernails dug crescent indents into my palm. The left hand hurt too much to do more than twitch.

I dropped my head, careful to keep my face everted until I was sure the last of the fogginess had cleared from my mind. "You're here." I couldn't believe it. "You came." My words were barely more than a rasp.

"Of course. You called me." Putting one finger beneath my chin, he tilted my head up and to the side, examining what was no doubt an impressive bruise. "Valek." He spat the word as he glared over his shoulder. "I'm so sorry, partner."

There was a body in shiny black breeches laying against the wall. Its exposed skin was charred and flaking like barbecue left over the flames too long. "Did you do that?" I asked.

Divinius had his hands pressed over the shackles binding my wrists, ignoring my question. "Khula," he muttered.

A metallic clank rang through the dungeon as they swung open. The ones around my ankles followed.

"Come on. Someone will have heard that." He tossed something into my lap. The cut on my thigh twinged in protest at the added weight.

I bared my teeth at him, refusing to acknowledge the concern that darkened his eyes. "You let them drug and torture me like I was some kind of common criminal. As if I hadn't saved your life twice." I snatched the belt he'd thrown at me and secured it around my waist. The comforting weight of my whip and sword settled into place.

"I had no choice. She's my mother. At least I managed to get here." He grabbed my arm, tugging me to my feet and into the hallway. "And I'm here now, aren't I?"

I shook out of his grip. That was a fair point. I wouldn't have escaped on my own.

What a laugh that circus would've been.

I glanced around. As far as dungeons went, this one was pretty tame. The walkways were straight and, though it hadn't been mopped recently, at least the floor had been swept clean of rat droppings.

"Hey!"

I looked to the side as we passed the cell the mage, Abram whatever-his-name-was, occupied. The old man curled forlornly in a corner, metallic cuffs resting in his lap, looking all the world like a sad puppy dog.

I faltered as something twisted in my gut. The male had been just another pawn of Orion's.

Divinius grabbed my upper arm. "Come on." He turned his attention to the prisoner. "We'll be back for you, just keep quiet about where we went."

My steps stuttered as I half-jogged to catch up to the long-legged prince. I glanced over my shoulder. "Div—"

His fingers hardened around my bicep. "I know. He was played, just like I was. But mother won't execute him until at least tomorrow. She wants to try out her new weapons first, then use his death as a final blow to the mage's morale."

Behind us, several voices cursed. Our footsteps echoed off the walls as we left the other prisoners to their fates. The air cleared of some of its stench and took on a damp, musty smell that reminded me of the sea. We must be approaching a body of water.

"Divinius, you know your mother's not..." I trailed off, searching for the kindest way to say it as he steered me around a corner in the passageway.

"Not fit to rule? Power hungry?" His voice had a hard, brittle edge to it I'd never heard before. He shook his head and chortled. "Valek. I know. It's just—" He met my gaze. "She's my mother. And I'm not particularly interested in assuming the throne."

I nodded and looked away. I hadn't been able to dispatch Orion when I'd had the chance, either. I dug my feet into the ground, pulling us up short as my brain processed the last of his words. "Wait. Why don't you want to rule?"

He stared at me like I'd grown a second head. "Do you have any idea how much work is involved in running a kingdom?" He studied my flat expression for several blinks before turning away and continuing down the corridor that curled around in a slow downward spiral. "Nevermind. I suppose you do. Once I'm king, I'll have no time to study magic."

The one thing he enjoyed most in the world.

He didn't need to say it. The words hung in the air between us.

"I don't want Obron's throne, either," I whispered, studying the floor that had switched from rock to dirt at some point in the last few minutes. "Too much pressure. I meant what I said in the interrogation." It struck me that he may or may not know what transpired while I'd been drugged. "An inn with an entertaining clientele and a competitive advantage with a reliable beverage supply other than arak, and I'd be happy." I paused. "As long as there was someone decent on the throne." Which was, unfortunately, easier wished for than achieved.

Divinius raised his eyebrow and flashed me a half-grin. "And who would judge the candidate as worthy or not?"

I snorted. "Me, of course."

His eyes sparkled and a faint smile graced his too-perfect mouth. "Can't trust anyone else to do the job?"

I ignored the warmth pooling in my gut and met his gaze with a flat one of my own. "No." With this stuff about his mother and what the warlords had done with their taste of power, he had to know that by now.

His smile dropped. "I'm sorry."

I looked away and swallowed, a curl of guilt mixing with sadness deep in my chest. Everything he'd discovered and lost in the last few days was a painful echo of what I'd experienced when Akre had killed my family. My heart ached for him. "Don't worry about your mother. When the time comes, I'll handle it."

He paused, turning to me. "Gin—"

I glanced over his shoulder, my jaw dropping.

He'd stopped us in front of a large room which was filled with row upon row of black powder barrels. At my expression, he turned. His eyes widened. "By Naraka…"

The columns went on forever. "She's imported more than one ship load," I whispered.

Divinius ran his fingers through his hair, pulling it tight against the back of his neck. "What is she going to do with all of this?"

I raised my eyebrow as my mind happily supplied a cascade of images, each one more horrific than the last.

"I saw one fistful of this nearly break a wagon axle," Divinius breathed. "A single barrel would…"

My gut solidified into a lump of iron and plunged to the floor. "A few barrels could destroy the Mage College. The entire room full…" It could decimate the whole city.

Divinius swung his head from side to side, as if seeking to confirm what his brain couldn't believe as he took in the sheer amount of powder. "How long has she been planning this? She couldn't have brought in this many overnight."

I stepped into the room and glanced over my shoulder. "Unless your father…?" I let my words drift off in question.

He shook his head. "No. Alchemical weapons aren't father's style at all. He preferred verbal discourse and diplomacy. He considered war a 'shameful waste of life for people who didn't know any better.' No. This is all my mother." His tone turned dark, reminding me of how Akre's voice dropped when enraged.

Suppressing a shudder as I fought the instinct to put distance between us, I studied the closest barrel. "I'd love to know where she imported this from."

"Me, too."

Synchronized footsteps echoed down the hallway.

"Come on!" I grabbed his arm and tugged him deeper into the storage room.

Ten steps in, I judged we were far enough back to be hidden by shadows. Grabbing Divinius by his robes, I dragged him in tight to me behind a column of barrels that protruded slightly further out than the others.

He wrapped his arms around me and pulled me close. I tried to ignore the press of his muscled torso against me, the warmth from his body chasing away some of the chill from the dungeons. We froze. "Bharama," he whispered.

The air nearby wobbled, as though it were waves of heat bouncing off a field of slickrock in the height of summer.

Several guards rushed by, the room momentarily flaring with brightness from the extra light crystals they carried.

I squeezed my eyes shut and pressed myself into Divinius' chest.

The scent of mint baking in the sun surrounded me and calmed my pounding heart.

This felt good. I could stay this way for a while.

Far too soon, he released me. I bit back a squeak of protest and stepped away, brushing my hands down my tunic to straighten it. My pulse was racing too hard—hopefully he hadn't heard it.

Divinius cleared his throat and shook out his robes. "Do you think they're gone? Is it safe?"

I glanced around the edge of the barrels. "It depends on our ultimate destination. Are we continuing down, or heading back up?"

"Down for now. There's a small river that flows beneath the castle. The entrance and exit are gated, but if there's a boat, the portcullis can be raised." He frowned. "At least, if memory serves."

My heart jumped out of my chest, pounding rapidly at the thought of getting into another watercraft. I swallowed, fighting back the rising wave of nausea and panic.

"A lot has happened in the last week," he continued, oblivious to my reaction, "and it's been a while since I've felt the need to explore the underbelly of the castle."

I eyed his new robes. This set was purple and somehow still pristine despite the jaunt through the dungeons. "Well, fingers crossed." I glanced over his shoulder and out the door, in the direction the guards had gone. "Let's give them a few more minutes to get ahead of us, in case they decide to double back."

He nodded. "Very well. In the meantime, perhaps we can get an inventory of all this?"

"And maybe find the weapons?" The repeating crossbows and ammunition would be much more useful than a bunch of explosive black powder.

"Twenty columns on each side, by four high." I paused. "One hundred sixty barrels."

"Valek." Divinius shook his head. "She could destroy everything."

My stomach plummeted and I turned, spearing him with my gaze. Either his mother, or Orion. The last thing anyone needed was an elven queen with designs on ruling the world pairing up with a warlord. "Would she?"

"Oh. Um." Divinius stroked his chin. "I'm not certain. I don't think so."

His lack of immediate denial was not reassuring. "My question is," I grumbled, "who else has some of this? If one monarch is importing it, there's nothing to say one or more of the others aren't, too."

Obron wouldn't survive warlords with access to enough alchemical powder to bring down a castle. I blinked. Or a city.

I shook my head. That was a problem for another day. "Come on." I waved to him. "Let's go, before they decide to come back and do a more thorough search."

He led me through a maze of passages, to the point that even my excellent sense of direction was confused. We encountered no more guards.

After several minutes, the refreshing scent of running water tickled my nose. The tinkling ring of flowing liquid against rock had me weak in the knees.

We'd made it.

Divinius escorted me through an archway and out to a stone platform. The precarious-looking rowboat rocked back and forth in the current. A cool breeze brushed a few stiff strands of hair off my face.

I blinked. "You want me to get into that?"

He strode to the far side of the space to a large wheel and gear I hadn't noticed. "Come on. It's at least as stable as the lifeboat from Astra's ship. And, as a bonus, it's not weighed down by barrels of wine and oil."

I studied the thing that could only dubiously be called a boat. "It hardly counts as a craft. The planks look like they could crumble at any moment."

Divinius bent at the knees and turned the crank. It screeched in protest and refused to move. "The alternative is wading into the water and kicking the raft in front of us." He bared his teeth and groaned as he strained against the rusted gears.

I shuddered. No way was I getting in that river voluntarily. I'd go back to the dungeons before that happened.

I ran to the other side of the gear and braced myself. "Ready? One, two, three!" I yanked on the wheel as he pushed.

With a shriek loud enough to raise the neighborhood, the mechanism shifted, releasing an orange cloud of dirt and rust. Three turns, and the portcullis lifted, dripping a curtain of seaweed into the channel.

"Hey! Down here!" The voice drifted up from the passageway.

Divinius shoved me toward the boat. "Quick! Get in."

I swallowed and stared at the raft. The ground beneath my feet wobbled as the image in front of me was replaced with Akre's water wheel and the sensation of a cheesecloth bag being yanked over my head just before I was bound and dunked into the pool below. I shook my head, stepping backward as I took a too-shallow breath.

My lungs heaved, fighting against the invisible bands that constricted them and forced the last of the air from my chest.

Warm hands grabbed my arms, bringing me to a halt as I backed into a muscled torso. "Gin?"

I ignored him, hardly caring if it was Divinius or the guards who had me. I couldn't go forward. Not into the water. A rushing noise pulsed behind my ears, in time with my heartbeat.

A blurry face came into view. His somehow always perfectly-styled dark hair curling around his eyes and angular cheekbones. And his eyelashes were so long. "Is Desert Rose, the world's most famous assassin, scared?" A teasing twinkle sparkled in his eye as one half of his mouth curled into a smile.

The sight of his blasted dimple pulled me back into the present.

Meeting my eyes, he squeezed my arms then leaned over and untied the boat from its mooring. Jumping in, he steadied it before holding out his hand to me. "Don't worry, I won't let us sink. Do you trust me?"

Footsteps pounded toward us.

The taunting question stabilized my trembling legs and rushed heat through my veins. I met his gaze and bared my teeth, steeling my spine. Because, despite everything that had happened, I did trust him. "No, I'm not afraid." I was terrified. But I'd come too far to allow something like fear stop me now. I put one halting foot into the boat just as a bolt flew by, close enough for the wind of its passage to ruffle my hair. A second one followed.

Those shots were too quick to have come from a standard crossbow.

I glanced over my shoulder at my assailant. The male held one of the new repeating crossbows, aimed at my head. He also had two batches of the special ammunition attached to his belt.

Without thinking, I vaulted onto the dock, tumbling in a somersault as a spray of bolts tracked me.

"Where are you going?" Divinius' voice echoed.

"I want that crossbow!" Not like we'd have time to float to freedom with soldiers firing at us from the river bank, anyway. Best to take these men out so we could make a clean escape.

I sprang to my feet behind the guard, grabbed his jacket and yanked it down, trapping his arms against his sides. Ripping off his belt, I snagged the two quarrels of ammunition and tossed them in Divinius' general direction.

The soldier aimed a kick at me. I ducked and rammed my elbow into his face. His nose shattered with a satisfying crack.

The male dropped his crossbow and flexed, tearing the seam of his blazer down the middle. Ignoring the blood gushing over his face, he snatched the collar of my shirt and threw me into the wheel we'd used to raise the portcullis.

My temple cracked into the metal as my sight exploded in a ray of stars. The gear shifted and the gate slammed back into the water with a wave that nearly tipped Divinius into the river.

The guard sprinted across the dock to where I leaned against the wall, shaking my head and blinking to clear my eyes. He wrapped his arm around my neck and squeezed.

I gasped as he pressed tighter, cutting off the blood flow to my brain. My vision went gray—I only had a few heartbeats of consciousness left. Glancing to the far side of the room, I met Divinius' wide-eyed gaze.

As much as I wanted him to throw a fireball or something and burn all the guards to a crisp so we could escape, he risked hitting me if he did so. That explained why he was standing there, frozen, staring at me. His chest heaved like he was breathing too fast. In slow motion, his mouth moved, forming my name though I couldn't hear it past the rushing sound in my ears.

He couldn't help me—it was up to me to free myself before I passed out. I dropped my weight suddenly and reached into my boot, pulling the dagger I'd kept hidden from Queen Lillia's guards.

I reversed my grip on the blade and slammed it over my shoulders into my assailant's eye.

He screamed, releasing his hold on my neck and dropping to the ground.

I gasped, sucking huge gulps of air into my lungs. Bending over, I braced both arms on my knees as the world spun.

"Aga!" Divinius' voice rang out behind me, followed by a flare of red-orange light.

I kicked the downed guard in the gut and dragged my dagger across his throat. I glanced at Divinius. A curtain of fire obscured the passageway. Men's voices cried out in alarm on the far side.

One male tore through the magical flames, looking like a demon escaped from beyond the Night Gate. He raced forward, knocking each fireball Divinius hurled at him aside with his blade.

I blinked as my jaw went slack. This man was too skilled to be a rank-and-file dungeon guard.

Divinius ripped off his robe and tossed it over the sentry. "Pharo!"

A cerulean ring encircled the newcomer, pinning his wrists to his waist underneath the cloth.

I barreled into the soldier from behind, tackling him just as Divinius released the magic, allowing us to slam into the floor. The male's sword clattered across the stone pier. I punched him once in the temple. He went slack.

Pushing to my feet, I glanced at the curtain of fire as I dusted my palms on my pants. My head throbbed, but not badly enough I couldn't push the pain away to deal with later. No one else seemed willing to brave the flames, though from the sound of their shouting, an entire regimen lay on the far side.

Returning to the gears, I clenched my teeth and cranked the portcullis back up. Grabbing the two dropped swords and repeating crossbow, I headed toward the boat, trying not to notice the liquid it floated in.

Divinius stood, feet in the craft, hands splayed on the stone platform. "Um, Gin?"

I paused, halfway crouched to slide into place beside him. "Yeah?"

He nodded at the puddle of purple laying over the last guard. "My robes, please?"

I studied his bare torso as though contemplating refusing just to see what he'd do, but really using the excuse to admire the scenery. He was built entirely too perfectly. Blasted elves, it just wasn't fair. Just as the corners of his lips started to turn down, I gave him a crooked smile and a wink. Retracing my steps, I ripped the robe away from the unconscious man and chucked it to Divinius before climbing into the boat, keeping my gaze focused only on the rickety wooden planks beneath my feet. "Shame, that."

"What's a shame?" Divinius pushed away from the dock and resettled the cloth over his shoulders.

I flashed him a teasing grin as I laced my own belt through the two quarrels of bolts. "That the robes were recoverable, of course."

"Ha, ha." He crossed his arms and stared at me as I secured the two swords at my waist and the crossbow over my back.

I froze, uncomfortable with the weight of his gaze. "What?"

He glanced pointedly at the oars. "There's only one set, and since I've done the lion's share of prisoner rescuing today…"

Silence stretched until I rolled my eyes and grabbed them. "Strain a muscle with all that fireball throwing, did you?" I was the one who'd been locked in the dungeon, then tortured.

"You have no idea," he mumbled.

I would, if he'd open up about the cost of his magic use. I pulled with more force than necessary, guiding us into the current, being careful with my wounded left hand. But the rhythm of the push and pull against my shoulders and back as the paddles slid in and out of the water was soothing, and it helped me steady my breathing. Slowly, my panic at being back on a boat receded.

A refreshing sprinkle of drips dusted over us as we scooted beneath the portcullis and to freedom.

When we were out of view of the gate, I released the oars and braced my elbows on my knees, leaning forward. "Well, now what?"

"Now," he said, "I suspect we'll regroup with your assassins and plot our assault. Mother plans to attack the Mage College at first light."

I glanced at the moon, hanging low in the sky. "We have a few hours left to plan our own offensive, then." Which was good, because tonight had gone to the sand demons.

He nodded. "Assuming your minions have done their job and found us a second way into the castle."

Chapter 29

Gin

A few hours later, I crouched in a clump of bushes along the south castle walls as the first hints of sunrise brushed over the flag of House Morganis on the uppermost turret. The conflict should be isolated to the far side of the grounds, closest to the Mage College. My initial impression of the castle's exterior had been correct—the outside was just as polished and smooth as the interior.

I kissed the grappling hook one of Sana's younger assassins had presented to me, studied the window several stories above, and threw it with all my strength.

The metal bounced off the frame with a clank and tumbled back to the earth.

"Sand demon's spit." I coiled the rope back around my arm in preparation for a second throw.

Divinius came up behind me. "Want some help?"

I raised an eyebrow and glanced over my shoulder. "Think you can toss this better than me?"

His eyes sparkled as he held out his hand.

I put the grappling hook in his palm with a shrug. "Sure. Just don't wake the castle doing it."

With a wink and a quick half-smile, he said, "Pakara."

It floated up to the corner of the window, where it fastened itself.

That was so not fair.

I tugged on the rope, confirming it was secure. I turned and gave him a silent but polite clap. "Must be nice, being a mage."

He flared his robes with a bow. "Always happy to be of service."

I bit my lips to hold back a laugh. "Show off." Shaking my head, I grabbed the line and started climbing. "Wait while I climb up before you follow. It's impossible to know how much weight this thing can handle until it's tied off."

He widened his eyes and slammed his palm over his heart in a dramatic display of offense. "Are you calling me fat? Or is it that you doubt my magical abilities?"

I rolled my eyes as the smile broke free. What a cluck. "Neither. Nevermind, forget I said anything. Just let me get up there first."

The rough fibers bit into my palms, but the climb went easily enough. I slid into the window and pulled the crossbow off my back. The room was empty for the moment, just as the Assassin's Guild had said it would be. Stacks of supplies, arrows, bolts and round leather pouches crowded along the walls. The room smelled of that sulfur stench the black powder had given off.

I checked the grappling hook. Just as Divinius had promised, it was embedded in the wood of the frame. I stuck my head out and waved him up. The line went tense as he hoisted himself off the ground.

Behind me, the door latch tripped and opened.

"Hey! Who are you?" The groggy voice echoed loudly enough to wake the entire wing.

I leaped across the room, slamming my fist into the guard's temple. He tumbled to the floor with a thud and a crash of steel over stone.

I winced. What was a guard doing on the roof wearing full leather and plate armor hours before a battle? Not that the metal would protect him from magical fireballs. I kicked him in the head again to make sure he was out cold.

I combed through the supplies shoved against the walls and found a stack of ammunition for the repeating crossbows. "Excellent." I secured two more containers to my waist. I had forty or fifty bolts now. I crossed my fingers it would be enough.

Divinius pulled himself through the window with a grunt. I was beside him before he had even tumbled to the floor, pulling the grappling hook up behind him.

I studied him as he lay prone on the ground. "What's wrong? Are you hurt?" My eyes skated over his robes, looking for any protruding arrows or patches of blood. I couldn't see anything, but with the dark purple color, I may well miss any wet spots.

"No." He gasped, inhaling several deep breaths. "I've just never been a fan of heights. Give me a minute."

I grunted. Hopefully this would be the end of our surprises. "Couldn't you have mentioned that little detail before?"

He stared at the fallen guard, then my waist. "By Naraka. How many quarrels do you need for that crossbow?"

I flashed my teeth at him. "One can never have too many going into a fight."

"How much more can you fit on your belt?"

I glanced at him as I tied the grappling hook to a free spot. He watched me with a raised eyebrow.

I winked. "Wouldn't you like to know?"

I shook my head. He was probably right, though. I grabbed one more quarrel, for good measure. "In all seriousness, never leave a good tool behind. We may need to make a quick exit." I paused. "Unless you want to be the one to carry it?"

He scowled. "No, thank you. It might snag on my robe." He snatched one of the leather pouches and upended it. Black powder spilled over the floor. He jumped backward.

I took a step back, my heart in my throat as I braced for the explosion. "Careful!"

One heartbeat passed. Two.

Nothing happened.

He rubbed his chin with two fingers. "I wonder what my mother is going to do with these?"

"I don't want to know." And the sooner we got out of here and away from the spill, the better. I cracked the door and peered outside. "But it might not be a bad idea to take a couple of them with us." Not that we knew how to use them, but I'd rather be too prepared than not. The battlements were empty, but that wouldn't last long with the approaching shift change.

With a sigh, Divinius handed me two leather satchels crammed to bursting.

I tied them to my belt, too. There wasn't room for much more. I'd have to make sure to account for the extra width in my hips when the fighting started. "Ready to make us invisible?"

"Of course. Just remember, invisibility won't help you if you run into someone, or they see us opening a door."

I threw him an irritated glare. "I'm not an idiot, you know."

He didn't bother to respond but instead reached behind and grabbed my hand. "Bharama."

The air wobbled around me like I was back in the high desert at midday. Our shadows, streaming across the floor in the torchlight, disappeared.

"Alright, let's go." He tugged me toward the doorway.

It was disconcerting, being led by a person I couldn't see. His hand was warm, the pressure reassuring, just like it had been in my dream. I tripped over a seam between two rocks and stepped on his robe as I struggled to catch myself.

"Careful," he whispered, the word a little harsher than necessary.

I bit my lip. "Sorry. It's hard when I can't see my own feet."

He guided me across the battlements to a stair, and down into the stronghold.

We kept to the edge of the hallways, where there was no rug to reveal the indentations where we trod, and less traffic to avoid.

This palace held the same organized chaos I remembered from the days of my father's reign. Servants bustled through the halls, preparing for the day. Some of the food they carried smelled divine.

I frowned. When was the last time I'd eaten? There'd been nothing after the angry stew.

Guards marched past, most heading toward the north quarter of the castle.

Divinius tugged me into a room. "My mother's chambers are this direction," he whispered.

He led me through a narrow hallway that wasn't nearly as crowded as the one we'd just left. Burgundy brocade tapestries and banners hung from the chandeliers and rippled in the breeze. A loud bang from the other side of the wall shook the windows and rattled the floor.

"What was that?" I hissed.

"It sounds like the mages aren't waiting until sunrise for things to get started," he said. "We need to hurry."

We reached the end of the corridor. Two sentries stood on either side of a mahogany door. Divinius pulled up short, causing me to slam into his back.

"Oof!"

"Halt! Who's there?" Both guards brandished their spears, their gazes bouncing back and forth across the hall.

I stepped to the right, making sure to give Divinius plenty of leeway, hoping the prince wouldn't move. Being careful to keep my footsteps silent, I pinched the sides of the first sentry's neck, blocking the large arteries to his brain. He collapsed without a fight.

The second man turned, eyes wide, and swung his spear in front of himself. "Darren! Darren, are you okay?"

I tumbled beneath the other man's guard.

He dipped his weapon at the last moment, catching my arm with the tip.

"Fates!" I popped to my feet, my hand slapping over the wound, applying pressure. A trail of visible blood splashed across the stone.

"Gin!" Divinius' disembodied voice echoed through the chamber.

The sentry opened his mouth.

I slapped my bloodied hand over the lower half of his face and yanked his head backward.

"Don't kill him!" Divinius said.

Another explosion rattled the walls.

I sighed and redirected my knee to impact the man's hip rather than snapping his spine at the waist. We tumbled to the ground in a tangled heap. I rolled onto his back and applied pressure to the left side of his neck—the only artery I could reach with my free hand.

It took far too many heartbeats for the tension in the guard's muscles to relax as he passed out. As he went limp, his eyes rolling to the back of his head, I pushed to my feet. Blood dripped down my bicep.

"Div, drop the invisibility."

"But—"

"I need to see how badly I'm hurt."

He mumbled something I couldn't quite make out and suddenly I could see myself.

I poked at my torn skin. A sharp sting lashed up and down my arm. One more wound to add to those I'd received tonight.

"How bad is it?" He stepped closer. "It's really bleeding."

Blast it, the guard had nicked a small artery. I turned. "Get out of the light, let me see."

He moved to the side.

A tiny knot I didn't realize was there released between my shoulder blades. "It's going to need stitches, but I've had worse. I just have to find something to tie it with for now."

Divinius tore the hem off the closest sentry's tabard. "Here, hold still." He wrapped the fabric around my arm and tied it off. His fingers brushed over my skin, sending tingles of a different sort dancing along each nerve. "How's that?"

The sensation faded, igniting a fire in my core. I blinked and looked away before the heat in my face betrayed me. No one back home had ever shown half the care he did in bandaging me up. And wasn't it sad that was all it took for me to take notice? "Good, thanks." My voice was far too husky for its own good. I cleared my throat and studied the men at my feet.

Flexing my wounded bicep, I glanced at the door. "I don't suppose we have any chance of sneaking in now?"

Divinius shook his head. "I'm surprised we're not covered in guards already, to be honest."

I flashed him a quick one-sided grin as my eyes dropped to his lips. "Benefits of being in the middle of a fight, I presume." I forced my attention away, mentally slapping myself upside the back of the head. The heat of battle was not the appropriate time to be fantasizing about how that mouth would feel on my skin.

Sand demon spit.

A blast of fire exploded against the nearest window, blinding me. The glass shattered, spraying across the floor. "Agh!" I threw an arm over my eyes, but the damage had been done—white after-images blocked out everything. I was blind, helpless until my vision recovered.

"Quit throwing fireballs at my castle," Divinius growled, running to the opening. He was silent for a few heartbeats. "It looks like the battle's in full swing."

I caught his eye as he came back into view and gestured toward the door. "Plan B?"

He nodded. "Plan B. Let me go first."

I bowed and waved him forward. "After you, highness-ness."

Chapter 30
Divinius

I faltered for a heartbeat before nodding and striding to the doors. With one last glance back at Gin, I threw them open wide and marched inside.

"Mother! What are you doing?"

Lillia Cordelia Morganis stood on the balcony attached to her private suite, surrounded by a squadron of elite guards as she directed the attack below. A large bonfire roared to her left. Each guard held one of those repeating crossbows Gin was so obsessed with and had at least one leather pouch filled with black powder tied to their belts.

Plenty of firepower to protect their queen.

My mother's face brightened as she caught sight of me. "My son!"

I glanced over my shoulder. Gin should be in the room by now, hiding somewhere in the shadows, waiting.

"Come on!" Mother waved me forward. The soldiers parted to make way. "The bombs are almost in place. Come, watch the marvels of modern technology!"

I allowed myself to be pulled into the queen's embrace, but my eyes searched the room. Shelves of books lined the walls. Ancient volumes my mother hadn't cracked in at least a decade. Her desk occupied most of the area in the middle of the space, along with a plush carpet in her signature burgundy. I couldn't see Gin anywhere.

Would she wait for my signal as we'd planned? Or would she take the first shot she had?

Desert Rose wasn't known for her patience, but I would never forgive myself if I didn't do everything possible to try to save my mother. Even after what she'd ordered done to Gin.

As our embrace drew to a close, I stepped back. "What's going on?"

No bolt flew into Lillia's torso from the shadows. The tension between my shoulder blades released. Gin was waiting, as we'd agreed.

Mother sent me a beatific smile. "Watch, my son."

A moment later, a flare raced through the sky and exploded into several trailing legs of flame. It reminded me of a flying spider.

I shuddered.

Queen Lillia clapped once. "That's the signal! Archers, fire!"

Four guards moved to the front of the bonfire, aimed their repeating crossbows into it and squeezed their triggers.

Burning quarrels lanced through the flames and toward the mages.

I grabbed my mother's arm as my jaw fell slack. She couldn't... I stared at the unfamiliar woman beside me. "Mother!"

She ignored me and slid to the right. "Aim higher! You're falling short!"

My intestines took a nosedive.

A rippling explosion set off along the closest corner of the Mage College. Wave after wave of pressure assaulted my ears until I lost count. Black smoke billowed outward, obscuring the building.

I screamed. "Mother!" Swallowing, I tried to force the lump in my throat back down into my stomach, where it belonged.

"Don't worry! That was only five barrels," mother said. "We have hundreds more."

An answering volley of fireballs took to the sky, arching from the mage's stronghold. Two hit the main gate, while the other three slammed into the castle walls.

I splayed my hands to the side for balance. "Please, call a parley, otherwise you bring the city and our home to ruin."

My mother whirled to face me, her features contorted in a rage I'd only seen the like of once before. That same wrath that had given me the lash scar across my back. "They killed your father, Divinius. If you cannot support us in this, then I'll have you thrown in the dungeon with that other traitor mage. Archers!" She pushed me away and turned toward the men. "Ready, position two!"

Half of me wondered if she knew Gin had escaped the dungeons. Would she care, at this point?

From the corner of my eye, I caught a flash of movement in the shadows as Gin stepped from behind a curtain and aimed her crossbow at Queen Lillia's back.

Every muscle in my body locked. No, we'd agreed...

After a heartbeat, Gin lowered the weapon to aim for the queen's thigh. My knees went weak. Not a deadly shot, but one that would incapacitate and allow me to take command.

A large fireball lit up the sky on a direct path toward our balcony.

I threw both arms wide. "Aga!" A blue burst of flames arched to meet the oncoming one.

The two collided in a dazzling display of color. The magics swirled as though fighting for dominance. Gold and cerulean chain lightning covered the surface of the sphere. The smell of ozone permeated the area.

"Well done, my son!" Mother glanced back at me and froze as her gaze met Gin's.

"Guards! Assassin!" She pointed. "Kill her!"

The entire squadron turned their weapons on Gin.

I tensed. Not even the famed Desert Rose could dodge ten repeating crossbows.

The click of each bolt as it released was as crisp and clear as if I were standing in a glade on a spring morning. The army of wooden needles flew toward Gin.

"Jhalaka!" I grabbed my magic and flung it in her direction.

A flash of teal wavered like a mirage in front of her. The bolts bounced off the shield and tumbled to the floor.

A headache burst between my temples as Gin gasped, her muscles going slack.

I'd never seen someone so surprised they weren't dead. I bit back a grin. The ground dropped out from beneath my feet as the sudden realization slammed into my skull. My mother had tried to kill Gin.

I whirled to face the queen. "No! Pharo!"

A lightning blue ring encircled her and every other guard on the balcony.

"I've had enough of this nonsense." I spun, using my magic to flare my robes dramatically and marched until I was nose-to-nose with my mother. "You will stop this assault on Gin, the Mage College, and the capital."

Her lips pursed into a thin line as her gaze hardened.

I brushed the wrinkles out of the front of my clothes. "Vadha." I cleared my throat and projected my voice across the city. "Lillia Cordelia Morganis, Queen of the Fae and Heir to the Rings of Reimar, before these witnesses here, the mages and the population of Elysia, I declare you unfit for rule, and remove you from the throne."

My mother bared her teeth. "You can't do that! You need a second, as well as the permission of the council, all of whom are dead."

"I, Taniela Shanera, second him." One of the guards removed her helmet and shook her head. Long strawberry blonde waves tumbled across her shoulders and ample chest. She nodded and grinned at me.

Had it only been a few weeks since we'd danced during my so-called birthday celebration?

"And I, Sapphora Saussec, also support him." Another guard pulled off her helmet, smiling.

From the corner of my eyes, I caught motion as Gin's jaw went slack. Her fingers twitched against her crossbow trigger.

Uh, oh.

I sent a tendril of magic toward her surface thoughts. I shouldn't have, but I couldn't afford for her to kill the two women who had placed their safety on the line to dethrone my mother.

Gin blinked and shook her head. *Was every elven woman so stunning? I'll never be able to compete. Wait, what am I thinking? I'm not here to rule Elysia, even if the elves would settle for a non-fae ruler.*

I bit back a smile as something warm and soothing settled in my stomach. I released the magic. Taniela and Sapphora were not in danger, at least, not immediately. Gin and I, it seemed, needed to have a different conversation. Which we would, but later.

Turning to the two nobles, I bowed. "Thank you, ladies. You have my gratitude." I dropped the magical hoop from around their waists.

Projecting my voice again, I continued, "Lady Lillia Cordelia Morganis, you are hereby removed from the throne and banished from the castle. You will be allowed to take up to five servants of mutual choice with you to our summer home in Adenasa, where you may live for the rest of your days. Away from politics, and in disgrace."

Tear trails ran down Queen Lillia's pallid face. "My son, what have you done? I'm your mother!"

I shook my head and moderated my voice to a more reasonable level. "No mother of mine would place her own desires above the needs of the realm, of the people." I glanced at Gin, then out toward the Mage College.

Taking a deep breath, I met my mother's eyes. "You fell for Orion Byre's poison and nearly destroyed everything we hold dear."

She opened her mouth, but I cut her off with a sharp wave of my hand.

"Don't bother denying it. I know what I saw in your head when I first arrived. You wanted a convenient excuse to eliminate the mages, the one source of power that could threaten your own. But, without the knowledge of the magic-users, Elysia would be vulnerable to the likes of Orion and the other foreign rulers who would seek to bring us down." I shook my head and swallowed the bitter taste climbing up the back of my throat. "I'm ashamed to call myself your son."

My mother gasped and leaned against the ring of magic binding her, as though faint.

I turned to the remaining guards as another fireball slammed into the edge of the balcony. "Vadha," I said, before turning in the direction of the mages and growling, "Hold your fire! By the order of Divinius Morganis III, King of the Fae Realm and holder of the Seven Orbs of Femora!"

The dust settled. No further attacks came.

I gestured to the two elven women who had supported my mother's removal. "Ladies, would you please arrange for an emissary from the Mage College to meet me in the Council Chambers?"

The two bowed, spun on their heels, and marched out the door.

"Now." I studied the remaining soldiers. Would they follow the rule of law, or support my mother? Sentries were sworn to protect and uphold the laws of the realm. Of course they'd back me. I dusted imaginary dirt from my palms and turned toward them. Taking a deep breath, I said, "Pharo" and released my hold on the magic.

The blue rings holding the patrol in place dissolved, leaving Queen Lillia the only one restrained.

"I apologize for detaining you," I said. "I hope you will understand it was necessary and forgive me."

"Guards!" my mother screamed, "Arrest the traitorous prince!"

As one, they leveled their crossbows at me.

Chapter 31

Gin

I squeezed the trigger on my crossbow, blindly spraying the area with bolts as I sprinted across the balcony.

The guards too slow to drop to the ground beneath my onslaught screamed as quarrels punched through their armor.

I grabbed Divinius' arm and hauled him to the side putting the bonfire between us and the rest of the squad.

"Come on, partner. Time to go!" I unfastened the grappling hook and glanced over the edge.

"Wait! No!" He struggled. "Let me talk to them."

"Even I know better than to take on odds of twenty against two." I tugged on the grapple twice to make sure it was attached and circled the rope multiple times over my wrist. "Come on! Hold tight."

He wrapped his arms around my neck, pulling close. The scent of baked mint and sunshine surrounded me as he squeezed his eyes shut.

I grabbed one of the leather satchels of powder from my belt and flung it into the bonfire.

The shockwave from the explosion shoved us off the balcony.

Divinius screamed as we flew through the air and slammed into the castle wall.

I glanced up at the grappling hook, which was embedded in a window frame. A narrow outcropping clung to the wall beneath us, approximately ten paces below and five to our right.

"Divinius, look down."

He shook his head, staring at the sky as though it was the most interesting thing he'd seen in his life. His voice trembled. "No way in Helani am I looking anywhere."

I narrowed my eyes and studied him. His face was pallid and a trickle of sweat worked its way down his temple.

Fates. He wasn't kidding when he said he was afraid of heights.

My shoulder screamed in its socket as the rope dug into my wrist. I'd have an impressive burn when this was over, but at least we'd live.

Voices rumbled from above. Queen Lillia's cries of "Find them!" rang across the area.

"Okay, don't look," I said. "But there's a balcony below and to our right. We need to swing that way before anyone comes to mess with the grappling hook. Think you can help me?"

He turned wide eyes to me. "Swing? As in, side-to-side?"

The corners of my lips hardened. Of course that was what I meant. "Remember how you pushed me into the ocean when the sea demon was attacking?"

His throat worked on a swallow as his arms tightened around my neck. "Yes."

"Consider this payback. Hold on tight."

He bit his lip and buried his face against my shoulder.

And blast it if that action didn't cause something in my core to explode into flames.

I shoved off, running along the wall as though I was holding onto a cable to swing over a river. At the height of the rope's arch, I said, "Let go!"

He firmed up his death grip, which was exactly the opposite of what I'd asked him to do. Blasted royals. I clawed at his fingers until they slipped from around my neck.

He tumbled to the edge of the balcony with an "oof!"

The rope pulled me in the wrong direction, toward the queen and her guards. Bolts flew past close enough I could feel their breeze. With one last cry, I sprinted along the wall, untangling the line from my wrist and doing a backflip.

I landed beside Divinius on one knee, my hands splayed out behind me.

He stood, shaking his robes. "Showoff."

I tugged him against the pillar, out of sight of the soldiers' crossbows and through the open balcony door. I jerked the heavy velvet curtains closed.

His blue eyes were striking as they stared into mine. I shifted my weight, brushing my palms down my tunic. "What?"

He brushed the last of the wrinkles from the thick purple material of his garments. "As if you didn't have the whole escape planned from the beginning."

I barked out a laugh, more than happy to take that credit, even if it wasn't warranted. "Well, I'd have preferred to leave the way your lady soldiers did, but I told you, you never know when you'll want a quality grappling hook." I glanced at the rope, dangling from the window above, well out of reach now. Hopefully we wouldn't need another one.

"Come on." He took my hand and pulled me inside.

"Where are we going?"

"The council chambers, of course. That's where the ladies Taniela and Sapphora will meet us. Helani willing, with the mage emissary and guards more loyal to the crown than my mother."

I blinked and studied him as he led me through the largest library I'd ever seen. The faint scent of vanilla and old parchments tickled my nose.

Gone was the impetuous prince in the jungle outside Tenara. In his place stood a king, one who'd just thrown his mother off the Elysian throne.

By the fates...

We'd done it. One coup to undo the other, if we could keep his mother from reclaiming power.

I swallowed a very inappropriate laugh. It felt far too satisfying to foil Orion's plotting.

"What are we going to do next?" I asked, glancing around the room we'd entered. There were several couches and chairs gathered in small groups. Empty tables where food or beverages could be placed lined the outer walls. Perhaps this room was used for tea or other social gatherings.

"I need to establish a Ruling Council, one that can validate my mother's removal." He met my gaze as he hesitated at the library's door. "Hopefully Taniela and Sapphora can muster enough influential people to constitute a quorum, and that we can put it to a vote before the queen and those loyal to her intercede."

I wrinkled my forehead. "A what?"

He paused as he glanced over his shoulder. "Fifty percent of the seats must be present for an action of this nature."

I shook my head. Whatever. The intricacies of Elysian politics weren't something I needed to deal with at the moment. Besides, it seemed like the prince—no, the king—had them well in hand.

I squeezed my crossbow hard enough to turn my knuckles white. "Let's do this. Put me at the door to the chambers, and I'll make sure you get your vote."

He studied me for several heartbeats, then nodded. "Thank you." He cracked the door and stuck his head into the hallway. "Quick, the coast is clear."

Chapter 32

Divinius

I waved toward the Council Chamber doors. "Khula!"

They swung open with a suitably dramatic bang.

"Showoff," Gin muttered as she turned her back to me, taking her position to the side of the entryway.

I bit back a smile. It wouldn't do for potential members of the new Ruling Council to see me smiling while I was working to dethrone my mother. But I sure did enjoy how the sparkle in Gin's eyes and the slight curve to her lips softened her features.

There would be plenty of time to explore that later. Right now, I needed to focus.

I marched to the conference table in the middle of the room. The cold marble matched the hollow pit in my gut. I shuffled through the layers of parchment my mother had left spread across the surface as I glanced over my shoulder.

It was unreasonable to expect Taniela and Sapphora to be here yet. It had been just a few minutes, after all. Word was no doubt spreading through the castle with each breath and heartbeat.

I checked the doorway. Gin wasn't visible, but she was there, guarding my back just as she'd promised.

This was probably the last quiet moment I'd have for some time. Days, weeks even.

"Gin," I said. "I never got the chance to—"

"Highness! I mean, Your Majesty!" Two men jogged through the door. Stopping before me, they placed their hands over their hearts and bowed. "We were told to report here to declare our loyalty to you, King Divinius Morganis III."

I nodded. "Thank you, Lord Suzac, Lord Belieu." They were minor nobles, but I had to start somewhere. And most likely, the heads of the major families had been killed when my father's Ruling Council had been disbanded.

I gestured to the parchments spread across the table. "As I'm sure you know, I've been away for the last few weeks. Please, would you fill me in on recent events?"

The stamp of multiple synchronized footsteps echoed through the hallway as a regiment of soldiers marched in, led by Lady Sapphora. "Your Majesty." She curtseyed.

Sana, the head of the Assassin's Guild, stepped out from behind the guards and caught my eye. She winked before she went to lean against one of the pillars that lined the room.

I sighed. The assassins had been instrumental over the past twenty-four hours. I supposed it was only fair to have one of them present. Besides, Gin wouldn't have let Sana pass if she didn't approve.

Sapphora approached. "Taniela is coming with a representative from the Mage College. Apparently they sent one to the castle as soon as you ordered the ceasefire."

"Excellent. Ladies and gentlemen," I turned to face the room, "as I'm certain you are all aware, I have declared my mother unfit to rule. However, that decree must be certified by the Ruling Council before it becomes valid." I met everyone's eyes in turn. "I find myself in need of advisors. Bear in mind that if my mother is victorious, anyone present today will be branded a traitor and most likely executed."

Taniela entered, followed by one of the two mages who had led us to the Mage College's sublevels only a few hours ago. How time flew.

Lady Taniela flashed me a wide grin as both women bowed. "Your Majesty."

I gestured to the magic user. "I apologize that I do not know your name, but I would like to offer the College a spot on the new Council. Will they accept?"

Wordlessly, she nodded and I waved for her to sit.

"Anyone else?" I glanced around the room.

Unsurprisingly, Taniela and Sapphora took seats at the head of the table, one on either side of the cushioned chair that had formerly been my father's and was now mine.

"Your Highness!"

The muscles in my upper back tensed at the sound of Taeral's voice. Slowly, I turned to find the man standing at the door with one of Gin's swords at his throat. My mother, ringed with several guards, stood further back, safely out of harm's way.

I sighed internally, bracing myself. "What is it, Taeral?" I asked, even though the answer was obvious.

The soldiers who had followed Sapphora into the room raced to the hallway and formed ranks across the entrance, spears drawn. I lost sight of Gin in the bustle. I took a step in her direction, but one thing she had proven over the past weeks was her ability to take care of herself.

She'd promised to buy me time. The least I could do was take advantage of it and trust her to stay alive.

I steeled myself and turned back to the first of my advisors. I nodded to Lords Suzac and Belieu, gesturing to the chairs. They may hail from minor nobility, but if they joined the council, they would be among the top ten most influential fae in the realm.

Belieu's jaw went slack and he paused for a heartbeat before lunging toward the offered chair. Suzac was only slightly more dignified in accepting his place. It was a higher position than either male could've reasonably expected under any other circumstance. I had the numbers needed for a quorum. The remaining five slots could be filled later.

"My son!" My mother's voice echoed through the chamber. "Please, I beg you. Set aside this treason. Stand down and all will be forgiven."

Nausea flooded me as I swallowed past the sudden lump in my throat. If only life could go back to the way it had been the morning of my birthday. There were so many things I would do differently.

Gin's clear words rang out over the throngs. "Take one more step, my lady, and your man here loses his head."

A tingling warmth spread through me, washing away the queasiness. Just over two weeks ago, I'd never met Gin, hadn't allied myself with the most notorious assassin in the realms. A large chunk of me wouldn't mind watching Taeral's head roll across the room, though wishing him dead strictly because he was annoying was petty, even for me. The man was loyal, even if it was to the wrong ruler.

I swallowed and cleared my throat, glancing around the room with its too-big table and gaudy burgundy banners. "Before this council, I charge you, mother, Lillia Cordelia Morganis, with failure to protect the realm, conspiring with Warlord Orion Byre of Obron, and the murder of my father, King Divinius Morganis II. I formally strip you of your title as

Queen and Holder of the Rings of Reimar and exile you to our summer estate."

I turned back to the faces circling the conference table. With barely enough for a quorum, I'd need every one of their support. I hid a shiver as I remembered the contentious debates I'd had the displeasure of sitting in on when my father lived. "Members of the Council, in accordance with the laws of Elysia, I put this matter before you for a vote."

"You can't do that until I've stated my case!" My mother's voice rang off the marble, reverberating through my head.

I sighed, but she did have a point. If this was going to be legal and by-the-books, I needed to accord her the rights given by law. "Very well, mother. You and Taeral can enter, along with two others of your choice. Your remaining escort will need to stay outside."

It might have been my imagination, but I could've sworn I heard the sound of Gin's blade sliding into its sheath as she moved back. Sapphora's guards split down the middle, allowing Taeral, Queen Lillia and two bodyguards through before they closed ranks.

I waved her forward. "Mother, you may approach the council."

Lillia tugged the cushioned chair out from the head of the table and sat with much fanfare as Taeral flitted about her like a butterfly, arranging her skirts to their best advantage. Then he stepped back like the perfect attendant he was.

I worked to contain my eyeroll. Power plays wouldn't win the day here.

At least, I hoped they wouldn't.

With a grand wave toward my mother, I pulled out a seat between Taniela and the mage and settled, ignoring the fact she'd usurped my place. Though, as I was sitting in a space designated for a council member, that implied I had voting rights, which would make her less than happy if she'd taken a moment to consider. "Mother, we are yours to address."

She cleared her throat and speared each seated noble with her gaze in turn, no doubt committing their faces to memory so she could condemn them to death later. The corner of her lip twitched as her eyes fell on Lord Belieu and Lord Suzac. "As I'm sure you are all aware, my son has not been present since the unfortunate demise of his father, as well as the great patrons who comprised this council before you. His information is flawed. He's being goaded on by that woman." She pointed toward the entrance to the hall. "Genevieve Trushade, of Obron. Yet, he accuses me of colluding with Miss Trushade's rival, Warlord Orion Byre." She gestured to the room. "How can he consider himself impartial in such a situation?"

She shook her head. "The sad truth is that the Mage College attacked the castle and killed my husband. My son, with his strong ties to the mages, refuses to see that."

My gut clenched, a sour taste rising in the back of my throat. My fingers turned white as I braced against the table. All she had to do was sew doubt into one member, and I was lost.

I could hardly tell them I'd read her mind and knew she was in on the plan from the beginning.

Sana strode across the room. "Majesties. Permission to speak?"

I nodded. "Of course."

My mother made a sharp slicing gesture with her hand. "No! I am speaking, you do not know your place, peasant."

Ignoring my mother's outburst, Sana reached into her pocket and pulled out a folded piece of parchment. "I would serve as a witness for the council in this matter, with the council's consent?"

"Who are you?" Taniela asked, her eyes narrowed.

Sana bowed. "My name is Sana Mistwater, former head of the Assassin's Guild." This drew a gasp from several people at the table. "And occasional courier for the Royal Fleet."

I blinked. What?

"I have a missive here," Sana continued, "that I was directed to deliver to Queen Lillia less than a month past."

My mother exploded out of her seat, knocking it over in the process. "You miscreant! You expect us to believe you not only opened a secret letter, but made a copy?" The chair slammed into the floor with a crash that echoed throughout the room.

The older assassin tilted her head to the side and raised an eyebrow. "When the sender is an Obronian warlord?" She exhaled through her mouth. "Of course."

I bit my lower lip, uncertain if I should be nervous or overjoyed.

Sana handed the parchment to the Mage College's representative, the closest council member. "It's proof the queen knew of the coup in advance and plotted with an outsider to frame the magic users and place herself in power."

My chest lightened until I felt I might fly away. This was it—exactly what I'd needed, what I should have sought, before overthrowing my mother. I glanced at Gin, trying to catch her eye. Had she known Sana was going to bring this forward, or was it a coincidence?

"This is a ridiculous forgery!" The last of the color drained from my mother's face. With a furious gesture, she scattered the parchments laying on the table to the floor. "I won't stand for this heresy, this slander. Not from the likes of this!" My mother pointed at Sana as she and Taeral backed away. "Guards! Kill her! Kill them all!"

The clatter of steel against armor rang out as sentries on both sides of the door leaped at each other.

I whirled to face them, my heart in my throat. "Gin!"

A dagger flashed in the light. Taeral pulled it back for a throw.

I raised my arm. "Jhalaka!" The magic curled around my mother's attendant like a lover's embrace before shooting toward the far end of the table.

The teal pearlescent shield popped up between the servant and the rest of the council members. The knife wobbled as it impacted the barrier and clattered away across the ground.

A headache bloomed inside my eyes as the magic's cost settled into place. One more burst blood vessel in my brain. One day, it would kill me.

But I would not die today.

A crossbow bolt rammed into Taeral's chest, fired from somewhere up in the balustrade on the second floor. He tumbled to the side with a wet gurgle.

"No, Taeral!" My mother lurched toward him before changing directions and seeking shelter behind her overturned chair.

"Call off your guards, Lillia Morganis." Gin's voice reverberated throughout the chambers. "And let the vote proceed, or you're next."

My stomach did flip-flops. "Please, mother. Exile is better than death." And if anyone could kill the queen, it would be Desert Rose.

Every clank of sword on shield echoed, too-crisp, as time slowed. The whoosh of blood past my ears with each heartbeat, the rasp of air through my nose, were all exaggerated to my heightened senses.

My mother pulled a leather pouch from her sleeve and stood, aiming at me. The faint stench of sulfur tickled my sinuses. "I'm sorry, my son. You've had your last chance—"

A quarrel sprouted from her chest in slow motion. She lurched, throwing the sack, which curved in an arc above my magical shield and headed for me.

"Get down!" I cried.

A second bolt punched through my mother's sternum, a finger's width away from the first. Her face went blank as she pitched forward.

I extended my hand toward the bag. "Aga!"

The smell of ozone filled my nostrils as the magic curled around me, temporarily dulling my headache, before it coalesced into a fireball and hurled through the air. It impacted with the black powder satchel.

I threw myself beneath the table as the rest of the council members followed my lead.

The room shook with the force of the explosion. Dust and bits of mortar rained down on us.

Someone sneezed.

My gaze locked on my mother's body, laying face down at the far end of the table.

Chapter 33

Gin, One week later

With a spectacular feeling of déjà vu, I dangled from my grappling hook above a marble balcony scattered with several potted plants. They reminded me of miniature palm trees, but Divinius had called them ferns. A breeze tugged an errant strand of hair across my face as it swung me a few feet to my left and back again. My braid was still damp from my failed swimming lesson.

The sting of the instructor's laughs less than an hour ago as I panicked for no apparent reason still stung more than anything I'd experienced since coming to Elysia. It was the perfect complement to my embarrassment at my failure to get more than waist-deep in the water before losing control of my body. Forget those lessons anyway. Once I returned to Obron, I'd never need them.

I strained my ears for any sign of movement in the suite below.

The sun peeked out from behind a cloud and cast my shadow along the wall and onto the balcony, revealing my presence to anyone aware enough to look for it. I pinched my lips together and sighed through my nose.

Hopefully Divinius was alone, otherwise I'd have some explaining to do.

I released the rope and dropped to the railing before jumping down, pressing myself against the doorframe.

Still no sound from inside.

I knelt and stuck a piece of silvered glass into the doorway, angling it so I could catch the reflection of the room.

Divinius sat at his desk, back hunched, as he poured over a stack of parchments. No one else was visible. A set of bracers made of white metal were next to the paperwork, orange light flickered as they reflected flames from the hearth, which was just out of view.

I stood and, stepping forward, leaned against the doorframe, making sure my shadow fell across his workspace.

"Hello, Gin," he said, not looking up from the letter he studied. "I was wondering when you were going to come by."

My jaw twitched as a burr of annoyance wriggled in my chest. "I tried to come earlier, the more conventional way." Twice, actually. Once before and again after swimming. "But your guards wouldn't let me pass." Had been downright rude about it, actually. His Royalness was lucky I had controlled my rage and avoided creating a political incident.

He put down his pen and turned to me with a raised eyebrow. "And that stopped you?"

The expression on his face had me breaking into a reluctant chuckle.

I gestured over my shoulder at the rope dangling out of his line of sight. "Clearly not. But I didn't realize you would be so flippant about me gutting your sentries." I cast a pointed glance toward the doorway. "I'll take the more direct route next time."

He chuckled, and the warm sound had another sort of heat unfurling in my chest, replacing the lingering humiliation. His laugh was, well...

nice. It made me feel toasty and fuzzy. And I hadn't seen his dimples in far too long.

"Thank you for not murdering my guards," he said. "As it is, I have few enough I can trust right now."

The latch on the doors at the opposite end of his suite clicked as the heavy wood creaked open. "Your Majesty? I heard a voice..." The guard's expression flattened at the sight of me. He flung the door wide and stepped inside, reaching for his sword. "I apologize for this intrusion, my king. I will remove the human at once."

Divinius waved his hand. "Stand down, Coram."

The male's face went pale, which contrasted nicely with the purple and silver of his new uniform. "But, m'Lord..."

Divinius speared the unfortunate sentry with a frown, and I couldn't deny the satisfying curl of pleasure that rippled through me at the expression on Coram's face. It served him right. "You're dismissed." Divinius' tone didn't leave any room for questions.

I smiled, tilted my head, and wiggled my fingers at him in a jaunty wave as I dropped into one of the chairs across from Divinius and propped an elbow on his desk.

The guard paused, then glared at me as he jerked the door closed behind him.

I glanced at Divinius. "I suppose I'm not making friends among the palace guards, am I?" Not like it mattered. They weren't mine, this wasn't my country, and I wouldn't be here long.

He shrugged. "Coram doesn't like to be made a fool, or to think someone would question his ability to perform his duty." Divinius studied me. "But do you care?"

"No, not really." As long as the man didn't decide to do something stupid as payback, like trying to kill me.

"Coram would never do such a thing."

I whirled on him. "Stay out of my head!"

"Sorry. You can't blame me. You were practically screaming."

I clenched my hands at my side. "Sand demon's spit, I was."

He sighed and reached into a drawer on the far edge of his desk. He pulled out a flask the size of two fists and tossed it to me. "Here. This is for you, as a thank you."

I caught it. The metal flashed white in the sunlight as the liquid inside sloshed around. "Thanks." I think. "What is this?"

His eyes sparkled as one corner of his lips curled up. The dimple made another appearance. "Taste it."

My eyebrows knitted as my resolve crumbled beneath the heat pooling in my core. That stupid dimple did unfair things to my insides. "You didn't poison it, did you?" I unscrewed the lid and sniffed.

He barked a laugh. "Poison Desert Rose? Is such a thing possible?"

I rolled my eyes and risked a swallow. Cool fresh liquid flowed into my mouth. I smiled and, tilting my head back, poured the rest of the contents down my throat.

And poured. And poured.

I choked, nearly spitting water onto Divinius' immaculate rug.

He burst out laughing so hard he had to grab the desk to keep from falling.

I shook the flask. It sloshed, soaking my hand. "What is this sorcery?"

He wiped the tears from his eyes and took a few deep breaths as he fought to contain his laughter. "Praise the mages! I think that was the funniest thing I've ever seen." I opened my mouth but he waved a hand, cutting me off. "It's enchanted to never go empty. That way, you'll always have Elysian water on hand. You won't have to drink whatever-it-was-called."

"Arak," I said, my lips pressed into a thin line. I'd gotten liquid up my sinuses, and they stung bad enough my eyes burned.

He nodded. "Never again, except by choice. You could use it to supply that tavern of yours." He swallowed and leaned closer, dropping his voice. "I request you don't utilize it on a large scale, though. It's linked to the main spring that feeds the Shermagne. It would be a shame for the river to run dry, after all."

I sputtered. "It could… do that?" How much was he afraid I'd drink?

He winked.

My heart did a stupid little flutter as my eyes started to burn in earnest.

I stared at the flask as my fingers tingled with warmth. I blinked, fighting to keep the tears from spilling over. "Thank you. This is the nicest thing anyone's ever given me." I clutched it to my chest. "Did you make it?"

He shook his head and waved the question away. "No, I'm not skilled with enchantments. And that was not an easy one to create. Abram did it as part of his penance to commute his sentence."

I secured the gift at my waist. "So, he's back as head of the Mage College?" That was quick.

"No. He's free but no longer in charge. Ayda, the magic user who sat on the Ruling Council when my mother died… I named her the head."

"Oh." Well, that was good, I supposed.

"She studied under Abram for years and is skilled in her own right. But she's younger and more experienced from a political standpoint."

I nodded. "A logical choice, then."

"Agreed. As it was for them to send her to sit on the council." Divinius glanced at the parchments scattered in front of him with a list of twenty female names. "Speaking of logical choices…" His voice drifted off.

"What?" I crossed my arms and stared at the fire that crackled away in the hearth for a few heartbeats before turning my attention back to him. "Are you finally ready to set sail for Obron with me like you promised?"

Swallowing, he gestured to the bracers on his desk, ignoring my question. "Also, these are for you."

I picked one up and frowned at it, well aware he was using them as an excuse to change the topic. But I was nothing if not a sucker for pretty gifts, apparently. It felt metallic, but weighed no more than a sheet of parchment. Intricate vines and Elven writing wove across the surface. "They're stunning, but they're too flimsy to be of any use. And metal tends to get too hot in the sun to be practical in Obron. And, I'll have you know," I said, wiggling a finger at him, "All the presents in Elysia aren't going to get you out of your promise."

Divinius picked up the twin to the bracer I had and tossed it into the fire.

My jaw dropped. He did not just do that. "Hey!"

We watched as the flames kissed it for several minutes before he snagged the bracer with a poker and held it out to me. "Go ahead, touch it."

I took a step back. "No way. Heat blisters hurt worse than a sand demon's bite."

He shook his head. "It's cool. I swear it."

I narrowed my eyes, searching his face for any hint of untruth. But there was no reason for him to lie—Divinius wasn't one to get off on cruelty or hurting others. I reached out with a finger and jumped when I touched it. He was correct—it was room temperature.

He smiled. "And, as for your other concern..." He placed the bracer on the desk and gestured to it. "Go ahead. Strike it with your sword."

I raised my eyebrow. "Seriously?" He nodded. "Okay." I pulled out my blade and sliced.

A peal like silver bells rang throughout the room. My weapon bounced off the metal. I bent down to eye level. "Amazing! They don't have a scratch."

Divinius' chest swelled. "Of course not. The Rings of Reimar are not so easily dispatched. And now that my mother is dead, they no longer have a guardian."

I ran my fingers over the intricate scrolled designs along the seams. "So, these are the Rings of Reimar." I frowned. "I thought they were jewelry of some sort. Like maybe a fancy ring or hoop earrings."

"Most people do." He paused, staring into my eyes. "Someone needs to guard them. I would very much like that person to be you."

Me? Ha! I raised an eyebrow. "Are you sure you can't find some pretty elven lady to be the next owner?"

He shook his head. "No one is more worthy. Besides, when my mother had them, they did nothing but collect dust on a shelf. With you, they may actually get some use."

I picked up the bracers, admiring them in a new light. The quality of craftsmanship was unparalleled. But I didn't know much about Elysian smiths. A small grin curled my lips. "They might."

I fastened them over my arms. They fit as if they'd been made for me. I had no doubt there were more magical properties to these things than their inability to absorb heat or get scratched, and Divinius was obviously enjoying withholding the knowledge.

He leaned close, his mouth near my ear. The brush of his breath against the fine hairs of my neck sent goosebumps across my skin. "Desert Rose... Heir to the Rings of Reimar."

The title flowed. I liked it.

I smiled. What would Akre, or Orion for that matter, think if they could see me now? Fancy new armor and all the fresh water I could ever drink.

Divinius glanced over his shoulder at the paper with the long list of names and swallowed. He turned back to me. "Gin... Forget about Orion, Akre, and everything else. Stay here, in Elysia." He cleared his throat. "Stay with me."

My blood froze. I bared my teeth and took a step back, clawing at the ice-cold bracers. So that was what this was about. "As your personal assassin? I already told you to go pick a fight with a sand demon. My answer is not going to change."

He shook his head as he moved toward me.

I frowned, reaching for the blade at my waist. "Coming closer is not the wisest thing you could be doing right now."

His eyes darkened, ignoring my warning. "No, not as that. As my queen."

I froze as my jaw went slack. A metallic screeching sound rang out. I rubbed my ears. There was no way I'd heard him correctly. "I'm sorry, say again? I must have misheard you. I thought you just proposed to me." In the least romantic way possible.

"I did." He gestured around the room as he took another step closer. "Think about it, partner. Our strengths and weaknesses complement each other perfectly. And you can't deny the attraction between us."

I put both palms against the flat planes of his chest and pushed him away. "Yes, I can. Besides, the court and guards barely tolerate me. They only do so because of you. I'll never be welcome here, especially if I steal the Most Eligible of Bachelors."

"The most eligible of bachelors?" He barked a laugh. "Please. I was kidding."

No, he hadn't been. "I'm serious." And if he would quit with the hysterics and think for a few heartbeats, he'd realize how… how preposterous the whole idea was.

He cleared his throat and met my eyes. The intensity in his gaze caused heat to flare below my navel. "So am I. You know what I think?"

I crossed my arms, giving up on drawing my blade and using it to threaten some sense into him. Instead, I cocked one hip to the side. "No, but I'm sure you're going to tell me."

He stepped closer, until there was no space between us. "I think you're afraid," he whispered, his voice was guttural and something deep in my core responded in a very inappropriate way. Ignoring the kernel of myself that wanted nothing more than to tear off his mage robes and crush my lips to his, I opened my mouth to tell him where he could shove it, but he cut me off.

"You're terrified. Of me, of being happy, and of letting go of the vendetta you have against Akre, Orion, and everyone else in Obron who's ever done you wrong." He brushed his hand through his hair, pulling the far-too-shiny strands away from his face. "By Naraka… forget them! They're nothing but a barrier holding you back. Let them go. Be happy, for once."

I staggered back, every word a hot spike driven into my heart. I gasped. I couldn't. Without that resolve, that steel in my spine, I would be nothing. Weak, vulnerable.

He grabbed my shoulders and covered my lips with his.

I froze. Was it acceptable to knee a king in the groin?

The smell of mint banking in the sun wrapped itself around me as Divinius drew me close. I curled my fingers in his robes and pulled them tight until he broke the kiss.

Ignoring the betraying wetness dusting my eyelashes, I rested my forehead on his chest as I fought to breathe. "I ought to kill you for that," I whispered.

"But you won't," he murmured, and I could practically see that darn dimple settle into place on his cheek.

I tilted my head to confirm and yep, it was there. Fates.

We stood, noses inches apart as our breaths mingled. Blood rushed through my ears in time to the heart that thumped against my ribs loud enough he could no doubt hear it.

Oh, forget this. Tangling my fingers in his hair, I pulled his lips back down to mine.

"Ahem." Someone cleared their throat.

I jumped backward, spun toward the noise and flicked my whip at the intruder before my brain caught up with me.

The youth wore the characteristic blue feather pinned to his tunic that marked him as an official courier. He scrambled out of reach, his eyes wide.

"S-sorry, Majesty," he stammered, eyes downcast. "The guards told me to come right in. I had no idea..."

I pursed my lips, arching an eyebrow and pinning Divinius with a stare. "Your men need a lesson in etiquette," I mumbled. Or my sincerest thank you. One of the two...

Divinius cleared his throat and brushed the wrinkles from the front of his robes. "No apologies necessary, young man." He held out his hand. "Do you have a message to deliver?"

The page bowed and fumbled at the leather satchel over his shoulder. After several heartbeats, he removed a scroll sealed with silver wax. Handing it to Divinius, he bent low again and retreated. The door closed with a soft click.

Divinius broke the seal, as though he hadn't just proposed and kissed me in the same breath. He scanned the letter and stared at the door with a sigh.

My skin prickled with suspense. "What? What's wrong?"

He glanced at me and back at the parchment on his desk before settling into his chair. "It's started. Warlord Byre has attacked Akre."

A heavy weight settled on my shoulders. "I need to get back home." I met his gaze, unspoken words hanging between us. *Come with me, please.*

I thought that last part very hard, in case he was still listening to my thoughts.

He studied me for several heartbeats. I fought not to shift from side to side.

Finally, he nodded. "Give me forty-eight hours to get things in order here."

My knees went weak with relief. He was honoring his promise, coming with me. I wouldn't have to retake Obron by myself. Taking a deep breath, I smiled. If we were leaving in two days, there were preparations I needed to make, people I had to recruit. I licked my lips. "I should go."

"Will you please send a page for Ayda on your way out?" he asked. "We need to decide which mages are staying here and which are traveling with us."

I paused as I reached the door.

"Our conversation isn't finished," he said to my back. "I want you as queen of Elysia. You're exactly the person the realm needs."

I froze, my hand on the door latch. "If that's what your heart is set on, I suggest you get used to disappointment."

"I've never been disappointed yet."

I clenched my teeth. Of all the smug, pompous, egotistical—

I gasped as my attention was drawn to the far corner of his desk.

A black long-stemmed rose lay there, tucked out of view from the balcony.

Ice flooded my veins as my throat dried. My head spun. I ripped the sword from my belt and whirled around, scanning the darkened corners of the room.

Divinius leaped to his feet, knocking his chair to the ground. "What's wrong?"

I pointed to the flower. "Where did you get that?"

He frowned, studying the onyx bloom. "I thought you'd sent it. Though, now that I see your reaction, I realize my assumption was incorrect."

He studied my face and stepped closer, laying a hand on my arm. "What is it?"

I shook my head and backed away as invisible bands wrenched into place around my ribs until I couldn't breathe.

Orion was here.

Acknowledgements

Gin, Divinius and Astra were characters in a roleplaying game in grad school (over a decade ago, at the time of publication). Rachel and Ryan Murphy asked me to write a story about them in 2020 while we were all at a mutual friend's wedding. And here we are, five years later, almost to the day. While the character personalities and names are intact, the plot and worldbuilding is completely different than what I suspect either of them were expecting. This manuscript has gone through more critique partners, alpha and beta readers, editors and proofreaders than I can possibly list out here. For everyone I forget, my sincere apologies.

To my wonderful Alpha Readers, Sarah Burchett-Cook, Irene Davy, Julie Nunez, Laura Matney, Livia Daniela and Kari Wood. I can't thank you all enough for your patience and willingness to read the rough drafts I gave you and for your enthusiasm that helped power me through the many writer's blocks. And my beta readers, John Gunningham, E. Marie Robertson, J. Logan C. Rice and Marc B. DeGeorge, who constantly push me to be a better writer. My editors, Elisabeth Moore and Hannah Vanvels Ausbury, thank you for your patience and guidance as this manuscript matured to something that could finally make its way out into the world. A special thank you to Elizabeth for her patience in explaining how to write in passable 1st person point-of-view, as this is my first major writing project not in 3rd person.

No book is ever complete without a good proofread. My sincere thanks to Rachel Murphy for hunting down all my grammar and verbiage mistakes. (I'm still convinced the computer randomly switches some of my typed words for others, just for fun.) I also salute all the stealthy typos that managed to make it through my countless rewrites, alpha/beta readers, editors, proofreader and ARC readers. For their diligence and fortitude, they deserve to remain and so they shall.

And thank you to Ravven (http://ravven.com/) for the amazing cover art. I am blown away at your talent and am so fortunate to be able to work with such a gifted artist.

And huge thanks to my readers. I hope you enjoy Gin, Divinius and Astra's adventures.

About the Author

Michelle A. Darnell started writing as a way to decompress after a long day at work. Working with the public in a science heavy field, sometimes it's a nice change of pace when she can solve problems by throwing a fireball at them. When it turned out people enjoyed reading her stories, she decided to publish her novels so others would have the chance to enjoy them.

She grew up in Western Montana before moving to the Spokane, WA area in 1999 for college. Michelle now lives in Eastern Washington with her husband and one incredibly spoiled cat. She enjoys hiking, especially when she can take her sisters and her camera with her. She also enjoys reading, painting and biking.

Also by

If you enjoyed **Shifting Sands**, I hope you will also love:

THE VAMPIRE ASSASSIN CHRONICLES

Castle of Blood and Secrets – Book 1

Cave of Blood and Bone – Book 2

Goddess of Blood and Shadows – Book 3

Streets of Blood and Dreams – A Prequel

THE SHIFTER QUEEN

To Kill a King – Book 1

To Save a Kingdom – Book 2

Coming in 2026

DESERT ROSE

Shifting Sands – Book 1